DEATH MASK

"The Face of Illys"

By

Raymond R. Bosnic

To my son Milan

PREFACE

"A death mask is a wax or plaster cast of a person's face taken while he or she is alive or near their death.
Usually the mask is created after the death of the person because of the danger imposed by its materials.
The making of a reproduction of the face of a dead person is an ancient practice whose origins date from the periods of the Romans and Egyptians. The process served as a reminder of the deceased for the family, as well as a protector from evil spirits, and is associated with a belief in the return of the spirit."

"In some cultures, mostly in African, Native American and Oceanic tribes, death masks are considered an important part of social and religious life. Death masks facilitate communication between the living and the dead in funerary rites and they create a new, superhuman identity for the bearer. Death masks can take form of animals or spirits, thereby allowing the bearer to assume the role of the invoked spirit or to fend off evil forces."

"In some tribes death masks are used in initiatory or homage ceremonies, which recount the creation of the world and the appearance of death among human beings.
For others where the link to ancestors is sacred, they are used to make the transition from the deceased to his or her heir of the family.
Death masks are also used as a tool to help the deceased's soul pass easily to the other life.
The respect of the funeral rites of mask dancing can also protect from reprisal from the dead, preventing the risk of a wandering soul."

"Guiley, Rosemary E. Harper's
Encyclopedia of Mystical and Paranormal Experience.
San Francisco: Harper San Francisco, 1991."

"I DO NOT REGRET OTHERS HAVING STOLEN MY IDEAS.

I DO REGRET THE FACT THAT THEY DO NOT HAVE THEIR OWN ONES."

NIKOLA TESLA

Table of Contents

PROLOGUE:

ALL AS ONE

6 – TH CENTURY BC, TRIBE OF DAESITIATES, DAORSON TOWN

(Modern day on territory of Bosnia and Herzegovina, near the town named Stolac, village of Osanici...)

Daesitiates Chief, named Bato step - out from his stone hut and slammed his heavy iron spear – Sibyna, engraved with bronze ornaments, three times against the gold covered circular shield which has been positioned above the entrance door. The shield represented his right to rule with this tribe. His grand – grandfather got it from Bardyllis their First King, as a reward, when his tribe together with others from Illyria conquered Dalmatian Islands and Greek colonies on the South. Above his right shoulder, tied on his broad back by leather made scabbard, was ornamented Wolf's Head handle of his Illyrian fighting sword named "Ulk"("Wolf") and two of his father's Sica, named "Abeis"(Snakes)on their leather belts. He gave a signal to his warriors to group themselves in the middle of The Square ready for a battle. He checked sentries above, on the megalithic stonewall five meters high, composed out of large trapeze stones blocks, which were surrounding their capital. He was satisfied with his Commanders and their trainings on their people. In order to survive they have to be strong, brave and proud.

They are One with the Land.

He was tall and well - build, more than two meters tall, with broad shoulders and strong hands, last weekend he crushed two skulls of his opponents in the training exercises with another Pannonii Tribe. It felt good and pump – up his rating among the Illyrians Chiefs. Warriors lined up in front of him and salute to him with their right open hand. Their fingers were wide opened which has meaning from their hearts and souls:

May This Hand Make You Think About Yours.

Each of them was tall as he, some of them even wider and bigger, definitely stronger and faster, but not bloodthirsty, unpredictable, turbulent and savage as him in the combat. He is their Chief and these were some of the reasons why he command them, but The Blood of his ancestors, size of his brain, his tremendous visions and his mind power were the real motive why he was chosen on the first place. He removed his Shmarjet, protecting metal helmet made of pure silver. His mind power expanded over them. He removed his gold Death Mask called "The Face of Illys", too. He wanted to see their eyes and their souls. He wanted them to see Him. Open minded and One with them and the Land. His green penetrating eyes swept across the faces, scanning with his brain their thoughts.

All as One.

Good.

One with the Land.

One with the Hand.

He shielded his thoughts from them and spoke with his musical, leveled and calm voice:

'I have already showed You the truth and our destiny through the pictures. I have seen more then You and my visions are correct. I give You my Soul as a gift and I know that you accepted.'

Warriors kept the same pose in front of him. They did not flinch or move for an inch.

'We are not going to survive this battle in flesh, but our Souls will be free. Letters will keep our secret. We must protect our Land with our Hand.'

The language has to be used, to remind them who they are, where they come from and where they are going. He could do the same with the pictures and letters, but the Word has a Power over them. He is not going to show them the end of his visions. He will make picture and letters. He will protect them with the Sign.

My Sign will be protected by Mask.

The Mask will protect my Soul.

My Soul will be protected by Hand.

The Hand will protect the Land.

CHAPTER I
Section 1.

NEEDFUL THINGS

August, 2009.

CANADA, ONTARIO, TORONTO, PEARSON INTERNATIONAL AIRPORT, ARRIVALS
AREA, GATE NUMBER 7…

The man was walking down the corridor unobserved by the others, just another face in an endless
row of people running for their next flight to catch. His attention was concentrated towards the
long legs of unknown blonde female which were couple meters in front of him, with full focus –
optical zoom on her bottom, moving shaking jelly ass. It was long time since he had a woman the
way as he liked and the small itching inside his groins remind him on that. After this job he is
going to treat himself with some meat, he will have enough cash for a high end whore. His high
cheekbones were classic genetic signature of his grand-grandfather's blood, somewhere from
Balkan peninsula, which was long time ago forgotten and erased through generations of his close
ancestors which lived in the New World for some generations. The man was not aware of this
information, same as he was completely unaware of some other pair of watchful eyes that were
following him from the moment when he stepped on the exit gate number 7. In the left hand he
had very thin briefcase, more look like notebook size, which was chained to his wrist, but
covered under his thin leather glove. The edge of his Armani suit's sleeve was covering
completely his chain and nobody was able to see that he was unbreakably connected to his
suitcase. The women in front of him turned sharply to the nearby, coffee bar, which had big sign
on its entrance:

"COFFEE TO GO - ONLY 3.99 $".

He followed her ass with his eyes as it was the last time that he will ever see that kind of miracle
in his life. He couldn't suppress incoming filling of loss, like a kid losing his new toy; he exhaled

slowly through his teeth and adjusted his hair with the quick stroke of his right hand.

His mobile started to vibrate on his belt sending the uncomfortable trembling to his jelly - belly, which grows every year like some selfish beast under his skin. He tried to lose weight with irregular exercise and some unhealthy diets, poisonous medical tablets and artificial chemical substances, but the belly spread his vengeance on them swiftly and without mercy. For the last months he was considering seriously some surgery as an option, but the tight schedules are killing his plans, too. If, the time is money, as they said, he never has enough of it, to build it with money and complete never ending magical circle. His concentration went back to flipping billboard for announced domestic flights and he searched the board through-fully scanning presented destinations and the time frames in which he can fit prescheduled meeting with the next available flights to Atlantic Canada. He has more than two hours between connecting flights and his baggage will be on his way to Halifax, NS (Nova Scotia). The money transfer will follow the same path after this short meeting and unnecessary delivering of the package. He preferred to deliver packages through DHL or FEDEX, but circumstances changed drastically in the last three days. The client insisted from him to deliver his merchandise in person. Ringing of his mobile phone has been set on "Meeting Mode" and he felt vibration inside his pocket, so he picked it up, before ringing sound started. He flipped his mobile and navigated with the cursor to Inbox messages. Pop up window blinked with its yellow light in the background.

> …

"Meet me at the Starbucks Coffee Bar at the Gate 3 area. I will have King's "Needful Things" book on the table. Face Up. 15 minutes."

...

How convenient name: "NEEDFUL THINGS." By Stephen King. Really needful things for you..., I have. And after all of this…I am going to be the King.

CHAPTER I

Section 2.

BOOM

March, 2000.

UNITED STATES OF AMERICA, CALIFORNIA, LOS ANGELES, RANDOLPH STREET, COLIN'S APARTMENTS, 8-TH FLOOR SUITE 203…

…

'Honestly, I love this job; it gives me strength to hate all mankind.'

He said and light up his ZIPP-o on his cigarette. The brown color of cigarette's tip changed to red. He exhaled smoke through his nostrils to kill distinctive smell of blood.

'You should give up smoking. There is much faster way to kill your-self.'

Young women with pony - tail black hair photographed the table in the kitchen, where they were standing, with two fast light blasts coming from her "EOS Canon Rebel" and gave him a quick push - kick with her right elbow. Chief Police Investigator, Detective Marc Arsenault has been too long in the force to know that some jokes release the pressure of the stress and refresh this morbid environment created by murderer. Also, he supported, that some rookies as Bonnie is trying to be useful in the situation like this, but his mood has not been changed since the first killing file appeared on his desk almost two years ago.

Nasty case...But justice has been served...

'Did you finish the job with your digital pal? Or should I …'

He did not have time to finish his sentence, he was interrupted by the blast of light, which cut his thoughts and brought the havoc on all eight floor area of an apartment building; which had been carefully secured, marked with yellow police tape. Explosion from Suite 203 shattered all windows nearby, sending their sharp fragments far away across the street to small park area.

CHAPTER I

Section 3.

BIRTHDAY CAKE

July, 1998.

CROATIA, CITY OF ZAGREB, CITY HOSPITAL "SVETI VID", GROUND FLOOR, MORTUARY ROOM…

Single twitch under his left eye would tell everything to someone close by about a temporary state of his mind. If there was anybody alive beside him in this cold place on the ground floor of mortuary room.

'Honestly, I did not have enough time to check every piece of information which has been delivered to me in this short time notice, but I've managed to put some leads together and I think we will be able to follow them to certain areas and narrow our investigation forward, towards some hard evidences, Sir.'

'I do not think that I can accept another of your excuses agent Willburn, and I did not expect from your department to deliver accusations and mambo-jumbo predictions, I can accept only hard data and clean reports. If, I ever want an opinion of some fortune teller old bag, I would go to India to get some advice on my cloudy future and football scores over next season games and forthcoming championship. What did you get till now?'

Agent Willburn nervously shifted from one leg to another, as he was there in front of the man on the other end of the phone line and he continued:

'Data is showing some interesting locations and documents which can prove my theory about the cult, also in my possession is a map, which were authentic one and the closest copy of original one which can bring us closer to hard data which you are requesting, Sir. I can send you through secure channels ASAP, together with the pictures of the body and detail markings on it.

I think that body itself has to be transported to secure location as you have suggested last time.

I have already made some arrangements with the local authorities to provide us transport and to secure parameter and the package delivery on our time and place.'

'Unacceptable, period. Local authorities are not reliable and trustworthy, any involvements from their side is a high risk for the data and the body. Use local thugs with cash on their hands as security and small private company for transport. Cover your tracks through the black market and avoid witnesses of any kind.'

'What about the tattoo?'

'Remove it from the skin, use something sharp, I want it in perfect condition, and bag it and bring it to me urgently. Is that clear?'

'Yes, Sir.'

'Do this clean.'

'Yes, Sir.'

'And another thing..., agent..., no witnesses.'

'Yes. Sir.'

The line was cut off. Agent Willburn hang up the phone and for a couple seconds was looking at it, as he was expecting to ring again, or it is going to explode in his face any moment.

The fear was clear in his eyes, but his mind was occupied with problems that cannot be resolved as easy as his Chief Brendan expected and ordered him to do. Brendan has been expecting from him to resolve this case in a month, but agent Willburn had different feeling inside his guts. And most of the time it proved itself to be correct at the end. He made his first cut on the flesh.

Slowly, sharp medical scalpel progressed through rotten soft tissue. It was almost like cutting the birthday cake. Without slightest difference in the beginning, but enormous similarity at the end.

There weren't lightened candles over The Sign. No breath blows and wishes to make. Birthday - Boy!

CHAPTER I

Section 4.

WHITE PIGEON

January, 1943.

UNITED STATES OF AMERICA, NEW YORK, NEW YORK CITY, HOTEL NEW YORKER, 33rd FLOOR, Room, 3327…

(Modern day – New York City, Hotel New York)

White pigeon was at the window in the same time and at the same spot as always. Like he has some internal clock on which he was visiting the old man, right on time like Swiss clock well oiled and right on schedule. The old man was also on the schedule all his life, working 20 hours per day for the last 70 years without rest and he liked very much pigeon's "right on time" behavior, actually he adored this small creature for his dedication and simplicity. Bird's brain are more developed then the humans know about it, his tests with the birds showed him that they can do amazing things, things that average human being cannot imagine. But the white one is really something special. That is the reason he has a special place in his heart and he gave him the special name, too. The old man hands were huge, but delicate. Bony fingers are long, but the first thing noticeable on hand is his thumb, unnaturally long for human being, even for the tall and large man as he was. Even his skull was unusually long, shaped as triangle, wide at the top and narrow, like a spike at the end of his chin. His face with the high cheekbones, hollowed eyes, large ears on the edge of the face and his wide mouth in the middle of it, gave him astonishing look like he doesn't belong to the human race, at all. But the most amazing were eyes of the man, grayish – blue on the edges with the wide dark pupils in the middle, with the light in the centre, flickering with high intelligence like a lonely star on the dark sky, eyes which were younger then the thin skin and white bones of the skull. Soul inside was full of youth, energetic and was radiating her enormous power. Through them, he mesmerized anyone who met him in person, and cut his soul like a laser and burn his radiance on their brain forever.

The man cannot be forgotten. He will be remembered.

He opened the window and the bird hopped inside together with chilly January's air. He gently strokes the soft, warm feathers of pigeon's light gray wings with long fingers and the beat of his heart changed the rhythm. Excitement and joy culminated inside him. He took small bowl with special ordered seeds from the shelf and he drops some of them on the palm of his other hand. The old ritual started again, between the bird and the man. Pigeon cooked his head on the side as if he is considering man's offer, he made eye contact with the man and bowed his head twice as he is accepting it with gratitude. The man smiled with the one corner of his mouth and bowed back to the bird as he accepted it. The bird crossed the distance between them with short flap of her wings and nested on the edge of the man's palm. She dropped the head and carefully took two-three seeds in a fast movement of her beak. The man was watching the pigeon and he patiently waited till the bird ate all the seeds from his hand, then he moved his huge head close to her and whisper some words to her on the strange language filled with some unknown accent which to the normal listener sounds like this:

'Chassst…kolko-lis-ashato…michi-se-na-to…ti…ashh-hcho-fata…michko-ni-tara…je…uv-ichere…'

Pigeon's white and light gray feathers trembled during these quiet old men's instructions, and from time to time he released some strange sounds from his beak like he is trying to make some conversation with the man and answer with his own suggestions to it. The scene continued, like in a slow motion movie sequence, until the pigeon's head dropped on his long finger and stayed there, almost minute or two, frozen in time and the old man's lips stopped moving.

Together like ancient picture taken by some anonymous artist, they were connected in the momentum, master and his slave, teacher and his apprentice, two secret lovers hidden in the hotel room. Suddenly, pigeon came to life as he was pinched with some needle under his wings and he spread his wings in attempt to rise from the man's hand. Old man raised his long body slowly and went back to the closed windows. He opened them with one swift movement of his other hand

and released the bird; actually, it was as if the bird in the same time released him from her grasp and in that second, small lightning came out from the man's fingers, something like a static collected between them, and both of them were connected through the air. The man's posture changed after that, he looked older as he was, like all these years went back to his now fragile body, his hand drooped beside his body like it was uncontrolled with no connection or part of the same body. Shoulders went lower almost immediately and his legs become rubber under him. He made unsteady steps backwards as he hit some invisible wall, he leaned towards the table and then like a ball he bounced back on the opposite side, and turned his head towards the open window. On his lips was the name. The name was spoken through his mind and his last breath was filled with it. He collapsed beside it like a puppet cut from his strings. Sounds from the street covered his short breaths like a blanket. Sparks in his eyes were blinking on – off in the same time intervals. He closed his eyes over wide opened windows.

CHAPTER I

Section 5.

LOONIE

July, 2009.

CANADA, ALBERTA, EDMONTON, WEST EDMONTON MALL, GROUND PARKING

AREA…

…

Coffee… Mmmmmmmm. Nothing smells better than that. I have to admit that I am addicted to it. I already know this is not good, but some habits are hard to kick – out from your life. What a treat! Small things come first. They are very important in our short life. Shit! Pager is vibrating in my left inner pocket of my jacket as he want to remind me that my lunch break is over and I should get back to my job. I checked the watch. Another three hours till the end of my On Call Duty Hours. This driving is killing me more than the job itself. Driving two and half an hour in one direction to fix problem in 10 minutes on the spot and then went back with the song:
"On the Road Again…"
I will change this job…

…

These were private thoughts of Melvin Dayer, Service Technician for photocopiers, faxes, printers and other peripheral computers devices, when he reached his Ford Taurus on the parking lot of Edmonton's largest mall, West Edmonton Mall, on the second level, and he was preoccupied with his own thoughts to see other vehicles around. He did not even notice large Chrysler van, until the last moment before it hit him from his left side and smashed his body between nearby parked car and the van. Driver of the van was dead, too, so it did not matter to him either.

RCMP Officer, Paul Thompson saw position of the bodies on the parking lot and figure that out.

Victim outside the van was clear as guilty to have a coffee break and his case is closed, but the other one, inside was free of charge, due to the fact, he was definitely murdered. And that is what is annoying about it. He will have to wait for forensics and other "cleaners" to figure out when, why and how. He has to be careful about the scene and watch for his steps around it.

Last time he unintentionally crushed some of them and he gets slapped on his wrist by his boss. He is not going to make same mistake again. He released small quite "Pffffff !" fart when he bend and crouch himself to the frog position to see what was flashing from the head of van's driver, when something heavy dropped on his shoulder and almost deliver him a heart attack.

'Jeeessuussss! You scared me to death! Do not sneak around me like that, buddy!'

'How are you Paul?! It's a hot day today, or not?! I think will we get some showers in the afternoon, hmmm…'

'Maybe, maybe…, You never know these days…, With all that climate changes and… Hey, look at these clouds over there…'

Paul raised his head to check up on the sky, but his "buddy" did not wait for his forecast report, he was already closing the distance between the van and Paul's meteorological improvised frog position - station. Michael Blaquier's blue eyes focused on the piece of metal that was inside left eye socket of the victim. He outflanked large oil smudge in front of the driver's door; which was spreading on the floor in hart's shape; he draw his "Leatherman's" tool, flipped over to tweezers and slowly, steady and carefully, like a surgeon he pulled out metal round shape from the orbit. He turned over tweezers and checked the other less bloody side of it.

'I 'll be damned! It's a "loonie" !'

He made a comment out loud for himself.

'Wha' did you said?'

Paul asked lifting his kilograms with major difficulty.

'Nothing. I am just talking to myself, as usual…'

Paul just waved with his hand and turned towards his car, where he left his coffee. Michael is here and from now on, Paul's jurisdiction is officially over. Investigator has a better salary then him, so it is time for him to earn his paycheck and bonuses. Michael realized that he made mistake with the coin, it was not "loonie" (one Canadian dollar coin) at all. It was some strange old type of coin; like these numismatic collectibles coins; on one side he saw dolphin for sure, but the other one, wasn't clear enough, dried blood and skull fragment stick to it, so he bag it in plastic pouch. He saw that other body was pinned between two cars and it was lying down between them like broken puppet, cut off from his strings, but another interesting detail caught his attention. Windshield of the wan was not smashed or cracked in regular patterns; there was strange angle of spider's web cracks on the surface. He bypassed the same oil pool again from the other direction and position himself in front of impact point. He saw that all spiders' net of cracks on the windshield had the same starting point. It was in the driver's line of sight, actually in heights of his eyes, on the same level where his head would be positioned during the normal driving. This meant that the coin flew through the windshields glass and rammed in his skull, precisely his left eyeball. The speed on impact was enormous and his death was instant. The poor guy in front of him didn't have a chance for run at all. He looked back to bagged coin in his hand. On the opposite side had some carved face of the man, "en face" positioned like an old Roman or Greek coins? Probably was the same origin, too. An honorable death of a man to be killed by old collector's coin is the most stupid death case up to now in his twenty five long police career.

But, as they said:

"People always surprised you after all." "Dead or Alive".

CHAPTER I

Section 6.

THE THUNDER

January, 2010.

SERBIA, BELGRADE, "KALEMEGDAN" FORTRESS, CITY - PARK…

Strong wind, named "Koshava" by the local habitants, was blowing from the north, the river Danube flickered with frozen patches of ice on her surface and the sun was trying to break through gray, heavy clouds from above. Winter was sharpening her teeth on the nature, which has been witnessed by frozen trunks of the trees in Kalimegdan Park, brave small birds – sparrows, heroes of the days, and some occasionally passing people hugged in their coats, running for the cover in the alleys and opened bars near buy. Miran Ivanovich , son of Zelimir, at the age of almost 18, was already close to 2 meter in height and 100 kg in weight, well muscled, build as an athlete and between his friends respected for his sport's skills and as well at Technical University as brilliant student with the score of 10.00 in all subjects. His last year is going to be finished after one more semester and he was already two years on advanced study program, which has been recognized and approved by his mentors and professors from the beginning on Belgrade's prestige University of Technical Science. He was rewarded more than once by university and local technical societies for his very high achievements on international competitions in mathematics, physic, chemistry and electro-technique. Beside this he completed four years of high school in two years which was amazing due to the fact that he did it almost effortless in compare to the others, also talented students from the other regions and surrounding countries which evolved from the ex – Yugoslavia Republics. But beside all this, he was modest, simple and quiet person, concentrated on sports and books, with his "down to Earth" attitude, which was most of the time for his boldness, simplicity and good nature, by mistake recognized as slowness, stupidity and naive by his girlfriends and closed friends. He did not care about that, and as a young person he was really open minded towards anything and everyone around him. He tried desperately to distance himself from the raging nationalism and collective primitivism which was influencing all regions for the last 15 years of his life, and he fought that battle with his inherited father's patience and birthed mother's courage. He crossed the park in almost straight diagonal direction from the fortress entrance to the beginning of Knez Mikhail's Street, covering distance in effortless long strides with even fast breaths from his huge lungs. His Aikido training session is going to start in 60 minutes and today he was excited and thrilled with a thought that he will take his first official attempt to pass First Kju (1st Kju). His Sensei told him to prepare himself for some surprises, which meant that the regular testing exercises performed for the last 100 days are going to be overture towards more difficult technical and spiritual challenges, which are waiting for him in their dojo. Sensei called him "The Thunder", on the local language translated as "Grom", for his movements, speed and power in aikido techniques, and "The Lightning", translated as "Munja" on local languages, for his reflexes, his intuition and perceptions on his opponents fighting tactics. Trainer suspected and felt on numerous occasions, but he never admitted openly in front of him, that he can read his opponents minds prior to perform their sparring combat training. Miran never relied on the "feeling" which he had from time to time on the training, and he focused more on experiences and lessons thought by his trainer. But he cannot rid off skin's tingling, flashes under his eyes, which in some moments distract him from his focus; and small pain between his eyes, more like slight pressure on the bone between his eyebrows. He felt that cold air on his face shaped the frozen mask on the surface of his skin, boiled blood pumped his cold hands under the skin's surface of his knuckles and steady rhythm of his heart pumping inside his temples. He was hearing his body music, cacophonies of tunes through his veins, small steady signals received from the stretched and strained muscles, micro-songs of his pulsing nerves and trembling ganglia. An electrified brain charged by adrenalin, which spread on the surface of his skull, was spreading his power to all parts of his body, initiating sparks in his joints, boosting his stamina and activating hidden body's energy.

Light as a feather he reached corner of Milosheva Street and turned to left speeding up from free run into the steady sprint. He will warm up his body prior to the test and he is going to reach their dojo on time to meditate on it and through meditation exercise prepare himself completely, together he will unite his body and his soul. He is going to be ready for any surprises, which his sensei prepared for him tonight.

CHAPTER II
Section 1.

BELA

May, 1992.

BOSNIA AND HERZEGOVINA, MUNICIPALITIES OF SREBRENICA, TOWN OF

BRATUNOVAC... CODE NAME – "BELA"("THE WHITE ONE" translated from Bosnian or

"BELLA" abr. From Italian Language: "The Beautiful One")

(Modern Day – Bratunovac, Entity of Republic Srpska, Bosnia and Herzegovina)

...

"Serbs are "Nation from Heaven"...

Our small village, near Bratunovac has been occupied by local Serbian paramilitary forces

together with JNA (Yugoslavia National Armed Forces) from Serbia that crossed river of Drina

at beginning of May, 05-th. 1992. Neighbors from villages nearby fully armed, masked came

together with Special Forces units named "Arkan's units" inside the village and collected us

from our houses, all together by force, and assembled in groups in front of local mosque. When

we went out from our old house, they tied my father's hand by steeled wire and kick him, hit him

over his body all the way towards our march to the center of the village. One of them, unfamiliar

to me said:

"You will be good... just perfect..."

He dropped pack of cigarettes in my pocket and said:

"I will take you with me, back to Serbia, and there you are going to be married for a Serbian..."

He continued:

"Serbs are "Nation from Heaven", you know..., and we are stronger than any other nation of this

world, by blood..."

As he walked beside me, he added:

"Maybe you don't know by now, but The Creator itself is Serb, too!"

Before we reached end of road in the direction of mosque in the middle of the village square, they separated men and women in two large groups. They beat everyone during our forced partition. There, among others Chetniks, I have seen two women, dressed in same type of uniform as JNA soldiers. They used to work as teachers, teaching our children, at our local school before the war started. They were Serbs, too. One of them, as the rest of them called her by her nickname "Bela" came over to group of men. The name or nickname of the other one I do not know. The first one, nicknamed "Bela" pulled out her knife and stabbed Nevzet in his neck. He bled to death in front of her and us. The other woman teacher took out her gun and she shot Nevzet's father point blank. Later on, before both of them killed another man, Saban Gerovic, they asked him how would he liked to be executed, where he would preferred to be stabbed, which part of his body. They killed together Camil Rizvanovic on the similar way, too. At first they asked him to chose direction and type, so when he did not answer them. One of them hit him with her gun in the head, and blood covered his face immediately. When he fell on the ground, in the middle of the road, teachers pulled out their knives and cut his throat simultaneously. Other Serbs – Chetniks detached two of us, from the large group, my first cousin H. and me, they pushed us on the way to the edge of the forest, nearby. First, one of them took H. and then disappeared with her inside the woods. Secondly, three of them grabbed me and followed the same path. When we were close to the edge, I saw the first Chetnik on the top of my cousin. He ripped off her underwear as she tried to defend herself. She was kicking and screaming till he pressed his knife on her neck, threatening her to kill her, when she stopped her struggle; he just continued and raped her on the same spot.

...

"If you give any sound at all, we will cut your throat instantly!"

The other three masked Chetniks brought me near the same place where were H; and one of them yelled:

"Remove your clothes! Fuck your mother..., and fuck your Alija Izetbegovic, too!"

As I refused to remove my clothes, the other one grabbed me, as he draw out his knife, and told me that he will cut my throat, if I do not take my clothes off at once. I realized that the third one was gone, as the other, two of them pushed me between themselves and removed my clothes and my panties. One of them pulled upper part of my clothes up to my chin and he held my hand. I struggled and tried to pushed them away from me; until one of them hit me hard in the face and in the head and I fell completely on the ground. Both of them raped me there, one after another, as they hold my hands above my head. Shortly after the third one showed up and he raped me, too. As they repeatedly raped me, always one of them held the knife close to my neck skin, frightening me with the words:

"If you give any sound at all, we will cut your throat instantly!"

I fainted more the once, during their rape. Helpless, I prayed to God, deep inside me to help me, as I was bleeding heavily. After they raped us both, they brought us on the same road as before. Beside the road, on the edge I saw killed people, Bosniacs, their bodies in the trench. I managed to recognize one of them Seco Ibrisevic, as we passé by. After all, what happened, I had been transported with all others Bosniacs somewhere close to Kladanj, where we have been exchanged for someone else, and then soon after to Tuzla. I do not know what happened to any of our men from the village, my father together with them was gone without trace. It is five years now, since these Slobodan Milosevic's savages from Serbia attacked us civilians Bosniacs. Nobody from our men was never ever found dead or alive up to this day. When Chetniks molested me and raped me, I had only fifteen. Today, I am twenty years old. All men are the same for me now. I do not trust to nobody. I do not believe in justice. It does not exist. I told my story. I used lighter and softer version of it .It can't be described by any words. I believe in God and I praise the Lord to give me the strength to hope, that one day the justice is going to reach them and punish them all, all of them in time.

...

Michelle B. closed her Apple Notebook and thought about this recently received file. It did not come through her regular info cell channels; it was send by one of her "sensors" located overseas.

This information will become crucial in her further murder investigation. At least she has a name, to play with it; actually, it is only a nickname - *"Bella"*.

CHAPTER II

Section 2.

B&B

September, 1998.

UNITED STATES OF AMERICA, CALIFORNIA, LOS ANGELES, 140 NORTH LA
STREET; MAIN DISTRICT POLICE DEPARTMENT, CHIEF'S DETECTIVES OFFICE...

...

"Hi, Marc, I have left some files in your office, on your desk in yellow envelope, please,"
browse" thru them and let me know if you find anything interesting. I trust you and your "hunch"
has been very helpful last time in Montreal with that "psycho" case. Sorry, I did not have a time
to stay over the weekend; I owe you a big one.

Yours,

Mic."

Marc read the note on his office door and considered these two possibilities:

One:

He should get inside, pick up that envelope and slide to his chair behind his desk and spent
another evening in his office alone, reading some psycho – maniac workout of another lost soul
and comparing theirs "signatures" with his previous semi – patients.

Two:

He should get outside, start his Toyota Corolla and drive to the first "Greasy Spoon" restaurant,
have a bacon with two "over easy" eggs and some warm hot cup of coffee, not that American
"washed socks" color coffee, but the real one, European, double espresso with the drop of high
level fat milk.

After second night in a row of his unplanned night shift he preferred the second option more than
the first one, but as always he chose the third option which has been mixed combination of these

possibilities: Use option number two with option number one, but without office. His concentration is not going to be good as in the office, but he needs some B&B (bed & breakfast) specials in reversed order. He picked up envelope from his desk and closed the office. He did not see that flashing light on his digital answering machine was steady red, which indicated full memory of received messages.

CHAPTER II

Section 3.

JOKE

August, 1998.

CROATIA, ISTRA REGION, CITY OF PULA, SIGIRIJEVA STREET…

Willburn was walking around these two blocks before the Forum, a great amphitheater in Pula, named "Pula Arena" , which was actually Colosseum ; for forth time during the last hour. He was scanning the area for potential exit points, check points and stake outs and he replayed different scenarios in his head in a case that scheduled "blind date" become too hot for him. It was shame that he did not have a time, some additional days, to see beautiful city of Pula and get to know some girls, women here are gorgeous and sexy, but he was not here on vacation at the moment, but he promised himself that he will make one after this assignment. "Rendezvous" meeting point is going to be Chapel of St. Mary of Formosa, small humble – looking stone structure build during Byzantine Empire's rule here and it was good spot, open green space between port and other small streets surrounding the chapel's area. He chose it on purpose, although the chapel itself was usually closed for visitors, it's occasionally occupied as a gallery space, most of the time it was empty and deserted as graveyard. He bribed local Archeological Museum employee to get duplicated key, of course not directly, through other local greedy bastards. Now, the only thing left for him is to take a peek at the chapel's interior and then wait, as spider in his net. He was inside the chapel waiting for currier to come. He was late.

You cannot expect anything on time in this region.

Inside the chapel was warm, maybe 20 to 25 degrees, but still five to six degree of Celsius less then outside.

Finally…

He saw bold man with sunglasses, in mid thirties, white shirt with yellow baggy pants, with both his hands in the pockets, he was crossing small area park with his head down. Under his left armpit was a small book as it was arranged signal – sign, through the phone. The man stopped in front of the chapel and he surveyed the area on more time. Willburn left him to fry on the afternoon sun for some time and then whispered through creaked chapel's door.

'Over here…'

The man did not expect anybody inside the chapel, and he jumped a little, surprised as a rabbit.

'Do not turn; just drop the book in front of you and leave…'

'But… I thought that we will…'

Accent was strong and locally colored.

'You think too much…'

He did not turn, but went rigid for a second.

'I change my mind… Get inside…'

Suddenly, Willburn did not like this situation.

Something changed… Not him… Something in the air…

'Okay, okay…'

Willburn opened the door and put his right hand on his back where was hidden his Glock 39. He positioned himself one meter on the opposite side of the door, far from LOS (Line of Sight) from the entrance, when the bold man entered.

'Closed the door.'

Man's thin mouth produced masqueraded smile. His eyes drooped to Willburn's right hand and back to his face. He closed door without looking back with his left hand; in the other one he was holding the book. He kept facial expression on his face and answered with dry, rasping voice of long - run smoker.

'This wasn't prearranged location…'

'I had to improvise… Anyway, this meeting face to face wasn't planned either, but situation changed. You have the book?'

'Yes, I have.'

'Put her on the floor in front of you.'

He put the book on the tiled floor still looking in Willburn's right hand.

'That will be all, now step outside and be gone.'

His expression on his face... Maybe he is stoned. Like he heard a joke, but he didn't get it.

'Okay, okay...'

Willburn move further from the man and the opened door.

'You know...'

Man stopped on the entrance with his head down and he turned his bold head to the left side, like he marveled Roman's tiled mosaic on the floor under his feet, and started sentence which he never finished.

What's going on?!

Willburn asked himself in the same second when the unfamiliar sound filled the air around the man.

"mmmmmmmMMMMMMMmmmmmmm..."

Circle of bright gold light appeared on bold - man's neck, his head went back in spasm, and then gurgled sound came from his throat and another second later his body fell, actually slide aside, and it happened in the same time, strange sound stopped and golden light dissolved, too.

What the fuck is this?

Next second, Glock was leveled with his eyes; both of them were targeting empty space on chapel's door.

No movements. There is nothing.

Body hit the old polished tiles and his head detached from it, like sliced piece of meat, it rolled several times and stopped in front of Willburn's legs. Willburn was fully aware of everything, his heart jumped and speeds up his rhythm, but his hands were steady, his focus stayed on the same spot, entrance door.

Do not move. Wait...

Drops of sweat rolled down his spine. Air inside the chapel become thick and hot. He licked his dry lips; he released his stomach muscles and slowly exhaled low steady breath.

Look at me. Look… Just look at me… He couldn't resist it.

…

Do Not Look Down! Focus on the door! Don't look!

Willburn's eyes moved for a brief second down on the head in front of his legs. Bold man's eyes were rolled up and white, but thin lips smile was frozen on the face.

He got it finally. He got the joke.

CHAPTER II

Section 4.

THUD – THUD

June, 1861.

AUSTRIAN HUNGARIAN EMPIRE, LIKA REGION, GOSPIC TOWN, VILLAGE OF SMILJAN …

(Modern day – CROATIA, Gospic, Smiljan)

Village of Smiljan was quite and calm, like everybody was sleeping under some magic spell or secret plan of his habitants to hide themselves from strange humid day, low dark clouds and warm crazy wind from the high mountains. Nikola was running with dry tear's scars on his face, through the woods approximately for half an hour or more, he was not sure and honestly he did not care anymore. He was not aware of coming storm above his head, which collected clouds like puzzles on the black board; his attention was concentrated on tricky path in the forest on which his legs bounced up and down, on his own rhythm, pulling him with every covered meter closer to his hidden spot. His secret place of solitude, where he collected all his dreams and hopes, his childish undeveloped ideas of future, the old church on the mountain's north side, his brother's favorite runaway destination called him clearly for three nights in the row, through his dreams, with church's ringing bells that doesn't exists any more. Rain drops started his drummed beat on the leaves above his head; they were speeding up like background music in his ears, their echo sounded to him like Danilo's voice in church's coir, high and strong. When he reached church's entrance doors, he was already wet up to his bones; his cotton shirt was soaked with water and glued to his bony shoulders giving him cold shivers under his warm skin. He run beside the wall, left of the entrance area, towards pilled wooden hogs and hidden back door beside them. Danilo and he discovered it by accident, when they run after greedy squirrel which hijacked their chestnuts prepared for grilling, and they abounded their blind race after her when they found small doors on the back of the church, through which opened their eyes towards unimaginable childish secrets. Nikola's thin limbs squirmed through small crack before the first thunder hit some wood near buy, and his deafening sound filled the forest. Like a small rabbit he hip – hop on four legs through the hole and raised himself on his trembling legs in half sitting position. With a quick instinctively glance towards blocked main entrance doors, he straight up his spine and raised his hands to his black hair pulling it on the back of his head in an attempt to dry it and remove some parts from his wet face. He moved slowly, when another thunder in the background announced his rage and throws his anger on surrounding forest, towards small closet room, right beside the altar, which has been used last time by Danilo as his intergalactic space command center. It brought pressure on his breast bone as he remembered their last game here. He missed him. He never imagined this emptiness in his soul. He cannot stand up before his father anymore. Sadness in his father's eyes is like endless pit of misery. Echo of his wounded soul filled his ears with unbearable silence. His mother's gentle touch and calm voice is roaring pain of mortally injured human being at the edge of madness. Legs felt stiff and unstable under him. Improvised chair made from stacked potato's bags filled with dry leaves and stuffed grass in their empty pockets become bigger and bigger, till it cover his view of the room. He was trying to remove his cotton shirt above his head when he heard the strange sound, some loud noise.

"Thud – Thud –Ud… Thud – Thud - Ud".

The light spread above his head, around him like thin transparent milky fog, layers after layers without direct source, visible from every angle, but without steady source and direction or origin.

"Niko, don't be afraid of this… It is not going to be painful…"

'Dane?! Is that you? How…?!'

"Shhhhh. Do not worry my brother. I will help you, just stay calm and with me."

'I did not have time to be with you, I failed you when…, You fell…'

"Niko, nothing is wrong with you, I am not leaving you again…"

'I miss you… Father said that you are with angels, up there…, but mother said that you will always be here, close to us…'

He had strange feeling in his body, as thousand, million ants are moving across his skin, tingling heirs on his head are stretched and pulled by invisible hands, one heir at the time and all of them at once. Something sat on the top of his lungs and it pressed his enormous weight against his fragile body. Ringing in his ears gets louder with every passing second, the sound of Dane's voice boomed in the background, till Nikola's voice has been lost and he lost connection between his incoherent thoughts and his broken voice.

'I ca…nt, … ss…ee…whaa…ttt…th…i…sssss….'

"I am coming to you my brother…"

He fell from above on his back and lost his breath on impact. His head was clenched between two hammers which are smashing each other.

"I am here… Niko."

I am here… Dane.

I am here…

I am…

I…

…

Thud – Thud – Ud… Thud – Thud - Ud… Thud – Ud… Thud… Thud – Ud…………Thud……Ud…
Thud…Thud… Thud…………Ud… Ud……Ud …………Ud ……………Thud.

CHAPTER II

Section 5.

MIRANDA

August, 2009.

CANADA, ALBERTA, EDMONTON, EDMONTON POLICE WEST SIDE; KINGSWAY AVE, NW (NORTH WEST)…

The phone was ringing. He did not have a wish to answer, but he was expecting laboratory results, so he picked up receiver:

'Inspector Blaquier on the phone.'

'Hello? Am I speaking to Mr. Blaquier?'

'Yes. I am speaking. And you are…?'

It's soft and calm female voice with a hint of unspecified accent.

'My name is not so important. Information that I have is more important. For you.'

'I do not play that type of game. No name – no game.'

'Ok-ay… Let's say… Miranda. Miranda is here.'

She is fast thinking, confident and calm.

'Ok. Now I am listening… Miranda.'

I am listening and switchboard is recording…

'I believe you had some dead man with a coin in his head. And no name attached to the body.'

'I see…, You are well informed for a housewife, let's say. We did not release anything on it, yet.'

She was there or she was part of it.

'Where I come from, housewives know everything what is going on in our neighborhoods. But trust me I know even more.'

'I would like to chat with you all night long, but we can cut the crap and get to the point. N'est – ce pas?'

I am tired of everything woman. Speak...

'Tres bien, monsieur Blaquier... I know who is your victim and real victim's name, so you can speed up your investigation.'

'That's charming; I can't stand the suspense... If you have some information about it, let's sit in my office for a while and you tell me whatever you have and I will listen. What about that?'

'I can't. It is not safe and I will give you now two names and you check it. That's it.'

Just a little more time and I can track you, baby...

'I can guarantee...'

'General Luis MacKenzie.'

Name sounds familiar.

'Colonel Brian Murhead.'

Couple of seconds more...

'Sorry, I didn't catch the name...'

Line was off before he can add anything else. He was standing with the handset in his left hand as an idiot.

She was gone for good...

He hanged up the phone and he was considering checking the phone log, maybe he had luck with the time frame, when the phone started his ringing, again.

Maybe, she changed her mind and she called again.

'Inspector Blaquier on the phone.'

'It's Mick from FIS (Forensic Identification Services) laboratory, Sir; I have sent you an email yesterday...'

'Yes,... What did you find?'

Its better be something good...

'Well, we have confirmation on DNA analysis and positive ID, too. It is confirmed that the man was retired military officer Major Claude Lévesque.'

Surprise... Surprise...

'You can send me his file by secure network e-mail.'

'Sorry, Sir I do not have anything except basic information, I think you should contact your supervisors, military channels or CSIS (Canadian Security Intelligence Service) office in Ottawa.'

Great! Fuck you very much!

'Thank you for an update and…'

The man on the other line interrupted him, before he had an opportunity to cut the line.

'Sir, the coin is very valuable; It was made in 4 -th or 5 -th century BC; and it was additionally shaped and sharpened to make a lethal damage.'

Even better!

…

Now I have a numismatic killer with his highly valuable and historically precious weapon!

CHAPTER II

Section 6.

EUROS

January, 2010.

SERBIA, BELGRADE, NOVI BEOGRAD (NEW BELGRADE) MUNICIPALITY, MIHAJLO PUPIN STREET, NUMBER 66…

The Yellow Taxi cab driver stopped the car in front of an apartment building complex. The street was jammed with traffic, passing cars, pedestrians and some occasionally bike riders were on regular scheduled route to their unknown destinations. He pressed control button and slide the window on driver's side down, then he turned the engine key off. Switchboard operator confirmed this destination as customers address and he double checked his mileage on the meter reader which was identical to his own calculations of covered kilometers. He received a call as high priority, and he expected high priority tip for it, due to the fact that he left another customer with his foot inside the car and his wallet outside on the street.

Leftovers for another taxi driver…

Older man in his sixties showed up beside parked vehicle on driver's side and asked him:

'Are you waiting for some customer or you just arrived here without schedule?'

'Sorry, I am waiting for customer and I am on scheduled time, reserved at this moment.'

'Thank you and goodbye.'

Man passed vehicle in front and turned to the other side like he is going to cross the street, but instead of doing that, he turned back towards the passenger's side of the vehicle and opened the door.

'What are you doing?'

He ignored driver's question and jump in the seat beside him and slammed the door. He turned his head for a quick glance across the street and then turned his head back to the driver. His blue eyes under his greenish cap, flashed with anger and fury when he told driver:

'If you start your car now and move it immediately, I will give you 100 Euros! Quickly!'

Cab driver opened his mouth to add something, but when he heard "Euros" in the stranger's proposal, he started the car and shift to the first gear without thinking. He pressed gas pedal and released the clutch, so the car jumped a little and then speed up, burning tires left two smudges on asphalt.

'Where are we going?'

Strange old guy checked the rear mirror and then his right hand grabbed the edge of his seat to prevent his body to slide towards the dashboard. He mumbled:

'Just drive...'

Cab driver corrected rear window with his right hand and then switched to third and then fourth gear, speeding up towards changing lights and passing through blinking yellow light on the first junction.

'I will turn left on boulevard ...'

Old guy added through his teeth:

'Yes, and get to the first exit to highway... In direction to Avala mountain ...'

'No problem...'

Next ten minutes cab driver was concentrated to avoid potential car crashes and to catch up as much as he could kilometers between the starting point and unknown destination.

He did not tried to start conversation with his unexpected customer and he did not like him either from the start, so he felt that this feeling is mutual, because the other person ignored him as he didn't existed at all.

They were already on the highway for fifteen minutes, speeding up 10 to 20 kilometers above the limit, when the radio station went on and switchboard operator jumped in with question:

"Hello, Cab 49, give me your location, I have..."

Old man grabbed the mike and pressed "Off" button, before the cab driver had a chance to react, and added:

'Do not answer and I will put additional 50 in your pocket!'

Cab driver was looking at radio station for a second and then answered:

'Okay, but we have maybe 20 to 30 minutes before "the shit hit the fan" on my side and it will be good to know where we are going…'

The man was looking thru the window and without any comment pulled out 100 Euro bill from his left inner coat's pocket and handed over to cab driver. The bill magically disappeared between them and ended up in cab's driver left front shirt pocket.

'Take the highway exit towards Mladenovac town, I will tell you later our final destination…'

Shark's smile on cab driver's face widened as he followed the signs on the highway. He answered:

'You just guide me, boss…'

CHAPTER III
Section 1.

STARBUCKS

August, 2009.

CANADA, ONTARIO, TORONTO, PEARSON INTERNATIONAL AIRPORT, GATE
NUMBER 3, STARBACK'S COFFEE BAR…

Nash Stevanovich did not expect this. This was real surprise for him. Across him on the table was
one of Stephen King's bestsellers "Needful Things" and beside the table, the owner of the book
was sitting and it was…, a woman?! The worst, actually the best thing for him was that she was
beautiful; her lean long legs covered with stonewash color of Levi's jeans were supporting the
chair in front of her. Leather tweed jacket covered her upper body and it was zipped almost up to
the neck, but her breasts were pushing underneath like they did not want to be covered at all.
Thin waist broke her body on two amazing parts and in the same time it shaped her all in one hot
goddess figure. He was not able to see her eyes, hidden by Ray – Ban sunglasses, but her full red
lips, with no lipstick on them, produce tingles on inner part of his thigh. Her red hair was tied up
under the "Nike" light blue baseball cap and her hands were hidden in the pockets of her jacket. It
activated a little silent alarm inside his brain, which he acknowledged it, but he ignored due to
initial moment of surprise and unsatisfied greed in his heart. She caught his hungry male look in
his eyes, but she did not show any sign acknowledgment of it, she was just sitting there, waiting
for him to sit on the opposite free chair of their reserved table. Her face did not change when he
flashed his perfect smile and offered his hand in open handshake across the coffee table.
'Mademoiselle, I am…'
He did not have a time to finish his sentence. His thought has been stopped in split second as he
hit an empty wall in front of him. His body continued his right hand movement through the space
between them for one or two seconds, and then he lost control of it, his hand dropped beside his

body like numb, dry branch, fell from the old tree. His mouth stayed open as he wanted something else to tell her, but suddenly he forgot what it was. Twenty meters left of them the "Starbuck's" bartender caught some strange movement at the end row of coffee tables closest to the exit on Gate number 3, but he was distracted by waitress's yelling order from front desk service:

"Two cappuccinos, low fat, no milk, no sugars, with whipped cream, no sprinkles, … " "Two times blubbery muffins!" "FOR HERE!"

"One double espresso!" "One straight!" "One regular - long shot!" "Three latte macchiato, with low fat milk, chocolate's sprinkles on the top!" "One carrot cake!" "Two brownies and two cheesecakes!" "TO - GO!"

Nash felt like under the water, his right hand slowly passed beside his hip bone and stayed there for a second, then in the low arc went back and stopped beside his right suit's pocket.

He heard his voice in his head, which sounds a little strange to him, echoing and booming in the same time, to sit on the chair in front of him. He listen his voice for some time and he had a wish to add something to that, more like suggestion, but he couldn't remember what… At first, he heard chair's scrapping noise and then he saw that his hand was dragging the chair on the floor and positioning it beside him.

How come that my body is faster than my mind? Usually it was opposite?!

Then he felt the chair under his butt, and it was wooden chair, but it feels like made of cushions and sponge.

What a good feeling…

He knew girl on the opposite side of the table, but he couldn't remember where they have met, before… He can't put her in the picture at all… Like she was part of him, his life, all along, from the beginning,…

The girl came closer to Nash like she is going to whisper something in his ear, something private and confidential. She touched his forehead lightly, as if she was removing braid of his hair from it and from that moment Nash lost himself completely, his brevity left him, he did not fell to the dark hole as before, he did not fell at all, he rose above, in the direction of the light and inside that light, he lost himself.

CHAPTER III

Section 2.

KRKAN

May, 1992.

BOSNIA AND HERZEGOVINA, BOSANSKA KRAJINA REGION, CITY OF PRIJEDOR...

CODE - NAME: "KRKAN"("SAVAGE")

(Modern Day – Prijedor, Entity of Republika Srpska, Bosnia and Herzegovina)

...

That night I was watching TV with my mother, in our living room, when I heard loud knocking on our apartment's door. I went there and opened it. It was Serbian Police patrol. I have recognized one of them, it was our neighbor's son Bata Kovacevich and two other males dressed as members of police. They ordered me to go with them immediately to the police station for some additional interrogations. One of them saw TV channel which was on in that moment and he made a comment:

"Watching Croatian TV channel?! Fuck You and fuck your President Tudjman, bitch!" "Where is your sister Amra?"

"Tonight, she is on her regular night shift at the hospital."

They pushed me downstairs towards Mercedes van which has been parked in front of the building. They put me on the back and started the engine.

I saw that they were driving in hospital direction.

"Where are my sons? Do you know what happened to them?"

"Shut up you whore or you are going to join with your brothers!"

I was scared to death and I did not dare to ask anything else. The van stopped after some time and it was in idle, maybe two – three minutes, when the door opened and my sister Amra was pushed inside. The door was slammed and we continued our nightmare drive. She did not have a time to remove her white doctor's outfit and she asked me quietly:

"What have just happened Alma? Where are we going?"

"I do not know..."

They drove us to Main Police Station and locked us in o n e small room without words. We were frozen by our fears and we were waiting all night for someone to interrogate us or come for us, but all that night nobody showed up. We stayed there almost all next day without water or food. Close to the same night, they came and forced us to the toilets, so we have managed to drink water there in the meantime. They loaded us on some military truck two days after that and drove us in the middle of the night. It was dark and late in the night when they stopped and pushed us out. Even with the weak moonlight in my eyes, I have recognized the place:

"Keraterm" Factory."

They opened iron's door" Number 1 Hall" and pushed us inside. When my eyes were adjusted to the semi - dark I saw horrible sight. The Hall was filled with only male prisoners. Place was packed with people, some of them had faces carved in mask of horror, scared faces, lost, empty eyes, blinking like ghosts at us some of them had scars on their bodies and their faces, dried blood on the limbs, heads and shattered clothes. I have heard some crying sounds, and even I am born in this area I couldn't recognize anybody in the darkness. One of them came to me and called my name:

"Alma..."

I did not recognize his face, but I recognize his voice, it was voice of my uncle. Very soon, after maybe half hour later, they have come in and told us that we have to finish some job for them, to take care of some upstairs rooms. They put me i n one room and my sister went in the other one. When I get inside, I realized there is nothing to clean and take care of there. There was not electricity power, only one candle gave some light to the place. At first I thought I made some mistake and entered the wrong room, but in the same second the doors were opened and the man entered the room. It was Zoran Sikirica, "intellectual" man, educated and he was famous, well-known person, respected in the city where I grow up. He entered, locked the door and welcomed me with the words:

"With God's Help, Turkish Woman!"

I did not answer anything.

"Remove your clothes! All of It! Slowly and Easy! Do it! Now!"

I was stunned by this, but I have managed to answer him:

"No! I do not!"

"Fuck You! Did you hear what I have just said?! Do it now!"

I couldn't do it and I did not want it, I felt strong resistance inside my soul... Zoran move towards me, he attempted to remove my clothes, and I resisted fearlessly and backed up until I hit the table and the candle fell off from it to the ground. Darkness covered the room completely. Suddenly Zoran grab me and I have get hard kick in my head, in my left eye. Blood splashed my face and I was almost lost at the moment. I was on the floor next second and immediately he continued his assault, hitting me harder and ripping - off my clothes till I was completely naked. I have tried to stand up in the dark, but I received another punch in my head, this time harder on the face. I was on the edge of my consciences, helpless in the dark. I heard his movements in the dark, he was removing his clothes and in the next moment, he was pushing inside me, like some savage and he raped me hard, on the most vulgar way. I was in my menstrual cycles and I had very hard bleeding. I felt pool of blood under me and I felt the bleeding from my head, face...

For a moment I think I lost my consciences and the animal continued it with his words:

"Fuck you bitch! Are you enjoying it?! It is good! You like it same as I, don't you, bitch?!"

Pain was unbearable and I vomited from the shock. I have got another punch in my face, and after this I lost my consciences completely. I do not have a clue how much time passed, when I heard rattling chain's noise on the other side of the door. It was still dark in the room and I tried to orient myself in the darkness, when someone brought the light through open door. I saw sunrise was up, by the light that was coming through open door. I thought it was Zoran, again, but it was another man. He watched me for some time without movements and said:

"Get Up! Get your things and dress up. Quickly!"

I was broken, but I managed to get up and collect threads of my clothes and cover myself the best as I can. The blood trailed my legs as we went downstairs. On the bottom of the hallway I saw group of soldiers lined up by the wall. At the end of it Zoran – The Animal was standing. He asked the man who brought me from the room:

"Did you treat yourself with the Turkish- Girl?!"

There was no response from the man.

"You son of a bitch! You don't have balls to do it! What kind of Serbian soldier are you?! You useless peace of shit, move away!"

Zoran moved quickly cursing and yelling in the same time, then pushed a man aside, grabbed my hand and he dragged me upstairs to the same room. The room looked awful, bathed in the sunrise light, overturned upside down and smeared with blood. This time he did not locked entrance door.

"Just for the record, your sons are here, too… And if you do not cooperate with me and tried to resist, I am going to kill them slowly and painfully in front of your eyes…"

I knew that bastard is telling me the truth. I did not resist anymore. He brutally raped me again, cursed me and savagely tortured me through it; he was making some inarticulate sounds, he bite me couple times on the neck breasts and arms and after he was done with it, I already collapsed under him, out of my strength. He called his guards and told them:

"Take her to the big hall."

On the daylight the big hall was picture of hell, creepy and scary. I realized that the hall been packed with old people and children together with the others prisoners.

They were watching me without words with the endless sorrows in their eyes, most of them know me very well, and I recognized most of them. Our eyes communicated wordlessly and told each other everything. I saw my Amra cuddled in one corner, covered with bruises, bitten and scratched, she was crying quietly. Every morning started with beatings, crying, tortures and killings… All you can hears some cars were arriving on the spot and after that screams, yells, curses and fires from machine guns. I couldn't see anything outside, but the sounds were telling us all what we did not want to know, but all of us knew it without our eyes. I heard some cries and begged voice asking them to stop beating him and kill him to stop his misery and sufferings. They laughed to his cries and they continued to torture him. Songs were echoing through the day:

"Who will be the second One, I will be the first One, to drink blood of Turkish - One!"

"Who was saying - Who was laying Serbia is small one, She was never small - She fought three times with all..."

Chetniks songs continued and in the hall new people arrived every day, but the others which have been dragged outside never return. Some other women were brought there, too. During the daylight, two of us, as females were not forced out, only after the sunset they would come for us. Others whose names did not know have raped us continuously, but we remember their faces and their body smells. Three days after Amra and me were moved to some other building in the compound where they 've told us that we are the spies of Alija (Alija Izetbegovic, President of BIH) and that is the reason they are going to execute us. I saw six soldiers, they prepared their guns and we were told to step towards the wall and our hands on the back of our head and turn our backs on them... Suddenly, I heard steps and cursing of Sikirica Zoran and his order to postponed execution up to some other day. Two days after, close to the evening hours four soldiers in Chetniks badges and uniforms came and brought me in the same room as before. After we have entered it, they pushed me on the floor; they took some ropes and tied up my hands on my back. They checked that they tied me properly and they stayed in the room without words...

Ten- twenty minutes after Zoran went in to the room and told them:

"Leave us. Get lost!"

He closed and locked the door after they left. He came on me and removed my skirt. I was terrified and in the same instant, I have got same symptoms as when I had my period. It just came out. He removed his clothes without words. He was ready for new sexual orgy. When he removed my panties and pushed himself in me, he felt the blood, stopped and screamed:

"You are disgusting... you Muslim – Whore!"

He turned his back to me and went to the table. There was a glass bottle on the table. He took it, *came back to me, watched me for some time and then he bent over me and pushed the bottle in my vagina, screaming with joy. He was turning and pushing with his entire strength glass bottle inside me. The pain was terrible and I could not stand it, I screamed and I have lost my consciences completely… I woke up close to sunrise, wet all over my body and numb. When I realized what happened and where I am, I fainted again frozen with fear. I woke up later in the morning. My hands were free. I was wet from my blood and I couldn't move at all. Beside me on the floor was glass bottle smeared with blood. Room door was wide open and Chetniks soldiers were getting in small group to see Bosnian Muslim women naked on the floor, some of them made a comment:*

"You're disgusting pig!.."

Some of them would come inside to spit on me, or kick me from time to time, and I was just laying there for them. After some time four females came, washed my body and put me back on my spot in the hall. After this two of us, Amra and I, they transported us to "Omarska" compound. We were together with the other 28 women in one room. Most of us knew each other, by our names or by our faces. Most of them brought have been there before us, all of them were thin, skinny, ghostly white, and speechless towards everything that was happening around and with them. We have not talked to each other very often and not for long periods; mostly we watched each other and shared our sadness, misery and fears through hopeless stares. Prison was horrible place. In "Omarska" compound was imprisoned thousand of Bosnian Muslims and Croats, men, old people and children. It was real Hell on the Earth. The same day when we came, we were sent to work on cleaning compound, rooms, toilets, kitchen work, etc… It was not allowed to speak to each other, and we were forced to watch all shooting and killings and after that we have to clean all bloody trace. In the endless rows of mutilated bodies I was looking for my sons and prayed to God that I am not going to find them. Every morning they would line up all of us and welcome us with words:

"With God's Help, Turks!"

We had to answer them:

"With God's Help, Serbs!"

One morning, one of mine close by neighbors, named Hajra asked me to borrow my scarf.

"Why?"

She did not answered to me, instead she pull up here shirt and showed me her large belly, hers skirt was unzipped, so she tied up her scarf to support the belly which has been growing every day. I have met here after that in some occasions and she was not able to hide it anymore under her cloths. Soon after, she was not able to move at all and the last time when I saw her, they dragged her to the "White House", as we called one building there, and nobody saw her after that... Every one of them, Chetniks, soldiers, had a right to hit us, torture, rape and do whatever he want it to do with any of us, day or night, whatever and whenever they chose on their free will. Sometimes, some of prisoners would beg them to stop with words:

"Please stop it, my brother... Just, shot me, please..."

They would answer it:

"I am not your brother; you Muslim mother-fucker..., Fuck your mother!"

The worst of them, was Mladjo Radic, nicknamed "Krkan" ("Savage"), bloodthirsty and cruel, he raped me and other women on many occasions in front of everybody, in the daylight, in the middle of prison's compound. Due to the fact that all our families were prisoners of "Omarska", he threatened all of us with words:

"I am going to kill your children, your mother, father... All your families... All of you!!!"

...

I have closed additional pages that were attached to the file and closed my eyes, too. I have only one wish now, to reach my bed and sleep like a newborn baby... My "B & B" especially first of" B", as breakfast was close to burst back on the surface of the table and I have felt the same ticking in the back of my skull when I was in Ruanda and Tanzania. Headaches will come later without any delay. I need to get out and take a long walk... Then maybe, I will be able to do other "B", bed and good, calm sleep, without nightmares and heavy dreams about the past and overseas wars.

…

Marc Arsenault went out from "Sandi's Home Cookin' House'" restaurant and took a huge gulp of unusually hot September's air. The day looked promising in the eyes of ordinary, hard working regularly stressed people. Marc took his first step and realized that his last wish is not going to happen for some time, not now at the beginning of his long walk to his office.

CHAPTER III

Section 3.

SMS

August, 1998.

CROATIA, DALMATIAN COAST, CITY OF DUBROVNIK, DOWNTOWN, STRADUN STREET…

The waiter checked his new guest again and his timing was perfect. Black colored man with gold rimmed sunglasses, dressed in simple white T – shirt gave him a signal to bring another double shot of herbal brandy called "travarica" on his table. He knew that brandy can hit the man hard and quick, but the following guest showed unusual resistance to it, without any side effects on his fifth order of 2 deciliters, pure homemade brandy. On the other side, he had very good supper, it started with "prsut", ham and special cheese from island of Pag and salted olives. Main dish was made of one large portion of " pashticada", beef stuffed with lard and roasted in "Dingach" wine and Mediterranean spices, and finished it with typical dessert in Dubrovnik, named "rozata", locally produced version of crème caramel. Waiter expected some tip after all, but from his previous experience with American tourists, he is going to have a big argument at the end, when he produced the bill… As customers, most of the time they are not happy with prices or missed "good deals" which they used to have back in the States.

Fuck them! They should pay the bill and we should charge them properly!

They want to sit on the main street, on Stradun, eat cheap, drink cheap and enjoy our sun and crystal clear sea, only for something like 1, 99 dollars. When I was in Paris, France, on Boulevard Des Chanselise, I paid 5 Euros for one latte macchiato! When I was in Rome, Italy, inside Vatican City, on St. Peter's Square, I paid 8 Euros for one small shot of espresso, and why not…

'Ante! Did you fall asleep or what?! Don't you see that man is calling you?'

The cook opened kitchen's door and he yelled on waiter, who was looking in the same direction, but he was frozen with his hand on the bottle of "Travarica" - "Brandy of herbs". Black man drop his left hand on the table after inefficient three signals to the waiter and he remind himself that this one is not going to get any tip from him, no way! He felt that brandy only warmed up his blood, his head was clear and his body handled alcohol very well due to additional fact that his supper was extraordinary big and good. He knew how much beverages he can handle and he did not expect any problems with it. He needed it tonight, especially after all that shit what happened back in city of Pula, two days ago. He sent detailed report to his supervisor at Washington, DC, together with scanned pages from the book, which contained another additional map of probable location of lost artifacts. Since he started this special assignment - crusade for these items, he met really weird people and strange things happened to him, here in Balkan. He has a feeling that as much as he discovered so far, things get more and more complicated with every following steps that he made; area of his responsibilities was getting bigger and bigger and soon he will require additional help from someone. Next time, he is going to make some suggestions to his boss and special equipment requirements from The Cell. He always preferred to work alone in the field, but now it will be wiser to have some back up personnel close by… Maybe, he is getting old for all this, after all… His mobile phone vibrated in his pocket only once. It's probably new Inbox message. He pulled it from the pouch on his belt and unlocked it with the code. LCD screen lighted itself and message pop up instantly:

"Cell is up and charged in full. Battery will not last long. Two - three hours maximum. We do not have a spare one. Get another there, asap. That brand is not available on our market. Seller's store was closed without notice. Original provider changed his primary location to overseas. You can try with local stores there, but we can only advise you to improvise till next delivery. Good luck with it!"

Waiter materialized in front of him with his order.

'Thank You! May I have the bill, please?'

Willburn pressed red button on his phone once. Thought about the message for some time and then switch off the phone. His worst nightmare has become reality. He does not have enough time to finish everything.

I am in the vacuum. I am sucked into the black hole. God, help me!

CHAPTER III

Section 4.

FEVER

June,1866.

AUSTRIAN HUNGARIAN EMPIRE, GOSPIC TOWN, VILLAGE OF SMILJAN, TESLA'S FAMILLY HOUSE…

(Modern day – Croatia, Gospic, Smiljan)

Milutin Tesla, priest, was holding his three fingers together above his eyes, on his forehead, and crossed himself three times across his chest, left and right shoulder and the end of his belly, and in the same time he repeated his prayers:

'Dear God, keep my son alive, I have already lost one, Do not take this one, I beg You as a parent, Not as a priest, Help him dear God…, To be better and live…, keep my Nikola alive…, Please…'

He kneeled beside the bed in his living room and closed his hands in front of him and he put his head on the edge of the bed inn silent prayer. His hands were shaking a little every time as he put his forehead on them. On the bed, covered with hand maid blankets and sheep's flattened skins was body of child, ten years old boy, with dark black hair, thin long limbs, his hands were under the covers and his legs were wrapped with the same blanket, too. Only his head wasn't covered, except the white linen cloth on his forehead, and his dried and cracked lips were moving, whispering some mumbled words without any meaning. His thin face was white mask, covered with sweat; eyes were moving left and right, from one corner to the other, under his eyelids, his all body was like a string, rigid and feverish, hot from his rising temperature. Milutin rise and uncover son's legs to check socks attached on his feet, full of potato's slices mixed with apple's vinegar, an old medicine to remove temperature from the body. At the end, when he was satisfied with that, he add wet cloth on his son's forehead and additional one under Nikola's shirt, soaked with pig's fat, this is going to collect temperature from his son's lungs. Gently he returned the covers on unmoved Nikola and kissed his forehead with prayer:

'God Bless You my son and do not be afraid, He will give you the strength to rise after this.'

Milutin pull out Nikola's left hand under the covers and he took it with his both hands. Nikola's blue colored nails look polished like, to the opposite whiteness of his skin; the veins on it pulsed with hot blood pumped from his strong heart and with wetness of his skin reminded Milutin on wet, long petals of some rare flower. While he was holding it in his hands, tears slide across his face and they dropped on Nikola's hand.

'My son, I promise You, that I will not push you as before to become a priest, you can go and study whatever you want, just stay alive and be well… I see, that I have made a mistake when I asked you to do things which you did not want… Just, don't live us… We love you… I love you….'

Nikola's eyes opened a little and he squeezed his fingers in his father's hands. It was light movement, just a small twitch of his hand that caused his father to raise his wet eyes from them to his son's face and asked:

'Nikola?'

Nikola's eyes were closed, only difference was that they went calm under his eyelids and on the edge of his left eye one tear stopped briefly and then continued to slide towards already soaked pillow.

'Nikola…'

CHAPTER III

Section 5.

FISHING

August, 2009.

CANADA, ALBERTA, EDMONTON, STURGEON COUNTY, CFB (CANADIAN FORCES BASE) EDMONTON, HQ BUILDING, ROOM NUMBER 23…

Inspector Blaquier left Master Corporal Roger Dew additional 10 seconds to "fry over easy", and then he flipped him over to the other side and pressed it harder. Man on the other end of the phone line got very nervous.

He should be. He deserved it.

"Take me to the river…"

'Claude Lévesque.'

"Put me in the water…"

'Never heard.'

The bait is on.

'Major Claude Lévesque?'

Something is "fishy" around here.

'As I said, never heard.'

Pull the string.

'Are you sure?'

Release a little…

'Positive.'

Turn the wheel…

'How come, when I have information that you've served together in Croatia, Bosnia and later in Kosovo?'

Roll the silk.

'What information? Who told you that?'

Pull it back.

'Colonel Brian Murhead.'

Release again…

'I do not know him.'

Roll the silk.

'1992. Stop. Sarajevo. Stop.'

Pull it hard.

'What's that?'

Pull it harder…

'Pale. Stop. Jahorina. Stop.'

Hook it.

'What are you talking about?'

Catch it.

'Mountain house. Stop.'

Pull it to the surface…

'What the…'

Grab it.

'Woman. Stop. Rape. Stop.'

In the net.

'Listen…'

On the floor…

'General. Stop.'

No air.

'…'

Trash and splash.

'Luis MacKenzie. Didn't Stop.'

Remove the hook.

'Man, I…'

Measure it.

'Let's have a meeting.'

Pick it up.

'Only under one condition. No recording.'

Put it back in the water.

'Deal.'

Clean the net.

'Deal. Where?'

"Take me to the river…"

'Muttart Conservatory, Tropical Pyramid, tomorrow at 3 o' clock PM. White shirt, cream pants and Edmonton's Sun in the left back pocket, front page faced up.'

"Put me in the water…"

CHAPTER III

Section 6.

BOHEMIA

April, 1918.

AUSTRIAN HUNGARIAN EMPIRE, BOHEMIA, TEREZIA, TEREZIN FORTRESS, PRISON CELL…

The Latin Bridge image flickered above the Miljacka river surface producing flashes of stars on her surface on this warm day of June 1914. Light reflected directly to his eyes and he tried to avoid them by adjusting his hat closer to his already wet brows. Sweat bite him under his armpits and sting his eyes with its salty – sourly taste. He heard an explosion some minutes ago and he knew that if Nedeljko missed the target, he was the last in line to defend ideas of their group "Union or Death", honorable "Young Bosnia" young government movement, made of Serbs, Croats and Bosniacs, that was committed to the independence of the South Slavic peoples from Austria – Hungarian Empire. Especially now when they rejected his membership to "komite" of irregular Serbian guerrilla forces of the secret society "Ujedinjenje ili Smrt"("Unification or Death"), known as Black Hand. Tankosic from Prokuplje personally told him that he is too small and too weak to become member of their elite Black Hand Force Group. He will prove to him and to all of them that he was more than equal to all of them and that he was destined to become a hero. His shadow stretched and rested on the wall of Moritz Schiller's café bar, when he heard exited people's voices, together with the booming car engine that drove past him and continued down the crowded road of Franz Josef Street. He spotted and immediately recognized Ferdinand's figure inside the car. Suddenly driver of the car put his foot on the brake and began to back up in reverse towards his spot, when he realized that he took the wrong turn. The car engine protested, stalled and stopped, the gears were locked instantly. He detached himself from the mass, using this unexpected opportunity, and stepped forward, pulled out his gun and fired once in the direction of incoming vehicle. Woman's light colored eyes met his in a brief second before the bullet got her in her abdomen.

"Why?!"

Her thought imprinted inside his brain together with the scream of dying child inside her womb.

"Eeeeeeeeeeeeeeeeeeeeeeeeeeeeeeeee...."

Scream of the child woke him up and he felt wetness of his own sweat across his bold head. This time he did not have time for another shot.

But I shot twice..., as I can remember..., And there wasn't any child there at the time..., Or there was...?!

Gavrilo, the postman son, opened his swollen, wet eyes and felt salty streaks of tears on his left cheek. The same dream hunted him for all these three years and ten months here in the Terezin's Fortress prison cell, dream of unborn child, his voice and thoughts followed by his steps behind Gavrilo's own steps every time when it's time for a walk.

It would be much better for me that I have managed to shot myself in the head, or that damn cyanide pill worked out...

He coughed heavily three times and swallowed bloody spit, and instead of sickness in his stomach and weakness of his breath, he felt warm liquid moisturizing his dry, painfully parched throat. He contracted tuberculosis long time before prison's doctor told him that, he knew that before an assassination of Archduke, that was the main reason why he had small physical stature. His non-existing fingers of his left arm, amputated a year ago by Austrian butchers, were still wiggling through his severed nerves which did not existed any more, but there were connected on the other end to his brain that tortured him for all this time after.

The Black Hand betrayed me, they've put weak cyanide for all six of us, Nedeljko and Mohamed tried and failed, same as I, to kill themselves, the rest of them were too weak to do it...

From the beginning, we were doomed, sacrificed in the name of freedom and justice, recruited to die, to become worm's food from the start...

Strange unfamiliar sound coming from behind his back broke his thoughts. It was some kind of buzzing, deep drone of heavy bumblebee inside his ear. It was humming and vibrating in the same time around him in an endless noise that pressed him inside – out. He turned around on his back and he saw female face closed to his own. The face looked familiar to him, as he met her somewhere before…

Sssssssss…, Seme… (Schematics…?) Seko (Sister)…

'Who…?!'

Mmmmmmmmmm…, Mapa… (Map?) Mama (Mother)…

'Are…?!'

Rrrrrrrrr…, Ruka… (Hand) Braco (Brother)…

'You…?!'

Tttttttttt…, Talisman…?! Tata (Father)… Smrt… (Death)?!

'I know what you are looking for… But, I am not going to tell you where it is…'

The Hand is safe… Hidden… Under… The… Water…

…

Gavrilo's body weakened by malnutrition, weighted around 40 kilograms and his amputated arm hung uselessly on the side, has been lifted in the air by female shape apparition. The ghostly image held him another three seconds like that and then returned his weak body back to the wooden bench. As the ghoul dissolved in front of his eyes, Gavrilo's last breath left his body.

CHAPTER IV
Section 1.

CLICK

September, 2009.

CANADA, ONTARIO, TORONTO, TORONTO POLICE SERVICE, MAIN BUILDING, 40 COLLEGE STREET,3'RD FLOOR…

…

Click.

Click. Click.

Click. Click. Click…

Michelle clicked on another Power Point Slide on the screen of her 32'' inch Dell monitor. Hard drive of her, also, Dell desktop computer, was humming happily under her office desk, all her calls are on hold at the moment, and her digital automated answering machine is going to pick up all emergency calls from the other departments or outside calls. She was looking through set of slides taken at accident report from the International Pearson Airport and even she read hard copies of Incident report, made by Security personnel of the airport. Medical Investigator's report and Police officer on the scene detailed description of the event, she couldn't rid off the feeling that something was wrong, something was missing or something has to be added to it. It was just an itch – thought in her head, just a small empty space between the lines on the pages, there were bugging her. The man, named Nash Stevanovich had an accident. He had brain seizure attack on the airport, on arrival gates, in the coffee shop area, where he landed with overseas flight from Europe. These things happened before, sometimes in the plane, too, but this time it was for some reasons different… Something was familiar to her, involving his face expression and the picture from the scene caught between the moments, it looks memorable to… She has seen this somewhere before… She has two more cases to analyze after this and three more on hold, due to additional crime scene revised versions reports and her inner clock was ticking on over time for last three hours. She was tired, that was all.

You can't handle the same amount of job as before woman! When are you going to accept the truth! You are not 25 years old anymore, you have more than 40 now; and you have to respect it, remember your age! Ten years ago, maybe your chance had been better then now, you had enough... Ooohhhh... My God! Ten years ago! That is It!

She jumped towards the phone, unlock it and she canceled all forwarding, pressing "* 86", after that she punched "archive" section's extension number and she grabbed the pen and notepad book ready for "rock-an-roll". Her right hand was shaking from an excitement.

My heart violently shook from sadness and sorrow!

CHAPTER IV

Section 2.

PROMISE

September, 1998.

UNITED STATES OF AMERICA, CALIFORNIA, LOS ANGELES, 140 NORTH LA STREET; MAIN DISTRICT POLICE DEPARTMENT, CHIEF'S DETECTIVES OFFICE...

Marc played the last voice mail message then he made notes in his pocketbook. Another day in "City of Angels" as they called it, for him on the everyday job he called "City of Devils". The thing is that his job influenced all his private life, so his perspective and opinion on the city name remind the same since he came here. He have got another call from South Central area, this time for district that runs south from Slauson Avenue along Figueroa Street – an area notorious for prostitution, drug crime and violence. Many of the cases had languished unsolved for years, buried among hundreds of open homicide cases that backed up in that area. A security guard found 21 – year – old Regina Williams, partially naked body in the back of a downtown Los Angeles business. She was Alexandria, Va., resident and she had been raped brutally; then strangled, the killing itself was recorded on a grainy surveillance videotape. This was the first time that they are going to have some trace to follow at least. Marc knew that most of the time, deaths of this serial killer will not drew virtually no attention when they happened, and the paperwork on them might easily have remind filed in police archives among hundreds of other old, unsolved homicides. He compared with other cases, too; all the names and dates that filled his answering machine memory; all victims ranged in age from their early 20s to late 40s, but most were around 20. Some were prostitutes, and several had struggled with drug addiction or they just lived on the streets of "City of Devils". The sheer number of cases to choose from and to track made his task daunting. So many had stacked up at one time in the LAPD's 77-th Street and Southeast divisions which were covering part of South – Central L.A., that other detectives believed several serial killers might have been involved. Over the last year, the detectives from other divisions kept submitting DNA samples from various cases to the main LAPD lab. It gave results after all. Nearly one in every six months they got hits and the number kept on growing, after five in a row for last month they start to ask themselves where is going to end? The earliest of these murders dated since the beginning of March 1996; as per Mic's files, and it was partly nude body of Diane Lyon, 21, she was spotted by two passing motorists at some construction area in the block of South Grand Avenue, near the Harbor Freeway. First, she has been raped and after she was killed by glass bottle in her vagina, as per detective's reports. The alleged rampage continued through the years up to this date. The partly nude or completely naked bodies of women showed up again and again, one every few months or years. Dumped in alleys and vacant buildings, or on roadsides and stairwells, they resurfaced again. Only one body was found in a better part of the neighborhood. All of them have been killed with the same similarity, some strangled with bare hands or garrote. Mic provided these additional pages with the file from 1992. Different continent, some other country, an additional city followed by the same bloody pattern across the ocean. Finally, now he had solid lead and the name behind these 25 victims so far. *Zoran Sikirica.*

…

At least that was his name back in Bosnia… Here, he is someone else… But,… I will find him… That is my promise… To all of them.

CHAPTER IV

Section 3.

THE STONE

September, 1998.

CROATIA, DALMATIAN COAST, DUBROVNIK CITY, OLD CITY OF DUBROVNIK...

...

It means that I am not going to get any additional equipment - weapon and there are no available agents to help me. I have maximum 2 to 3 days to find that hidden, sealed room, here in Dubrovnik, if there is one at all. I do not have any time to explore other locations, in Herceg - Novi, Montenegro and hidden site at Canyon of Tara River, due to some unexplained deadlines... Plus, they have lost contact with Professor B. L. at USA, L. A, and all documentation from his house and office disappeared, the only option is to go back to Canada, Niagara Falls and find Fitzgerald Francis's notes and compare them with FBI files from 1943 found at New York's hotel. The worst part of it's that I have to go back to Pocitelj, to that shit-hole of Bosnia! I don't like that place at all! I still have scars from the last encounter with them and it took me six months in Swiss hospital to recover from injuries! I don't like it at all! Fuck it! Fuck them all!

Agent Lionel Willburn cursed under his breath climbing the stairs on his way to Dubrovnik's Fortress of Minceta, located on the north side of the City Walls which were protecting Dubrovnik Republic and the city for centuries, the most massive tower within the Old Town. On the city walls which are surrounding the Old Town usually there was endless lines of tourists with cameras, sunglasses, colored hats and bags packed with souvenirs, but this late afternoon there was only handful groups of them on the wall. Maybe, weather's forecast for the late afternoon and evening discouraged most of them to climb the stairs, together with raised strong wind locally named "Bura" prevent the rest of them to take initiative and follow their path.

It was even better for him; he did not want to be disturbed by noisy, annoying bunch of idiots running around him, clicking with his "idiots – cameras" and making moronic comments like:

"That's great!" "That's great!" "A lot of history!"

The wind was getting stronger here on open space area and his long sleeves cotton's sweater wasn't his best option; he suddenly realized that according to the mapped drawings, he should see the stone with the Sign carved on his surface. The stone should be around the next few meters after this curved edge of the wall… His eyes surveyed the area closely, the long shadows made by coming sundown just complicated things, polished by foot, washed by the sea and rain and shaped by winds for centuries; he knew that it is going to be hard task to find old carvings made by unknown man long time ago. Cracks and scars on the stones are deep, wide and there is so many of them, if he did not have to concentrate only on this particular area, his search will become extremely difficult…

Wait a second…, There is something… There… Yes…

He pulled out his flashlight and concentrated the beam on the spot. Picture was weak, shape of the wolf's head had been barely visible; but pictogram distinguished itself on the white surface of the stone. He checked the area again, before he reached small tools attached to his left leg, under the trousers. It will be disastrous that someone can see him to demolish stones one of UNESCO's World Heritage Sites tonight… It took him almost one hour to excavate particular stone from the wall, even with highly concentrated muriatic acid and diamond's head chisels as grounding tools. He avoided making noise as much as possible and with less frequent passing tourists, he managed to remove it after additional 30 minutes. There was additional free space under the stone and when he reached with his hand inside, he felt leather pouch under his fingers. He pulled out pouch, which was partially disintegrating under his fingers and he gently opened it. Some kind of polished gem or stone was inside it, surface was smooth and it was oval shaped surface under his touch. For a second he pressed the button on his small flashlight to see it. It was black.

Bingo! The first gem discovered…

CHAPTER IV

Section 4.

VISION

May, 1870.

AUSTRIAN HUNGARIAN EMPIRE, TOWN OF KARLOVAC, THE MAIN TRAIN STATION…

(Modern day – Croatia, Karlovac)

Tesla was happy to see Mara again. Mara was working at his uncle's house in Karlovac as a cooking lady for some time, until his aunt fired her, after she caught Nikola and her in the pantry kissing each other. Mara hugged him and squeezed him between her hands and her large breasts. It was good to feel women's body again, but he was in the same time embarrassed by her publicly opened adoration and revoked desire from his loins; that flushed blood in his colored cheeks betrayed him in the middle of train station square full of people. She told him that she would always remember him and she gave him piece of paper with her new address in Zagreb. She lightly kissed him on his forehead and disappeared through endless mingling mass of coming – going passengers on the departure gate of Karlovac train main station.

Women – Creatures build of love and hate. They love you with the same energy and they hate you with the same love. They float above us as angels of mercy, protecting us from evil spirits, but if you ruin their trust and failed to love them, they will become the same evil spirit and your angel of death.

He checked time on his watch; he had 30 minutes before train's departure. Someone beside him passed and hit him with his elbow. His black umbrella, horizontally attached to his bag, slide from it and it descended to the ground… The white light filled his eyes. On the edge of his eyelids appeared some blue lines, pressure on his temples increased with every second, his jaw tighten and he clenched his teeth in pain. His vision blurred with purple flashes, eyes sockets get heat from inside, burning sensation spread through them inward to the back of his skull. His inner voice was lost, his thoughts blocked by buzzing noise in the background; small voices are telling him to be careful, they guide him to find his focus, to keep balance on the edge between his lost sanity and found insanity. Other part of him standing beside as his shadow of the light heard an announcement:

"Train from Belgrade arrived on Gate 5…"

Picture of long tube, filled with liquid – gas, like flute without holes, shape was trembling in the middle of white light, it was rotating in the place, his view of it changed with every second, from inside to the outside in three dimensions, taking different angles. Childish voices whispered words through his head:

"Aluminum cylinder…3 bar…,pressure…vacuum inside…diameter… 25…,long… 2…,width…, 1, 8…, 5% of…"

Drums were booming, thunder and lightning hit the flute with deafening noise, cracked picture of attached wires to it, ripped with flashes of red, with floating balls of gold in the middle, levitating in the air, buzzing around, rotating itself in the opposite direction…

"Train to Vienna departing in 15 minutes…"

Foggy image of his watch appeared in front of him, at first he was on its surface between the numbers, seconds were clicking around him, and then it was above him. The watch was large as round swimming pool, next moment it become size of bike's wheel, rotating itself, then transformed itself as balloon floating in front of his face and at the end it was shrunken to his normal, regular size attached to his right hand. Tesla blinked with his eyes, opened and closed his long fingers in the fist, just to get blood running through his numb right hand, when in the same time, his umbrella hit the ground and it clattered with his wooden handle in front of him.

He was confused and stunned when he realized that 15 minutes passed since he lost track of time and he fell inside void of his uncontrolled visions again.

It happened again…

Beside him, someone's thick male voice whispered:

'I beg your pardon, I sincerely apologized you for your umbrella…'

CHAPTER IV

Section 5.

GENERAL

June, 1992.

BOSNIA AND HERZEGOVINA, CITY OF SARAJEVO, VICINITY OF PALE… CODE - NAME: "GENERAL"

(Modern Day – Sarajevo, Entity of Federation, Bosnia and Herzegovina)

…

I was on the bus to evacuate my one - year old baby and myself somewhere far away from three months shelling, shooting and fighting for blocked and occupied City of Sarajevo. Transport was "organized" by The First Children Embassy – Medjasi and I was on it, (under the name "Lidija Goldbaher"). The place which has been paid in cash for 2000 DM (German Mark), reduced price due to mutual acquaintance and local's connections; when we were stopped by the road blocks – check point of Serbian Reserve Forces on the exit from Ilidza, suburb of Sarajevo.

They lined up us in front of the bus and after document's check out, told me to move aside with the baby and wait. One woman, Croatian by name, tried to protect me by begging them to release me and let me go has been" rewarded" by one of Serbian Reserve's soldier's two-three slaps on her face which was immediately covered in blood and she hit the ground.

'I did not ask for your comments or opinions, slut…!'

He said and I recognized Miso Bajic – nicknamed "Crnogorac" (Montenegrian"), who lived in Sarajevo, in our neighbor's area and I knew that he recognized me… He put finger on the women on the ground and then to the other passengers:

'You…, and the rest of you! Go back inside the bus!'

They put me in their vehicle and drove to the Main Police station in Ilidza. There I have spend night in the prison cell and early in the following morning, we continued across road to Pale and after that we reached Vogosca, another suburb of Sarajevo. We stopped in front of the "KON –

TIKI" Restaurant, nick - named as "Sonja", too. My baby cried very loud and often. One of them

made a comment:

'Fuck your mother Turkish Girl, if your bratty child doesn't stop crying, I will slam it against the

wall...'

They locked me in one of the rooms above the restaurant. Some man had occupied room; his

clothes were in the room. Hour and a half passed when door was open and two of them and one

woman came in.

'Give the baby and all his belongings to this woman, without any questions!

I went numb and very much scarred.

"What will happen with my baby?"

I tried to calm myself by thoughts that the baby will be OK, that they just want to investigate me

and after that, I will get him back... Child started to cry very hard, screaming when the woman

took it from me. I thought:

"They will change his diapers; he is wet and hungry..."

When women disappeared with my baby through the door, they told me to follow them. We went

inside the next room in the same corridor. Inside, two other men, around 35 –40 years old, in

military outfit were sitting there. Another woman in front of typing machine was sitting there, too.

'Jackie, are you ready?'

Man on the left asked the woman. She confirmed with the node of her head.

'You..., wann'a a cigarette?'

'I do not smoke.'

'Do you "smoke" anything else?'

The other man asked with the smile.

'You wann'a a drink? Something,... Strong?'

'No, thanks.'

'So, you are running away to Zenica?! Going to your Turkish fellows, friends?'

'No. I ...'

The one on the left side added:

'To your husband in "Green Berets", or he was in "Patriot's League"?'

'I don't know, as I know he is not with them, these organizations, he wasn't part of them at all...'

'Do not lie to us, we know everything, we are going to kill you all... If you are not with us, you are against us, what relatives you have in Zenica? That politician Salchinovich? Tell us!'

'I do not know any Salchinovich and I told you, I do not have anybody in Zenica!'

The other one slammed his fist on the table and yelled:

'We are going to confront both of you very soon, Turkish! And then you are going to "sing" different tune to us!'

Interrogation continued for hours, with questions about my family, attacking Muslim's politicians and glorifying Serbian politician Slobodan Milosevic, insulting me, cursing, insinuating and at the end they told me, that they are not satisfied with me, specially with my answers, that I have been laying all the time and that I am real peace of work. They brought me back to the same room where I was the first time with my baby. Room was empty and different this time. On the top of one of two sofas it was fresh ironed military, JNA jacket, with yellow stripes and one star sew it on an epaulets. Exhausted from investigation I set on one of them and curled in the corner. After approximately one hour, they came back and put me on the same chair in the same room, again. Questions were repeated again, with additional insinuations regarding my spy's activities and connections, with only difference that there were another two male "investigators", new faces with the same attitude...

'This is the proof of your subversive activities against us...'

One of them gave me the paper across their desk. I saw that it was on English language written and with a short look; I realized that was only some private family letter addressed to someone... I read some parts of it, when the same person took it from me.

'Do you know English?'

'Yes, I have some knowledge of it.'

'How good is that "some" knowledge?'

'I can read and write and I have basic conversations skills…'

Both of them smiled with satisfaction.

'We knew all this before, so we are just testing you. Your child is good and safe. It is up to you what is going to happen to him in near future… Only up to you… Understand?!'

I started to cry and I have begged them to give me back my child.

'It will be better for him to stay where he is in this moment. You are lucky one, you know… You should be in "bunker", with all others…'

One of them said and then they left me inside the room and locked the door. I stepped to the window and I saw two soldiers with guns on the entrance door. It was raining hard and heavy outside. In the evening, the man entered inside, he was dressed in JNA military uniform, approximately 45 years old, salt and pepper hair, medium height and build and addressed me as Major Vlado. He was speaking Serbian dialect and he told me that I am here only temporary, so I should be more cooperative with the other officers – investigators and that they are not satisfied with my answers and my attitude.

'We have already checked your background and we have some information about you. You are English teacher and you are teaching foreign language in the school… In addition, you lied to us that you are nurse, you are actually English language professor and you were working as translator for English Permanent Observers of European Union, these "ice cream delivery boys"…'

'This is nonsense! I am not English professor! I am not old enough to become one…'

'Shut Up! You Turkish whore!'

He quickly closed the distance between us, grabbed me and slammed me with his right hand two – three times across the face. I was not prepared for this and before I managed to give him an answer or react at all, he turned his back on me and left the room. After one hour, he was back with some clothes in his arms and threw them on sofa.

'Try them all now!'

'But, I can't...'

'I said now! If you continue to make troubles for us, you are not going to see your baby, ever!'

I went quiet and I have tried all women clothes. He was sitting on the opposite sofa during that period and after I finished with it, he chose one skirt, two blouses and one dress, put them aside.

'Soldier!'

The door opened and young soldier came in.

'Take these clothes back, and go to Milena, pick up an iron from her and bring it here, quickly!'

Soldier disappeared and after five minutes, he was back with an iron.

'You are going to prepare all this clothes that I "ve put here, put this dress on and I'll be back in twenty minutes! Better not be late!'

He was back on scheduled time and I did everything as he requested. We went outside to the parked jeep vehicle, with two soldiers inside, one was the driver, the other one has an automatic weapon with him and he was sitting on the back seat. It was dark outside, maybe early evening hours and after one hour drive they stopped in front of some mountain house. I think we were on the mountain of Jahorina, somewhere... He brought me to the room on the second floor and told me to take a shower, get dressed and be ready for half an hour. I did as he requested and soldiers came in and escorted me to restaurant look like area. They brought me to the table occupied by two people. One was a JNA officer, maybe colonel, and the other was 30 year old woman. The presented themselves as Stevo and Slobodanka and they were finishing their dinner. Soon I have got my dinner, too, it was "pljeskavica" (grounded meat like hamburger) and some salad. Music was coming from the speakers and some other two - three couples were dancing on the floor. Stevo and Slobodanka were dancing, too. Everything was quiet up t o 23:00 hours, when some other people came in. It was six to seven persons, all of them military personnel and two civilians. Two of them had foreign uniforms and the rest of military personnel were in JNA uniforms. One of them was approximately 45 years old, brown hair, taller and he had familiar face. I have seen him somewhere before, but I couldn't remember... Restaurant's staff had put two tables together and new arrivals seated near buy. Through Stevo and Slobodanka's *conversations I have found out that one of foreign officers is Luis MacKenzie, Canadian's General, commander of UNPROFOR's forces in Bosnia and Herzegovina. Then I have realized that I saw his pictures in local newspapers and his face on local TV almost every day, he was well - known, celebrity person in some way. Close to midnight, Major Vlado came in and quietly ordered me to go back my room. He escorted me to the room and locked it. I was too tired, but I was not able to sleep after all, I tried to lie down on the bed, but I couldn't sleep, so I set in the chair instead. I was sitting there and I was listening drank men's voices and their singing through the night:*

"Who was saying, Who was laying Serbia is small one, She was never small - She fought three times with all..."

After all, after some time, exhausted I fell asleep on the chair... I woke up in the morning, lost and confused, thinking about my baby, where is he, how is he and am I going to see her ever again... In the middle of that day, on MP soldier brought me food and after that I stayed in the room all day long. In the late evening Major Vlado came in, brought me plastic bag with used, but cleaned underwear and told me to prepare myself immediately. After I was ready, we sat in the same jeep vehicle, with two soldiers inside and this time he drove us to some other mountain house in the same area.

'If you play right and you are smart one this time, you will see your baby soon... One gentleman, foreigner will pay you a visit and he is a powerful man, he can help you, if you help him, so be smart... It is up to you now...'

He locked the house and he was gone. I looked around the mountain's house; there was huge living room, with TV and radio, a bathroom, on the ground floor, and three small bedrooms upstairs on the first floor, more like an attic floor. I sat there in the living room area, scared for myself, but scared even more for my baby. Maybe around 22:00, I heard vehicle's engine noise outside. House door were open and entered by foreign military officer with two other military personnel. I have recognized Canadian General, Luis MacKenzie's face and he crossed the room with outstretched hand and he offered me a handshake and said:

'Miss… '

In his other hand, he had red rosebud, which he "planted" in my hands quickly, and I was surprised, scared and unprepared for all of it. In meantime, two men from his escort went out and locked the door of the house. He asked me:

'What is your name?'

I was quiet.

'Where did you come from?'

I was pretending that I cannot understand him at all and I backed up a little away from him.

'Miss, I know that you understand me completely and that you speak English language.'

He smiled politely and continued:

'I am here to help you. This is in your best interest and of course, you are here to help me. This is in my interest, too. Love inspired by mutual interest is the strongest love.'

I realized my situation finally. I was fully aware of it. I was locked here, I was a prisoner all this time and I cannot play games anymore. In addition, it was not only my life on a stake here; it was my baby's life, too.

'I think you know what I am talking about…'

General concluded his speech without any additional remarks. I did not resist at all, it will be useless, and it will make things worse, for me and for my child for sure. If I did not have a child I would fight till the end, but in this situation any confrontation, provocation or additional talk was pointless. I had someone who was dependable of me, who cannot defend himself and I have to get focused on that, this will be my goal and my target. I will survive… General touched my shoulders with both hands and came closer. Defenseless, I have closed my eyes with the only thought…

"My baby…"

I felt his breath on my neck. It was short and hot.

He said:

'Good girl…'

It was repeated and going on for roughly twenty days in total, he would come from time to time seven to eight times for this period and finished his job. I was collecting my misery, pain, and shame emotionally inside me and I was counting days, nights and visits till the end, when I am going to see my son... I asked every time before he left the house:

'When I am going to see my son?'

He answered:

'Be patient... Soon...'

And he was gone.

'When we will be free?'

He answered:

'Soon enough...'

And he closed the door.

'Can you ask them to bring my baby?'

He answered:

'I will see...'

And he left me.

'When...'

The answer was:

'Tomorrow, be patient...'

After that period two soldiers brought me to Major Vlado. I was in "Sonja" another ten or more days after. Major Vlado and other two soldiers there have raped me continuously. I think it was the end of July, 1992. Around 21-th, when they brought my son for the first time... He lost some weight and he was weak. The following day they released me to the foreign soldiers of UPROFOR forces, commanded by Canadian General Luis MacKenzie's...

...

He press minimizes bar – button of Word's document translated file, and locked his computer with the password made of nine characters long. At least one number, one capital letter, small letter and at least on special character; as per SOP, but he did not feel at all more safer, secured or assured that he worked in unerring environment, even that he lived in unfailing country. He considered his options. Connection with the case exists, but investigation is dragging on for too long. He will pull out his trump from his back pocket and they will play this round on his terms, but on their territory. It is going to be interesting to play the game.

The show must go on…

He was singing his tune:

'Yeah, the show must go on…'

Michael unplugged memory stick from his desktop computer and he put it in his jacket's right inner pocket.

CHAPTER IV

Section 6.

TEST

January, 2010.

SERBIA, BELGRADE, SPORT CENTER, MARTIAL ARTS, AIKIDO ACADEMY BELGRADE...

Miran shifted his balance from right to the left leg.

"Hidari Hanmi No Kamae."

His three opponents circled around him as hungry pack of wolfs. He dropped his eyes in front of his feet; he inhaled short breath and slowly exhaled long breath with his stomach. He remembered one of "Osensei Ueshiba's" famous quotes:

"Do not stare into the eyes of your opponent, he may mesmerize you. "

The first one charged as a wounded wild boar at him. He rose his Bokken aiming to Miran's head.

"Yokomen Uchi Aiki Nage"

He stepped aside partially, as he initiated false blocking movement towards his opponent's Bokken, and then avoided their contact completely in a split of second, as he threw him using his momentum and applied technique. The man flew beside him, when Miran used power of own hips to push attacker behind, adding an additional force in smooth half circular hand's movement above his shoulders. Bokken miraculously ended up in his hands now and he continued his movement against second one, who was now closer to his right hand side. The second man was in the middle step of *"Ai – Hanmi"* step position, partially of his balance, surprised by Miran's speed and his unusual tactics, holding tanto with his right hand, horizontally positioned in front of his abdomen. The third one returned one step back, changing his footwork from *"Ai – Hanmi"* to

"Gyaku – Hanmi", as he positioned his Jo in front of himself. In that crucial moment Miran's vision got blurred, images of his opponents stretched, twisted and resolved themselves in front of him.

What was happening to me? I AM BLIND!

CHAPTER V
Section 1.

CSIS

September, 2009.

CANADA, ONTARIO, OTTAWA, PARLIAMENT HILL…

Red haired woman in 30s, good looking, dressed in light grey business suit, which couldn't hide her body curves, step out from the bus on Langevin Block Station and then she crossed Wellington Street, in front of Federal Parliament Buildings on Ottawa's Parliament Hill's. Through her sunglasses she surveyed the area and she continued her walk between Bytown Museum and 73 North Restaurant Lounge, turned left beside Dixon Jewelers shop; surprisingly she did not stop in front of it as most of the women, then Inter-art Evaluation shop and she entered Chapters, book shop. Air conditioned book store was wide and open – space designed, so when she entered nobody paid attention to her, except few male looks between flipped pages of open newspapers or books in front of their noses. She removed her sunglasses and slide them in her blue leather "no named" simple vertical laptop bag. Her light green eyes searched the area carefully and she was pretending to read labeled rows of bookshelves in front of her, after she confirmed that everything is all right only then she went towards belletristic book's section - magazines section, took last edition of 'Chatelaine", Canada's favorite women magazine. On the front page printed letters whispered her name:

"FRESH FOOD FAST + 5 best meals in minutes" "How to allergy – proof your home"

"CANADA'S BEAUTY 100, 4 TH ANNUAL EXPERT GUIDE TO THE BEST SKIN – CARE AND MAKUP PRODUCTS + WIN THEM ALL!"

She understood women's wish to stay young and healthy, but she never believed that advice from magazines will improve her self-confidence and she can "wholeheartedly" agree on all their anti-wrinkle and plastic surgery bullshit, which they present in them.

Just purportedly "celebrating" women's beauty; kiss my ass!

On the cover was picture of beautiful older woman, Karen Kain, ballet dancer, with inevitable standard operating procedure of computer's airbrushed face, with statement:

"Karen Kain defines gorgeous at any age (she's 58!)"

She sat at comfortable chair between the isles and thought about her mother's face, same age as Karen, which was also shaped beautifully with lifeless expression in her eyes, hunting her in her dreams, delicate face given by bloodline, inherited from her. She hated her sad, never smiled eyes, soft, calm and god – loving voice, gentle touch of mother's hand above her head and overprotected words from her full-mouthed lips. She doesn't have a mirror in her apartment because of her. She will never have a man because of her. She would never live full life and have a child or her own family, because of her. She was here because of her. She will never get her mother's true love, instead of this cursed gift, which she never asked for. Her eyes flashed with anger for a second and Chatelaine's September edition flew from her lap and hit the bookshelf across her. She quickly calmed herself, looking for potential witness, but nobody was near her. She went there, picked up magazine from the floor and she sat back in the chair.

You silly girl, somebody could freak out, if anybody see it in a broad daylight. Control yourself!

She unzipped her computer bag, reached inside and took out SolidTek's digital notepad, size 6" x 9" inches, which she found in briefcase. She managed to download all data to her home computer, together with pictures and digitalized maps and she made additional two copies which were secured, one in a bank's safe deposit box and the other one in fireproof chest buried on other location. Now she has to double check information which she collected from Ottawa's Security private agency and briefcase's files from the airport - man. Then she will go to scheduled meeting with Mr. J. P. Touchette from CSIS (Canadian Security Intelligence Service) in 12:30 p.m. at "Parliament Pub", next block down to the Sparks Street. He was eager to hide his personal tracks with dirty games that he played with others and military involvements in "unofficial" undercover investigations overseas. Anyway, he is just another step on the ladder which is going to lead her to her final goal. She will take everything that he has to offer and more...,

Much more...

CHAPTER V

Section 2.

PROFESSOR

September, 1998.

UNITED STATES OF AMERICA, CALIFORNIA, LOS ANGELES, WESTWOOD AREA,

UCLA, MANNING DRIVE…

Professor Bronson Leonard adjusted his thin metal glasses on his nose, scratched the edge of his black trimmed beard and dropped his sad – puppy eyes on the large bag again. It was looking like overstaffed turkey on 4-th July celebrating dinner. All files that he collected during the last 20 years of his Tesla's project have been in this bag. All copies of registered 122 patents of Tesla, from John Kerr's Lawyer firm where Tesla made deposit of his inventions papers, together with Tesla's personal Lawyer Thomas Byrne's paper works related to transport sources of energy on the long distance. All pictures collected from 'Sarony Photographers" Company and "Commercial Photostat Co."; where Tesla copied his registered patents in order to protect them from fraud and protect his invention's rights. Historically papers were priceless, but emotionally for him, they have additional value, value of last 20 years of his life. He took a deep breath, picked up the bag, his coat and went out of his office. He punched security code and activated the alarm system, and he closed automatic locked door with his left elbow. Tweedy jacket had conveniently attached leather patches on the elbow area for situations like these, he called them semi – automatic patches and they have multiple purposes, like wiped coffee stains, activated elevators button or they could be used for opening back door to the parking lot. He crossed parking area under his office building and dropped the bag beside his four wheel drive Toyota Runner, when he heard some strange sound left of him. He drop his head a little down and squeezed his small brown eyes above the edge of his glasses, cocked his square shaped head like rooster to the left side where the sound came from.

"Pfffffffffuuuuttttt!"

That was the last sound that he heard, then concrete ceiling of the parking lot filled his focus and become final view of his world.

CHAPTER V

Section 3.

DOD

February, 1943.

UNITED STATES OF AMERICA, WASHINGTON, DC, DOD (DEPARTMENT OF DEFENCE) OFFICE...

Lieutenant Colonel Denmark, USA Army Officer, Chief of DOD Office, surveyed documents provided by FBI Field Agent Frederick Cornels who was in charge for Tesla's operational tracking unit. He was not happy with his final report on surveillance procedures, tactics and collection of Tesla's personal items. The man died a month ago and a lot of his belongings were missing. He gave orders to his operatives to identify and apprehend certain individuals who have been in contact with Nikola Tesla for last two months in order to gather additional information about his private notes and unpublished, unknown experiments and inventions. It seems that last two weeks have been quite busy in his life, like he felt his death at the end. He picked up a handset of the phone on his desk and he dialed number at New York, N. Y., number which has never been registered or associated with any agency and hidden even for government high officials.

'Hello, Lieutenant Colonel Denmark here. I have his files from Niagara Falls, Sir.'

'Good job, Colonel. I have got his notes from this end, found at his hotel room in Hotel New Yorker, so we can compare them together and then start with the project.'

'Of course, Sir. I have already made arrangements with engineers and technical support staff on our sites at Canada and Europe. They made both prototypes and they finalized preparations for final tests.'

'You have found suitable test areas?'

'Yes, sir. It is going to happen simultaneous at two separate sites, as we planned.'

'Ground zero will be at residential areas?'

'Yes, Sir, this is the only way to collect information from the first hand, only on active testing subjects and in the real environments, under full experimental force and power.'

'What about the affected subjects - residents?'

'They will be isolated for some time, first for their and our safety; anyhow the real side effects on them will start together with fully functional individual developments, which will come much later, but we are going to monitor all subjects individually with detailed analysis, till the end of their physical lives. The real fun starts after.'

'Define "much later" time frame. For how long?'

'Well Sir, it is hard to predict it, but approximately between 60 and 70, by Tesla's mathematical calculations.'

'Days or Months?'

'No, Sir. Years.'

CHAPTER V

Section 4.

BOTANIC GARDEN

October, 1875.

AUSTRIAN HUNGARIAN EMPIRE, GRAZ, GRAZ POLYTECHNIC SCHOOL, "BOTANIC GARDENS"...

(Modern day – Technical University of Graz, Austria)

Tesla had a long walk from his room in Attemsgasse number 8, to Schlossberg Castle, the one standing on the hump of a hill in the middle of the city center. He walked down the street, under green shadows of chestnut trees in a row which were just beginning to drop their chestnuts on the ground; then he went up the winding wide road, through the sunless forested hill. The air was cool, forest heavy - sharp and scented with pine trees and decaying leaves. He enjoyed walking and it stimulated his brain. He was on the top of the hill and city was sleeping under him, vista of red – tile – roofs, resembling a sea of new copper coins, an endless colors and shapes of windows, city a thousand years old. He followed the path to the middle of "Botanic Gardens" park and he sat on wooden bench. He thought about his study and he was satisfied with everything; he finished his first year with the highest grades, he passed nine subjects, twice more than required and he was very proud that he became fluent in German, Italian, French and English. He was sleeping only four hours per day; he was thirsty all the time in this shrine of knowledge, endless rows of books to read with too short classes to attend. He was thinking about Gramme's Dynamo Machine and he felt deep in his soul that he was right and Professor Poeschl was wrong. Machine did not require commutated wire brushes. He did not find solution for that yet, but it was constantly occupying his mind. He had some ideas, but all of them were fuzzy, unfinished and undeveloped inside his head. Suddenly, the light in the garden dimmed and died under coming shadow. Something dark enveloped his soul, dark shape covered his vision and he felt the cold touch of death on his skin. From his mouth came mute scream of horror. He closed and reopened his eyes in total darkness; his teeth shattered from cold and frozen breath of white cloud was produced from his opened mouth. He was sitting on the edge of endless pit dark as hell. The Voice filled the void and chilled his spine:

"You summoned me."

'I did not.'

"You have called me."

'I did not.'

"You released me."

'From where?'

"You want me."

'What are You?'

"I am You."

'I do not know You.'

"You want to know things."

'What things?'

"The price has to be paid."

'What price?'

"You are first class star."

'I am not.'

"You follow your nose."

'What are you talking about?'

"I want to play."

'I do not understand.'

"I want to drink."

'I don't.'

"I want to live."

'I have a life.'

"I want more."

'I don't.'

"I will have all."

'You can't.'

"Yes I can."

'Who are You?'

"Who are you?"

'I am Nikola.'

"I know."

'Who are You?'

"I have told you."

'WHO are You?'

"You already know."

'WHO ARE You?'

"I am You."

'WHO ARE YOU?'

"I am Dane."

CHAPTER V

Section 5.

CONFESSION

August, 2009.

CANADA, ALBERTA, EDMONTON, MUTTART CONSERVATORY, TROPICAL PYRAMID…

Air was hot and humid. He followed the path between the green jungle look like wall that was spreading around him. He didn't like this lush, green and fragrant environment, but inspector suggested this site through the phone as a meeting point. Some couple with two kids just passed him making the noise with their exited high pitched voices and uncontrolled clicking of their cameras. He stopped beside the green settee positioned on one of the corners of inside walking path and he sat on it. Exhausted by warm air inside artificial pyramid's climate, his eyes were filled with bright tropical rainforest, grasslands and showy evergreen plants around him. Bird or something similar in the trees above his head made sound like she is going to die instantly. Something flew through the branches without the sound, just couple meters left of him. Sound of the waterfall cascades with small fishes and water lilies in the center of the glass made pyramid added wild life atmosphere and strong smells many orchid varieties perfumed the air around him. Opposite of scheduled tour's direction man in white shirt and cream pants was approaching his hiding spot. Corporal Dew armed himself with tanto – knife secured on his hip, under his long sleeves shirt. He was prepared to act if something goes wrong. The man had light blue eyes, wide fresh shaved face and short haircut. His hands were large and strong, but empty. He reached his left back pants pocket, produced "Edmonton's Sun" newspapers and he presented himself to him: 'I am Inspector Blaquier, you can call me Michael. I assumed that you are Corporal Dew Roger, right?'

Roger got up and step forward.

'Correct.'

Inspector offered him a hand.

'Nice to meet you.'

Roger responded and took his hand. Firm handshake connected them for a second.

'May I call you Roger? I preferred off the record conversations.'

'It's fine with me. I had too many official statements in my life.'

'Good. Then, we agreed on that one. Please, have a seat.'

Michael gesticulated toward the bench beside them. He dropped newspapers on the edge of it.

'Only one thing left. Then we can start.'

Michael pulled up his shirt up to his neck and turned around slowly in circle. Deep scars on his back flashed white under green shadows of the trees. Four circular spots in diagonal line from right shoulder down to the left kidney marked him across his wide chest.

'Satisfied?'

'Not completely.'

Roger checked Michael's legs and around his waist, too. He confirm with the nod of his head.

'Now I am.'

'Me, too.'

'Another thing… Just to clear up everything before,… I am not going to testify against any of them.'

'I am not going to ask that, either…'

Roger nervously sat on the bench and Michael calmly joined him.

'So, when we cleared up all angles of our "close relationship", I can shoot my questions?'

'Fire Up.'

In that moment, 40 years old women with wide straw hat, dark sunglasses, baggy green and white pants and shirt came around the corner with open book in her hands. She produced sound of surprise:

'Oh, I am terrible sorry for my interruption gentlemen, did you see, by any chance, a couple with two lovely kids here, recently?!'

Roger answered her question eagerly:

'Yes m' am, I met them, they just pass us a minute ago and they continued on this path's direction.'

'Thank you very much for your help, Sir. Have a nice day!'

'You're welcome!'

Michael waited until the woman disappeared around the corner and then he added:

'Do you know that Major Claude Lévesque died?'

Roger did not fake it; it was real surprise on his face.

'What do you mean died? How?! When?!'

'At the beginning of last month. During the weekend days on the parking lot of West Edmonton's Mall. Killed by 5-th century BC, old coin.'

'What?!'

'I am telling you the truth, Roger! I've pulled it out of his eye socket myself. It was sharpened on the edges to penetrate easier.'

Roger dropped his head down and he took a deep breath.

'There is another one, Colonel Brian Murhead.'

'He is dead, too?!'

'No, he is gone. We cannot find him. He evaporated in thin air.'

'Anyone else?'

Michael watched Rogers face looking for some false reactions or genuine lies.

'General is still alive. He is in his home town at the moment.'

'What do you want me to do? Why did you contact me?'

'I want to know. You were there.'

'It seems that you already know everything, …'

Roger resignedly put his back on the bench.

'I want to hear from you.'

'Why?!'

'I want you to hear yourself.'

Michael put his right hand on Roger's left shoulder. Roger felt like someone added additional

hundred kilograms on his back. Michael continued:

'I witnessed much worse things then you, and I have kept everything inside me. It almost killed

me.'

Roger turned his head to Michael. His light brown eyes were filled with tears.

'I lost my wife and my daughter because of it. I almost killed myself with it…'

CHAPTER V

Section 6.

DO NOT DISTURB

January, 2010.

SERBIA, BELGRADE SUBURB, TOWN OF MLADENOVAC,; "SELTERS SPA" MEDICAL REHABILITATION CENTER…

The air was crispy and icy cold. It was windy outside in the park surrounding the main building with 30 centimetres thick snow on the frozen ground. Through the window of ground floor room of "Selters Spa Wellness Center" light was passing and falling on the white linen sheets of the bed. Bed was empty, unused and freshly made by housemaid. Beside bed on the night stand was a Bible, glasses and glass of water. These were the only things that indicated that room was occupied. On the opposite side of the bed was a chair. In the chair was a man. Man's head was on his chest. Someone would think that he fell asleep on the afternoon nap, until he come closer and see dried blood on his neck. The cut was clean and swift. The man was dead. Outside, on the entrance door of his room number 8 was a sign: "Do Not Disturb". The cleaning lady was pushing the cart and she stopped beside his door. She was looking at the sign on the door couple of seconds and then she passed by down the empty hospital corridor. She was busy with her own thoughts when fire alarm started. She stopped in the middle of the hallway, left her cleaning cart and then she went back to the door number 8. She produced the key from her right pocket and unlocked the door. She opened it and she carefully stepped inside. After six seconds, she added her shriek to already activated fire alarm screams.

CHAPTER VI

Section 1.

THE BASEMENT

September, 2009.

CANADA, ONTARIO, KINGSTON TOWN, ELLIOTT AVENUE…

Colonel Brian Murhead woke up tied to the iron chair in somebody's home basement at Elliott Avenue, number 89, at Kingston, Ontario, Canada. At first he was not sure where he is at the moment, until he saw his son's bicycle on the opposite wall, bicycle that he bought him for his fifteenth birthday; it was hanging on the wall's hook. He knew that they were on their way to the camping site at Rideau Acres Campground. He was totally naked and his arms were tied on the long metal bars of the chair with some rubber like rope and he felt that his legs were also tied with similar rubber rope to the iron legs. His mouth was gagged with his wife's socks. His legs were bent and fixed to the inner part of the chair, so he was in a half sitting half bending position. He felt that under his ass there wasn't any support; that his ass, his penis and his balls were hanging in the air hole between the bars. He felt coldness on his skin and he tried to move his fist and fingers, but there were already numb from the cold air and broken circulation. He made test with his toes, but legs were even in worse shape than his arms. He touched with his toes some rubber mattress under the metal chair. He tried to remember what happened with him and her wife and son after and how he got here, but everything was blurry, surrounded by fog and his thoughts were incoherent in his head. He even had a difficulty to remember his wife's name and his son's name, too. He was sure that he will remember later, but at the moment he can't and some other things he couldn't remember at all. Like he was drugged or one part of his memory was erased. He was thirsty, too. He heard footsteps on the ground floor above his head, maybe his wife? He mumbled some words through the socks in his mouth, but nothing came out. He shook the chair a little, but his attempt to overturn it did not get any results. He was too weak to move.

If his wife or whoever is there can hear some noise from the basement, they are going to come here and then…

DO NOT MOVE!

It was inside his head.

What was that, I did not hear any voice?!

It wasn't his own thought, he was sure about it.

I SAID, STAY WHERE YOU ARE!

There it is again! It is getting louder. What's this, am I crazy?

'No, you aren't. You just hear my thoughts. And I can hear yours.'

He did not hear the door or her steps on the stairs. She just showed up in the basement in front of him.

'I can hear all your thoughts. You cannot hide anything from me. And do not try to do it.'

He realized that he knew somehow even from the first moment that it was her not him.

'I am not going to be in your head all the time, I just want to ask you some questions and I want correct and honest answers from you, so I am going to remove socket from your mouth, okay?'

He drop his head twice shortly as confirmation. He saw only her skirt and long legs when she came and remove gags from his mouth. By voice and her body she is older than his son, but younger than his 40 years old wife. He wiggled his tongue in his dry mouth and he licked his cracked lips.

'There is another thing to remind you that I have power over your brain but also over your body.'

Suddenly, he felt like thousand needles hit his spine, his all body was vibrating, his muscles were shaking, even his eyelids seems to vibrate, pain speeded through him like a wave in solid never ending motion. He tried to close his screaming mouth, he heard himself distantly, like he was in some echoed space where his voice bounced to eternity.

'This is an overture to cacophony of pain that I can produce for you.'

His body was twitching in muscles spasm and he was ready to lose his conscience, when he felt splash of frozen water on his head and shoulders. The shock cut his breath and brought additional pain inside his brain together with strong spasm of his all body. It brought him back from the edge of darkness.

'You see, I can extract everything from your brain, but in that case you are not going to feel pain and appreciate value of your own life, you would be an empty sea shell without pearl.'

He heard her voice from distance. He was not able to answer her, he just fight to get his breath in seconds.

'What have you felt was small version of Nikola Tesla's Oscillatory testing equipment and I have initiated the lowest vibration level; and you are lucky that your body and the chair have been isolated from the ground by rubber mattress under your feet, so if you aren't this house would collapse on our heads instantly.'

His thoughts went to his wife and son.

'Don't worry about them, there are upstairs in the bedroom, stoned by drugs. They will have a huge headache after this episode in their bored uncomplicated life. Now, enough of chit – chat, I will ask you some questions and you're going to answer them, or I will use oscillator again…,

And again…,

And again…'

CHAPTER VI

Section 2.

TWENTY SIX

October, 1998.

UNITED STATES OF AMERICA, CALIFORNIA, LOS ANGELES, SOUTH L.A., VERMONT SQUARE…

…

Number 26… The room smelled hard on blood and urine. Parameter was secure with local forces and lab technicians just finished their part. My nose was staffed with medicaments to protect my nostrils and prevent my stomach to return my inside out stuffed with Chinese chicken – bolls, egg – roles and others goodies from "All You Can Eat" Lunch Buffet Specials for 9, 99, USA $, two blocks from this crime scene. Scene was irritating enough without the smell; body of something that used to be a woman, unrecognizable shape of human being, carved with scars and bathed in own blood was more than enough for someone who never seen anything like it in his life. But even for me after all these years in the field, was hard to watch and take professional unattached analysis. On the other side some sick, pervert and self torturing feelings woke up every time on the crime scene, some unidentified urge and wish to remember every detail of it, which I can use later as a motive to push my efforts, doubled my strength and sharpen my focus to nail low life creature who did the killings. I tried to use my photographic memory gift to catch all details which cannot be recorded by digital cameras pictures, make my own brain protected private collection of them, which are not going to be filed and numbered at the end. One thing is definite – he is getting more and more cruel and bloodthirsty with every killing. There is only one way to stop him – with the bullet. There is no recovery time for him and there is no psycho therapy that can change him, help him or medical institution which can hold him inside and change his wild nature? He deserved death more than once…

...

'Detective Marc Arsenault?'

He turned around to face DNA laboratory technician John, he couldn't remember his last name, who was working all night long to get as much as he can get from the scene. He smiled, but his tired eyes stayed too long on the dead body to get honest one, so he ended with something between apologetic and funeral expression on his face.

'Hi, I am John Boggs, from DNA Lab, may I ask you something?'

'Yeah, shoot.'

'Do you have someone's face to attach to these murders?'

'No face yet, but his profile and "expertise", yes.'

'I thought about something that was crawling through my mind last night...'

'Yes, spit it out.'

'He rape them and beat them hard, before he make his "special treatment" with the bottle at the end, but last two times I have found someone else's DNA samples beside his own and victim's on the scene.'

'So, he brought someone with him? An apprentice?'

'It seems to be, but his DNA and other one were related to each other.'

'Relatives? Cousin? Brother?'

'First relative, like son, daughter, maybe sister or brother, even father or mother.'

'I would like to meet his father and mother and ask them some questions.'

Yes, you are right on that one, man!

'He found some company to support his job.'

'It is younger person, up to 20 to 25 years old, and it is male for sure.'

'His DNA is on the victims, too?'

'No. But he is around during the "session".'

'Maybe, he is making some photos or video collection?'

'Yes, it will be good to check these "kinky" sites, especially "darker one". Maybe we are going to see his work published on the net.'

'Good idea. I will get on it. Thank You, John.'

'Don't mention it.'

'Have a good one!'

'You too, man… You, too!'

Little was known about this serial killer, till he got his ex – name, original one from Bosnia, Zoran Sikirica. Through Interpol and Europol departments they are gathering data on him. It seems that he kept himself busy in Europe, too. The seven detectives on the task force, beside him are working on the case, and god knows how many people in the support. From bodily fluids he has left on the crime scenes, they know his DNA. Exhaustive comparisons to genetic profiles stored in felon databases, however, have produced no matches. Up to now, we had his face as a dot, a dash and a line on the screen, but now we have a name to go with it. Soon we are going to have a picture, too. He knew that even with that, it is going to be needle in the haystack, but there is a chance that someone is going to find it, even if he changed his face with plastic surgery. Detective Arsenault was not under no illusions about his chances. Despite heavy demands on his unit, he kept up running a grueling schedule, running undercover operation and surveillance on various corners of South side districts, during the daylight hours and other times in the middle of the night. They managed to make Serology Section inside LAPD's Scientific Investigation Division. Plus, they developed strategy called "DNA dragnets" which was first employed in Europe, where authorities have swabbed thousands of people and solved dozens of crimes. German authorities undertook and create one of the largest dragnets; collecting samples from 16,400 people in the search for a man who raped and killed an 11 – year – old girl. At the end they found him. Marc picked up his mobile phone and dialed number at LAPD Cyber Crime Center. He didn't like an idea that killer's apprentice developed skills to become a copy – cat killer or even worse…new natural born killer raised by another skilled serial killer. He made a promise to himself and he had an intention to keep it.

'Hello? My name is Chief Detective Marc Arsenault, LAPD Homicide Division…'

CHAPTER VI

Section 3.

AN ISLAND

September, 1998.

CROATIA, DALMATIAN COAST, CITY OF DUBROVNIK, ISLAND OF LOKRUM, THE
SAINT BENEDICT MONASTERY…

Lionel whipped sweat drops from his forehead with his rubber gloved left hand.

I am sweating like a pig!

He was moving ten to twenty centimetres per second inside the stone corridor – underground
passage for last 45 minutes on his elbows and knees. Passage was not wide enough for his huge
body and he struggled to keep pace on the cold, hard and wet stone under him. Lamp bulb
attached by rubber strip on the top of his head gave him clear view of greenish, wet walls in front
of him; the air was filled with rotten, decaying dumped alga, mixed smell of sea salt aroma
together with his personal body smell. He was not claustrophobic at all, but closed space like this
gave him unnerving couple of seconds of strong feeling that all these stones above his head will
collapse any moment on his head and that he will never find way out from this tight corridor. He
kept pushing his hands and knees in the same dead end rhythm, rhythm which woke up hidden
energy to double increased his efforts to finish this race against the stone and time.

I hope there is another way out at the end of this shit-hole!

After additional 5 minutes of snail's speed struggle through tight space, the corridor in front of
him bent slightly to the right and he felt on his face light breeze of fresh air, which gave him
additional stamina to push herself further and reach the end of it. He saw small square window of
dimmed light in front of him, closed with metal bars in shape of big "X", and air that was coming
through it has been clean, cold and dry. Rotten metal bars gave away two minutes after he used
acid on their edges in combined force of his large hands and full body pressure. He switched off

the light bulb on his forehead and crawled out on his knees and out of the hell corridor and he was breathing heavily under strained muscles, he happily laid flat on the hard surface of the stones for some time getting the fresh air in his lungs.

I am definitely getting old for all of this!

He crouched and surveyed the room. It was circular shaped like a tower and the light was coming from the top. All together towered size of the room was maybe four to five meters in diameter, less than one meter in front of him was a small wall, 100 - 120 centimetres tall, build from small egg - shaped stones, similar to each other, with same diameter and unbelievably same size, maybe same weight, too. He stood up in his full height with additional pain from leg's muscles through his joints to his bones. Circulation of his blood was cut off for long in his arms and legs, that he had small nausea in his throat and weak dizziness in his head. Wall was made in the same circulated way and it was following tower's shape, from inside out, so the pattern of egged size stones were continuing all the way around. The thickness of that "inner small wall" was around 30 to 40 centimetres with three rows of egg- sized stones. Inside the small wall was something similar to altar, about one meter in diameter, 80 to 90 centimetres high, made of the same egg - shaped stones. He saw some kind of circular cake shaped box in the middle of it. He came closer to the small inner wall and he put his left hand on it for support to cross – over to inner circle of it. One of egg shaped stones on the surface cracked under his weight, but the wall stand still when he stepped inside inner circle. He touched the surface of the cracked stone with his rubber glove, intrigued he switched on the lamp and looked at small beam of light.

I'll be damned! It's a human skull!

He looked closer to the surface of it and realized that it was polished with some liquid or artificial neutral colored paint. Actually, the size of the skull was smaller than average human skull, it looked like skull of the pigmy, dwarf or some small midget man…

Children! It was skull of a child!

All of them in the inner part of the towered walls were children skulls, like on the inner smaller wall and the altar itself. He raised his head and beamed light touched the surface of inner circled tower wall confirming his thoughts. He turned around, the tower wall from inside was filled with children skulls to the top, where his beamed light couldn't penetrate, but polished skulls gave him their positive reflection on every spot where light touched them. He got sick feelings in his stomach.

There is hundreds of them, thousand, maybe couple thousands of them!

He stayed on the same spot three more seconds, frozen from the site and then he turned his attention to the altar. Circular shape of it was made from skulls, too, but in the middle was not cake shaped box as he thought before, it was more oval shape stone, more like a hump in the middle. When he concentrated light on it, he saw some kind of inscriptions, letters of some unknown hieroglyphs, more like pictures, combination of both of them, carved in the stone from every angle on all four sides and on the top of it. He wasn't able to see the pattern, where it started or where finished it. The more he looked at it, the more he got confused by it, lines, empty spaces between them, pictures, numbers and shapes like, changed their positions, angles and in one second get closer to him, the other one they are further from him, at the end he got dizzy from it. He closed one eye.

Calm down. It is the same trick when you are driving from tunnel towards the light. Close one of them before you enter or exit the tunnel, the rest will be take care by your brain and the body. One eye will adapt to the new environment and to the light and angles. Just open it slowly. Open your left one. Yes. That is it.

He peaked out with his left eye on it and he saw that oval sized stone shifted to right a little, which was trick of eye, but some letters were gone and some of them remained on the same spot. He switched to his right eye closing the left one in the same time. Now he saw signs instead of letters, letters were gone. He repeated test slowly two- three times looking for some clues and logical connections between them. If there is some, he couldn't see it or he just couldn't understand meanings of signs and read the strange language –letters. He can spend all his life here and never figured it out.

Take another approach to it. Think... Use your brain.

He touched surface on the top with both gloved hands. He applied small pressure on it, he tried to push, to pull, to move it left or right, rotate in different directions, shake it, slide from different angles – nothing. He was starting to be frustrated by this at the end. His diving suit kept enough heat to his body, but he knew that, if he took the same path back, he is not going to have enough time and strength to cross the sea the same night between an island of Lokrum and Dubrovnik's opposite coast. At least his diving gear and some food which he left on the entrance of the church will be there, the bottom line he can stay on island maximum two days, and then go back to his hotel the following day. He released secure belt and took the knife attached to his left leg's thigh. He made a move towards the hump - stone. Tip of knife's edge wavered in his hand a little and then stick to the surface of the stone and stayed glued on it.

Magnetized! The stone is magnetized metal!

The color of it resembled the stone, but it was pure metal underneath. He used both his hands to remove the knife away from the surface. He checked the compass attached on the top of knife's handle, needle inside went ballistic, turning in circle unable to attach itself to the N - north. Knife was magnetized to maximum and he needed some grounding to remove it, but around him he didn't see any metal to use it.

Unless... The inner circle which looked like the wall, maybe it is metal underneath.

He turned around and waved the knife on the surface of the inner wall. Nothing happened even when he passed around the altar and closed the circle on the same spot where he started. His theory didn't work this time, so he sheathed his knife back in plastic holder on his thigh. Immediately when he removed his left hand from the knife to check metal humped stone, the knife itself flew out from his sheath, turned upside down in the air and then flew up. At the same time bluish sparks showed up on the surface of the stone – oval box. He heard humming sound and oval stone surface cracked with gold light underneath. He instinctively threw himself above the inner wall, out of the inner circle and he landed painfully on his right shoulder, but he managed to put hands in front of his face and protect his head. Humming sound became loud crack with bluish light in the middle of circled stones. Light flashed up like blue and gold beam of energy towards the skylight window somewhere on the top of the towered structure. Lionel was on his back looking at the beam which stayed in the air one second, then in the second one, like a laser disappeared through the sky. Next second metallic thud sound reminded him that his knife fell back to him from above.

What was that? It looked like giant laser beam! The magnetic field initiated it!

He stood up and surveyed the scene. The inner circle wall was blackened from inside by the force and the altar was black oval shaped monolith. Black metal monolith, instead of humped oval shaped stone in the middle, had gold metal piece on the top. He bent over and picked up his knife, but in the same second he dropped it on the stone floor before his feet.

Fuck, it's hot!

Plastic handle melted and disappeared forever, but released energy .blackened the blade together with handle part. Lionel looked at Gold Sign on black altar flickered under the night sky light. Lionel's heart quivered a little by his hidden greed. He couldn't remove his eyes from it.

CHAPTER VI

Section 4.

HAPPY PEASANT

April, 1878.

AUSTRIAN HUNGARIAN EMPIRE, SLOVENIA, TOWN OF MARIBOR, THE HAPPY

PEASANT PUB...

(Modern day – EU, European Union, Slovenia, Maribor)

Nikola waved back with his long right hand to two passengers for Ljubljana, in the far corner of "Happy Peasant" pub and he put small amount of money in his pants pocket, which he had earned playing chess with them. It was easy money for him, only half an hour simultaneous chess party game with two of them, brought him the same amount of money - 15 forints, that he earned all week at Master Drusko engineering company, where he worked as a draftsman all last year. He was happy at the moment with everything; his temporary employment gave him a freedom to relax and make some initial schematics on his alternating current machine which has been on his mind for long time. He knew that his invention is going to change life on the earth and beyond; it will bring free energy for everyone, and no one will have to pay any forints for it. Also, he was very satisfied that his headaches stopped when he made a deal with Dane, and this time spent at Maribor enlightened his spirit, calm down Dane's soul and refreshed his body. The only thing that bothered him was his father's visit scheduled for this Saturday at his apartment at house of Teggetthofstrasse, his father Milutin was for sure disappointed by his temporary break from Graz's University and he will try to influence him to continue his studies there. Tesla had refused the church calling, military calling, which were his family professions for centuries; and now after everything that happened between them, his father is going to question his technical profession and his engineering dreams were in doubt. He was determent to deject his father's, Milutin proposal whatever would be. He will follow his own path with his own will on this world. He loves his father very much and he respects his work, he is an honest, hard working person who thought him the most importing thing that a man can learn:

"Use your brain and live your life free".

He is going to remind him on his words. He will never tell him that Dane is alive and that he is always inside him, that his sons are going to stay together as always, in good and in bad times; that they will make him proud on them in the near future.

CHAPTER VI

Section 5.

PEACHY

August, 2009.

CANADA, ALBERTA, EDMONTON, MUTTART CONSERVATORY...

Woman which presented herself to Inspector Michael Blaquier as "Miranda" on the phone, passed through exit door of Muttart Conservatory building and she removed her wide straw hat from her head, but she kept dark sunglasses on her face. She reached in her right pocket of baggy green and white pants and took out Nokia mobile phone, punched the number of her last received call. She waited ten seconds for an answer. Male voice on the other end answered:

'Yes.'

'Blaquier and Dew are together.'

'Good. Leave them be.'

'Should I proceed further?'

'No need for that.'

'Blaquier is on the hook.'

'This will keep him active for a while.'

'He is not a quitter.'

'I know, but do not worry about that now. I will take care of him later.'

'I do not like him.'

'I know that he is not your type, but we need him to do the job.'

'I can do his job easily.'

'Yes, you can but he will do it on his own expenses, and at the end he will pay the price.'

'Still, I don't trust him and he is an idealist.'

'Reason more for you to keep your distance from him. If he believes that what he is doing is right, we are not going to have problems with him.'

'And what when he figure it out?'

'Then, we are not going to need him, anymore.'

'I would like that. Can I have him?'

'He will be all yours, honey. I promise you.'

'I can't wait.'

'Now you have more important things to do.'

'Yes?'

'I need you in Niagara Falls next week. To pick up a package and take care of his owner.'

'Procedure as usual?'

'Yes. And another thing…'

'Yes?'

'Trophies are yours for your private collection.'

'With pleasure.'

'The only thing I want from his collection is the Black Stone.'

'You will have it. Anything else?'

'Keep all his gadgets for yourself as bonus.'

'Peachy.'

Line was off, but she still had a smile of predator on her face. She flipped through memorized contact list numbers in her phone and she dialed another one.

This one answered almost immediately and this time it was female voice.

'Hello, my dear sister.'

'Hello my love.'

'Pack your bags we are going on short trip.'

'Business or pleasure?'

'Business with pleasure.'

'Where?'

'Ontario, Niagara Falls.'

'Nice.'

'Bring the camera with you.'

'Another video? For our collection?'

'No. This is more as an investment and our insurance in the future.'

'You don't trust our 'Big Brother"?'

'I don't trust to any male.'

'Amen…, To every man, my sister!'

CHAPTER VI

Section 6.

CLOCK TOWER

January, 1986.

MONTENEGRO, CITY OF HERCEG NOVI, OLD TOWN GATE, CLOCK TOWER…

The sun reflection hit his eyes in full. Glare from the window on the first floor of the stone house on the left blinded him completely for a second. In this brief moment, he realized that he made fatal mistake. He shouldn't come here at all and he should bring at least two additional thugs with him. An early evening call from Belgrade interrupt his sexual exercises with his new girlfriend. She was barely 16 years old, but that was never issue for him, he always preferred younger one as much as possible and it was not a problem to get one in a land of traditional patriarchal society where economy problems dictated human's behavior. He called them fuck – friends, due to the fact that they performed sex only without sufficient talk. He did not felt tremble of fear through his body for a long time, since the last war at beginning of 40-s and it brought him sweet and sour memories at the same time. He run from an invisible assassin that eliminated two of his bodyguards at castle "Forte Mare", up the hill, armed with the strange lightning whip –weapon used at these science – fiction movies. Decapitated head, sliced body at half in front of him were imprinted in front of his pupils together with buzzing sound and shrieks of men in the background still echoed inside his ears. Artifacts, two strange shaped identical blades found inside the Fortress "Stari Grad" ("Old City") walls, buried under the stone marked with wolf's head engraving on the top; where now in the hands of an unknown killer. He knew that his only chance lied inside the "Sahat – Kula" (Clock Tower) at the Old Town Gate, if he is going to be able to reach it. Tourists mingled around the area all day and night and he assumed that killer is not going to attack him on an open ground and in front of all people after all. He leaned against the warm sun bathed stonewall behind him catching the air in his short breaths. Suddenly, he lost it. The air is gone. Through his wide - open nostrils, he inhaled the subtle fragrance of yellow and green mimosas. An enchanted scent of thick greenery of tropical flowers filled his last breaths.

CHAPTER VII

Section 1.

E – MAIL

September, 2009.

CANADA, ONTARIO, TORONTO, TORONTO POLICE SERVICE, MAIN BUILDING, 40 COLLEGE STREET, 3'RD FLOOR…

…

RCMP Detachment, Ottawa Center,

Ottawa, ONT, CANADA

To:

Chief Investigation Unit, M. Bamford

Good Morning,

I am just forwarding this e-mail information on behalf of our Chief Commander. We just want to inform you that Mr. J. P. Touchette had an accident, heart attack failure at Parliament Pub Bar near his office at approximately 14:00 local time. Investigation is ongoing at the moment and we are going to inform you on our results. CSIS officers are collecting witness statements and detailed report will be provided for you. We are sending you medical exam report and detailed file report on investigation cases on which Mr. Touchette worked last month. Please, if you have any additional questions you can contact us through secure lines or through an e- mail on secret classified network.

Best regards,

Central Repository for Criminal Investigation Unit

Officer Cpl. Francois Bagard

RCMP Office Ottawa, Central Division

...

Michelle's opened e-mail computer screen flickered once and then went black. In front of her monitor is a wireless keyboard with the yellow sticker note attached to Space Bar. Dark letters gave her a message:

"Michelle, Official report form Ottawa's Security Private Agency is waiting for you at the front desk. Mike."

CHAPTER VII

Section 2.

SAVIOUR

November, 1998.

UNITED STATES OF AMERICA, CALIFORNIA, LOS ANGELES, SAN FERNANDO'S

VALLEY, BURBANK...

…

'Steve, how many times I have to tell you to stop that game on the fucking PC and come

downstairs to eat!'

'Mum, I have told you that I am not hungry and that I have things to do!'

'If you do not want to eat, what I am cooking, then you can go to that shit – eating – factory Mac-

Shit and eat there!'

His mother slammed the kitchen door and continued her monologue inside. Steve smiled for

himself with the end of his mouth, and closed his chat box. He chatted with his game - pals for

last two hours about new game from Blizzard, named "Diablo", which occupied most of his time,

out of his part time job at "Wendy" as fast order cook. The game was good, something new that

revolutionized previous versions of tactic's games. He loved it. The only thing better then game

was his father's game which he started "to play" three months ago.

That was the real stuff. Amazing!

Beat of the heart filled with pure adrenalin. He couldn't wait for another session with his dad! He

just played video first time, but he remembered his emotional excitement that his father allowed

him to be there with him; to be "on the ground"; after all these years of training and recorded

sessions which his father played for him since he was five years old.

First time when he saw it, it looked like puppet show, black and white, like these old Charlie

Chaplin's and Buster Keaton's movies without sound, and they look funny for him. His father showed them at the beginning, only on special occasions and later on, when he gets more familiar with theme and action. After some time he was relaxed; and his father played them on every occasion when they were together. It was their bound and their secret, father's and son's moments of happiness and joy. His dad was genius. He invented new series of suspense and horror, he made these sessions as Star Track episodes and they watched it together over and over. He realized that his father is an artist; that all these women enjoyed his performances and they asked for it. Some begged for it. Some resist it. But at the end all of them took part of it. He liberated them of their own misery. He showed them the purity of life and love. They embraced him as a Savior. His words were:

"I saved them from the World."

Yes he did. They were low life before they met him.

"I gave them purpose to exist in this World."

He guided them to their deaths. He was beside them till the end. And they loved him to the end.

"I helped them to accept who they are."

He did not judge them. He accepted them for who they are. They accepted him who he is.

"They are food for maggots."

Yes, there are. Even before, they knew. Then after, they knew. They know it today, but they don't accept it.

"They are bodies without souls."

Yes, lost souls in weak bodies. When he shattered the body, the soul got free. He saw it in their eyes.

" I collected them and save them for their afterlife."

He is their Savior. He kept their souls for later. He guarded them from themselves.

"They loved me like nobody else in their life."

All of them said the same at the end, that they love him. He was their life, their love and their God.

His mobile's vibrations broke his thoughts. He rotated it on the table, so he can read the caller. It was his sister Milena.

What does she want now?

'Hello?'

'Hay, it's me. Can you come here to see me?'

'What's it wrong?'

'Nothing. I just want to see you.

'Why?'

'You didn't come here since last Friday!'

'I was busy. Somebody has to work, you know?!'

'I know! I am just missing you, you know!'

'Okay, okay! I will be there in one hour.'

'Bring me the toys!'

'No toys this time!'

'Pleeaaseee!'

'Okay, okay! I will bring them!'

'I love you!'

'Love you!'

He switched off his mobile and he went to his closet. He slide hidden, false part on the inner shelf and reach inside the plastered wall.

One bag will be enough for tonight. Two of us will have fun. She will beg him for more! I will be your God!

CHAPTER VII

Section 3.

THUNDER

4 - TH CENTURY BC, TARA RIVER GORGE, DARDANI TRIBE'S, NORTH – EAST

TERRITORIES…

(Modern Day – Canyon of Tara River, Montenegro)

Cadmus was standing at the edge watching the coming sunset. Under his feet 2,500 leaps on the bottom of deep canyon, the river flickered in the light, running wild and free; remind him on silver snake from his tribe's legends, whispered secret stories beside his grandfathers cave fires. Enchelei tribe tried to push them deeper into the mountains, but his Dardani warriors slathered them to the last one. Taulanti and Dessaretae tribes already felt Dardani's power and broke their teeth on their shields and spears, so this time they did not tried to attack them from the back. Now Dardani dominated through their expanded territories from the Wide Blue Waters on the South, to Zot's Mountains on the West, Djall's Finger Mountains to the East and Epona's field to the North. Only Illys – The Mighty One will know for how long they will have this freedom time and knowing the Gods: Dualos, Mezana and Zis, it is not going to last long enough. They will try to take their land and destroy us - People to the last one. Human blood is their drink and our meat is their food. He came here to prevent them from coming back and walk on earth again. He touched golden torque on his neck, to protect him from Teuta and her ghost's Army of Darkness. *The Sign of Illys is there. It will be hard to drop over there 300 leaps down with breast armor, graves on my legs and helmet on my head. I will leave them here, together with my shield and spear, and I will bring only my Sica. The rope will cover first 50 leaps and after that I have to use my arms and legs. The cave is hidden from the top, but it is there. I have to enter the cave in daylight and, if I am late – I am dead.*

He dropped the rope down and removed all armor and weapons to become lighter. He adjusted his Sica on his back and he slowly started his descend on the rope. He used his legs and arms to go faster and save the time. After the rope length, he slow down due to hard stone surface, which made deep cuts on his stomach and his chest and his inner thigh legs and the minimum supports for his already bleeding hands and fingers. When he reached entrance of the hidden cave, he was already covered with his own blood and two nails were missing from his fingers. Most of cuts and bruises were artificial on surface of his skin, except two of them, one across his left breast and on his right leg thigh, which were going to leave nasty scars for the rest of his life. He took the leaves from his medicine bag attached to his belt and applied them on the wounds with his own blood. He took another two of them in his mouth and chewed them slowly, sucking the juices slowly and breathing heavily. His arms muscles were shaking under the strain, but he knew that after 30 – 45 breathes of rest, he would be ready to continue his task. He prepared his modified torch made from the broken spear's handle and leather stripes soaked with Black Pool's blood. He initiated sparks from the Fire stone and torch blazed with golden light. He turned his back to the entrance and coming night; he removed his Sica from scabbard and he stepped deeper inside the cave. His eyes adapted to the light of the torch and he was able to see four to five leaps in front of him. He kept torch in his left hand, far away from his body in a case of an attack. Blood from his hands has dried, but he attached the Sica's handle firmly with leather thongs to his right wrist arm, so he cannot be separated from his weapon, unless someone cut his arm completely. Slowly, he advanced through the narrow passage. Only sound were his feet crunching the small stones disturbing the dust collected by centuries. After 100 leaps he came to the wooden door. On the door it was carved image of Horseman. In his left arm he had shining disk – shield and the other one long tube like spear which he pointed to the left corner of the door. Cadmus came closer to the door, shined it with his torch, so after 10 breaths, he found the spot. The hole was bigger than his fist and he couldn't see anything else inside. He thought to put his hand there for a moment, and then he changed his mind and he inserted handle of his torch inside. He heard some "chunk" sound, then grounding noise and the door started to slide to the right. The inside of it was lightened from the ceiling by some liquid gray light. The light floated on the edge of the ceiling and spread it's whiteness on the stones, so it looked like all upper part was floating in the fog. Cadmus touched again torque around his neck with the tip of his Sica and continued his exploration. Space was five times wider and longer then his village square and in the middle was some type of altar. Altar was squared shape stone, black as his wife's hair and smooth as her skin. Something shined from the center and reflected the light of his torch. He came closer and looked at it. It was gold metal Mask smooth on the surface with two holes instead of eyes. Eyes were shaped as olives. There wasn't any support or rope around the mask, but still object was floating in the middle of the air. It was just three hand distance above the surface of the stone altar.

It was witchcraft! God's game for mortals! There must be some trap behind this!

Cadmus raised torch above the mask and the fire spread like liquid on the top of it, stayed there for some time and then distinguished itself. He repeated his test one more time. Then he tried to touch it with his Sica. The blade vibrated, become heavy in his hand and spark of gold and blue fire circled around the edge and continued across Sica to his hand, all his body shook from the impact, then it jumped back on the surface of the Mask. It gripped him with invisible force and held him there. He had feeling that his heart stopped and that he is going to see The Mighty One. He remembered his oath to the People and with his last strength, he waved his torch, hit flat his other hand and closed the distance above the Mask and his Sica. Sparks continued their dance between him and the Mask. Sica connected with Mask; stones under his feet vibrated from the sound.

Thunder is between Sica and the Mask!

He saw once as Thunder hit and punished abounded wood in the field, the same wood collected hits from time to time. It created the fire that burned tree and the land around it. Blazes of fire ate the wood.

Thunder ate him! Wood will collect Thunder and I will collect the Mask! The Sign of Illys...

His body burned with heat and he saw the light flashing through the altar. He closed his eyes to protect them from fire. He heard that Mask screamed with his voice. The burning smell of wood and meat filled his nostrils. The Face of Illys laughed to him. He fell in arms of Teuta and her Army of Darkness embraced his Soul.

CHAPTER VII

Section 4.

SHADOW

September, 1880.

AUSTRIAN HUNGARIAN EMPIRE, CITY OF PRAGUE, CAFFE NATIONAL…

(Modern day – EU, European Union, Czech Republic, Prague)

It was foggy September evening at Prague; chilly air collected around his long legs, but the man didn't care about that, when he was sitting outside at coffee - bar – restaurant Narodni Kavarna (People's Caffe)" at Vodickova's Street. His face was dark, pale and long with clever, bright, intelligent eyes, enclosed with strong black hair on the top of high forehead. He held coffee cup in his long delicate hands, looking towards the Karluv Most (Charles Bridge), whose architect made a deal with a Devil to repair it. The long walks through the city helped him to release pain and sadness after his father died, and even is more than year since then, he dreamed about him, and he knew that his father is visiting him through his long tortured dreams. Story about Golem that laid in the attic with genizah, Houses for Dolls from Zlata Ulicka (Golden Lane), Doctor's Faust House at Charles Bridge no.40, Astronomical Clock that nobody was able to repair it, Mala Strana (Little Side), Stary Zidovski Hrbitov (Old Jewish Cemetery). Or, the secret venue of the Elders of Zion, Certovka (Devil's Stream); "All the Seven Devils" house and legend of devilish natured Woman , Singing Fontaine with Lilies, stories of thirty years long War, and any other endless history facts and legends couldn't occupied his mind completely from the fact that he missed him more then he wanted to accept it. Only one thing kept him concentrated and it was his vision of free wireless energy implemented on these streets of Prague, which were still lit by gaslight. He was learning foreign languages, and he was grateful that he inherited his faculties from his father, which helped him to finish this year at university very easy, even with Dane's wish to play cards, chess or his unbeatable games in billiards from sundown to sunup. Tesla struggled to keep Dane's soul controlled, but he was learning to use both parts of his brain simultaneously and to use Dane's energy and power for developing his ideas and his ongoing experiments. It drained him out every time when Dane is trying to take over his body and push his soul aside. Last time he collapsed in the middle of his university lectures in Analytical Geometry and Experimental Physics and before that, it happened in front of his unheated, sparsely – furnished room at Smeckach street number 13. Nikola felt some change in the air around him and in the corner of his right eye he caught shadowed movement. The coldness spread from neck through his spine, on the tip of his fingers static electricity build charges and he felt like he entered magnetic field, bluish circular charge pushed leaves from him, initiated from the center of his body to his legs and arms. Charging snapped its lightning through his fingers to the ground and he felt some strange ecstasy in his body, speeded from his stomach to his head, which kept his energy boosted on his skin's surface. He was expecting Dane's voice in his head as before, but this time he could hear only his own thoughts and electrical sensations on his body amused him, so he embraced them with adoration and mild fear. His tall, athletic, straight figure stretched and shined on the edge, in contrast with dark gray background of the building behind him. Shadow separated itself from his feet and stretched across the street, then slide it back to the wall beside him and stand up leveled with him. It positioned itself "en face" to him in his own height and he saw his own image made of darkness.

Who are you…? What are you…? What do you want…?

CHAPTER VII

Section 5.

CHEERS

October, 2009.

CANADA, ALBERTA, EDMONTON, 102 – STREET, APT.203, NORTH WEST…

Inspector Blaquier, sat in his "Lazy - Boy" chair, put both his feet on the sofa in front of him and he opened another "Budd", six pack can of beer, till his Toshiba laptop processes digital voice record of Corporal Dew Roger's unofficial "testimony". He was smart enough to tape that thin digital gadget inside 'Edmonton Sun" newspaper; recorder was so thin and light that it was actually invisible between the pages, he masked with other "Cut and Paste" copy of the same page glued above recorder, so even if Roger shook the "Sun", it wouldn't fell out. Luckily, for him, man occupied by his guilt that he did not pay attention to newspapers on the bench. Recording had perfect quality and it was clear and understandable even with the background noise. Roger's monologue confirmed story of unidentified women from Michelle's files, file which has been recorded on protected witness testimony from International Court's record, of ICCY (International Crime Court for Yugoslavia), at The Hague, Netherlands. How Michelle had her hands on these papers, he really didn't want to know, but it helped him a lot. She was amazing woman, brave and unique, even in her age good looking, but above all, real professional and the best female investigator he ever met in his career and his life. He is going to visit her on his first chance of official or unofficial trip to Toronto. He was worried about other woman, that "Miranda" on the phone, she was unknown player and unidentified factor in his investigation, and he never liked to have some of them. They're the weakest link of any investigation, but always they dangerously influence it and at the end create chaos, he used to called them "Moloch of Truths". They deliver our madness to perceive and to observe their blind justice.

"The truth will set You free."

He took draft from the can.

Cheers!

CHAPTER VII

Section 6.

AN ACCOUNT

January, 2010.

SERBIA, TOWN OF MLADENOVAC, BELGRADE'S COMMERCIAL BANK, LOCAL BRANCH OFFICE AT DRAZA MIHAJLOVIC STREET…

…

'Mr. Jovanovich, I am quite confident that your account is empty. I have already checked twice with our main branch at Belgrade office and they have confirmed that your account has been closed and cleared three days ago by your wife, Mrs. Slobodanka Jovanovich, and this is the copy of her signed paper which we have just received by e-mail.'

The bank teller showed him the paper which clearly stated that his savings account has been cleared completely and the signature on the paper did not mean anything to him, because it did not belong to his wife at all, but his money belong to him and now it is gone. The only good thing in all of this mess is that camera were installed in the banks everywhere, so at least he can trace her face with his money, which is going to be good lead to catch her and to catch others who helped her to do this.

Then she is not going to have the face at all. None of them!

'May I have a copy of this paper; also, I would like to have a word with your supervisor or manager of the branch. Could you please, call him?'

He kept his posture calm, and his eyes leveled on the paper, but the skinny bank's whore across him felt his rage instinctively and she couldn't hide it when she dialed the number with her trembling hand. Maybe she guessed that the money has been removed by mistake, but he was able to smell her fear, it was emanating from her same as always when he interrogated people in his old army days. It felt good to have that power over them, even for a second now.

'No problem, Sir, please sit over there and he will come in a few minutes. Thank you.'

20.000 Euros was not small amount of money, but he killed the people for less and without the money at all in the war fifteen years ago. Whoever made this move against him after all this time, expected that this will crippled him financially, but they did not knew that he have larger amount of cash and other decent stash of gold concealed on two other locations.

They have a good connection through the government channels to do things like this and they are going to make another move on him soon, but he is going to activate his own network as contra measure to their moves. He still had some hidden aces in his sleeves to play this game.

'Mr. Vlado Jovanovich? Our Branch Manager is expecting you at his office please follow me!'

Skinny bank teller appeared in front of him and he tag along with her on the way to glass door at the corner.

CHAPTER VIII

Section 1.

LE CHATEAU

October, 2009.

CANADA, QUEBEC, QUEBEC CITY, FAIRMONT LE CHATEAU FRONTENAC…

…

'I have tried to reach him for some time, but I don't have any respond from him through regular channels, so I used military contacts later, but the results were the same. No response.'

Small bold headed man said, pick up his coffee mug and he swallowed two short shots.

'If I do not have positive confirmation on his status, I am not going to start anything, is that clear to you?'

The other, bigger man with brown hair and moustache in "Wolf skin's" rain jacket took two of cheese fingers, dipped them in Greek Salad dressing sauce and chewed squeaking cheese with pleasure.

'I think that Brian had some unfinished business with old Department and that is the reason to become temporary out of their picture, until dust settled down on his file.'

A small man breaks one piece of Chocolate Chip Cookie and adds another shot of coffee after it.

'I don't care what type of unfinished thing he had with the government, as I have told you before on the phone, I owe him nothing and I am not going to start investigation, because we have been together in only one mission.'

He licked his fingers and took another two cheese fingers.

'I didn't expect anything like that from you, but for God's sake Doug, we have been the best buddies out there…'

'I said what I have just said. It is the end of discussion.'

Doug finished double fingers in support of his statement.

Two of them sat in front of The Chateau Frontenac, on the bench watching the River St. Lawrence and continued their hush – hash conversation over their snacks. Twenty to twenty five meters of them, beside the old black canon, pointed towards the outer walls of Old Town of Quebec City, woman was standing with her small Sony camcorder making her amateur movie on Quebec City castle. Tourist group of ten to fifteen people spread between them on the free benches and railed fence to watch the sunset on Laval's side of the river. The noise of their yapping overtook seagull's songs above their heads. Woman turned her camcorder on two friends on the bench, stayed no more than two seconds focused, and then she continued her zoom on wooden staircase, which leads to the top of fortress. She switched off her camcorder and packed it in her brown leather rucksack. She opened tourist guides book of the city and browse through pages, keeping an eye on two fellows.

…

'Doug, you should consider some other possibility, that someone is targeting us.'

'Listen Marty, you just take care of the staff that, I have just told you and everything will be OK. Keep your mouth shut and let me handles the things.'

'As you said so… But I am not convinced that…'

'Marty, do I have to repeat myself? Which part is not clear for you?'

'No problem Doug, see you then in couple of weeks. Have a good trip and take care of yourself! See you!'

'See you later – Wally - Gator!'

Marty left Doug and followed the path through little park near buy. Doug turned around and he went in the other direction down the hill. Woman waited until he reached the edge of the park and the she followed him keeping 40 to 50 meters distance between them. She couldn't wait to confront him and find out where is the general. The general was the key to open her secret door to the truth. The truth was her path to the freedom.

CHAPTER VIII

Section 2.

VISA

November, 1998.

UNITED STATES OF AMERICA, CALIFORNIA, LOS ANGELES, LOS ANGELES TRAVEL AGENCY…

Detective Marc Arsenault slide his "VISA" credit card through the machine with concern that is not going to be accepted. He already purchased some Christmas gifts at "Sears" store this morning with the same card, so his budget was considerably shorter after this air ticket purchase at Los Angeles Travel agency. He did not planned this trip to Toronto, Canada, so soon, but he felt lonely, as always around this time of a year, the Christmas time, and he is missing her all the time. Last time they have been together in August at Channel Islands Beach Resort on diving and snorkeling weekend and he felt attached to her more than ever before. She was the first one after his wife died, that woke up real feelings in him. At the beginning, he thought that their relationship is not going to last more than two – three date times, but after they have sex together, something broke inside him, and she felt it, too. He had feeling that up to that moment he had only gymnastic exercises in the bed with other women. He was scared and exited in the same time, scared of his own hidden desire that something like this can happen to him again and exited with the thought that he is going to start to love again, for real. He couldn't keep his mouth shut and he told her what he felt with her. She did not react at all at first, but later she flouted in the same cloud of love as him. She completely let go herself to him, it was as she has been captured bird inside her on cage of life. His boss complained on his short notice leave request, but due to good results with ongoing investigation on the case, he used his bonus points and score ten day vacation with extra plus Christmas long weekend. They knew each other very well after all these years and his chief accepted his "out of blue" change of plan, when he used his "hunch" to resolve situation and get results in very short periods of time. It was the same with his private life and plans, since he met Mic. Actually, she helped him on various occasion with her expertise, her police experience and connections with RCMP and Canadian police forces to speed up, resolve and get some additional information in some cases. He returned her favors any time he can from his side; too. Because both of them have been in the same type of a job for years, that was additional connection to their relationship all these years and instead to break up. They were more and more, deeper connected between each other, through respect for each other and their friendship as first layer and their love was on top of it as second layer. Love glued all other similarities between them and kept them together as one. Marc dialed her home number and left message on her answering machine. It ended with the same words as it started:

"My love…"

CHAPTER VIII

Section 3.

VACATION

October, 1998.

UNITED STATES OF AMERICA, WASHINGTON, DC, UNITED STATES DEPARTMENT OF DEFENCE…

General T. Brendan dialed phone number of his field agent at Croatia, Dubrovnik. He was pleased with his work and now they can raise project on the second level when they have the Sign, he hoped that it is authentic as they heard from foreign experts. Detailed check and analysis will confirm that. The phone ringed twice before agent Willburn answered.

'Hello, agent Willburn, I have one good one and one bad one, which you prefer first?'

'Well Sir, hit me with the bad one first, the good one can come later.'

'Agent Willburn you have 96 hours till the show starts again on Balkans.'

'Is that official statement from us?'

'That's official, but unofficially I can tell you that action will be swift and very punishing, because their President Milosevic filled Balkan's graveyards on his promises before. We deployed B - 52 already in the area.'

'Are you expecting problems across the border?'

'Not really, but since you are closed to it and you have already finished major part of our job there, it will be good for you to take some vacation and go somewhere else.'

'Sir, are you suggesting the real vacation time, or it's just transfer time till other assignment starts?'

'What do you think?'

'I think I deserved some vacation time after all.'

'Good. Take two weeks off, but stayed close to the area, in a case of emergency.'

'I did not expect any better deal, but I am in.'

'Before you start with it, send me an artifact from Dubrovnik.'

'Through our regular channels or diplomatic post?'

'No, I am sending two of your kind, one to be collected and delivered, and the other one to continue your job.'

'Where I am going to meet them?'

'There are already there in Croatia, in Dubrovnik. They will contact you at your hotel.'

'Good…'

'Good - Buy - Agent Willburn!'

Line was dead as usual in the middle of his response. Willburn slammed the headset on the phone. He was piss - off by that asshole's attitude for a moment, but then he recollected that his vacation time is going to start officially tomorrow and his mood changes from worse to bitter. He is going to have a shower and then nice supper before other two agents will arrive at his hotel.

At least he isn't deployed at Kosovo at the moment and the site at Montenegro can wait for better days to come…

Better to check that Sign relic before they come…

CHAPTER VIII

Section 4.

VISION

May, 1881.

AUSTRIAN HUNGARIAN EMPIRE, BUDAPEST, VAROSLIGET PARK (CITY PARK)…

(Modern day – EU European Union, Hungary, Budapest)

The world was shaking around him. Ms. Martha Varnai, his property owner, green-eyed and blond haired middle-aged woman whispered about his strange sickness to the other neighbor in front of her apartment building. Their words were booming through his head like two giant bells of Budapest's St. Stephen's Basilica. The clock in the second room, two stairs down of his neighbor's living room hit him on the top of his head like a hammer; ants moved their feet in the basement with grounding noises; sun's rays of light split his skull in half and under his skin light flashed when fly landed on the coffee table. All his senses overpowered by noises from everywhere, oversensitive to the smallest change of air, sound, smell or touch, tormented his body without the end, night and day. Through the fog and lightened pictures in front of him, marched gout bearded, shrunken faces of doctors with silver glasses and monocles.

This is something…, Unknown…, Never seen before…, Unbelievable…, Not possible…, Unexplainable…

Antal Szigeti , his best friend here, raised him from the dead emotionally by his unbreakable spirit, never-ending jokes and physically out of his bed by his strong hands, athletic body and steady exercises, long walks through the green outside open fields, Budapest's wide parks, far away from city's noises and people's voices. He guided him through his love adventures from Budim across bridges to Pesta and back, through famous city bordellos, small attic female student's rooms and lonely ladies in big houses, paid by their job stranded husbands. Tesla was still shaken and weak from the strange sickness that shattered his bones to the core and brought enormous headaches on his brain, but his everyday long walks and rigorous exercises with Szigeti refresh him completely, so now he was able to enjoy the sunset evening in Varosliget – City Park of Budapest.

'Nikola, sometimes I am breathless in front of beautiful woman that I was not able to make normal, regular or civilized sentence, the only things left there, were my heavy breathing, eyes flashed with desire and rigid muscles on my body. How come that you can control all this sexual energy; which has been poured by God through our soul and body to torment us till we died?'

Szigeti turned his head and he saw Tesla's profile clearly on the evening sun. Nikola was concentrated on the sun and to Szigeti; it seemed that Tesla's soul crossed again into one of his own universes, worlds that existed parallel with this one. He was scared for Tesla's health, but more than that, he was scared to death that Tesla's soul tormented to eternity will stay somewhere there forever.

'Nikola, are you listening me at all? Look at me!'

Tesla's face was a mask of fire, burning under the closing sun. He was statue of red shadow frozen in time.

'Tesla! Look at me!'

Szigeti raised his voice to one octave more, honestly concerned for his friend.

'Look at me!'

Tesla repeated words without real feelings for them and then he added:

'I am turning…, I released the switch and it is going on reversed side…, There is no sparks…'

'What are you talking about?'

Szigeti asked him with the small twitch in his left eye, unsecured on Tesla's well being.

'My motor is using two magnetic fields to control the force and the force is keeping flow of electric switched from one direction to the other one, holding the motor in the grip of the force…'

Tesla's dark eyes flashed with bluish sparks inside his pupils. He kept looking at the sun as the source of his imagination.

'Look, I will make a picture on the ground, so you can see the same as I see it….'

CHAPTER VIII

Section 5.

IMPOSSIBLE

September, 2009.

UNITED STATES OF AMERICA, WASHINGTON, DC, WASHINGTON, "BIG BROTHER"
OFFICE...

The old man was reading much older pages in front of him.

...

Three years since his mother death Tesla didn't stop to work for a second, he even slept two

hours less than before to complete his tests on his "telautomatons".

The amazing energy burst of his tests on wireless lights vacuum tube activated by high –

frequency coil, showed him very wide types of usage and new possibilities opened to this new

tube types. He produced test machine on wireless tele - control that was able to activate

telautomaton 10 kilometers away from the source, they contacted him by military contacts at

DOD (Department of Defense) to prepare an additional copy of this machine. He was not happy

about it, but he desperately needed the money to finish his last version of prototype "Teslatron",

another new patent based on wireless energy transmission that was not transferring electrical

current energy only, it was transmitting small mechanical and physical objects from one spot to

the other one. He managed to transfer different objects up to 5 kilograms without the problem

and the prototypes assembled last week should be able to transfer up to 100 kilograms.

Clemens suggested that he should tried transfer human body through the machine and he

volunteered for it, but Tesla rejected his idea completely due to his determent decision not to use

other human or any alive animal, or any other creature for his tests. Tesla made most of his tests

alone, and on himself, but this time he called me to assist him. Tesla stepped inside the wire cage

tree meters high with the metal frames attached from the ground to the ceiling and he closed improvised door with his rubber glove. He performed this test on dead tissue and on some hard

objects, inside the lab only few meters apart, with smaller version of the same machine. But this

time he built identical cage on the other site at Niagara Falls, Canada and even he send some of

his personal belongings and some early staged equipment there, this will be the first time that

living tissue – himself is going to be beamed on the other side.

'I am ready, Crawford. Initiate the test!'

I scratched my moustache, which was recognizable signal for Tesla that I was very nervous and

deathly scared.

'I am going to count Sir, up to three…'

I said.

Tesla adjusted sleeves on the edges of his suit, as he is going to give another lectures to the

Franklin Institute at Philadelphia.

'One.'

He took deep breath.

'Two.'

He exhaled it slowly.

'Three.'

Two and half million volts hit the cage with high ten meters sparks of electricity connecting the

cage with metal frames, ozone filled the air around Tesla's body, purple, blue and yellow

lightning's bolts hit the grounding of the cage creating the magnetic force.

He was standing in the middle of large sheet of fierce, blinding flame, his all body enveloped in a

mass of phosphorescent wriggling streamers, which like tentacles of an octopus connect him to

the cage. Bundles of blue and white light stick out from his spine, as he stretched his arms under

the force, thus forcing the electrical fluid outwardly, roaring tongues of fire leap from his

fingertips and the deafening noise filled the room. The cages around him bristle with rays,

emitting strange musical notes and sounds, like singing the song on his own, glowed with energy,

growing hot and red. Tesla was in the middle of it, little elevated from the ground, in the centre of

more curios actions, which were invisible for my eyes blinded by light. His all body has been bombarded by the surrounding electrified, magnetized air and dust particles floating around him. Sensations on his skin were indescribable. In both his hands two bluish circles of light appeared, they grow steady from his hands and they covered him completely, his body was invisible at the edges and it melted itself into the giant ball. Loud clap of thunder filled the room. I pressed my white, sweaty palms in pain to my ears. I screamed and closed my eyes as another one hit the cage walls. Tesla disappeared between two of them. Bluish giant thunder ball of light stayed one more second in the middle of the cage and then evaporated in small electrical beams. The cage cracked from power and electricity and the high-pitched tune continued five seconds after. Sound of silence filled the room space and I felt that pressure on body of mine is gone. I was standing there as castaway on the island watching the rising tide on horizon. My limbs shook from the shock as I made my first steps toward the cage and then I whispered to myself:
'Impossible…, this is impossible…!'

…

Crawford was a fool… But still he was fool enough to kept the record in his private journal this event, which was final proof that "The Machine' existed, and now I have found location where was hidden for all these years since 1895…

…

The old man nicknamed "Big Brother" smiled victoriously aloud inside his office. He smiled as tears of joy were filling his eyes.

CHAPTER VIII

Section 6.

TARA

December, 1998.

MONTENEGRO, THE DURMITOR NATIONAL PARK, MOUNTAIN OF DURMITOR,

CANYON OF TARA RIVER, "GLOBA GLAVA" AREA, "LEDINA PECINA"…

…

"The Tear of Europe" That was her name, how locals refer to this remarkable stretch and sight of the river in front of me. They were right… She is violent and wild as my life it has been through all these centuries, yet pure and clear as a teardrop, as I have tried to keep my soul at the spinning course of the time…

Tanya imagined the time when river of Tara has been sculpting and scouring its path through the soft limestone surface of the land and rock, with its great water strength made of winter snow and seasonal rains, through continued erosion creating 82 kilometers long canyon, when the human being inhabited these lands and respected it as their Mother. Of course, even now after all this time, water kept its quality and purity, any traveler at any point of its journey through its limestone abyss can safely and freely drink it in the length of 140 kilometers. She was tracking across Mountain of Durmitor, from "Globa Glava"("Round Head" or Head of Globe") to "Ledina Pecina"("Cave of Ledo" or "Ice Cave") team of mercenaries hired to find an artifact buried for thousands of years or hidden somewhere between the Tara River Gorge's banks. The Tara River Canyon was second deepest and largest chasm after that one of the Grand Canyon of Colorado at United States, 1300 meters to the valley floor, and for sure, they did not come here to consume the water and enjoy the sightseeing. Not in the wintertime season… For last twenty - six hours, she was following company of five of them, all the way through thick forest of mostly black pine, eastern hornbeam, black ash, elm, linden, cork oaks, and sycamore and beech trees. Vegetation was so dense and thick in some areas, that sometimes she lost them completely in the black pine forest, between the tall and thick one, some of them more than 50 meters high and over 500 years old. Snow instead of moss unhide and recovered their tracks, as on huge carpet of white – green colored cover, endless sounds of continuously cascaded dripping water were wrapped around her, that without activated "body scanner" she would lost them inside depth often additionally camouflaged by the raising, dissolving fog and dense cloud formations on the top of mountain's peaks. One of them, the man in the green jacket had some kind of a digital map, which guided them on the way to correct cave, where relic eventually would be. Without the map, the time spend to explore approximately 200 caves, from which 80 of them were large enough to hide more than small object as mask; with almost similar interior description, measurements, location descriptions and well hidden inside rocky, steep cliffs above the river, so the possibility to find the right one would be zero. Some of them were so deep inside the mountains, that after all these centuries they stayed undiscovered by humans and probably they took vast of their lives only to become visible to the naked eye. The man was obviously German, tall, well build, in very good shape for a man in his late 50-s, with his blond thick hair, white skin and stony cold blonde eyes, even without his thick accent, anyone would guess that. Others called him Kirk, if that was his real name, he was the leader and evidently, they were scared of him. The other one, in blue jacket, shorter, with stocky shoulders, wider and heavier build, like wrestler, in his 30-s, short black hair, wide cheekbones and black pearl eyes was Kirk's bodyguard or probably "hired gun" from some foreign agency. Accent was strong, South Carolina American, with a hint of Latino blood on his semi dark skin. He was calm, very quiet, professional and very keen for a kill, which he proved twice on a deer and wild goat, when they fell inside his shooting perimeter. They called him Simon. Two of them where natural twins, close to their 40-s, large, bulky, heavy moves as professional bouncers or semi - pro weight lifters, both had shaved bold heads, dressed completely in black, similar Slavic face structure, with locally colored Serbian accent. Very noisy, rude and arrogant near everything and anything. They were nicknamed as "Brale" ("Bro'" – short version of "Brother") and "Profa" ("Profe'" - short version of "Professor"). The last one was a woman, skinny, light - weight, thin figured, like long runner athletic, brown eyed and brown haired, in her 30's, dressed in gray jacket and pants, very knowledgeable about the area, used as a guide, but extremely shy and calm, there was something more than appeared personality underneath. She gave her creeps for some unknown reasons. They called her Jackie. She did not have particular accent at all.

It started to snow again. They are going to camp in 15 minutes. German is right on a clock. He pushed them hard today. Twins were not happy about that.

She switched to "stealth" mode as she approached them from the east. In order to get detail information, as much as it was possible, about their employers, their locations and organizations, she had to get closer, up to 100 meters for mikes to work, to collect records of everything.

Since they moved far away from marked footpaths, their speed decreased due to snow, but mostly because they get closer to the source and it look like their map is useless last hour. Since they crossed "Djavole Lazi" ("Devil's Lanes"), very narrow riverbank path, where they were able to leap to the other side of the river, their progress was painfully slow through fords and vertiginous riverbank. The snow is going to show her movements openly to them in a case that some of them detected her. At least darkness will cover her in her warm blanket of secrecy. Durmitor name derived from Balkan Romance dialect that meant, "Sleeping" or "Dreaming", cognate with English word "dormitory", but I preferred another etymology that could be from Celtic meaning "Mountain with Water". It is more suitable for it. Tanya checked her locator and realized that if they are going towards "Zmajeve Pecine" ("Dragon's Cave") direction tomorrow, she will be "in - out" of retraction beam range, which meant that in a case of emergency, perhaps she is not going to be able to transfer herself back to her hotel room at Zabljak, where was her receiver.

It's a reason more for me to be more careful when I approached them… OK, the mike is on…

…

CHAPTER IX

Section 1.

BON APPETITE

December, 1998.

CANADA, ONTARIO, TORONTO, CABBAGETOWN, PARLIAMENT STREET,

PEARTREE RESTAURANT...

Detective Constable Michelle D. Bamford sat comfortably inside the cozy, pleasant little restaurant nestled in among various local clothing shops on Parliament Street, and she was resting on exposed red brick wall above her head with warm coffee mug in her right hand. Her left hand was on folder - files of an unsolved murder. Coffee steam smell tickled her nose and it felt good under her cold fingers, compared with outside occasional flurries, which were dancing with snowballs on the north wind. Her thoughts went to her dead colleague W. J. Daniel who was assigned to the Special Investigation Squad, Brake and Enter detail, stabbed recently on his undercover assignment in the north - east section of Toronto. It was too late when they transported him to Sunnybrook Medical Centre, even with Emergency first aid applied on the scene, he lost too much blood and he succumbed to his injuries. There is ongoing investigation in progress, but until now it did not give any results. Unidentified woman stabbed him on his back, when he was attending a store in the area to obtain a cold soda pop, per eyewitness near buy there is another female involved with it. Stab wound was unusually wide and deep; like the killer used some strange long shaped knife or machete. She knew him very well from Academy, they have been on the same class, married recently beautiful blue - eyed girl and they have small baby girl together. She felt sorry for her and her child, it will be tough to raise the child without one parent, and she knew that very well from her own experience. Her father, police officer, died on line of duty when she was eight, under strange circumstances and case that hadn't been solved for all these years. Although, it happened in 1983, she felt the same pain as it was yesterday. She struggled to keep her tears inside her eyes under her eyelids.

'Miss, are you OK?'

Passing 20s years old waitress, with curled brown hair stopped in front of her table. She brought her order and watched her with her light brown "Bambi" eyes.

'Yes, I am thank you.'

'Are you sure? If there is anything I can help you…?!'

'No, thank you very much, I am all right.'

'Okay, "bon appétit" and enjoy your meal.'

She wiped rolling tear from her left cheek and she smiled back to waitress unconvincingly. Soft bittersweet jazz music in the background put Michelle in melancholic mood for some time. Pasta, "Spaghetti alla Carbonara", smelled deliciously inviting with mixture of raw eggs, cheese, olive oil with fried pancetta. Beside the plate there were three small dishes filled with sour cream, mushrooms, broccoli and Parmesan cheese. With all this, one glass of red French wine will be good as the smack on the fool's face, but she is going to pick up Marc from the airport in the afternoon and she wouldn't allowed herself to drink and drive, specially on this slippery, snowed streets on Christmas time. She ate slowly enjoying the taste and spices on her tongue, breathing the smell through her nostrils. Her heart - beat was faster, warm liquid spreading feelings came from her stomach and she felt first date teenaged excitement through her legs. Marc woke up that in her and she became addicted to it from the beginning. She loves him fully and completely, and she was considering an option to move to the States with him. She will find a job easily there due to crime rates are much higher in L.A. then here in Toronto. She is going to propose this to him tomorrow. Food calmed her stomach and coffee added positive caffeine energy shot to her body. She felt energized and ready for Christmas Holidays spree of love and joy. Her pager biped twice and started to vibrate on her belt. She slide out it from his holder and checked incoming message.

"Call me at the office... We have another carved sample at the morgue. Todd."

CHAPTER IX

Section 2.

THE SPIDER

December, 1998.

UNITED STATES OF AMERICA, CALIFORNIA, LOS ANGELES, UCLA HAMMER MUSEUM...

Markus Artmann, nicknamed "Die Spinne" (The Spider) open the third file cabinet drawer searching for the key. His source gave him right information, accurate to the last detail. Of course, the man with smashed toes and chopped eight fingers on his legs wouldn't provide false information after all, but from his experience most of them confess well buried secrets from their skull, once he start his other "specialties" on them. Professor Bronson wasn't unreasonable person, after all he confessed everything after one toe and two fingers, but Markus continued his special treatment just for fun. He used car battery cables on his genitals to break his spirit completely and it felt good to take Bronson life, when he cowardly begged him before the end. He found false wooden bottom of the drawer, masked with lighter oak's markings, and he used his bayonet to open it. Wooden plate creaked under blades pressure and he broke the edges with bayonet's iron handle. Inside hidden drawer, he found small polished mahogany box. On the surface was carved wolf's head made of bronze. He opened it. On the red satin sits polished black gem. Stone looked brand new after all these centuries and his almond shaped edges had small letters on it, indicated that it was part of some bigger object before. He closed the box and put in the black bag under his left armpit. Markus slide bayonet in his holder on inner side of his left forearm. Now he just had to contact his Cell and report his positive results. He heard steps were echoing through the corridor. He left drawer opened and moved across the room to the sliding entrance door. Through cracked door, he saw security guard silhouette outlined by light from the hallway. The man was most likely, on his regular night shift tour through the building. Markus blended with the darker background beside the door. He drew out his bayonet from its sheath.

The security guard was a big fat man weighted more than 100 kilograms and almost 1, 80 cm. high. With his heavy walk, the man approached Markus and slightly opened door. Markus hold his breath and he elevate his weapon in line with his left shoulder. Guard followed by his instincts stopped in front of the screened door and stayed immovable for some time.

Go away. Just continue your stupid low paid exercise route. Go on. Continue it. Go away!

The guard touched door handle with his right hand, grip it for two seconds and then closed it. He stayed in front of it another three additional seconds, taking into consideration his private thoughts and woken up instinct and then he continued his walk down the empty passage. Marcus stayed in the same position until security guard's steps fade away in the distance.

Good Boy!

CHAPTER IX

Section 3.

TOWER

November, 1998.

BOSNIA AND HERZEGOVINA, TOWN OF STOLAC, POCITELJ OLD CITY, CASTRUM TOWER...

Old tower glommed under the midnight moonlight, circular carpet of fog was spreading its tentacles around the bottom edges, and to agent Frank Dillon it look like broken sharp wolf's fang raised upside down toward the night sky. He was standing at the edge of monolith block of stone, which remind him on some of his grandfather's tales about Stonehenge and his legends. Frank accepted this assignment as temporary due to fact that other agent has been trapped with a job at the moment; anyway he thought that in two – three days he will be back on his regular graveyard shift at Zagreb's Embassy. This place gave him creeps and his skin tingled from the strange electrical charging in the area. It was too warm night for this time of a year here, as per locals, but his hands and feet were cold as ice for last fifteen minutes, like some cold box of air from the north stayed above his head and locked itself on this place. He decided to wait half an hour more, so if his local contact doesn't show up, he will abort the mission for tonight and make some other arrangements for delivery. He changed the meeting point as usual, giving them new location half an hour prior to their schedule to adopt, and he was expecting that they are going to be late. He heard some strange sound above his head. Clock was ticking. He looked up above his head and did not see anything except the moon's milky light spread on the surface of the tower's stone. The sound stopped suddenly and in the next second, another one started.

"mmmmmmmMMMMMMMMmmmmmmmm"

He caught flashing light in the corner of his right eye and then hot short pain went from his right shoulder across his chest to his left elbow. Instinctively, he aimed with his right hand for his gun under his left armpit and his eyes drooped down. His left arm detached from his body and his left shoulder with his gun followed the left arm. Blackness enveloped his thoughts. His dead decapitated body slide on the left side like broken doll. Shadow detached itself from the wall behind him, followed by gold – blue flickering snake at the end of its left hand. In a second shadow and the snake disappeared in a thin air. Only moon above the tower watched it as a witness.

CHAPTER IX

Section 4.

WAX

September, 1882.

FRANCE, ILE – DE – FRANCE REGION, PARIS, "MUSEE GERVIN", BOULEVARD MONTMARTRE...

(Modern day – EU, European Union, Paris, France)

Hands of the thin, transparent man in front of him were making the face from warm clay, shaping the nose, cheeks and ears from nothing and brownish color of clay sprinkled with water, assembled colors on pastel's surface of canvas behind man's back. Picture was made of black - red chalk with yellow pastel chalk, and it was Isabella d'Este by Leonardo de Vinci, as he remembered correctly from his history of art classes. His small delicate fingers were like spiders legs, moving on top of it, touching, pressing, removing and adding small portions of material in silenced musical tempo, dancing on their own rhythm, stroking the surface with sensible, gentle touch of his fingertips. Tesla was looking how in front of him the face of long time ago deceased person became alive again through the hands of Monsieur Gervin. The Wax Museum has just has been established in Paris in January this year and it served as an important nexus for new invented medias in Paris, as early cinemas performances and projections, offering itself as a "living newspaper" on the one hand and hosting Tesla's electricity demonstrations secretly to the other. Tesla is welcomed guest at "Musee Gervin" at Boulevard Montmartre, since he helped Monsieur Gervin to electrify his house and build the magical Palais des Mirages (Hall of Mirrors). Hexagonal room that has very special effects with the lights and multiple reflections from the mirrors that go from floor to ceiling and it completely surround you; which appeal stretched images of the person far and wide. Tesla made his new build motor presentation, at Baroque styled Hall of Columns, which impressed people, but nobody was interested to invest money in his invention, so he was already considering possibility to go to America and test his luck there. He was working for Continental Edison's Company at Paris, last couple of months and he already have got very good rating between engineers and technicians in the city due to his innovative, fresh and hard work on electrical and mechanical problems on his everyday job. Salary was very low, however once in a month when he would received his salary, he would go to café "Oncle" (Uncle) and he would order dozens of different delicacy aperitif meals with the main luxury meal of "Rabbit in Lemon Sauce" with the glass of sweet sparkling champagne, and treat himself as a king. The rest of the month he used his money very carefully through the never - ending month, eating at the cheap places like small tavern "Two Brothers" with their everyday specials of Goulash Bourguignon and cheap red wine, drafted at small half a litter long neck bottles. He knew deep inside his soul that someday he is going to turn upside down this world with his inventions and ideas, which were nesting above his deep-set eyebrows.

'Monsieur Tesla, May I invite you to drink one glass of our finest cognac with me and celebrate our friendship together with your triumphant future, which is ahead of you in the following years.'

'Dear, Monsieur Gervin you are going to spoil me with your kindness and your generosity…'

'Monsieur Tesla, as a token of my small gratitude towards your unselfish hard work and your honest friendship between us, I would like to make a wax portrait of your intriguing, mysterious and magnificent face for my own private collection, if you allowed me…'

'Well, Monsieur Gervin, since I have to travel tomorrow to Alsace to resolve some technical problems at the Strasbourg's Main Railways Station and I am not quite sure when we are going to have similar situation like this in our unpredictable cloudy future, I accept your offer gladly. You may proceed with your magical scheme of thrilling technique of waxing my face, but I warn you, you will need a lot of wax to cover my long face, large nose and my wide ears…'

Monsieur Gervin honestly smiled to Tesla's comment as Santa.

'Ho – ho – ho…, ho-ho…'

CHAPTER IX

Section 5.

MINNIE

October, 2009.

CANADA, ONTARIO, NIAGARA FALLS, ST CATARINES DISTRICT, LINCON AVENUE...

Woman's brown haired ponytail pops out and in the same time, her creamy colored hat flew from her head, when she received front leg kick in her face. She tried to balance her body for a second with both her hands, rowing through the air backwards and then she hit hard on the floor with her bony ass and the back of her head connected with the edge of wooden coffee table. Her nose sprayed the blood under her chin and on her pink Minnie Mouse T-shirt. Deep growling noise came out from her mouth in her attempt to speak, her eyes went up and rolled on the left side, her face got expression of boringness and she lost her conciseness for time being.

'You, son - of – bee – eee - eech!'

With vengeance – scream – call on her mouth, the other woman in her forties hit the man with full strength, adding her 60 kilograms of weight, to the speed of her trained muscles, on his left temple arcade.

'Aaaarr - gghh!'

The punch of her leathered - gloved right hand sounded like released Champaign' screw, and the man's head went aside, it's impact send him flying from bar-chair where he was sitting, parallel with the bar, ending on metal garbage bin right of him. His hands were useless, tied by police handcuffs and they couldn't provide him any protection against the metal garbage bin edges and hard polished tiles underneath. Without any sound from his mouth, he rebound from the floor and collapsed on his stomach when he fell. Older woman hit him additionally twice with her left spiky cowboy's boot in his left kidney and his ribs. She would continue her raged pumping revenge, if she did not heard other younger' woman moan from behind.

'Stella?!'

She turned around, covered the space between them in two long strides and kneeled beside younger woman's head. She took her bloody face in her leathered palms and called her name again:

'Stella? Can you hear me? Can you move?'

'Yheess, I phink…, I bill be okay…, Bhat happound?'

Swollen upper lip and her broken nose made her talk strange, but her eyes were clear now and focused on older woman's face.

'Bastard hit you with the leg in the face; I managed to repay him a little…'

She produced a smile on one side of her swollen face and added:

'Bhut, he is alivfe?'

'Ah, regrettably yes, we still need him for some time, do not speak, let me take care of your face and nose…, Just lay down for a sec, I am going to bring some things from our car, do not move!'

'Bbeth, be carupfhull…baybe someone bhu - rdnoise…'

Older woman, Beth turned around, gave her one wink with right eye and she disappeared through house's entrance door. Woman named Stella pushed herself to sitting position and wiped the rest of her blood from her face with the bottom of Minnie's shirt. She looked like special force commando smudged face prior to action. She touched rising bump on the back of her head with her left hand and she was watching man on the floor with hateful bloody look in her eyes. The man didn't move and his face was turned to the bar, so she couldn't see, if he was just pretending or he was for real unconscious. They started to investigate him one hour ago, after they caught him by surprise at his house. They had lured this Dick – Head in their trap by Ontario swinger's web page on line club, which was his secondary full time entertainment, between his bank's real – estate advisory job and single man jerking sexual private life. Nevertheless, he had an access to bank deposit boxes, which contained some old hidden files of Fitzgerald Francis notes of Nikola Tesla's wireless electric energy from a year 1943 and allegedly some Tesla's inventions hidden there. In addition, Niagara Falls Hydro secret documents from 19 - Th. century, some Black Stone together with some other stuff that has been very important to their employer from Washington, DC. "The Big Brother", as they called him between themselves, Beth and Stella, kept his tracks well covered and till now they couldn't trace him, but at least he compensated them well and on time with cash for their assignments. However, both of them were fully aware that unnecessary spectators as them are going to be converted into expendable gear, eventually for Mr. Big. That was the reason that all this time, they were recording their entire moves, on every freaking mission, which they have got from him. The man on the ground moved slightly his head. She stood up sustaining herself with her hands on the sofa near buy. Her head hurt her, but she managed to come closer to the man.

'You…fub – huking asshouule, I wbill kill you…'

Man seems to take notice of her incoherent speech and her movements, so he turned his face, scrapping his nose on the floor in his effort to turn his head. His swollen, blue and red, left eye followed her unsteady approach.

'Oh, Sleeping Beauty woke up! Something happened to your nose, sorry I can't understand you! Hah, ha – ha, hah – ha, …'

He smiled with the pain spreading beneath his left ribs.

'You are labphing, ha! You' ayv not goving to lapbh pov long…'

Stella came closer and removed bottle of 12 years old "Glenfiddich" Scotch Whisky which was hanging upside down from one of dozers above the home made bar. She was coming on him from the top. She swung the bottle in green parabolic falling arc headed for man's head. The man superposed on his belly at the floor; he was starting to kick with his legs as a dead fish in a boat. The only thing he succeeded is to move two to three centimetres on the right before the bottle hit him hard in the head. Instead, on his exposed face, bottle smashed on his left part of the skull, one centimeter above his left ear. Impact shattered bottle in hundreds of green sharp pieces, some of them shredded his left ear and cut his left cheek deeply, whiskey liquid burned his closed eye and his skin slashed by the glass fragments. His scream filled his living room and he felt that warm blood splashed his face and ear. Fifty-degree strong alcohols bite his new opened wounds mercilessly. His scream continued and leaped to the kitchen ceiling.

'Whu-ay you av – not laphing nov…?'

Stella added with crocked smile on her face. Her swollen nose shortened the view between her eyes and she struggled to keep tears inside her over - filled eyes. The man stopped screaming and moaned under her feet. She screamed at him:

'Ham – on,… Laph at meee….!'

The door burst open and Beth marched inside with small berretta gun in her right hand. She glanced through the room at once and called Stella:

'Stella…, I am here. Look at me… Stella!'

Stella was mumbling some words for himself and she fixed her eyes on the man. Beth put a handgun on her trouser's wide leather belt and dropped the bag from her left hand to the floor, then she run for Stella. She embraced her in her arms and she tenderly kissed her swollen lips.

'Shhhhh…. I am here, Stella… I am here….'

Stella drop her head on Beth's left shoulder and buried her face in it. Tears sting her eyes but she hold Beth around her waist and sniffed two – three times in her shoulder. Beth slowly detached of her, ignoring Stella's stained blood on her white shirt, and she wiped part of blood streaks from her face with her back hand.

'I have some things at first aid box, from our car and I am going to clean your beautiful face…'

'He diftroyed my boutifall pface… He waf laphing at me…'

'Do not speak now, let me see what we can do about it…'

Beth stroke Stella's hair, smudged and soaked with her own blood, and guided her to leather sofa beside the window. She kindly helped her to sit on it and then she went back and she closed and locked the door after she double - checked left and right down the empty street for some snoopers. She came back to the man and checked his wounds, too. He had one deep wound on his head were whiskey bottle landed and one part of his left ear was missing, but the rest of it were artificial wounds on his skins surface and they were not life threatening. She kicked him with her booth, and he moaned in response, so she figured out that he is alive. Nonetheless, he can wait his time, after all; he started the mess, plus he is a male and there were never priorities in her life. She moved back to her Stella and gave her full attention that she deserved as her lover and her friend. After 10 to 15 minutes, Beth managed to put back together Stella's face. Now Stella looked like hockey player with a big wide band – aid tape across middle of her swollen nose and the bleeding from her mouth stopped completely. Beth applied antibiotics powder on her wounds and with some additional double dose of pain – killers Stella came back from the land of zombies in one peace. She had difficulties with a speech, but she was good to go and in much better mood then before. Beth nodded with her head that her job was well done and she dedicated her attention to the man beneath.

'Now, we can take care of our beloved entertainer and wake him up for second round of our conversations, but I can guaranteed that he is not going to like it, as we are, isn't it, my sweet loved Stella?'

'Yeessss,… Phe imph not gon'a like it…, But whee av gon'a enyoh it…'

CHAPTER IX

Section 6.

SAVAGE

March, 2011.

SERBIA, TOWN OF OBRENOVAC, BASEMENT OF THE HOUSE AT VUK KARADZICH STREET, HEADQUARTER OF LOCAL TERORIST CELL "THE BLACK HAND"

…

'What did you do?'

Brown eyes behind black rimmed glasses flashed with open anger.

'I did it for our cause, for our organization, for our fatherland, for my country, for people of Serbia!'

Spit from young man's mouth uncontrollably flew in front of his face; it ended on brown - eyed man's shirt which was standing across him. He registered it briefly as he held the younger one's black hair in his right fist.

'Which part of your moron's brain did not understand our direct order and developed an idiotic idea like this? What was the order?'

Fat older man shook his right hand up and down so violently, that strings of black hair broke from surface of young one's head and curled ends stayed knotted between his fat, meaty fingers. Younger man cried in pain as his strong beloved hair has been removed from his scalp. His eyes filled with tears and he answered through his clenched teeth.

'To install and activate the bombs in the house and in the car…,

Nnnhhhhh…'

Fat, wide, chunky left fist landed on youthful unprepared abdomen and he folded on half and drooped to his knees. His face was leveled with old man's right lap. Black rimmed glasses owner did not miss a chance when he see it. He crunched young man's nose with his left knee and kicked him in the chest as blood covered the face of a boy.

'Urrgghhh…'

Older one produced Zastava handgun pistol M57, caliber 7.62 mm from his back, pulled out under his shirt, in his right hand and he aimed at the young one spread on the floor.

'Noooooo!'

Two shots banged through the closed space like thunder cracks deafening both of them instantly. The first bullet hit the boy high in the chest and stopped him in the middle of the air and second one hit him in the middle of his forehead throwing his head widely back. His opened mouth produced whooshed sound and reminded open when he hit the floor. Eyes stayed wide unbelievably opened, an expression of his face shocked, as he couldn't believe what had just happened to him. The killer with glasses slide his warm barrel gun back at his previous position coldly as he just drink a glass of water and he pull out Samsung mobile phone from his front shirt pocket and dialed the number with his thick thumb finger.

'Hello, it's me…, I am done. Send your guy to clean…, No…, I do not have it; I will collect it from Predrag later in the evening…, See you in the club! Later!'

He switched off the line, turned around and headed to the basement's exit door. He stopped in front of it, like he had forgot something to say or to do, and he turned his head in the direction of the dead body laying on the concrete floor. He spat on it and murmured some words through his teeth:

'Now, you know who am I and why they call me "Krkan" ("Savage")!'

CHAPTER X

Section 1.

EARTHQUAKE

November, 2009.

CANADA, QUEBEC, L' ANNONCIATION, COWBOY PAINTBALL FIELD, 219 ROUTE
117 SUD...

...

Bitch is coming!

Doug Burke's fingers shook, as he was loading his gun. He was angry on himself, high on
adrenaline, shivering from cold and wild – eyed because of her. In the middle of nowhere, on
randomly chosen spot at the Cowboy Paintball Field of L' Annunciation vicinity, he stumbled out
of his Chrysler Pacifica and he run in direction of a storage wood – house with the gun in his
right hand. His fuel tank was on reserve when she started to chase him across Hwy 40 and an
alarm started when he reached Road 117, just before Mont – Tremblant, and he realized that he is
not going to reach Mont Laurier, so he kept running the engine until it stopped here.

What I was thinking?

He knew that, if she laid her hands on him he is going to tell her everything, no matter what he
remembered or not from his past. She is going to dig out all his secrets from his head, all
information which were hidden under hypnosis, which cannot be activated without secret word,
he was sure that she will find a way to reach inside his head and collect them like a candies from
broken cookie jar.

I should kill myself as in that Japanese honor's killing, what was the name...?

No, he is going to kill the bitch before she catch and killed him. He tried to reach Lt Colonel
Andrew Marlow on his mobile without success, so he left recorded message on his office phone

at Mont Laurier, maybe he will get it on time to come and help him. She's got Henry in his spa sauna centre and she drained him like a vampire. He stayed alive as "vegetable", without any physical control and self - awareness or any knowledge of who he is and where he is. He is not going to finish like him.

She will pay for all of them!

He slammed the door and he hunkered down beside the large pile of paint ball suits staffed in the corner of the storage house. The space was packed with paint ball weapons, targets, and other equipment. He found the spot three meters opposite of entrance door, so he would be able to cover all area with his weapon. Luckily, he had additional box of ammunition with him in the car. He was ready to make his last stand.

I am ready, come and get me!

He heard that other car, which has been following him through Quebec's roads for last three hours, Henry's Pontiac Vibe stopped in front of the modified storage house. Silence covered the area like a blanket. He tried to concentrate on the sounds, but he did not hear anything from the outside. It was as the nature itself discontinued to exist and it withdraw itself from this time and space.

Where is she? What is she doing? What is she waiting for?

Tremble under his feet started first as rumble in the distance and then it multiply itself all around him, until the deafened sound roared through his body. He impulsively put his left hand on the ground to steady himself, but very strong tremor continued and spread on his body like an uncontrolled wave. Ground under his legs cracked and all building structure screamed above his head.

Earthquake?!

Screeching sound of broken wooden walls filled his ears and he dropped his weapon on the ground, he tried to balance himself, but already cracked land under his feet collapsed and his right leg slipped inside the gaped hole up to his knee. He cursed when piled equipment slithered on his right shoulder. Rumbling noise elevated to the point that he could not detect collapse of the roof above his head. Something hit him across his back and he stayed pinned to the ground by it. All air from his lungs exploded. He felt breathless and dust filled his nostrils, he coughed in attempt to catch a breath through his mouth. Ruptured ground shook for third time and then it stopped. He felt cold air breeze across his exposed back and icy, chilled touch of the snow on his face brought him back from the foggy rushing noise inside his head. He elevated his head five centimetres above the ground and craned his stiff neck to see around, but dizziness filled his head and weakness of his body forced him to lie down and stay calm. He was not able to move at all under roof debris on his back.

What the hell happened here?

He heard scrapping sound similar to as somebody or something is pulling large metal sheet apart, metal screeched resembling pterodactyls call for a hunt. Pressure on his back lifted itself and his immovable body felt free again. His right leg was inside the hole, trapped by gashed ground, but he was able to wiggle with his toe and fingers inside his boot. He opened eyes when he heard crunching steps in front of his face. The black boot spoke to him with sexy, mild, smooth voice: 'Well, Mister Burke unquestionably you were shaken, but doubtfully you are going to be baked, too.'

Doug Burke never found out that, Natural Resources Canada's Office at Ottawa registered an Earthquake at L' Annonciation, Province of Quebec, with magnitude of 3.3 MN, which has been felt by Western Quebec residents on November, 2009…

CHAPTER X

Section 2.

MMMMMMMM

December, 1998.

UNITED STATES OF AMERICA, CALIFORNIA, LOS ANGELES, SAN FERNANDO'S

VALLEY, BURBANK…

…

;Ohhh, …., Yes!…, Stevan….'

He moved up his hips catching her rhythm. He felt her vagina muscles contraction on his penis.

Her spasms hold her on top of him. She was following his movements with her curvy ass,

rotating, moving and rubbing against his lower stomach with her hard firm bottom.

'Ahhhhh, …'

He caught his breath, he moved his left hand across her hip, and he grabbed her left breast firmly.

She moaned when he grasped her nipple and twisted hard.

'Mmmmmmm…, My God! Aaaahhhhh!'

She went up on his penis, stayed on the top of him for a brief second and then she humped back

swallowing him with her vagina. She dropped on his sweaty chest trembling like a leaf during her

orgasms.

'Aaaaaaa…, aaaaaa…, mmmmmm…, aaaaa…, ahhhhh!'

He couldn't hold it anymore and he filled her with his sperm kicking her three more times in his

final body convulsion. He released her nipple and he licked her sweat from his fingers. She

shuddered on him for some time electrified with her sensations and emotions that flowed through

her naked body.

'Mmmmm…, Aaarrrggghhh!...'

His right hand stroked her blonde hair, which resembled their mother's except large curls on the edges. She stayed on him breathing deeply; she listen his drummed heartbeat, until his penis shrank inside her and drops out from her. He called her name as in vain:

'Milena…'

Her brother's left hand stroked her belly and stopped on her piercing ring, playing with his forefinger on the surface. She touched his hairy thighs with her left hand and buried her nails on his skin. She scratched him.

'Mmmmmm…, My wild cat…'

He grabbed her golden hair and pulled so hard that she felt some of them separated from her scalp. A tear slithered down her cheek due to pain. He grabbed her neck with the other hand pressing her windpipe. Grasp was cruel and hard. Unprepared for this she struggled to get fresh air in her lungs. Instead of speech from her throat, it came out hissing choking sound.

'Ssssss… hhhhhh… nnnn…'

Her brother seized her neck towards his face. Malicious line passed across his lips. Something wild, unknown to her before, flickered in his eyes. She grabbed his hand glued to her throat, with both her hands and pulled, but his madness, coldness of his stare blocked her thoughts. This man was not her brother anymore; he was chocking her with brutal strength of a madman, with vicious twisted smile on his face.

'Hhhhh… uuuu… gggg…'

She buried her nails in his arm, which brought blood on the surface of his skin, and in the same time she supported herself on carpet with her left leg, the right one was kicking the empty air, so with her final struggle she pushed their bodies from the couch to the ground. They hit the surface embraced together and she fainted under the pressure applied on her neck. Dark crimson blanket fell across her eyes.

CHAPTER X

Section 3.

ANALYSIS

November, 1998.

UNITED STATES OF AMERICA, WASHINGTON, DC, UNITED STATES DEPARTMENT OF DEFENCE, GENERAL BRENDAN'S OFFICE…

...

Hmmmmm… Nothing here…

...

…"ANATOMY ANALYSIS,

Sharp object, long curved 30-35 centimetres blade, probably long knife's, was penetrating wound of right half of the chest middle lobe of the right lung, right and left ventricles of the heart, and the lower lobe o f the left lung. 2000 ml. of blood is inside both parts of lungs. Knife's penetration made wound present at half of the chest, sternum, left lower rib's cage part of the stomach, liver and right spleen. Weapon's penetration made wound of left lower arm bone, two through lower arm bone and tangential. Internal and external bleedings were involved."

…

General Brendan flipped fast through the pages in front of him. He picked up an external analysis of autopsy report from pathology expert and read:

"… AN EXTERNAL ANALYSIS

The white female's body height 169 cm, age: 22 years old. Bones and muscular structure is medium size developed and she was medium fatten up. Corpse's stiffness of the body is strong at all joints. Corpse's spots are at the back of the body, drained, light bluish colored and there were lost after applied pressure of the unidentified hard object. The skin is light grayish colored. Lymphatics of the neck, armpits and thighs are touched with the blade.

...

Agent Mitchell was good looking woman when she was alive, but in death she would be even better, if I am horny pervert who want to have a sex with a corpse...

...

Hair is black, colored, 30 cm. long. Forehead is medium high and without wrinkles. Eyelids are half closed and they are not swollen. Connective tissue of the eyes and eyeballs are smooth and bloodless. Corneas are transparent. Lips are light pink color and they are cracked. All teeth are in good shape and healthy without any missing. The neck is cylinder shaped and usually movable in all directions. The chest has cylindrical and symmetric shape. Angle of ribcage is narrow. Breasts are size of women fist, on cross section normally developed and shaped. The nipples are rigid and there's no fluid in them after applied pressure. Abdomen and the belly are under the chest level and with flat front wall. Pubic hair is normal for a female. Mucous membranes surface of outer labia and inner labia is smooth and bloodless. Upper and lower extremities are without deformities, slowness and without conversion of vessels. Nails on hands and foot are well manicured, without any damage. After detailed investigation, there was not any trace of needles on the skin surface.

...

At least, she was not drug – needle addict, except occasionally sniffed white powder, and for that one she has been punished last year with six months probation time at Iraq's semi – suicidal mission, which kick her butt right on track...

...

At the right area of shoulder blade, on the lower edge of scapula and 130 cm over the shoulder blade level there is a hole, defective part of the skin shaped octagonal 70 mm. in diameter, irregular shaped, blood clotted, positioned to inside with his sizes and edges. Around the area is vertical shaped wound, 200 mm in diameter, the skin is without epidermis, epidermis is dry with dark red color (an entrance wound). From the wound there is blade's made channel to the right half of the chest, left, easy down towards front (height difference is 10 cm). Inside the skin of front left part of the chest, on 120 cm. Over the shoulder blade level and 17 cm. left of middle line, at the level of 5 (fifth) rib, there is defect transversal shaped diameter 100 to 70 mm., with rolled up to the outside formed edges, from which is leaking blood and pieces of under skin fatty tissue (an exit wound).

...

Hmm, so he impaled her on the blade to have a private chat with her for some time and probably she was singing like canary, when he twisted the strange blade inside her…

...

CLOTHES:

Black shirt with short sleeves, black pants, black polyester lady socks, white underwear, black deep shoes, two rings on second (2) and third (3) fingers of the right hand, and earrings made from the yellow metal. At the back, clothes pieces are full of blood, with holes on them. We forwarded it to the crime ballistic expert investigation.

...

Shit! Shit… Artifact is gone for good. We have already checked her rental car on DC airport and her rented apartment under false name… Nothing. He took The Stone and The Sign with him. There were lost again after all my hard work and sacrificed years!

...

General Brendan skipped detailed report of the head, neck, chest, stomach and bones external and internal injuries and he was paying attention on the conclusion at the end of coronaries report:

...

"THE CONCLUSION:

Death was murderess and violent. Cause of death was internal and external bleedings due to blade penetrations to the chest, lungs, heart and liver. There were six curved weapon wounds all together – one perforating wound in the chest area, one penetrating wound on the left part of chest and stomach, one perforating wound on the right part of the stomach. One perforating wound on the left lower arm bone, one penetrating wound on the right breast and one reverse perforating wound on the left lower arm bone. It is possible that these wounds were from slashed and stabbed points at least four different angles from the close distance-using sharp, curved metal object, as long knife or short sword blade." …

…

He likes slice & dice game and he took a time to introduce himself to her, like a lover on her first time bride's night. He really enjoyed it. He was proud of his work.

…

His phone desk started to ring. He lay down the file of Agent Mitchell's murder on his desk and he took the headset. He exclusively said his secretary to cancel all his calls except an emergency calls. Emergency calls are problems, and he already had enough of them lately.

'General Brendan speaking.'

'Sir, Sergeant Simpson here, from CJ2, International Operations, we have a red alarm on Balkan's Zone! Agent Dillon executed in the field mission. TOD (Time Of Death) is eleven hundred Zulu time this morning.'

'Info confirmed by local authorities or our Embassy staff?'

'Embassy confirmed his death and initiated cover up procedures through our regular channels, so local authorities and their media were blind on spot, Sir!'

'Good. Pack & Bag his body, send it here ASAP. (As Soon As Possible), notify his family and relatives with usual info and proceed with drills for back up story.'

'Affirmative, Sir.'

'Find me, Agent Willburn and activate him immediately! Give him details on situation and update him with instructions. I will send them in one hour, sharp.'

'Yes, Sir. Anything else?'

'Yes, bring me HAARP project documentation and research files. Urgently!'

'Yes, Sir!'

General slowly close the line and slammed his left fist on his mahogany desk. The force shook desk's surface. He felt pain on his knuckles and he felt good for a second.

I am not going to lose this game! Maybe some moves on the table, but not the game!

CHAPTER X

Section 4.

THE EMPEROR

June, 1883.

FRANCE, ALSACE REGION, STRASBOURG, ELECTRICITE DE STRASBOURG…

(Modern day – EU, European Union, Strasbourg, France)

It was raining hard when Nikola reached the gate of "Le Gare de Strasbourg", the rain was beating hard on the cobbled square in front of the Strasbourg's Main Railway Station and Nikola's shoes were soaked with water, the left one started to make squealing sounds from watered leather. His knowledge of German and French languages helped him to find solutions between never-ending negotiations between French stubbornness of Inspector Monsieur Averdeck, and German thoroughness of Ober – Inspector Hieronymus, in resolving the problem of an incandescent lamp of 16 c.p. installations in a hallway ceiling 6 centimetres up and down of the spot which was already originally chosen by Tesla. After two hours of debate between them Ober – Inspector shattered Tesla's hopes of final solutions by his sentence:

"Regierungsrath Funke is particular that I wouldn't dare to give an order for placing any lamp without his explicit approval!"

Tesla shrugged with his bony shoulders and decided to go back to his small mechanical workshop at the Strasbourg Main Train Station and continue his private work on his motor which operated on alternating current. He already assembled and tested five different models with different magnetic fields, and motor worked perfectly, rotating inside magnetic fields and alternate current flowed through the coils as well through the air. Last night he called former Mayor of Strasbourg, Monsieur Bauzin, his only friend here, with few of his close friends and they were watching his alternate current motor, but Nikola could see that they did not understand the value and future capabilities of it. One of them, Professor of Theoretical Physics, Karl Ferdinand Braun from

Strasbourg University showed his interest in the electrical conductivity and Tesla discussed his ideas with him, gave him some hand written sketches of his wireless connectivity, electrical materials, metals, gasses, liquids and an air tube, which can be used as possibilities in the near future.

'Monsieur Tesla, what will be your final goal with this engine, excused me alternate – motor?'

Professor Braun touched his groomed large moustache with his left hand manicured nails.

'The object, which I have pleasure to, present here is a brand new system of electric distribution and transmission of power. Electricity would be now available to everybody; it can transfer energy at long distances, to illuminate all our cities, houses, to run industrial machineries and factories. This machine will bring prosperity and fortune to our future.'

'Would this machinery is going to put working - man out of work?'

Other concerned, round full belly individual with thin hair across his forehead asked.

'We can change the future with our actions. The final judgment it is not in our hands.'

Monsieur Bauzin added.

'It is hard to be man of original ideas, Monsieur Tesla; our inventor Louis Pasteur had his hard times, too and looks at it today, everybody loved him!'

'Applause is a gift of gods. A new idea must not be judged by its immediate results.'

Tesla smiled sadly and touched his alternate motor with his long fingertips.

'That will be all gentlemen, now I can invite you to my house this evening…'

Monsieur Bauzin waved with his hand theatrically through the air and bowed to his guests. Tesla went to his house last night and stayed up to three o'clock in the morning. On his way back to his room at Weissthurmring number 8, he felt positive charged sensation through his brain, as if his all brain has been caught by internal fire. He saw a light with two small Suns located inside his skull, they burned with high intensity spreading their energy through his neck to his all body, that the rest of the night he applied cold bandages on his tormented head. Now he felt much better with all this rain and ozone in the air. Dane fell asleep inside his brain and body for last four months and he was glad for that. Probably he wouldn't stand another internal energy and soul struggle between them in the same time with his visions applied inside his brain. He saw an

envelope attached to his workshop door; his handwritten name was on the surface. He recognized

George Stout's signature at the bottom when he opened it. He read it. Stout, who is going to be

his predecessor in the Strasbourg power plant offered him first engineering contract as a manager,

supervisor, technician, supply purchaser and chief engineer. He was installing cables, poorly

made insulation conduits, lamp sockets, lamp bulbs which lasted only a few hours. He was

repairing water and energy pipes, overseeing all repairs since fiasco at the Railroad Station in

Strasbourg, when during an opening ceremony of the new lightning plant; a short circuit

destroyed large part of the wall and endangered the life of Kaiser Wilhelm I (The First), The

Emperor, who attended the opening celebration. Tesla repaired and restored the power to the

ticket office, the post office; the waiting room and platform areas and had repaired even the

heating system. Tesla knew that his time is coming and as any young person, he had his dreams

and he was confident that not all of them, but some of them would come through. He closed the

letter and he placed it inside his inner right jacket's pocket. He smiled to himself with a thought:

My belief is firm in a law of compensation. The true rewards are ever in proportion to the labor

and sacrifices made.

CHAPTER X

Section 5.

RUNNER

November, 2009.

CANADA, ALBERTA, EDMONTON, CITY OF ST. ALBERT, LACONBE LAKE PARK…

Roger was running his regular 5 kilometers through Lacombe Lake Park at City of St Albert, suburb of Edmonton. He was getting in good shape, he lost 10 kilograms since his last medical check, but he wasn't quite happy about the fact that his body doesn't respond to the exercises as before, his joints and leg's muscles were not flexible as before, so after three kilometers of running he can feel the pain in his left knee. He has to slow down and shorten his pace; even he has energy and feeling that he can run the same distance for half shorter amount of time.

The outdoor rink at Lacombe Lake Park were filled, on this mild winter evening, with lots of kids strapped on their blades just skating, playing some fun games or playing pure hockey on the frozen shiny surface of outdoor natural skating facility. Breath from his mouth warmed his cheeks, crisp, cool air refreshed his body and he felt alive on this breezy November evening. Snow was crunching under his running winter shoes and he was stepping on his own tracks left an hour ago. Light from near buy lamp post stretched his shadow in front of his feet, so he was chasing his own reflection on the bright white surface last 30 minutes. He checked his watch for time.

I will speed up before the finish line. The parking lot is at the end of this semi – circle pound, so these last 800 meters I should cover for two, two and half minutes max…

He speed up ignoring his left knee pain and the street – lighting columns headed for the opposite direction faster beside him. After one minute he felt light pain signal from his spleen, but he kept running, and he pushed himself for last 400 meters harder.

You can do it! Come On! Go on faster! Faster!

His chest rose and pulled his ribs; hands followed the legs in the same rhythms, his breath got shorter and shorter when his lungs pumped chilly air inside, his all body stretched to maximum endurance and he was on the edge to collapse. Blood rushed into his ears and temples; his legs got heavier with every step and all his movements appeared to him as in slow motion movie. His heart pumped blood through his brain, so he heard it Thump – Thump, Thump – Thump, sound inside his skull, vacuum stuck in his lungs and he lost his balance on the ground. His left leg went sideways by her free will and all his body followed her after. He had time to position his left arm in front of him, so his elbow met frozen land instead of his face, but laws of physics applied on his body were merciless. When he touch the ground his left shoulder pop up with loud dry wood crack, his left side of the face connected with frozen surface and ripped off the skin from his cheek, ear and chin. His scream echoed through the park. His head hit the wooden stump of the parking marker sign. Instantly he was unconscious.

CHAPTER X

Section 6.

CAVE

December, 1998.

MONTENEGRO, THE DURMITOR NATIONAL PARK, MOUNTAIN OF DURMITOR, CANYON OF TARARIVER,"ZMAJEVA PECINA" ("DRAGON'S CAVE"), AN ENTRANCE AREA…

North West wind bluster above many tall, more than half centuries old "Crna Podas" ("Black Pines") trees that were prevalent in this area of Canyon of Tara River, above 1000 meters, and Tanya find them very valuable to protect her exposed body against an incoming gust of wind. She followed them, the group of five mercenaries all morning, without any problems through solid milky fog, across precipitous slopes of thick snow, with the sheer physical effort, until they reached the rim of graphite gray cliffs, some two – three kilometers west of a cave named Zmajeva Pecina" ("Dragon's Cave") area. As she gaze across white ravine in front of her, the line of people spread parallel to the rocky, steep and bear point leading to nowhere except to the bottom of abyss that started along the canyon's sharp edge.

Last night their leader Kirk, German, got some additional instructions from the other side of comms satellite link, from someone named Jeurgen, geo - coordinate to the last detail about exact spot of cavern located somewhere inside the precipice at the deepest point of canyon. The mean fall of the rock face was 350 meters down the steep cliff and the hidden cave was reachable only from that direction. There will be only one entrance and exit for them, as well for me, too…

Well-equipped team adjusted the ropes length; they prepared their mountaineering equipment, climbing tools and accessories and in fifteen following minutes were ready to move downwards the rock-strewn wall to their final out of sight destination. Simon, an American, bodyguard of Kirk, dropped to void, down the rope length, without hesitation and vanished from the site.

Tanya watched as Kirk, one of the twins and woman named Jackie, one by one fade away across crag's murky edge, until only one of them, the other twin nicknamed as "Brale" or "Profa" stayed alone above deep hole. Jackie had confrontation with Kirk regarding their approach to an artifact site and protection of piece eventually found inside the vault. She had serious concerns about ancient traps, unknown cave's environment, so she insisted that all of them wear protection oxygen masks all the time down there, but Kirk completely ignored her call, labeling her as mythological female nutcase obsessed by archaic myths and local legends. Tanya trusted woman's premonitions, since she saw enough of bad omen sites through her time travels, and above all, she deeply believed and highly respected forewarning from our ancestors. She attached her mini breathalyzer around her neck and activated "the shield", as she moved closer to the pine's edge. Snow whooshed around energized magnetic field. She did not care what was his name, when she impaled one of the twins, ruptured his heart on her blade, so the man was dead before his soundlessly body dive ended at the end of the canyon.

An arrogant Aryan raised individual, as Kirk will blindly lead them to their deaths, only to fulfill his selfish desires, insatiable greed for gold and never - ending lust to get an uncontrollable power of remnant.

The ropes trembled under her invisible progress and they were wavering on their own rhythms above the cave's gap as she reached three meters wide lending spot above. The entrance was spacious and empty. Flurries of disturbed snow coat, under her boots, broke her cover in a split second, when she dropped to the left side of an opening. The roar from the river's cascades heard on the very peaks of the canyon, swathed Uzi's fire. Silencer attached on the weapon made whop – whop - whop sounds and only chips of the broken stone alarmed her that someone was shooting at her. Bullets buzzed beside her right shoulder and around her legs as well.

Careless…! Stupid…!

Large bulky shape, a little darker then the background behind came into the sight, revealing itself by short flickering flames from his weapon. The scream of wrath boomed above an entrance:

'Eeeeaaahhhh!!!'

The other twin brother lost his initial surprise and an advantage of darkness, when he burst out on open for revenge, yelling to the light silhouette made of snow particles:

'You fuck! You killed my bro… th… ggggrrrlll…'

Tanya used given opportunity with lightning speed. Her knife materialized from whirled cloud of nothing, in blurred motion of disturbed air, it slashed – crushed Bro's windpipe. Uzi – the machine gun in his right hand quivered, delivering another short burst of bullets on the icy surface in front of his legs and his left hand grabbed metal knife's handle attached to his thick neck.

As a twin, probably he felt death of his brother, the special connection between them stayed active after all…

She delivered another knife on the back of his exposed neck, at the bottom of his bold shaved skull, cutting the nerves, separating connection between his huge body and his eventually small brain. As an old oak, he slammed beside her on ice-covered hard stone.

Surprise attack is gone forever down the drain… It is time to play a different game!

CHAPTER XI

Section 1.

MORGUE

December, 1998.

CANADA, ONTARIO, TORONTO, ST. MICHAEL'S HOSPITAL, 30 BOND STREET...

Detective Constable Bamford closed the door of the morgue. She took two steps further and her stomach erupted upside down. Nausea from inside shook her body and she steadied herself with her right hand on the elevator door. She breathed slowly pulling the air through her clenched teeth inside her lungs and she was exhaling slowly with her nose holding her brow on the light metallic exterior of the elevator door. Exhaled air from her nostrils made condensed circles on the cold metal surface.

'Are you all right?'

He asked her.

'I know seeing that body in the morgue was rough for you.'

'Yep.'

'I am sorry, Michelle...'

'Are you, Todd? I think you are not. You brought me here with purpose.'

Her comment produce small smile at the corner of Todd's thin mouth.

'Well..., that is the truth in some way..., but on the other hand...'

She opened her eyes and saw his distorted face reflection on the silver surface of the door.

'You want me to see this disfigured body to remember...'

'Of course... Yes. In time, you are going to learn to control your stomach and your emotions, too...'

'I am confident that I will master my emotions control, but I am not sure that it will apply on my stomach in the same time.'

This conversation gave her some pause. She felt better.

'I want you to nail this bastard, but not out for some cheap sense of vengeance. It has to be for all other victims before and after, for you and for all the other people whose lives have been destroyed.'

Michelle said nothing to this. She waited for some other devoted speech, but none came.

'You know, this is fourth in the row. In period of a year, he accomplished them with the same style and the same signature.'

'Why you assumed this is a male? It could be female.'

'That is correct. Yet, the strength required pulling the body in upside down positions and nailed it up on the wall cannot belong to the female. It has to be male.'

'Unless, she and some other person are involved, they worked in pairs.'

Michelle turned around and faced him. He remained silent. He was thinking about the possibility.

'That is the reason why they chose you between all of them on the screenings for this position.'

'What are you talking about?'

'Your insight, your approach to the problem, your natural instinct to find its solution.'

For the first time she saw Todd's full mouth smile. It looked creepy, although perfect for morgue.

'What those suppose to mean?'

'It means that from now on, you are officially assigned on this case. Permanent, until you solved it. Congratulation, Detective Constable Bamford!'

Shark's smile appeared on Todd's wrinkled face. His eyes were black and expressionless, dead, as a fish.

Then, he bites me.

CHAPTER XI

Section 2.

CELL

December, 1998.

UNITED STATES OF AMERICA, CALIFORNIA, LOS ANGELES, WESTSIDE, BEVERLY CREST, NORTH BEVERLY GLEN BLVD, MOUNTAIN COTTAGE...

Markus scratched scar on his left cheek with his right hand's forefinger while he was looking at the photographic images taken by their Cell's overseas operatives. The body cut in a half across sternum from left to right was lying in the pool of own blood. The cut was clean and man's death was swift. If he did not have data on the file, he would think that mastered cut made by samurai's sword – katana or some other similar cold, sharp weapon would produce similar effect on the human body, but this one was more than that. It was act of electrical charged particles, similar to the laser's strength and power, applied on the human flesh tissue ionized by unknown source and type of the weapon. Cell's analyst gave them detailed report on chemical and molecular structure, but he was not able to describe or identify physical structure of mysterious weapon. Two other Cell's experienced inmates were eliminated in Croatia last month and others were scared to death over there.

'The pictures cannot show you everything, but with zoomed detailed photos of the body wounds, you are going to get the better picture on strength, energy and magnificent power of that weapon!'

Eighty years old Juergen Schuster, had white strong hair, grandfatherly face and moisten blue eyes, so mistakenly he appeared as a person with perpetual compassion. Under his earnest looks of trusted, affectionate person lay hidden, cold-blooded killer, person totally opposite of his first exterior impression.

'These deaths were not the only one in the same area?'

'Of course not, there were much more, but all interested parties were covering their losses and tracks well to initiate serious investigation of local authorities, plus all that area is suitable for corruption and at the end you have land of deaf, blind and mute.'

Markus closed plastic file cover with the code name: "DEATH RAY". He watched Juergen's unassailably good natural mask with his musical, gentle voice, and he wondered how many people he executed by his strong arms, before they realized at their last breath, the truth under his lies and chameleonic face. He heard for Juergen's passionate obsession to strangle his victims. Stories are legendary topics in all Cells.

'Americans, Russians, Chinese or some other Europeans intelligence offices and agencies?'

Schuster produce an enigmatic smile on his lips. He moisturized them slowly with the edge of his tongue.

'Many of them were trying, through the last 60 years to get their hands on it, without success. But, we are close now. Closer than others to hold it in our hand's grasp.'

'We are close to the source or to the weapon?'

'Both of them are irrelevant compared to this. This is Alpha and Omega!'

Some strange eerie luminosity passed through Schuster's blue eyes. Repossessed look on his face, loneliness in his gaze removal of any wisdom from it, lunatic flash of his wide black pupils destroyed last trace of his humanity. He exclaimed parole with a high pitching voice:

'"DOPPELGANGER "WILL RISE AGAIN!'

Markus watched Schuster's transformation with frozen face expression and he sat calmly, patiently till insanity has left Schuster and he transmuted himself back to normal. He did not show any emotion on his face, since he knew that any twitch on his face could mean death in the presence of Jeurgen poignant outburst.

'Our re – activated Cell in Serbia is taking steps towards our final goal, they are going to fulfill the prophecy at this moment they are on their way to artifact site to collect object d'art. At last, it will be in our hands again!'

'Where that would be?'

'Canyon of Tara River, Montenegro.'

CHAPTER XI

Section 3.

THE SIGN

December, 1998.

CROATIA, DALMATIAN COAST, CITY OF SPLIT, OLD CITY, DIOCLETIAN'S PALACE, HOTEL MARMONT...

Wolf's Head was the size of the small plate, roughly 20 centimetres in diameter and made of some light material like aluminum, but strong, hard like iron, gold plated on the surface, shaped to the last detailed curve by unknown master artist, nearly identical to the real wolf's head anatomy. From inside it gleamed differently, bluish, red and gold; depends on the falling light's angle on the surface and of type of lights applied to it, artificial or normal daylight. The mask itself can fit children's face, not the face of regular size man, but it did not have anything to attach itself to someone's face. He already applied it to his face and an instant after, he felt dizzy and it developed hard headache on the back of his head, so he quickly removed it from his face. The eyeholes were almond shaped which reassemble the size of polished black gem which he had found at Dubrovnik.

The gem was lost now, and that was sure as it is, as per General Brendan's report on DC killing, gone together with another agent's life, too, and Chief Brendon was confident that the object itself has been lost too...

Nevertheless, Willburn did not deliver an original artifact to female agent Mitchell; he planted the fake one, copied by local artist who made identical one for two thousand Euros, of course gold plated real aluminum, home Made in Croatia. Why he did it? He didn't know and he did not have a reason for it, maybe his greed has been activated at the Island of Lokrum when he saw it, or it was just premonition to facilitate what he felt when he touched for the first time. He had strange hunch inside his head, it should belong to him by his unwritten rights, which it predestined to be his, so nobody deserve the right to have it, except him. He stroked polished surface of it with his left forefinger and balmy sensation spread through his body, nearly sexual excitement aroused inside his abdomen. He is going to continue with his mission officially, but he did not have any intention to deliver this relic to General Brendan, after all, he earned it based on his dedicated hard risky type of business. He read detailed coronary report on agent Mitchell's pared body and one thing wedged his attention, the wounds on her mutilated body were analogous to the wounds on the male body from Zagreb's hospital few months ago. Same curved strange weapon were used in both cases, which point out that the killer or killers would be the same. The other case of agent Dillon death at Pocitelj brought shiver through his spine and cold sweat to his forehead, the fear griped his heart when he remembered his experience at Pula. Petrifying weapon was used again against bureau agents and he could be there lying on the same spot in Pocitelj, instead of Dillon, if he didn't use his vacation time at Vienna, Austria. Picture of devastating lethal weapon's power over human body carved the image in his pupils forever. Killer's frightening skills to reach them without detection, no sound or any indication of his presence close by, confirmed his suspicion that they are dealing with highly sophisticated alien weapon in the company of well-trained, dexterous professionals. Instructions from Brendan were clear: avoid any confrontation with unknown enemy forces, especially on their ground, if the contact is inevitable chose and use location prepared before as an advantage and act as a group, or in pairs at least to increase your chances. Use sat link, recordable devices, hidden spy cameras, GPS (Global Positioning System) activated and gain any possible data on unidentified subject and their secret weapons. Any type of detecting device and tracking bug activate after first contact, so the back up team will track you immediately and initiate their support. Do not act alone and do not take any risk in this case! Do not play heroes! Agency deployed two more teams in the area, one active and permanently assembled and assigned to him and the other team close by, inactive, temporary on standby and reassembled in three pairs. Together twelve people plus him.

Team "A" is tracking him 24/7 with two surveillance checkpoints and one bodyguard, sniper close to his parameter. First team introduced to him prior to his arrival at Split and they identify themselves, and second one stayed "in the shadow". All of them were skilled professionals, operatives in the field more than 10 years with significant trainings and achieved results. Agent Willburn put his precious piece – The Sign, inside room's small metal protected vault and he install and then activated his booby – trap in front of it. He closed the closet, set up additional traps on the window and room's entrance door, before he reload his weapons and left hotel's room. He activated his earplug and check connection with others operatives in the area. They confirmed their active status. Now he is going on hunt on rare species bred inside secret places, under the code name of an "Invisible Man".

CHAPTER XI

Section 4.

PARIS

May, 1884.

ILE – DE – FRANCE REGION, PARIS, LA COMPAGNIE DE LA LUMIERE EDISON A PARIS, BOULEVARD CHAMPS – ELYEES...

(Modern day – EU, European Union, France, Paris)

Tesla put his long hands in his empty pockets and thought about the time that he spent on equipment's installation and his innovation on the old regulators at Strasbourg. All the time that he invested here in Paris to improve their own electrical systems and after all other networks that he innovated, rebuild and created, he was disgusted by their games when they send him from one to another door, for days, almost begging for his rightfully earned money. They played with him as he was a mouse attracted by the smell of a cheese, but from the beginning, he realized that he will never be able to get it, or even to see the real cheese settled between his paws. Only Mr. Charles Batchellor, Manager gave him an emotional support and suggested him to try his luck overseas at the United States in the office of his good friend Mr. Thomas A. Edison at New York. Tesla stopped at the corner of Avenue Jeanne d' Arc and Boulevard Saint – Marcel and he stretched his long legs a little, watching the green trees lines that was spreading down to the Boulevard toward Pont d' Austerlitz and river the Seine. At the end of it, directly below was a statue to the Maid of Orleans, brave girl, clothed in a peasant heavy tunic and hard, heavy shoes, her sword sheathed beside her legs, her shield at her other side, with a raised banner in her right hand holding a white dove with a scroll in its beak. Sunshine flickered through the trees playing with the leaves, making their shadows alive, dancing on sidewalks, in the middle of the street, streamed down the avenue at the statue of the Deliverer reminding Tesla on his early five o' clock mornings, when he walked to the Seine for a thirty minutes swim in an outdoor swimming area. He walked slowly after that up and down the wide avenues, enjoying the smell of morning coffee prepared in the passing by shops, having rich, mouthful breakfast at "Ivry" and listening bird's songs, watching pigeon's fluttered and strutted moves that create around him peace – bearing aura. He really loved Paris, the city's romantic aromas stayed attached to his soul. Dane was quiet and calm. It seems that lullabies of Paris worked on him. Beside city natural charm, endless beauty and immortal richness, there was nothing else there for him; he cannot live without the money. He knew more than others, he have all these great ideas, but nobody gave him a chance to show all his potential, maybe is time to move on further across the ocean, to present himself to famous Mr. Edison, who is going to have understanding to his alternate motor, current and other machines that floated in his mind for years. It will be better to make his move now, before he lost all his money, because he will never see anything of it that they owed him for his hard work. Maybe, United States is going to be real land of opportunity and place of freedom for him, as it become for many people who went there before him. Tomorrow, he will get recommendations papers from Mr. Batchellor, he is going to buy a train and boat's boarding tickets and he will prepare himself for a trip to America …

Maybe, my brother Dane would like to stay in Europe after all, so it is better for me to hurry up before he is going to wake up and changed his mind...

CHAPTER XI

Section 5.

PARK

December, 2009.

CANADA, NOVA SCOTIA, TOWN OF TRURO, VICTORIA PARK…

The man in Canadian Goose parka was standing on top of the steep wet snowed covered cliff, casually leaned on wooden poll on the top of Jacob's Ladder, a 175 – wooden step in Victoria Park at Truro, Nova Scotia. He was looking down the hill wrapped in the white blanket, where on the cold December weekend day like this, people gathered to enjoy skating, snowshoeing, cross – country skiing and sometimes, even golf. Today, there is some small group of "first timers" very young, smiling, pink – cheeked children who were giving their first steps at sleigh rides and sledding down the nearly vertical slope close by. Occasional flurries supported by North West wind were making perfect weather conditions for outdoor activities in the snow, but he was not here for that. His assignment here was investigation of suspicious death that occurred last month in the same park, on the same spot, where he was standing now. Police officer in charge of investigation did not have any additional information, or any leads on it, for him the case was an accident and it was officially closed under the same definition of that word. Actually, David Tarver, police officer who was first on the scene was quite eager to avoid him for couple of days and finally when he confront him face to face, he did not have wish to investigate any further. As he had some hot potato in his mouth, his answers were short, dry and slippery that all situations around this case have been "fishy" from the start. His mobile phone ringed twice before he managed to remove it from the jacket's inner pocket.

'Hello, Inspector Brad is speaking.'

'Hi, Brad how are you? Michael is here.'

'Hey buddy, thank you, I am fine. How're you doing?'

'Not bad my friend, you now Christmas spirit floating around us…'

'You were right my friend, you were right…'

'How was the weather up there on Atlantic? Lots of snow?'

'Ah, not so bad, we have only one blizzard storm which last three days, but we get to use to it, you know… How was there?'

'Oh yeah, iced and chilly as usual, dry and windy as always in Prairies, it was minus 26 with wind-chill.'

'Here is minus 10, it feels like minus 17 due to the moisture in the air.'

'Welcome to Canada…, eh?'

'You know, you where right about this case, there is many strange things here, my friend.'

'Like what?'

'First, the body was already cremated, so additional autopsy is impossible. Second, everybody is polite and friendly until you start asking questions. Third, I am on the crime scene and I can tell you immediately that broken neck is not the only thing that you can break here when you fell from this famous Ladder.'

'You 've read coronary report?'

'Yeah, it was clean as a whistle, school sampled, copy and paste from an instruction book. I have spoken with first officer on the scene today and I can tell you that he was scarred; he wiggles his story, but I read between the lines, somebody was with his foot on his tail, for sure.'

'What else?'

'Apparently, he found the body at the middle of the stairs, but the strange thing was that victim's neck was broken at second and seventh cervical curve. As per medical examiner this can be achieved mostly by applied pressure on them physically by hand, due to fact there weren't any bruises from the fall on the neck, neither any other parts of the body. I assumed that body was "staged" there prior to discovery. Strong force broke his neck like a twig. He was dead before he reached the ground.'

'As I told you before, Keith Stanford, the victim, was very close to our main suspect professionally and privately, so that was the main reason I've asked you to check up on the case.'

'You know man, you owe me one; after this... I meant a beer. One for you and one for me at our Scottish pub at Dartmouth, Halifax.'

'Deal it is! I promise; that I will be there on the East Coast, make some reservation on my next summer holiday, one pint of each one: "Opa", "Knot Ale", "Jamieson's Dark "and "Split Crow Select. "'

'I am counting on it!'

'What is about our general theme - General?'

'The general is celebrity here, national hero of 12000 inhabitants, homemade star with very good connections through the government, military and police forces, other municipality offices as well, so any further investigation will be obstructed gladly from the local communities.'

'I am aware of that as well, so I will give you advice: do not shake the tree to much; there are a lot of rotten fruits on it.'

'Yeah, probably you are right; in any case, I am going to be careful as always. I took a week off to investigate this, and then I am back in my unit in Halifax. I will let you know what I have found in meantime. Did you get my e – mail with pictures and reports on it?'

'Yes, I have it, thanks. Brad, please be careful over there!'

'Michael, I am old, but not stupid and careless!'

'I know my friend! Additional extra measures are always welcome. In this weird case death list increased rapidly on every turn and lead that I have made so far.'

'Is that so?'

'Trust me on this one, every person directly involved as a witness or he was deeply connected with the case turn out to be dead before I was able to get him, or when I reached him he suddenly have some "accident" that transformed him in the stiff, cold, missing fresh corpse.'

'This meant only one thing my friend that they're tracking you're every move and they were cutting your lead and trace to another dead - end. You have to find a way out and take an initiative steps in the opposite direction, towards next level on your own course of action.'

'What are you suggesting?'

'Improvised your next action and change their moves against them.

Blend in the background behind them and wait for their mistakes. If they did not make one,

provoke them to make one. Change the rules at least for short period.'

It is payback time!

CHAPTER XI

Section 6.

CALL

June, 2011.

SERBIA, BELGRADE, MUNICIPALITY OF VRACAR, S. MILUTINOVICH STREET NO. 36., GROUND FLOOR APARTMENT…

The bed was wide and long enough for two of them. It almost filled the little room completely except two strips of empty space on its sides only a half meter wide parallel to white freshly painted walls. They lay completely naked breathing steadily humid air, between two of them, drugged with incoming heat of the summer evening, exhausted from wild and short intercourse, smiling, staring at each other face as they were trying to remember all details on them or seeing them for the first time. Small lantern "Made in China", bought on the local flees market, flickered light on their bodies stretching their shadowed images along empty walls. Miran touched with his right forefinger Natasha's curled blonde hair, unfastened, spread above her shoulders like a cape, without any word exchanged between them.

She is so beautiful...

Natasha lay silently, listening her lover's steady breathing, enjoying the touch of his caressing hand. She leaned closer to him as a cat, buried her face behind his left extended hand, on his hard biceps edge biting his muscle with the tip of her front upper teeth. Miran felt her left hand on his penis, caressing him as some kind of pet. She wiggled like lazy cat, as he ran his right hand down her body, slipping down to touch the thick patch of hair between her legs. He found it wet, like she had been dripping from the bath, ready for him.

'Wait...'

She hissed through her teeth, pushing his hand away.

'Let me...'

She brought her fingers to her full mouth.

'No need for hurry...'

Natasha hushed him by cupping her hand over his mouth, and kept it there briefly, before she slid her head down to his genitals.

'Wet me with your tongue...'

Obediently she kissed his left testicle and licked the right one, holding it between her lips till he moaned with pleasure, but then he felt her mouth start working fiercely, he saw her cheeks sucking inward, with a harsh little sound she started to suck his penis. Once more he felt her hands on his testicles, squeezing it firmly.

'Come...'

Miran raised himself on his left elbow, preparing to mount her from above, but she shook her head, mumbling and pushed his shoulder flat against the bed with her right hand. Straddling him, she rose quickly and slipped his cock inside her. She was moisturized by heat and her desire, and she spread herself wider and settled farther down, concealing herself firmly on the top of him. Tensing her leg muscles, she slowly moved herself up and down, hissing and breathing in the same time.

'Tsssssss....ssss...aaaaahhhhh...'

He felt himself gripped as by fist; there was a roughness inside her, something that abraded his rod.

God, she's so tight and strong..., like...

'Don't rush it, please...'

He whispered, drawing her mouth down to his, as her lips remained clamped shut for a moment when she resisted it. Natasha held him tightly, and without warning her mouth barely opened under his pressure and she got out her tongue quickly inside. She bite his moisturized lower lip a little, released herself, pushing her hands behind her back, grabbing his upper leg muscles with both her fists. Her nails scratched his skin removing some hair with her finger's grip.

'I...., Nooooo...'

The moment came. He felt that sperm surged up through his erected penis, the trance of incoming ecstasy took him over. She was catching his rhythm with her hips, rotating around semi circularly, up and down pushing her left forefinger in her anus in the same time, when he ejaculated in her.

'Oooooo...hhhhh...'

She was weary, her lungs were gasping for air, totally exhausted she hold to her sexual climax desperately, her right hand went up to her hard dark right nipple, enjoying final shudder on the top of him. Miran trembled underneath her left breast that hung before his open lips, blood was humming in his ears, when ringing sound filled their bedroom. The ring continued in the background for another five to ten seconds, before he managed to get a phone handset and he answered to an incoming call.

'Hallo...'

It took him another two - three seconds until he recognized the voice on the other side. He struggled to concentrate himself, as Natasha spread her torso on him, pushing her breasts heavy, fully against him, still straddled to his penis which started to shrink inside her vagina.

She stayed attached to him during his forthcoming conversation, purring and caressing herself on his naked body, in the most sexual, alluring and seductive way covered in their sweat.

CHAPTER XII

Section 1.

MALL

December, 2009.

CANADA, NOVA SCOTIA, TOWN OF TRURO, TRURO'S MALL…

She was watching out of the window of the coffee shop when the middle - aged man walked in.

She looked up a little surprised and concerned that he tracked her for the last twenty minutes, but

he was concentrated on displayed varieties of muffins in the store, and he did not registered her at

all. At least he was pretending very well as trained professional police officer to cover it. His

body language did not show her any signs of it either, and he was standing too far away, from her

to read his thoughts. His strong dark brown hair collected strips of gray through the years, strong

wide jaw moved slowly when he spoke with the waiter. His brown eyes moved in her direction

only once, when he was paying for his order, but it was enough for her to detect his interest for

her, as a woman or as a potential suspicious subject, she did not cared and definitely she did not

liked it. The Truro's Mall were jam - packed with people on this windy winter's day, the food

court across the coffee shop have been jammed with lines of hungry, overweight figures which

were waiting for holidays specials portion of their daily poison food. She belong to "the skinny

people" branch, so in this small town like this, she was visible as black sheep in the white sheep's

flock on the wide opened green field, not only by her light figure, plus her red natural hair even

covered with the neutral black cap, brought negative attention from passing mall's visitors. That

was the reason why she did not like the idea to come here, where she can be easily remembered

and identified by any handpicked eyewitness, however she knew that her only chance to track

general's whereabouts was to come here and find his childhood's friend Keith Stanford. Doug

Burke's brain contained interesting information on secret military program code named " Five

Eyes", which has been initiated by ECHELON project, which described SIGINT (Signals Intelligence) agreement between five signatory states (Australia, Canada, New Zealand, United Kingdom and United States). Also known as AUSCANNZUKUS, described as the only software system that controls the download and dissemination of the intercept of commercial satellite trunk communications. The system was created to monitor military and diplomatic communications of the Soviet Union and Eastern Europe Bloc during Cold War, or hunts of terrorist plots, drug trafficking plans, political and diplomatic intelligence. It was capable of interception, content inspection of telephone calls, fax, e – mail, other data traffic globally through the interception of communications barriers including satellite transmission, PSTN (Public Switched Telephone Networks), Internet traffic, and microwave links. Nevertheless, his active knowledge of General MacKenzie's activities and exact location of him has been unknown to him. Stanford's name appeared also, in connection with the missing Nikola Tesla's files, equipments and tests performed at his laboratory from 1895 to 1896 in Niagara Falls, which were hidden by some mystery man whose existence was questionable, Mr. Nathan Thoma. Anyhow, Keith Stanford turned out to be dead, when she came here, killed under distrustful circumstances, which were investigated by Inspector Brad from Halifax City Police. He turned his head again at her direction and stayed there looking at her for four – five seconds. Inspector Brad just took his afternoon "coffee to go" with what was look like, double portion of blubbery muffin as a fast snack on the road, and he was on the way to exit, when he suddenly stopped, turned around and retraced his steps to the coffee shop. He crossed the food court, zigzagged between the passing people and went directly to her.

I knew it! He tracked my movements! I become reckless and arrogant after all!

…

No, calm down! You did not blow out anything!

His brown eyes met with light green of hers, the smile on his face confirmed his thoughts. They were cleared as his white wide teeth, to her.

You are fucking good - looking woman!

'Excuse me, m' am, I just want to ask you one simple question. Do you want to have a dinner with me tonight?'

And sex after that, which would be good!

'I know, this looks maybe cheap, but I couldn't resist, honestly!'

That is the truth honey!

She removed her black plastic fake optical glasses with her left hand and she looked up at him as a cold fish. Her posture did not change, but her coldness struck him boldly as he was outside on the December's wind-chill of minus twenty.

What a difference!

'I think your face expression would mean no?!'

What a face and the body she has, but cold-hearted soul!

She concentrated herself on her breathing to calm down her thoughts, to receive only his, and block the power within her, buried deep under her skull, hidden inside her head.

What a waste of life!

'I am sorry to bother you again!'

I really feel sorry for you!

'I apologized myself sincerely!'

You are dead, but you are not aware of it!

She realized that she was holding the cup of hot tea for too long; skins on her fingers were burned under the emanating heat from porcelain surface. The pains have been registered on the edge of her previously numb brain.

What a hard cold blooded bitch are you!?

Rage burst from her resembling uncontrolled wave of emotions under her calm frozen unexpressed face. She whispered his name through her clenched teeth:

'BRAD...!'

He was half on his heel to turn his back to her, when he heard his name for the first and last time. He felt radiated dangers from her for a brief second, through his brain a thought of his mistake just surfaced, when he felt light touch of her forefinger on the back of his neck. It felt like static electricity charge applied on the surface of his skin. It brought havoc to his brain and shock to his body. She released her power on him in a second. She heard his scream inside her head and flash of blazing light came from him. She cut his connection with her in the next instant and his body collapsed in front of her as a tree cut at his foundation. Without any sound coming from his mouth, he hit the ground together when two muffins rolled out from his bag across the polished floor and spilled coffee from his paper cup splashed her black boots.

CHAPTER XII

Section 2.

MY LOVE

December, 1998.

CANADA, ONTARIO, TORONTO, SCARBOROUGH, PACKARD BLVD 54…

Her clitoris trembled again under his finger's soft touch. She cried for more calling his name. Her left hand buried her nails at his left butt producing mild scratches on its surface.

'Ahhhhhhhhh, Marc!'

He filled her with his sperm, his long last agony prolonged through fast movement of her hips ended in total ecstasy. He collapsed on her gasping for air through tangled hair in his face.

'Mmmmmmmmarc…

Sticky sweat, oily smoothness of her skin, smell of her filled his nostrils, burning sensation between his legs spread inside his body, all together paralyzed his mind completely. Time sense was lost and place did not exists. He was perplexed in sweet tormented seconds physically connected with her, emotionally filled with emptiness that last for hours, creating their own void of existence in time.

'I love you Michelle…'

The sentence broke the spell between them. He forgot that he was able to produce the word "love" inside his mouth. Thought about it existed in his head for long time, but he never exhaled openly to any woman before.

'I know Marc…'

She slides her right hand diagonally across his back collecting drops of his sweat with her soft palm. She brought his own wetness on the back of his neck when she hold his head and kissed his mouth.

'I love you Marc…'

He glided above her wide opened legs and curled beside her right breast. He touched her right rigid nipple with his mouth. He sucked with joy of a year old boy.

'Uhhh…, you devil…'

She moaned, stroked his head, tangled her fingers in his hair and pushed him lightly closer to her breast pressing his lips to her skin.

'Do not stop…'

Marc switched to the other one that waited from him. He sucked her left nipple all at once pressing her between his tongue and his upper lip. He used his teeth as a support for his upper lip to get better grip at her already hard nipple.

It produced additional mumbled sound from Michelle's throat that sounded something like begging of tortured soul.

'My…deeeaarrrr…, My…, Ooohhhh!'

Suddenly, he dropped his head between her legs and buried his face on her warm, pulsing vagina. Small pubic hairs in the middle tickled him under his nose and he inhaled through it the air filled with almonds smell, his mouth opened to give a hard kiss to her outer vagina's lips. His hands played, stroked and squeezed her breasts in the same time when he started to kiss her clitoris. She screamed from pleasure, producing delightfully high pitching voice, grabbing his head with both her hands.

'Yesss… No! Do not stop! Kiss me!'

Without additional word, she pushed his face far away from her vagina for a moment and he continued his kisses inside her wide opened thighs. His penis to get hard when she called his name from above:

'Marc…, My love…, Kiss me, please...'

CHAPTER XII

Section 3.

TEST ONE

June, 1943.

CANADA, QUEBEC, UNGAVA REGION, CRATERE DU NOUVEAU – QUEBEC, ("CHUBB CRATER") - PINGUALUIT CRATER, TESTING SITE NUMBER ONE…

J.P. Marchant removed his backpack and he laid it at his feet. He breathed heavy under his 60 years weight over his shoulders, but he felt much younger in his soul and much lighter in his body, after he spent all day outside in the fresh mountain air. He had only two beers at the "Auberge" - local tavern down the road, but the alcohol spread through his body and reached his brain much faster this time, because he didn't eat anything all afternoon, and now his legs were rubbery, unsecured and unsafe support for the rest of his fragile body. He struggled for nearly a minute to fit his key into his front house door. He hadn't shaved for days and his beard was itchy on his dry, sun burned skin. He scratched his chin with the house large entrance key when he opened the door. He was swaying a little in the hallway and then he diagonally crossed it, stopped at the kitchen counter and switch on the radio. Radio seems to be ranting about the War at Europe, when he saw strange intense red glow on his windows curtains; that spread its shimmering light on his kitchen draperies. Radio was upset by strange magnetic disturbance, cracking strange low murmured voice continued his broadcast and when he tried to switch off the radio, he received electric shocks from it. He saw high shape of a pure red arc above his house, lightning noise without the clouds on the evening sky, and some kind of a mysterious beam of greenish light, in shape something like a cigar, and many degrees in length bloomed across the horizon. J.P. pinch himself on his electrified left arm to confirm that he was awake and he wasn't dreaming. The flickering light rose in the east and crossed the sky at a pace much quicker than but nearly as even as that of sun, moon, or stars, till it set in the west two minutes after it's rising.

Then after a few minutes the mysterious voices vanished, a gold corona was observed at zenith. Black out of radio stopped suddenly, as it started and the news program continued his gibberish talks. He felt dizziness, weakness in his arms and legs and before he was able to reach couch in his living room, he collapsed one meter in front of it. He did not register swaying shadow on the door of his bedroom. Four-year-old boy held his teddy bear across his chest, whispering unknown words to himself or to silent brown toy in his small hands. Child had a look of coma – patient; who just woke up from permanent vegetative state.

'Gland – Pa?'

CHAPTER XII

Section 4.

FIGHT

June, 1884.

SOMEWHERE BETWEEN AN OLD CONTINENT - EUROPE AND THE NEW WORLD –

AMERICA CONTINENT, ATLANTIC OCEAN, THE SHIP NAMED "THE SATURNIA"…

…

Watch out!

Huge fist flew through semidarkness in the direction of his unprotected face.

What a thrill!

The fist was closing on him.

Look all that blood!

Wide knuckles were smirked with someone's blood.

I love this!

It is going to hit him directly in the center.

Move aside!

He stepped aside as in dance and bent his left knee.

Now it is our turn!

The fist passed his face less than one centimeter from his right cheek.

Nikola now!

He reacted without thinking.

Now!

He made contra move at his attacker who was unstable shadow in front of him.

Crush his skull!

His left hand impacted with the man's ribs and he realized that he was real.

Hit him!

This time he moved much faster than his opponent.

Yes!

The shadow – man grunted as he repeated the same move with his right hand on his other side of the unprotected ribs cage.

Come on!

He pushed man in front of him with both his forearms and he crumbled in front of him.

Watch for the other one!

Another one slammed something against his left shoulder and one part of his exposed back.

He has a weapon!

The object made shocked pain to his shoulder bone and all his left hand went numb from it.

Hit the bastard!

He swung with his right elbow using additional force of his rotation backwards and he felt crunched nose on the end of it.

Crush him!

Second man cried in pain and dropped his weapon cursing on some foreign language, which Tesla did not understand.

Finish him!

He smacked the man across his left temple with his open right hand and it sent him aside.

Break his bones!

The first one was on his knees when Nikola hit him with his right leg in the face.

Nice move!

The man yelled probably for help on his native unrecognizable language.

Hit him!

Nikola shook his left shoulder, checking it with his right hand. Nothing was broken.

Now! Make your move! Finish them when they are down!

...

It is enough Dane! I am done.

Nasty mark will probably appear on his damaged skin and it is going to change the colors as rainbow through the following weeks.

Come on you coward! Kill them! Kill him!

When they are going to reach a land on the other side of the Atlantic Ocean, it will disappear from the surface, but his bone will remind him in his older days on this episode.

NO! I TOLD YOU!

…

Blast from the gun filled his ears. Every figure stopped, frozen on the same place where they were. Picture shimmered in front of his eyes and he blinked twice before he wiped sweat from them, after that he saw Captain of "The Saturnia" steamship clearly in the middle of it, with his weapon above his head.

'I SAID IT IS ENOUGH! YOU'RE LAZY LEECHES AND ROTTEN MAGGOTS FROM THE OLD WORLD! WHO STARTED THIS MESS?'

CHAPTER XII

Section 5.

OFFICERS

January, 2010.

CANADA, ALBERTA, EDMONTON, EDMONTON POLICE WEST SIDE, KINGSWAY AVE, NW...

Blaquier's light blue eyes analyzed reports on now opened investigation on Brad's brain stroke accident from Truro's Mall. Eyewitness stories on the spot covered each other up to the last detail and they saw roughly the same scene from different angles and did not have some specific additional information except one, which caught his attention. Interesting detail about red haired, tall, young woman who was on the scene prior to Brad's accident woke up his curiosity. Some older lady who was inside Wang Express store, next door to Tim Horton's coffee shop, saw that Brad had short conversation with the young woman in her 30s, in dark blue jacket, light blue jeans, with optical glasses on her face preceding his death. Old woman, named Sarah, thought that she saw young woman touched gently back of Brad's neck before he collapsed on the floor, but due to the fact that elder 87-s woman with an impaired low vision glasses, cannot be reliable witness, her statement was questionable as per local investigators. The fact that local police force and investigators couldn't find anywhere red haired above mentioned woman, together with his guts feeling activated alarm on the subject, Blaquier made some remarks inside his notebook. If he was not busy with other three following cases here in Edmonton, he would be there on the next flight to Nova Scotia.

It was my case after all, on which Brad broke his teeth. He bitted it, like a bulldog and did not want to let it go. I would do the same thing on his place, and I would be there instead of him... There is no point to think about that, it will be now up to me to continue this investigation and I will get to the end of it! I lost another friend and only that matter...

He picked up handset of his desk phone and dialed the number of ex - Brad's Police Office at Halifax, Nova Scotia. He checked his watch, there was 2 to 3 hours difference between them, Toronto is two hours ahead of him, and Atlantic Canada, Halifax or Truro are three hours ahead, so the chance to catch someone on an Atlantic Coast and Toronto office are very good. The phone started to ring, when there was knocking on his office door. He hung up the phone in the same time when the person on the other end answered his phone call.

'Yes, come in!'

Two men entered his room; both in civilian clothes, but distinctive movement of their eyes, position of their bodies together with his experienced hunch, told him immediately that they are active military or police personnel. Once involved with these professions life of the individual continue in the shadow of their abounded previous jobs, body language, trainings, discipline and expressions in the eyes stayed with the person for all his life. As he getting older with every year, he recognized these signs on himself, too. Imprinted signatures of military and police academies made their invisible tattoos on their skins and blood. The first one on the right came closer and offered his hand to him.

'Inspector Blaquier, allowed me to introduce myself to you, I am Lt Colonel Andrew Marlow, from Canadian Army Special Ops. Ottawa HQ, currently stationed at Mont Laurier, Quebec.'

His handshake was hard, firm with stretched opened fingers. The man's light brown eyes went directly to Michael's blue ones to get an additional connection between them.

'This is my colleague, Major, Olivier Marceau from the same section, but stationed at the moment at Quebec City.'

The other man gave him strong, but a little crooked handshake mostly with his fingers. His black small eyes were moving somewhere between Michael's short haircut and his wide fresh shaven face, without eye contact.

'Sir, it is my pleasure.'

His voice was high, with a hint of French Canadian accent.

'Nice to meet you, pleasure is mine! Please, seat yourself!'

Michael offered those two – seat couch positioned left from his desk. Colonel Marlow sat on the couch and Major Marceau took the chair beside it. Anxiety and impatience radiated from both of them.

They are not happy to be here. They do not like it at all.

'Before we started anything, please just call me Michael. If that's all right with you so, what can I do for you?'

'Well if you feel better that way, we can proceed with the same, it will be more convenient for all of us, you can call us by our first names, then Olivier and Andrew, as well.'

'I assumed that you already prepared yourself for the tasks and you did some homework on me, so it will be unnecessary to introduce myself to you, am I right?'

Colonel Marlow gave him an interested look and smiled only with the right edge of his wide mouth.

'I see that it will be our waste of time to proceed with that and judging by your direct answers I know what kind of person you are, so I will cut the chase and go directly to the core of our issue.'

That's it my man!

'I completely agreed with you Andrew.'

Michael answered and a moment passed before Colonel continued.

'Well, we have lost more than one of our ex - operatives officers recently, as you were fully aware of it, since you are responsible for investigation of their deaths, and their cases get complicated with every following day. We have found another of our man dead from brain seizure at Quebec, L'Annonciation, his brain was "burned to ashes" as our medical expert figurative expressed to us.'

Blaquier's hidden alarm went on.

This cannot be coincidence. There is more in it.

'His name was Doug Burke and he was part of team, an assignment overseas, a decade or more back, in the same group with the other people, some of them you already know: Claude Lévesque, Brian Murhead…'

'Yes, I "have met" Claude Lévesque at West Edmonton parking lot, he managed to kill another man there after his death, so he was quite amazing man...'

'You have strange type of humor Blaquier, but we did not come here to hear your "Best Off Michael B.", we came for some information which can help us to catch his killer...'

Major Marceau stopped his speech, when Colonel Marlow gave him short sharp look. He turned back to Michael with readable expression on his face: "Young, but stupid" and he continued:

'The other man, Brian Murhead have been found by our military police unit in Ontario, his body was discovered in September last year in the basement of one house at Kingston, together with his wife and his son, they were heavily drugged, exhausted, but found alive on the first floor inside that house. Murhead's body was mutilated and it suffered broken bones, internal injuries and bleeding as well; he was tortured by some strange method; that I have never seen before, it looked like all his body has been exposed to an enormous pressure and vibrations. Our investigators are trying to put lost pieces together.'

At least I know who was in charge here in a case of an emergency.

'Did his wife or son remember anything? Any additional witnesses in the area?'

'They gave us very confused answers, literally there were lost in time and space. Brainwashed apparently both of them, we are not sure, but probably something similar performed on them.'

That was really an interesting detail.

'There wasn't any other witness in the area, but there was some strange ground noise detected in the area, apparently during Murhead's time of captivity, something as light earthshaking through the neighboring block of houses.'

'An earthquake?'

'Yes, something similar, on the other case, murder of Doug Burke, there was a real one, an earthquake which was felt through the same regional area of Quebec. This is the reason for us to believe that killer or killers are in possession of device that simulated the same conditions on earth.'

'You are telling me that these killers have something like artificial earthquake machine and they have used it already in more than one occasion in Canada?'

'As for now, we connected only these two cases so far with that possibility, considering world - wide panic with terrorism, we are going to bloom as international haven – garden for new inventive terrorist weapons testing area in the eyes of international community, if this information reached news columns through the country. This situation present opportunity for the government officials and agencies, military and civilians to initiate an additional pressure on us to speed up our investigation and use all our sources to conclude this as: "Search and Destroy".'

Tell me about it. Only in your wild and wet dreams!

'You mean "Grab and Bag", more or less, as I understand our government policies so far.'

Michael turned his right hand and rotated it in a manner of "hocus – pocus" with finishing move at his right pocket. During his performance, he added confidentiality wink to both of them. Marceau restrained his impatience as Marlow simply stood and watched for several seconds.

'Murhead gave us brief description of person who tailed him through Quebec City and attacked another man, who ended up in coma, brain dead, too. Apparently, it was female, in mid thirties, good looking; red haired, slim, tall, in jeans and leather jacket. She is psychic definitely with extraordinary powers and abilities and we came here to compare our info with yours in order to catch her and eventually apprehend to justice her partners.'

My guts are still active, after all.

'Yeah, I have some new developments from Truro, Nova Scotia and I will gladly share it with you…'

CHAPTER XII

Section 6.

ASSIGNMENT

April, 2010.

CANADA, NEW BRUNSWICK, FREDERICTON, DOWNTOWN AREA, IRWING GAS STATION…

Small drops of rain were sliding across the big glass surface collecting the dust and invisible traces of salt spots left from previous night heavy rain. Miso Bajic – nicknamed "Crnogorac" ("Montenegrian"), got urgently need for his every hour cigarette looking through the closed window of Irwing Gas Station on the corner between Queen and Northumberland Streets, on his second graveyard shift. He hated this job, this place and this country. Since he arrived here five years ago he was working only these minimum wages paid jobs, shifting from one to another one, in an endless closed circle of night and day shifts, which were taking toll on his health and age. He was struggling with writing and reading on English, but he is able to understand almost everything on this language, except when some honky accented dummy – ass started to speed up his mumbling in his direction. He squint with his black small eyes checking the time on digital clock above the fridge with Baxter's dairy products. Five fifty five AM. Another two hours till the end of his job. Suddenly his Nokia mobile phone started to ring. It took five seconds for him to reach it across the table. Voice on the other line was not familiar to him.

'Montenegrian, you don't know me, but that doesn't matter at all, you know who helped you to come here. You know who gave you new life and new name. You know who I am even you never met me.'

'How did you get this number? I never…'

The voice laughed on his remarks and added:

'I know everything about you and your family, too…'

'Don't you dare to touch my family, you son of a …'

'I can do anything to you and your family…, The same things that you did to someone else's family back in Bosnia…'

'Listen, you mother fucker…'

The man on the other end of phone line broke his sentence with his angered voice:

'ENOUGH! YOU LISTEN TO ME!'

Miso - Montenegrian stayed with an open mouth over his handset.

'I have a power to destroy not only your life, but the life of your family as well, and their future, their plans and dreams…,

So you are going to listen very carefully what I have to tell you, because I am not going to repeat it again, is that clear?'

Miso closed his mouth and answered through his tighten teeth.

'Yes, it is… Clear…'

'Good, now you are going to be good boy and do everything what I am going to ask from you…

The first thing is a package that you have to pick up from someone at Niagara Falls and second is that you have to kill someone else at Toronto, which is not going to be problem for you since you have practiced both of them before...'

CHAPTER XIII

Section 1.

SHE – KILLER

January, 1999.

CANADA, ONTARIO, TORONTO, RESTAURANT "LE PETIT DEJEUNER", KING ST. EAST STREET…

This Sunday morning her mind was torn between their last conversations about their plans for the future, and dead end murder's investigations on the case that engaged her working hours and her weekends, too. The only subject outside her work that preoccupied her mind is Marc's promise to move here in Toronto, Ontario to live with her and share the rest of their life together; in fact the feeling that came out from her was that she loved him infinitely. When Michelle was fourteen years old, her mother was killed in a head – on collision on the highway 417, between Montreal and Ottawa. Since then, she never refuse call from her father, who was still at Ottawa, now retired police officer, and used every opportunity to talk with him through Skype for hours. Michelle discovered soon after the wreck that everybody will eventually die, sooner or later, and that present has to be shared with your loved ones as much as possible, because when you have only one parent alive beside you or no parents at all, you are handicapped for the rest of your life. She naturally, as a kid, tried to transfer her anguish, pain and loneliness on something else, which is going to fill the emptiness in her soul, void between her heart and soul, like athletics, sport that occupied her free teenager time. She dedicated all her time to trainings and she managed to swallow her pain of loss through Spartan's exercises in the field. She achieved excellent results on middle range and short distance athletics' routes, especially on 400, 800 and 1,500 meters. She won medals, rewords, certificates, recommendations, sometimes money, too on different provincial and state level competitions, but she was into it, until she exhaled and emptied her bowl of pain. That took almost six years of her life. Her father understands her urge for it and he gave her his maximum support. When she told him that she applied for Police Academy, he was not quite happy about it, which he clearly and honestly stated directly to her, but he respected her decision, helped her to overcome her natural fear of firearms weapon, even trained her by himself cold weapon's combat, which completely removed her dourness toward knives and blades.

Now, she was waiting for Investigator Todd Stamford to come, ten additional minutes stretched like hours, above the empty reserved table at "Le Petit Dejeuner" Restaurant at King St. East Street. She checked her Ford Explorer across the street, illegally parked on the curb, angled into a narrow space in front of hydrant, its rear half – blocking an alley entrance, facing the restaurant. Inside, tables were mostly occupied, late risers and earlier lunch -breakers were struggling in for breakfast. Light slanted through tainted glass windows, across tiled floor, wooden chairs then sank into a deeper gloom of breakfast's rear where she heard sentimental music over the kitchen sounds of fraying and cooking food. When he finally walked up on the breakfast, Todd noticed her clouded, dreamy look on her face, which he attached to the long working hours of unscheduled shifts, with unsatisfied, unproductive investigations results. The case, unofficially named "Bat – Man" between them, due to all victims post – mortal positions, upside down nailed to the wall or ceilings, was running in place, on neutral, through total investigative darkness. All leads were followed to every possible branch or version of it, which end up dead at the end. As always, the light will showed up at the end of the tunnel.

'Sorry, I was not sure where to park…'

She looks tired.

'No problem, Todd.'

Michelle turned and faced him smiling at him.

'I am not so hungry, after all…'

Todd sat down and he opened the menu when a cheerful waitress appeared beside the table.

'Green tea, please…'

He said and looked up at her.

'Toast, and let me check…; The fruit salad, without anything on it, just plain.'

She scribbled something on her notepad and hip – hopped to the kitchen.

The clatter and conversations from other tables around formed a constant background noise that gave the place warm atmosphere, loud enough to get comforting feeling like at home.

'I have already ordered English breakfast with regular coffee for me.'

Michelle answered to his obvious next unspoken question.

'It is nicer here then back there at our offices, anyway.'

Todd added looking iced ornaments on the frozen edges of the wide front window.

'I am glad that we are out of that cubicles mad house.'

'Me, too. I have got report from Montreal City Police, on similar crime scene, case three years old at Montreal – Est, Tetreaultville, in March 1996-th, male, mid 40s, similar position of the body, but only on the floor instead on the wall. It looks to me that was his first murder. That was the only one like that from that year and since then, up to our cases this year, he was quiet, he stayed somewhere on cold, left on the ice or he just hibernated all this time between them.'

'Yes, let's assumed that it was he, instead of she, and it could be that he was institutionalized between them, he went somewhere outside the country, overseas or he was just focused on something else which prevented his urge for killings.'

'I have already gathered data on "Institutionalized" potential suspects and checked more than half of them, but I did not get any similarities with this one. In any case, I checked all suspects on probation time and on free weekends, as well, compared their times, their alibis with murders, places and profiles, there wasn't any match.'

Steam from innumerable coffee cups around them drifted the aroma - cloud above their table.

'Hmmm. Coffee smells provocatively good. I think I am going to order another one.'

'Michelle, are you listening anything? What are you thinking? You seemed to be somewhere else, not here, as I can see.'

'Todd, I have some issues concerning my private life. You know, some of us have a private life!'

Todd made so realistic grimace on his face that a waitress stopped with his food plate in the middle of her path genuine concerned about him.

'That was low kick! Ouch! Thank You!'

Michelle saw it and it produced very wide honest smile on her face.

'I have to do it. You wouldn't stop! I have calculated dates between this year murders and the first one from Montreal and you can guessed what I have found!'

Waitress slowly continued her carefully steps on her invisible path to their table.

'What?'

'It was exactly one year and nine months between them!'

'Which means what?!'

'We have female killer, nine months pregnant, plus she was a year pause on her maternity leave!'

CHAPTER XIII

Section 2.

PRAVDA

April, 1979.

SOVIET UNION, EAST GERMANY, EAST BERLIN, ABOUNDED WAREHOUSE…

(Modern Day – European Union, Germany, Berlin)

The morning fog was dissipating from the ground surface and it left a high thin overcast above the area. Markus tied up his bicycle with the iron chain to the lightning pole with the simple cheap padlock. If anybody from this neighborhood decided to steal his old bike, he is not going to need anything harder then large stone or any other hard, heavy object to break that padlock and he will spend rest of this afternoon day on his long walk on foot back to his home. A month ago, he passed his tenth birthday and thin shadow under his nose made of puberty hairs marked him as an early teenager, and he did not like it at all, especially when he received undeserved smack on his face from his mother because he went to the school without washing his face first. His father was constantly drunk to notice any changes on his son, and he stopped to care for himself long time ago. Only good things from him that were left for Markus were chocolate bars half melted in his inner left father's coat pocket stained with alcohol and vomit's smudges, constantly smelled on urine and tobacco's sweat. Except occasionally fights between his parents and regularly yelling, braking things inside the house, most of his low life time his father spent in the bar's lined up between steel factory where he worked and his house where he slept. Last four years were worse than before because his father got sick, delirium attacks repeatedly came back, sometimes in waves of three – four in a row, they influenced his work and human behavior, which resulted last time that his father hunted him through the house with a knife totally unaware of who is he, where is he or anything else. He stopped him with wide baseball's home swing of shovel across father's skull. Numerous times he would drag him home from the bars or find him in the ditch beside the road, robbed, penniless, half frozen, left to die by his drinking comrades. Once, Markus considered possibility to left him there to die, but the pain in the middle of his chest prevent him from that. He was not quite sure is that love that it hurts or just the hate sitting there inside his lungs, preventing him to release father from his misery. The school did not go well either, he passed with minimum grades, avoiding classes as much as he can, but kept his absences from home frequently longer each time and he couldn't wait to leave for good. The only thing that got him focused on was membership in their "Hund's" Club -(Dog's Club) Youth Club which have been major hung around place for kids like him. He wasn't aware that registered as hunting sport club, presenting themselves, run by local community volunteer mostly retired military personnel, creating an image of sport union, but it was actually semi – private organization recruiting Neo-Nazi supporters under their wing. He liked things what they did teach them there, very cool things, like how to survive in the woods, making partial weapons and explosive materials from ordinary groceries, use of knifes and clubs in self defense, fitness trainings, but the most appreciating for him were long talks between them about their problems, families, school, their imaginations, wishes and dreams. He felt relaxed, trusted and important by the club's owners and his new friends and today he is going to have a special training session with his tutor Mathias Kirk at club's premises. Markus entered gray building which had been in ruins last decade, since KGB fist loosen its grip on Eastern European countries under the "Iron Curtain", places like this were collecting points for semi – military organizations and mafia families. These types of properties have been "purchased" with bribed sum under the local politician table. He closed steeled gate – door with a huge red letters in the middle of it, "PRAVDA" (JUSTICE) and entered gloomy dark corridor in front of him. Dim light from weak, rarely unbroken light bulbs on the ceiling gave him feeling that he was entering through gate of hell. He clenched his fists couple of times to remove stiffness and shaking from his hands, the fear which cradle his heart with silent whispers. His light blue eyes adapted to the shadows and darkness around him and now he was able to see much better, when he reached end of it.

'Come in, come in Markus do not be afraid!'

Mathias Kirk's shadow stretched across the path to the spot where he entered large storage area. Markus squinted his eyes to adjust brightness that temporary blinds him.

'Welcome to our testing arena, we were excepting you!'

Kirk was dressed all in black, from head to his toe, his blond, almost silver yellow hair made frightening contrast with his clothes and his white wide face made an impression of levitating in the space between them as he spoke to him.

'Markus embrace your destiny and accept who you are! Take your life and shape it at your own will!'

'I do not understand, I…'

'You accepted it without doubts long time ago, now you have to act! Make a move before it is too late!'

Something flashed from left to the right, in front of his eyes, and bites him on his left cheek with its coldness. Some warm liquid spread under his left cheekbone and in the same time, the pain surfaced on his skin. He yelled surprised and tried to touch his cheek with his left hand. Another flash of silver line ended on his exposed elbow, producing another line of pain on his flesh, which has been confirmed by his curse.

'Fuck me, what was that…?!'

'It is our sister Death, her kiss was on your cheek!'

Kirk's voice echoed above him, when he saw own blood on his fingers. In the same time at the edge of his right eye's perimeter, he caught a movement. He managed to move to the left before silver streak passed three centimetres in front of his chest. He saw only the knife attached to the hand instead of person in front of him.

'She is making love to you Markus!'

He ignored Kirk's voice that distracted him completely from the beginning and he tried to focus on his surrounding, but strong light blocked his vision completely around him. He dropped his gaze instinctively to the floor and detected shadow attached to his left feet. He crouched when knife slashed his left shoulder muscles instead his left kidney. Desperately he sprang with all his strength towards the passing blade and he grabbed outstretched hand with both his hands. Swing of his body, together with his weight and last strength waken by his fear pushed the shadowed man aside. He felt hard bone and soft flesh under his fingers.

'Dance with her Marcus! Yes!'

Contact with the live person produce extra strength in him and he kept pushing the man forward in front of him, locking his elbow arm between his chest and his arms tangled around, so he hanged himself completely with all his weight on opponents stretched arm. The man grunted under his pressure, lost his balance and skidded across the filthy floor. He hit concrete surface with both his knees simultaneously and he uselessly tried to protect his face with his left hand on the impact.

'Meet your Creator at last! Embrace Him!'

Kirk's comments were mixed with his fast breathing, man's yell in vain and the noise of their struggle on the dusty floor. Impact of their fall brought clattering sound of the metal to Markus, weapon detached itself from man's grasp and landed beside them. Without any active thoughts, he grabbed it with his free right hand and he swings it in the wide arc above his head.

'YES! TAKE HIM!'

He stabbed the man on the back, between his shoulders two centimeters left of his spine, and he felt electrified spasms under his arm. Sound of exhausted air came from the body when he punctured the body under him next time, now a little higher above, closer to the man's shirt collar. Blood erupted from the wound and sprayed Markus face. After third stab, he lost himself completely.

'YES! MEET HIM!'

He continued to puncture the man under him until he had strength in his right trembling arm. He did not hear Kirk's enthusiastic yelling in the background and he was not aware that man under him stopped moving. Somebody grabbed his right arm and removed the weapon from his numb hand. Some other hands pick him up in the air above dead body and hold him there, where he floated as he was supported by invisible strings attached to his fragile body.

'LET HIM GO!'

Kirk's heavy hand grabbed his left shoulder and he held him there as a puppet attached to it. The blood in his temples boiled and pounded his head from inside, so Kirk's voice was coming from the great distance.

'SHOW HIM HIS WORK!'

Strong, muscled hand with unrecognizable tattoo form on it entered his view and grabbed dead man's body at the bottom of his legs. His heart skipped inside his chest when he saw man's face frozen in death's mask of agony in front of him.

Father…

His thought flashed on the surface of his shocked face and his legs gave up under him. He dropped to his knees as an empty sack beside his father's corpse. Vomit erupted from his trembling mouths spraying above his father's left shoe. The right one was missing and his right bare dirty foot was lying beside left one as reminder of his act of violence. The sickness speeded through him when he heard Kirk's voice that was filling the void above him.

'Today, you are reborn again…'

Then he embraced incoming obscurity and he collapsed beside his father.

CHAPTER XIII

Section 3.

SPLIT

January, 1999.

CROATIA, DALMATIAN COAST, CITY OF SPLIT, SAINT THEODOR - THE CHURCH OF OUR LADY, BELL TOWER…

…

Now let's go!

She pressed "ON" button and felt familiar prickling on the surface of her body as always when the magnetic field energized itself around her. Through black silk stretched across her body and thin poly - mask on her face she saw bluish particles of ions as they were spreading in front of her, covering the space around her as "the shield" activate itself with low humming sound. Nipples on her firm breast get hard and itchy under electrical current that was circulating through her and her hair gave cracking sound in respond to it. It grew very fast from August last year, and it seemed to recover itself much faster when she shaved her head completely, instead when she was keeping it shorter. Anyhow, she was not in prime of her youth anymore, but the side effects of time travel is getting on her as well, and she was aware that sooner or later her other parts of the body will deteriorate same as her skin started since that episode at Pula, Croatia. She did not have any illusions about that, last time in 1984; when she saw "Philly – Man" from 1943. He looked like mummified parchment of itself, dried under the sun of eons and winds of past centuries. She knew and confirmed last time with Tesla in London 1897, after they performed medical check and an additional psycho – physical research through intensive and detailed training in his laboratories at New – York, Grand Falls and London, that she had only three – four time frames left after her wounding accident from 1992., together with her daughter's birth on 2012. Tesla reminded her on psychological aspects of time travel and climate – pollution effects which influence her health and health of her child and her grand children as well. She promised him that she is going to finish her task on time and reach 1897; before is too late.

I have to find The Sign in order to initiate tracing sequence! Without the Sign I cannot get The Mask! I am going to find The Mask before New Millennium start! This is our last chance to stop the end of our world!

She removed "String" from energy box attached on her leather belt and checked the charging on it. Indicator blinked "Full" twice confirming it and she programmed the weapon on its maximum potential. She is going to need every energy blast to stop agents which were closing their trap around her.

It's Game time!

CHAPTER XIII

Section 4.

HUMORIST

July, 1885.

UNITED STATES OF AMERICA, NEW YORK, EDISON'S NEW YORK HEADQUARTERS COMPANY, SOUTH FIFTH AVENUE, EDISON'S OFFICE...

(Modern Day – New - York City)

...

'Tesla, you don't understand our American humor!'

Edison's eyes flickered with pride above lighted brown cigar in his thin mouths. Partially opened mouth were showing his already yellow edged teeth which bite cigar and kept it there as bulldog kept his fresh dig out bone.

I have told you.

That was the sentence Edison gave him after all his eighteen day every day work, almost a year, at Edison's New York HQ on South Fifth Avenue. He was watching this man and he remembered how he marveled Edison before he met him, when he cross the same door with Batchellor's recommendations papers in his hand. He felt betrayed at first, but then he felt relief that finally he saw Edison as who is really are. An arrogant, selfish, manipulated man whose greed fed on his rotten character as the leach fed on human's blood.

I have told you.

After he saved Edison's reputation of the company through his job on steamship "Oregon", when he repaired his machines, innovations on the engines and motors on his new generating stations through the city, patented twenty four dynamos improving quality and productivity on old machines, increased their electricity output and lower the cost of them. Edison himself promised him 50.000 dollars after his job is done, and now months later he tossed and broke his promise, as it was prank, after tremendous amount of Tesla's overtime, he pissed on all his new designs, inventions and on him as his employee.

I have told you.

Edison lifted his eyebrows as he was saying to him:

'Well, what are you going to do now my little Parisian?'

Tesla did not have anything else to say to this man except two words:

'I quit.'

I have told you.

...

Yes, Dane you have told me.

CHAPTER XIII

Section 5.

HOTEL

January, 2010.

CANADA, ONTARIO, OTTAWA, HULL, RAMADA HOTEL, FORTH FLOOR...

Stella looked at her teeth lined up perfectly beside each other in her full mouths edged by "Scarlet Siren" of Estee Lauder's lipstick. The large mirror in the hallway on the fourth floor of Ramada's Hotel gave her self-assured image of true herself reminding her that she was an attractive woman yet after her 30-th birthday. There wasn't any trace of an accident that happened at Niagara Falls three months ago, no signs on her beautiful face, there was an emotional scars inside her soul, but she overcome that one as well with her sweet revenge on the man who made them. Her vengeance culminated when the bastard swallowed his own testicles, after she played with them with electrical pliers for forty minutes, and she choked him with garrote in after-time. Maybe she would finished him much faster, if Beth did not guide her rage to last longer than usually, helped her to channel her hate, she woken bloodthirsty retribution inside her. Everything at the end culminated with their multiple sexual orgasms between them beside his disfigured dead body. She smiled to herself with full satisfaction remembering that unforgettable episode. She had her smile on in front of exposed herself in front of the mirror when she heard "bing – bing' bell of arrived hotel's elevator. She switched off her smile when she stepped inside red carpeted elevator, then she pressed "M" button and checked her brown hair again before another mirror in the elevator itself. Now, she was ready for rendezvous with another potential buyer of the strange machine, as you can call it, which they found at one of the storage rooms at Niagara Falls. Beth went to see Big Brother's associates in their facilities in Washington, DC and deliver them some old files which contained some lunatic schematics and technical drawings of that long time ago dead scientist Tesla. The Big Brother gave her an order to deliver personally these documents directly to his thugs at DC office together with all other documentation and machines prototypes which they have found hidden at rented storage space. The problem was that it contained much larger amount of files, folders, documents, boxes and machines, apparatuses that they expected to find there, so Beth had to hire a moving trailer company in order to collect all items that they were stored there for years. Anyway, they kept some of them for themselves as Big Brother suggested before, but not only the technical gadgets and large chunk of money stashed from the dead dickhead's apartment, but also some items, which caught their attention and seemed valuable on the market as well. She stepped at hotel's foyer from opened elevator door when two bulky men grabbed her both her hands aside and pushed her back to the same elevator. She struggled to get free from their grip and she opened her mouth to protest, but the only sound that she heard, before she collapsed unconscious on the carpet, was whispered order on German, Dutch or some other similar language that she did not understood.

CHAPTER XIII

Section 6.

TRAP

December, 1998.

MONTENEGRO, THE DURMITOR NATIONAL PARK, MOUNTAIN OF DURMITOR, CANYON OF TARA RIVER, "ZMAJEVA PECINA"("DRAGON'S CAVE") AREA, HIDDEN PART OF THE CAVE…

...

'Simone, I think your time has come. Earn your money!'

The man removed his blue ski – jacket and carefully folded; put it before gray pillar on dusty floor at the bottom of huge stone double doorway. His black eyes briefly touched Kirk's icy blue stare without any word. His Latino blood boiled inside him and protested against ongoing repeated insults from "German Sheppard Dog", as he secretly nicknamed Kirk, but trained professional subdued it with single thought:

After this, you will be mine! Payback time is coming!

Kirk collected openly emanated hate from Latino's eyes and he enjoyed moderate change of color, if that was possible to detect, on his dark Mexican skin.

'We have unexpected guests in the entrance area, so it is our duty, as good-natured hosts, to prepare them a warm an entertaining welcome! What do you think Jackie?!'

An athletic, thin figure of women remained focused on glimmering light that was coming somewhere between overgrown frozen stalagmites that grew up, up to three meters long, hanged from twenty meters high ceiling.

'I think we should find The Mask and get out of here!'

Simon turned around and entered the long corridor, which they passed less than twenty minutes ago. He remembered one perfect spot, somewhere in the middle of it, which will be ideal to set a trap for incoming intruders. EMI (Electro Magnetic Interference) inside the cave was too strong to use any electronic device, so they have to switch off all technical gears, including communicators between their own team members, plus there was some other type of unidentified energy field around the artifact as well.

From now on, that is their problem; my only focus should be to eliminate team from the opposite side, quickly and quietly, or at least kept them outside the cave, until the end of daylight, for God knows what reason, as Kirk read from ancient script – map delivered digitally to his laptop last night. The man obviously has some serious issues regarding old legends, like his superstitious fear of ghosts from the past and other mambo – jumbo shit inside his crazy head…

Narrow path of stoned corridor was turning to the sharply left and curved section of passageway left some natural out of sight landing, as the large stone boulder has been removed from that area, which was positioned almost two meters high in the ceiling. Simon situated his heavy build body inside concave space above, supporting himself in the air by his stretched legs, as he was spider – man attached by some invisible strings to the top part of passage. In his left hand Berretta, an automatic pistol with silencer, with fifteen bullets in its magazine, gave him an additional confidence inside his semi – dark stratum. His other hand was resting on handle of long curved knife called "Sica" attached across his breast, which he acquired as trophy since August this year, after he killed undercover "con – man" at Zagreb, Croatia.

He was a fierce fighter, but without patience. At the end, he paid the price for that with his life… The real delight was an American agent… What was her name? …Mmmmmmmm…, Mitchell, yes…, She gave me great pleasure…, We spend together some time, gorgeous moments… I carved her body with my signatures, from her shoulder, stomach, arms and legs, but I saved her beautiful face until the end, but the bitch lied to me! She had a gem in her possession, but stupid whore gave it to the other one, agent at Pocitelj… Somebody deceived her, … And I finished my mission empty handed! Mmmmmm… Mitchell… Mmmmmm?

…

'*…mmmmmmmmmMMMMMMMMMMMMMMMmmmmmmmmmmmmm…*'

Circle of bluish light appeared underneath him and broke his reflections of past events. He did not hear any steps or breathing in the hallway prior to strange sound that filled the air around him. Small hairs on his neck get rigid from unknown feeling that multiply it through him.

Is this…, "The Fear"?

Berretta was steady in his calm hand when he aimed for white – bluish target. His forefinger pressed the barrel of the gun in the same time as streak of light flashed at his outstretched right leg.

Whup – whup – whup. Whup – whup.

He heard that one of his bullets found the target and hit something, when his right leg gave up its support.

Clink – clink – thud. Clink – clink.

He hit the floor sideway, with his left shoulder, instantly dislocated it and his extended left broken sidearm protected his bare skull to be as melon crushed on gray rock floor. His gun Berretta jangled on hard surface as he rolled on his back. The pain enclosed his body as well as he released it through shriek:

'AAAAAAAIIIIIHHHHHHH!!!'

His severed stump was surgically cut precisely above his knee as right leg's main artery sprayed its blood on rough surface of chiseled wall.

My leg! You fuck! You cut my leg!

At the edge of his right eye's perimeter, he detected trace of blood, which was wavering and moving across opposite wall. Revenge filled scream on his crooked mouth, while he grabbed Sica's handle and managed to get half of the blade length out of leather scabbard, when blue lightning snake leaped in front of his face. His decapitated head rolled down the corridor as blur of radiance extinguished itself above his dead body. Only sound from leaked blood vessel and strong unsullied odor of blood were filling passage area.

CHAPTER XIV

Section 1.

EXIT

January, 2010.

CANADA, ONTARIO, TORONTO, 49 WELLINGTON STREET, GOODERHARM

BUILDING, SOLICITOR'S OFFICE…

...

Look at me!

Man's eyes were empty. Pupils were trembling on their edges. His thoughts were wide open to

her.

How many of them?

He answered her truly. Openly she extracted everything from him, everything that he knew, since

he has been assigned to this unit. They have assembled special unit a month ago to capture her.

That was intriguing to her.

All right… Now you are going to do everything as I told you before! You will wait here three

minutes, after I am gone and then you are going on the ground floor.

She was holding him for the neck, as he was some small dog, a puppy of her, not grown up man

almost two meters high and 120 kilograms in bones and muscles weight. He confirmed her

thoughts with his head. The blood vessel on his massive neck was pulsing under her light touch.

His eyes were close now; his lips were moving slightly producing some hushing sounds under his

steady breath. She released him from her power; he shook his head left and right as something

was on the top of his head. She went back to the end of office's corridor on the third floor in front

of emergency exit doors which showed the way to fire escaped staircases by its explicit yellow

and red illuminated sign "EMERGENCY EXIT". She opened the door and peered down the stairs first, nobody was there, she glanced upstairs and she did not saw or heard anybody there. Agent Killroy said there would be another one here stationed in a case that she tried to run off from their closed trap. Agent Killroy gave her everything that he had and now he is heading to his glorifying death. He is going to buy some time for her, which she desperately needed to escape from general's men ambush. Other agent will guard the exit door at the bottom of the stairs and almost certainly, he is waiting for her like a spider in his net. Another detail that was working for her is precise order of their commander –leader named Marlow, to get her alive, which was the reason why all of them are equipped with stunt weapon or sleeping dart - guns, as per Kilroy's "scanned" mind pictures. All together, there were six of them, one positioned on the roof of the building, one at the bottom of fire escape route, one guarding the elevator floor and main entrance area and one on each floor of the office building. Killroy was decoy, positioned instead general in his lawyer's office prepared to catch her when she showed up. Luckily, for her they were not aware of her third psychic power of reading minds of the people which were close to her, so she "sensed " Killroy's thoughts in the office's corridor through the closed door and separating wall. His thoughts were incoherent, connected to his ex- girlfriend, Myra and their struggle to keep their relationship alive with - without casual sex. His concentration on the task was shattered in pieces by her unwanted pregnancy and the looming shadow of the child. It was easy for her to use his emotionally naked feelings, create false pictures in his mind and produce mental image in his head of his girlfriend in front of general layer's door, his mind was confused only for ten seconds, which has been more than enough for her to implant him vision of her girlfriend face. When she identified herself as corporate office layer, which arrived on their scheduled meeting, and he opened the door to shoot her with stunt gun she emanated Myra's reflection in front of him instead her own face. He was bewildered for additional five seconds, which was like an eternity for her to grab his thick muscular neck and take control of him completely. His internal confusions lasted a bit longer than normal, his sub – consciousness revealed itself through surprise and rage in the same time, but his brain already trapped by her power, tried to escape through his own seizures as always, which brought paralysis to his body.

Aware of everything, like a coma patient, but unable to move, to command with his body, he felt her power through his brain, how she searched through his memories, stealing his life from him, taking pictures, knowledge and ideas from him and erasing them completely inside his head. She injected him her own, filled the gaps with false memories recreated from his broken ones, using his unfinished mental creations to initiate rage and revenge inside him for all his broken dreams, sexual fantasies and hidden secret desires. She channeled his unhappiness, frustrations, losses and pain into clear, pure, blind concentrated rage. Filled to the top with it, she sent him back to his emotional creators and physical makers. She closed the door after her and she took stairs up leading to the top floor and the roof area. They were expecting from her an attempt to escape through the main entrance or some other options as windows and back door entrances on the ground floor of the building, not the roof. As she remembered schematics of nearby buildings and photos taken from the air, the roof of this one has connecting point to the other building, first on the left and that will be her exit point. The fresh chilled air met her behind the last door. Wind-chill added his minus ten Celsius to already negative temperature of the air. Two pieces business suit did not protected her from the frostbites. After she passed only ten meters across the flat snow covered area, she regretted this decision and an improvised back up plan did not look so prosperous to her. Fire escape metal stairs in front of her were leading down, some ten meters downward the wall to the lower level and after that was wide gap of four to five meters between the buildings. She was on the top of railings when she heard male voice behind her back:

'DO NOT MOVE! STAY WHERE YOU ARE!'

The gunshots from the ground floor boomed all the way through an open exit door to the roof. She felt agent's thoughts of hesitation and his broken concentration; she did not turn her head to check opponent's position, without any doubts, she jumped over the edge in the same time when his name surfaced over her brain.

Marlow.

CHAPTER XIV

Section 2.

LESSON

January, 1999.

UNITED STATES OF AMERICA, CALIFORNIA, LOS ANGELES, SAN FERNANDO'S VALLEY, BURBANK, BACKYARD OF THE HOUSE…

…

'Steve, when you're goin' to learn?'

The old man moved as a lazy cat, from one side to the other, shifting his shoulders up and down together with his hips left and right, as he was dancing in broken rhythm, somehow struggling to keep his balance between the steps. That was only his trick. Old man's movements were pure deception to the boy.

'Probably never.'

Younger one stayed at one place pretending that he is calm, but every part of his being screamed to run away from the old man's reach. He felt drops of his sweat rolling down his spine. His armpits were full of onion smelled liquid. The fear emanated from him strongly together on the surface of his sweat.

'Then boy…, I am goin' to teach you a lesson!'

Older man stopped one meter away from the boy, crocked his head to the right, semi parallel, turned en face to him, he was looking somewhere between Stevan's wide positioned legs. Stevan answered to his father agitatedly as he was able to make his false treats through his fast breath.

'I 'd like to see that.'

He answered in vain. Now, he was scarred for real.

'Watch and learn!'

His father answered to him and moved surprisingly fast for a man in his 60-s, catching Stevan's left side of the face with his right fist. Stevan's eyes perceive blurred movements on the edge of his vision parameters and he had a time to drop his head a little before father's fist crashed on his face. Blow was hard and strong that Stevan lost his balance for a second which gave his father additional time to add another one with his left one which ended on his son's neck.

'Uhhhhh…'

Black dots filled Stevan's eyes and he lost the ground under his feet. He collapsed on his ass first and then connected his skull with snowed white surface of their house backyard lawn. Two seconds later his right side ribs received the shot of his father boot. Frosted air entered his lungs when he grasped for it. He buried his face in the snow appreciating its coldness and freshness for a split second. He got another shot in his left kidney which cut his breath away.

'Father…'

He whispered through his teeth into the cold, wet surface in front of his nose. He opened his right eye just enough to see shadow of his father's figure in the snow in front of him. Another kick of the boot landed somewhere between his shoulders. He groaned.

'AS I SAID BEFORE, I WILL TEACH YOU A LESSON!'

The voice filled with anger and hate dropped to his ears distorted by his blood pumping - constant ringing in his head. It was as his father entered one part of his brain, the rest of it get anesthetized by his voice, and he took control of his thoughts, feeling and control over his body and soul.

'AND YOU ARE GOING TO REMEMBER IT!'

Next kick in his face send him to the land of the shadows where his father ruled above them all. He grasped his last thoughts and gripped them as drowned man to the straw, before darkness covered him completely.

Does he know the truth? Does he know about us? Does he know…?

CHAPTER XIV

Section 3.

THE SHIP

June, 1943.

UNITED STATES OF AMERICA, WASHINGTON, DC, DOD (DEPARTMENT OF DEFENCE) OFFICE, FILE'S NOTES FROM "PROJECT RAINBOW"...

(Modern – Day, Incident called "Philadelphia Experiment")

…

The field was on. The green fog slowly enveloped the ship from the bottom to the top. Waves stopped ten meters around the ship, splashing invisible barrier about the ship, sea color in the region of the ship changed from crystal blue to the purple – blue – green. Generators hummed like a giant bees and the stern of the ship was dissolving in front of my eyes. Structure of the objects become translucent under the spreading green vapor, wherever the mist touched and reached, the things become fluid wavering, unstable surface of nothing. The man ten meters ahead of me screamed as he become invisible to himself and through his transparent image I could see anchor of the ship. His apparent shadow runs through the metal wall on the left. Some other man screamed above my head, but an incoming steam concealed his body totally. The spree rolled across the deck in my direction like it was alive and it had own substance, purpose, life. Instinctively I retreated backwards until I hit the metal wall. Greenish substance of film reached my outstretched arm and I have felt static building on my skin, faint outline of my body remind visible in the air. My head get dizzy, nausea spread through stomach to my throat, weakness in my limbs stretched through my all body parts and it shook me from the head to the toe, as I am electrified. The feeling of the time was lost completely, it last in seconds for real, but my sense of time told me it started minutes ago. I melted as butter throughout the solid wall; I floated through the air, lost support on hard surface, panic filled my brain and my soul shrieked for help. Dreadfully, I have tried to catch something to hold on, but all ship was ghost structure drifted in space. Misty surrounding suddenly blasted itself into the orange ball of fire and blinding white light. I lost myself within vortex of light, buzzing sounds inside my head and thunderclaps of darkness. In one second, I was floating up through the endless darkness, in the next one I was falling through eternal tunnel of light. Lost in time and space, between the realms, nightmares and fears from my childhood went back from the darkness, hunted faces, and distorted screams of inhuman creatures around me filled my brain.

...

Again, I was on the deck of Destroyer Escort, U. S. S. Eldridge, DE – 173, deck materialized of nothing, dropped from somewhere to now here, from nowhere to over there, inside the green pool of bluish mist around me. The fog dissolved more or less few meters around me and I saw gigantic magnetic coils mounted on the deck in front of my face, I was on the other end of the same ship without any movements. Groan, unidentified sound came from my left side and I turned my head towards it. I saw one of the sailors faces fused within the coil's surface, the face gesticulated unheard speech, but from his mouth came only moaning cry for help or rage; it was difficult to understand syllabics of grumbled words. His eyes were double from regular size, round with broken capillaries inside them; pupils were wide, black full of madness. Scarred, I tried to move far away from him, but my legs were not under my brain's command. I dropped my blurred vision down to my left leg instantly frozen by the sight. Both my legs become part of metal coil's housing, there were inside the metal above my joints together under the flat gray metallic surface. Nightmare continued when I saw some other soldier's arms coming out from the floor's surface next to me, his fingers were moving as he tried to grasp something more than cold, dump, empty air, but the rest of his body was somewhere underneath, buried alive inside hard floor shell. I opened and closed my eyes as an attempt to wake up myself from a dream, but I realized that I am indifferent reality where dreams and nightmares can hurt you, not only emotionally, but physically as well. I concentrated harder in my mind and tried to force myself with an additional thought to free my trapped legs, still convincing myself that all this was just my imagination. I grabbed my right leg with both my hands and pulled hard as I could; twisting my upper part of body left and right, but the pain inside my leg's bone produced by struggle brought me to hard cold certainty. My voice sounded to me as replayed voice of the damaged type, twisted, stretched and deformed by skipped parts of my own speech, lost between the broken wheels which were turning triple slower than usual. In the next instant of time, I heard booming sound of thunder again above my head. This time dark blue cloud came from the top, together with the green haze, covering ship's deck like a warm blanket of transparent smog. It chocked the air from my lungs in one short instant as I was forced under the water surface, my heart skipped in effort to catch my short breaths and the pressure increased inside my skull. I have a feeling that my head will explode any second, when an electromagnetic pulse from the huge coils hit me like a fist directly across my chest and in the middle of my stomach. My whole body trembled under high pressure, an electric field and resonating sound from magnetic coils. I felt like every centimeter of my body has been impale with tiny electrified needles and each of them applied sharp vibrating puncture on my brain. The flash of light paralyzed my thoughts and for a split second, I did not feel the pain at all. Humming sound overwhelmed my senses and my arms broke apart as shattered puzzle in front of my eyes. Echo of my scream was lost inside an incoming void of darkness. The field was off. I came back from the darkness into the light called by name. Familiar name it should be mine. It was hard to remember. It was easy to forget. I was on the floor…, No … I was in the bed. I looked at my feet. They were there covered in bandages. They looked solid under the green light. The green light? Oh… My God!

…

General Brendan closed page of the file, made some quick reminder scribble on his notepad and then dial a number, which did not exists in any registered phonebook on the globe. Phone was ringing for some time and it switched to an automatic voice mail - box system without any introductory recorded welcome message. After two – three seconds of delay, Brendan left his message to the other side:

'Initiate "Aurora Borealis" program on twelve hundred Zulu – Time. Minus Ten, One, Nine,

Eight, Nine, North America, Canada, Ontario Region, Ottawa and plus Ten, Two, Zero, Zero, Nine, Europe, Norway, Northern Norway Region, Tromso,...'

CHAPTER XIV

Section 4.

EXPERIMENT

August, 1885.

UNITED STATES, NEW YORK, NEW YORK CITY, TESLA ARC LIGHT COMPANY,
RAHWAY, NEW JERSEY, IRVING STREET…

…

Interesting, really an interesting behavior…

Tesla was looking through the improvised glass cover at his modified arc lamp of high efficiency,
which was powered by carbon electrodes attached inside metal framed cylinder, controlled by
electromagnets instead of solenoids, as it was implemented in his previous version. He released
the simple clutch mechanism that was closing electrical circuit inside the cylinder and he did not
believe to his own eyes. Electrodes initiated bright illuminated light around them as they were
floating in some kind of milky – fogy liquid substance of own, but electromagnetic field around
them initiated particles of small bluish lighting – balls that flew through the cylinder and gained
their speed with every second. He was sure that an automatic fail switch will cut the current in a
case of overheated cylinder or overcharged electro – magnetic field is going to reach its
maximum power. As always, in his experiments, he prepared two - three identical models, which
were testing themselves in the same time under different electrical, electromagnetic and
environmental fields. He initiated the second cylinder that was powered and connected on
separated power supply by his alternating current motor, separated from the first cylinder with
one meter high and wide, five centimetres thick steel barrier positioned between them, physically
blocking each other completely in the corner of his testing room area. Basement of the Tesla
Electric Light & Manufacturing company contained three separated areas where he performed his
tests on his brand new innovations and his unregistered patents. Licenses required money, which

he did not have at the moment, even with the fact that company earned money, but most of the capital gained by his inventions went to the hidden investors and ultimately the same financial investors very often disagreed with Tesla on his plan for an additional experimental time on already developed equipment. The fact of improved capabilities and advanced performances of the same invention did not mean anything to them, when he invented his first version that is operative, useful and profitable machine, engine or any other equipment. Any modification or alternate version of it was waste of time, money and his talent for them and they were explicit and definite in their demands.

Fools, bloody arrogant fools…

Buzzing sound from the first cylinder filled the room as electricity charge filled the tube. The second cylinder repeated initiation procedures of the first one adding high pitching reverberation on its own. Bluish energy blast arced through the space between them, thin as a human hair, it stayed frozen between them for one – two seconds as fast written pattern on the steel barrier, like unknown God's signature imprinted on the surface of hard metal and then diminish itself inside. The first cylinder exploded sending the glass and other parts across the room, but the other one continued it was glowing for another two-three seconds in which his alternating current motor got on fire, gold and silver glimmers burst and ignite themselves on the end of its connection to the grounded wire. Tesla jumped behind protected glass headed for it, when screeching noise of metal cut his long legs movements. Iron barrier between them wield itself like a flag and then collapsed on the second cylinder crushing it under with all her weight. Metal sliced in two pieces following the curves of unimaginable signature pattern of bluish energy flare stand there as some kind of monument or carved imaginative sculpture of lunatic artiste.

That wasn't exactly what I expected, but my calculations were right, the field was energized and an energy flow was strong enough, but not channelized and controlled yet enough to support my additional tests on particle beam weapon. I should consult Dane regarding this issue; maybe he has some additional idea…

CHAPTER XIV

Section 5.

MESSAGE

February, 2010.

CANADA, ALBERTA, EDMONTON, CITY OF ST. ALBERT, MAIN HOSPITAL, ROOM 14...

Inspector Michael Blaquier was sitting at St. Albert's hospital hallway and he was reading medical report on an accident at Laconbe Lake Park. He couldn't believed at first that Roger had an accident at all, his first assumption was that he was attacked by someone or his fall had been pre-arranged and staged to look like Roger's own mistake. However, there were no grey areas in medical detailed report and it proved that Roger acted as complete moron at the end. He deliberately pushed himself over the edge and end up in coma since November last year.

I am not going to have a chance to chat with him ever again. He can be "veggie" until the end of his life, if his family decides to keep him in this state. Of course, everything depends on the money, as always... New developments on the case linked General Luis MacKenzie permanently to the case, but one of my crucial witnesses managed to put himself in coma, out of my range. Evidences collected were mostly useless without any live witness to support them on a trial in the eyes of the law. Specially, here in Canada, the land of freedom, our native land...

Pager attached to his leather belt beeped once as confirmation of incoming voice message. He dropped medical report on the main front desk and went outside entrance area to the phone boot. He picked up receiver and dialed his phone voice mail box number entering his security pin code. *Click.*

...

"Major, Olivier Marceau is here. Unfortunately, I do not have very good news to tell you. Marlow is dead... In addition, other five operatives from our Ottawa team, as well. Trap did not

work, we have underestimated girl and we paid high price... She is much stronger than we thought, she has multiple powers, more than three as we confirmed so far. Shortly before the trap is going to be completely secure, one of our agents, Killroy was influenced by her powers and he turned against us killing three of our other agents positioned at entrance and ground floor on the site. Two of them, Marlow executed before he killed himself, too. I am going to send you detailed report regarding this in the following days... I have to go now. Just be careful..., and if you get any new info on her, let me now. You have my number."

...

Click.

CHAPTER XIV

Section 6.

WIFE

May, 2010.

SERBIA, BELGRADE VICINITY, TOWN OF MLADENOVAC, NEW SUBURB AREA …

It was warm night, with crescent moonlight printed on the cloudless bright, full stairs sky, around 23:00 hours when Vlado Jovanovich pressed all buzz buttons in front of him except an apartment number 10 marked under the name of Filipovich. Six stores high building was last building in the row at the end of the street, which still did not have finished parking lot and it was part of new build apartment's complex in the town of Mladenovac suburb. All region was peacefully, partially isolated from other segments of inhabitant's sections by large football and basketball fields and semi finished green park area parallel lined up with unfinished part of new Belgrade's highway. Some angry voices mixed together with other impolite answers questions and curses came out from interphone speaker as someone in the same time activated electronic circuit and released locked door. Vlado slipped inside before anyone was able to open its window and spotted him outside of the new building entrance. He stayed hidden under ground floor staircase when an upset neighbor from the first floor went downstairs to check door and punish some teenagers for a practical joke, pranks that were very common among today youngsters. Bold middle aged man cursed under his breath as he locked twice front door and returned to his flat slamming an entrance door behind him. Vlado stayed patiently under the stairs for another two-three minutes when hallway lights automatically switched off on his own time interval.

Now, it is time to visit my "dear wife", named Mrs. Slobodanka Jovanovich, who owed me a little more than 20.000 Euros…

Slowly, using weak street light reflection between base levels, counting the stairs connecting mid-levels, orientating through dimness to some extent on passed stair's railing, he advanced towards his final destination on the last sixth floor, residence number 10. He stopped in front of an apartment door and kept his breath in darkness, as he was listening sounds behind neighboring door.

Someone is fucking neighbor's wife, he gets lucky same as I am going to become tonight with "mine"! Honey, I am home!

CHAPTER XV

Section 1.

TO

June, 1992.

BOSNIA AND HERZEGOVINA, MUNICIPALITIES OF KONJIC, TOWN OF KALINOVIK, PRISONER'S CAMP, DETENTION UNIT KALINOVIK... CODE NAME – "EMINA"(Modern Day – Kalinovik, Entity of Republika Srpska, Bosnia and Herzegovina)

...

The hardest time for me is the night, when I am again alone; I closed my eyes and pictures of hell surfaced in my brain. During the day, I stayed focused on some other things, but with the night hard memories, heavy thoughts and painful memories were running in circles through my brain. I am starting to lose my mind in them; they were following me through my dreams, when I am awake, when I lay down in my bed, anytime when I am alone. In one moment, I am back there in concentration camp, I can see the wire fence, I can smell Chetniks sweat, his beard. I can see their faces again and in the next moment I am running again through the minefield, barefooted; listening bullets buzz around my legs and body, I heard their laughing in the background when they pushed us into the field. I woke up bathed in my own sweat, lying in the bed collecting my thoughts after the screams of raped children, girls, my daughter Emina filled my ears. What a horrible pain tortured me and what are my tears for? There is no medicine that can heal my wounds, there was not anything that can help to ease the pain, and nothing exists that can help me in these moments... Concentration camp "Kalinovik" where I was imprisoned with my four children with approximately 800 other women and children looked like the end of the world place for all of us there. Terror, hunger, tears, fear and misery become unbearable with arrival of Pero Elez and his Chetniks group to the camp. They would come any time during the day, pull out women, first younger, like me, then later older, above 60 – 70 years old, too. They would come and pick up like on the market:

'You, this one, that one, you,… you ,too…'

Some of them disappeared completely and we would never see them again, but most of them they would be brought back next morning, or the following night, chosen again and again after some time. I have recognized between them some of my neighbors, like Zoran Susica and others, but the worst was when Dragan Lakovic was on the duty. They started with me the following night after they brought me to one of the rooms nearby; they pushed me to the floor, ripped off my clothes. I started kick them with my legs and my hands, but there were three of them at first, they hit me with their boots and hands at first then they threatened me with knifes and their guns, whispering:

'We are going to kill your children first, if you struggle…' 'You are going to bear a little Serbian, Turkish woman…' 'I will cut their throats and drink their blood woman…'

There after these words my struggles, my fight stopped… There were no words to describe all my pain, shame, fear and humiliation that I have felt after they gang bang me one after another, third one… They smelled on Rakia, their mouths were full of it, their stinking armpits, stained clothes, dirty hands and unwashed bodies were on me, inside me, around me all the time. Hard floor's dirt under my naked body rubbed my back, hips, spine and my hair, glued to my sweated boy, mixed with the air that smelled on urine, blood and male semen brought nausea through me, but they did not stop it, they continued hitting me with their hands all over my body and face. I remember that they drag me back to the main camp hall and they left me there in front of everybody, tortured I did not have strength to move. I did not have wished to look at their faces and through my half closed eyes, I saw that others turned their heads and dropped their necks down at their site of me. I felt someone's hands on my bruised body, carried me to the hard concrete floor after some time they covered me with some cloth and I have collapsed into darkness. I woke up surrounded by my children, Esma, Emina, my daughters and my sons, Adil and Edin. I saw their eyes; they stared at me without the words. They knew everything…

'Why? Why our children? Leave them alone! If you want to rape, rape me, rape us, please, leave them alone...'

I begged them and yelled at them, but the other women hold me on the ground when I trashed and kicked them in my useless attempt to free. They hold me...

"They will kill you..." "They are going to kill them, too..." "You cannot do anything..."

One night they came for my Emina, my child... She was only eleven years old...

I couldn't do anything... I just watched when they took her... My heart was broken in pieces, my never - healed wound opened... Just imagine how mother can stand the pain of the fact that her child is going to be mutilated emotionally and raped, only pain, unspeakable pain is the only feeling that was left inside my soul and nothing else surfaced my mind at that moment. Time between was never ending. I have heard her scream through the night. My head was between my knees and I have covered my ears with my palms, so I cannot hear screams of my daughter through that the worst night of my life. Some of the girls were so young that they couldn't comprehend in their minds what was happening with them. I took my son Adil and hugged him closer to my breasts, hold him there and I cried...I cried endlessly through that time and I thought that my heart would break from the pain. I had feeling that I am going to die from it. After couple of hours later, they brought our children back, so we can continue with our unspoken screams on and on through other following nights. After that night, they collected them many nights after that and my Emina never spoke again after that. She took her staffed doggy toy in her arms, wrapped her tiny arms around him and she was sitting in her corner looking somewhere and nowhere in the same time, for hours without any words coming from her. She kept her pain, her secrets and her fear between them, everything stayed with her and her imaginary friend dog. One night, I have overheard her that she was whispering to her toy:

'Only You my little dog, only You have right to touch me. Never ever again, any man will touch me...'

...

It is very hard today to look on our beautiful city of Sarajevo after all these horrible years. How I can enjoy this life and live the life when you are only 34 years old, but you feel like 64? All beauty of our Bosnia is around us, but my soul was lost somewhere behind, my wounded body and spirit stayed locked forever inside my Emina's nightmare where she lost her youth, childhood, she was left only with her disfigured soul trapped forever inside. One day when we start our new life in America, maybe her wounds will healed by additional time and distance. I live for that moment, to see honest smile on her face, again, after all these years, to see sparks in her eyes, light in her pupils, again... Maybe... Perhaps... Maybe... I hope that these words and my testimony will help me and all people like me to continue with their lives. Only God is going to be rightfully judge to all of them and to us all, good and bad people together.

...

Michelle put partially highlighted, sticker marked, stapled pages back inside its green file cover and closed her eyes for a brief moment. Her hands trembled when she touched her burning face. She felt overwhelmed by incoming emotions. She took deep breath to calm herself, but she was not able to control tears that were filling her eyes. She buried her face in her trembling hands and her shoulders shuddered under released sentimental pressure that burned inside her heart for all these years. For the first time in her life, she cried without any sound. Through her brain, only one thought scorching its path which filled emptiness with unbearable pain:

Baby... My baby... Oh, my dear little baby girl... Where are you now...?

CHAPTER XV

Section 2.

SHUT UP

February, 1999.

UNITED STATES OF AMERICA, CALIFORNIA, LOS ANGELES, 140 NORTH LA STREET, THE MAIN DISTRICT POLICE DEPARTMENT, CHIEF'S DETECTIVES OFFICE…

…

Since I have come back to L. A. everything seemed to be less and less important to me. The whole thing about the job, related to it, floated at the edge of my brain, as I did not belong here anymore, my concentration dropped together with my interest to follow my regular daily tasks, all of them reached the dead end. So, this supposed to be - the thing, what they called love…

Detective Marc Arsenault shuffled through the papers on his desk, but he did not see them at all. Mechanically he stashed them and rearranged them in small piles in front of him as he was putting things together and cleaning his old overburden desk.

I missed her more than anything… It is a very strange feeling, it's like I haven't live at all before I met her…

His office phone ringed three times in a row, before he realized that some sound filled his office space, where the buzzing noise is coming from. He watched perplexed as his right hand, on his own, pick up the handset, stopped the buzz and put telephone receiver beside his ear.

'Hello? Good Morning! Is this Chief's detective office in central police department?'

What kind of accent was that? What do you mean by "good morning", it is a late evening now!?

'Yes…, Yes it is…'

Focus yourself!

'Is this Chief Detective Mister Marc Arsenault speaking?'

Put yourself together, man!

'Yes…, yes, I am speaking.'

It is a long distance call…

'Hello! My name is Christoph Erber, Chief Fusion Cell of EUROPOL JIT (Joint Investigation Team) Division from Belgium. I am assigned to HVT (High Value Target) Unit at The Hague, Netherlands as Coordination Officer between WCO (World Customs Organization), Europol and Interpol international Agencies and I have an updates on some cases partly assigned to you and an individual's that was the main suspects in them….'

I should be impressed by all that?

'Yes, please continue, I am listening.'

'After we initiated comprehensive search on 18 premises in more than 6 countries, a joint operation focusing on the organized crime group that was led by international terrorist group named "The Black Hand", we tackled their network which has led to arrest of 126 individuals. During the operation our section provided 13 analytical reports and one specialist report to Europol and Interpol investigators…'

Are you ever going to finish your sentence?

'Sir, I am sorry to interrupt you, but I really had a bad day today and I am in the middle of something at the moment, so could you please cut the chase and give me a brief report and results of it?'

The man on the other end of phone line stopped his briefing evidently surprised and confused for some time, by Marc's sharp interruption and his open spiky comment.

Two seconds passed before Arsenault tried to recover awkward situation made by his blunt response.

'Could you please, send me an e-mail regarding your detailed investigation through our crypto cell secured channels, so I would be able to see summary of reports?'

Shit, Why I couldn't keep my mouth shut!?

'Well…, I can do that…'

It is obvious that I am an idiot and an asshole, too!

'And do not worry about size of an attachments file…, I am going speak with our Sys Admin to increase my Mail Box and to adjust filtering option on our Firewall before you send me the data…'

Just keep running on and digging your own grave moron!

'That would not be necessary; I will zip the file…'

'I really appreciate everything you have done so far, so allowed me to give you my office e-mail address and just in a case that you need, my private home e-mail address as well…'

Oh, for God's sake, just shut up you imbecile!

…

CHAPTER XV

Section 3.

ENTRAPMENT

January, 1999.

CROATIA, DALMATIAN COAST, CITY OF SPLIT, SAINT THEODOR – THE CHURCH OF OUR LADY, BELL TOWER…

Lionel Willburn crouched well hidden behind one millennium old stone - wall, heard as the last member of his "A" team screamed from the darkness and fired two shots from his Uzi in an attempt to save his life. Silence covered the church area with its wide blanket made of fear and desperation patches. He surveyed his parameter around him one more time before he put night vision goggles above his face. The green covered image appeared in front of his pupils, already irritated by pitch-black gloom, removing spots of nonexistent lights at the edge of his mental picture. He adjusted sharpness and focus of the lenses before he moved in the direction of squared set of steps that were only available path to upper levels of church's tower. Entrapment had been well prepared and organized for an incoming "Invisible Man", movement sensors arranged around structure's parameter, laser beamed detection points targeted all entrance and exit points of the area, traps were activated prior to assignment and agents were unmovable, assigned on their posts covering all main positions. Five of them, four agents and him should be more than enough to catch or eliminate any treats, but we did not expected third party involvements and we had overestimated our foe definitely. Lionel adjusted himself on small landing above first ten steps of tight and narrow stairs, which were like a spiral curved around broad pillar that supported upper clock tower. He heard only his breathing as he inhaled air filled with dust and musky smell of blood. Night vision goggles did not revealed anyone around, in front of him, and anything movable in the marginal area of his vision. Nothing was unusual as he peered around bent wall behind his back as well. He tried to steady himself and get a better position before an enemy approach. Willburn removed earpiece which had been totally useless from the beginning, while he recollected previous events, how everything started on the wrong foot tonight...

At first, I thought those other two thugs that showed up at main entrance where part of the same team; an "Invisible Man's" team, brought here as support and make some decoy for him. Nevertheless, since they had positioned themselves inside the church in similar manner and they situated themselves far from an entrance, as they were expecting arrival of somebody else, I figured out that they were hunting the same individual as we. Both of them were blonde, big, wide, pumped with steroids and iron, totally opposite light skin colored from locals, out of space and time, visible from the moon and it did not bother them at all, as they didn't care. Confirmation of an additional two of them, with same physical features as clone brothers, located outside the church, at surrounding square vicinity came through my earpiece bug. Sniper positioned on the highest elevated spot covered them immediately and I ordered him to be on standby and wait his orders. Three of us were already inside, one mingled between small group of tourist – last visitors, one hidden inside confession box and one positioned in the middle, undercover dressed as a priest in black. I was waiting in one of niches at the rear end of small church altar, behind large thick curtain and the last one was on the top of the church bell tower, at the very end of these same stairs, he was surveying all area of our responsibility. Scrambled communications channel died under strong unknown blockage, an interferences which started immediately after an "indivisible one" arrived. He materialized himself from thin air, upstairs in the church tower and they've got positive confirmation when an agent sited there yelled alarmed, surprised and dead in the same time when his body plummeted from the balcony above. His body landed on an inner courtyard's white cobalt stone spraying its surface with his blood. Both new arrived "blondes" pull out their pieces together simultaneously after we lost our first agent, even I gave immediate order to all "A" team members to not response, rock & roll started as first shot came from upstairs. Actually, I realized that it wasn't aimed to nobody and the main purpose was to initiate, provoke others to take an action in already too long, stretched nerves situation.

"Invisible One" made correct initial move on chessboard, so we have lost advantage in the game, before it started at all. House of worship's real visitors panicked for real, as "our" priest shot one of "blondes" in the neck, one nearer to him in close range. The other "blonde" fired in priest's direction and succeed only to kill one of tourists nearby; female in an orange dress, before our second agent from tourist group eliminated him with two shots, one in a chest and second in the head. Screams resonance through church as another two shots from above ended in priests back and he fell behind tourist's stampede that washed out our agent between them. I got out from niche as two things happened in the same time, first electricity went out and all church dropped into the black hole, second thing, about two seconds after, gunshots from outside echoed through an open cathedral door. An additional panic yells and shooting spread through external darkness. The rest of our team remotely continued with their private party business with the rest of "blondes". Nothing moved as I advanced diagonally, blindly through the dark, on the way to stairs located on the opposite side. I tripped over overturned wooden bench and that dislocated object saved my life. I felt at first, then I heard two "Zing – Zing" that flew beside me and they ended somewhere on the opposite wall. I used initial motion of my body and rolled sideways twice across my left shoulder gaining speed as I stayed low and covered more space. I end up lying beside an old stone sarcophagus of some unknown church's saint who temporary protected me.

Silencer attached to "Invisible One's" weapon was so smooth and soundless that only groans from our third agent, after he revealed himself making unnecessary noise, inside confession box authenticated that he is dead. Three thuds, "thud – thud – thud", on the surface of wooden wall confirmed it definitely. Last agent managed to get on his feet, somewhere close to exit chapel's door and he made an effort of lunatic, as I heard his desperate frenzy challenge to our invisible opponent.

'Come on, you fuck…!'

CHAPTER XV

Section 4.

FEAVER

December, 1886.

UNITED STATES, NEW YORK, NEW YORK CITY, BRONX, THIRD AVENUE...

...

NIKO, STAYED WITH ME.

'He's going to fain't it again!'

The bulging eyes on red capillary face with missing upper front four teeth produced ugly but honest smile to him, followed with bad breath smell of mixed chewing tobacco and cheap brandy.

Who is going to faint again?

Rough and large handgrip landed on his left bony shoulder as support and it shook Tesla's posture after every day's 14 hours of hard labor work of digging trenches.

What they are going to do with me?

DO NOT GO.

His hands half frozen and both his feet numb from frostbites were more like hard wooden sticks unable to bend, without flexibility to support him on his traitorous walk upstairs to his small room in the attic. Without his colleague's help, he wouldn't be able to reach it.

Why I do not feel my legs anymore?

George Everett, an Irish descendent, nicknamed "Sponge", by his amazing ability to drink large amounts of alcohol in a short period of time, was holding – carrying him like a baby through tight, dark corridor.

Did I fell inside the trench again?

Behind him, Giovanni Brielle, an Italian immigrant, fresh from Sicily, was holding Tesla's worn out shoes soaked with snow in his left hand, mumbling something to himself on Italian language like: miseria…, finito…, la furca…(sadness…, end…, the grave…).

Tesla plunged through an endless pit of nothing. The wind in his ears screeched as he hollowly fell into everlasting darkness.

DO NOT LEAVE ME, MY BROTHER.

'I t'ink 'iz goin'g to die!... mortale (deadly)… 'is not lookin' good anymore!'

Giovanni added and put his middle finger, inside the hole of Tesla's left shoe, which perfectly sealed it.

Did I have one of my "blackouts" as usually?

'Oh, forr God's sak'e, shut' p your pie hole and open the dam'n doorr at once!'

"Sponge" yelled on him, panting and puffing in the same time at Tesla's exposed neck.

I AM HERE FOR YOU.

Italian produced the key from his left pants pocket and unlocked the door making an additional comment:

Si,… Si,… 'iz not to live t'is day,… Domani… (Tomorrow…).

'Keep them ope'n and stay overr – therre!'

Where are we going?

George hauled Tesla over his right shoulder inside the room.

I AM COMING NIKO.

'Giovanni, put his shoes down forr luv'e of God!'

Who is talking?!

"Sponge" dropped thin blanket across stretched Tesla's body on the bed and he wiped sweat from his forehead with his right jacket sleeve.

'It' iz very strange here…, some forza invisibile… (Invisible force…)'

'Just get out ov herre, you crazy motherr - fuckerr!'

Who is calling me?!

George grabbed Giovanni's right hand and dragged him out of the room. He slammed door behind them, smacked back of the head of his partner with his left open hand and said:

'Now, we hav' to call Mr. Brrown and tell 'im wha't happen' herre! Nikola is verry sick…'

NIKO, DO NOT WORRY, I AM HERE!

As both of men descend to the lower floor level, they failed to see formation of luminosity of purple belt light under the door.

CHAPTER XV

Section 5.

MEETING

February, 2010.

UNITED STATES OF AMERICA, WASHINGTON, DC, WASHINGTON, "BIG BROTHER" OFFICE…

Beth did not like the man on the other end of mahogany table at all from the beginning, but an amount of money inside small "Samsonite's" leather pouch, placed in front of her on the table, just few centimeters out of her left hand reach, made it bearable at the present.

'Well, as you already know my client insisted that you personally deliver an artifact here. That is the main reason for this unscheduled meeting between us and another reason was, beside the fact that you preferred cash payment instead of wire transfer, to make sure that no one will witness this event except two of us. Am I right?!'

Totally grey haired head of late 70-s old man did not turn in her direction to acknowledge her present during their initial introductions; even after they continued their conversation, he kept his back to her since she entered his office on twenty - third floor of the building.

'You do not have to answer anything, which has been obvious, and my client completely understands your wish for privacy and respects your confidentiality in these matters. Please put the gemstone beside the leather pouch on the table, so we can exchange our valuables openly and evenly.'

She pulled out small red velvet bag, containing the Black Stone, tied around her neck, hidden by her wide black woolen scarf and she placed it on the table, as the old man requested.

'Good, now Miss… Beth?, if you allowed me to call you by your first name, like that informally? If that is your real first name?!'

What the fuck you are talking about?

Beth's stomach turned inside out under suddenly provoked pain deep down. She tried to calm down after her alarmed body screamed for an action, her right arm instinctively tried to reach her gun under her left armpit, the pistol removed by two bodyguards in front of the office door. She still had metal hairpin attached to the back of her skull, holding her hair on, as the last resource of defense. She managed to answer calmly, but not swiftly as before:

'Yes,… Please, feel free to call me…, Beth. After all, I preferred an informal conversation between us…'

As the old man used already well-prepared and staged situation, he turned swiftly on his heel and faced partially astonished Beth, with his blue-steeled cold stare. He pierced her with his eyes enjoying the split second of her unexpected emotional outburst betrayed by her right arm grip on wooden armchair.

'Or, should I call you Bella?!'

In that instant Beth recognized that, the game is over and she reacted unrestrained knowing that she does not have anything else to loose, except her life. She reached for metal hairpin oiled by neurological toxin that would paralyze younger man right away, but probably would kill the older one as that one in front of her. Her right hand was reaching half away above the table, aimed to the old man's unprotected neck, when a hard kick from a side connected to the nerve inside her elbow, so the pin instantly fell from her numb arm.

"Eiiiiaaaahhhh…!"

The Japanese man appeared from nowhere beside her right side and pinned her on the edge of the table, kicking her left knee simultaneously and holding her bended left hand across her back in a firm grip by his bony hand. One twist of his hand attached to her crocked wrist produced cracking sound and unbearable pain down through her arm to her left shoulder. She screamed again as pain increased her voice additionally by blind rage.

'Kintaro! Let her breathe for time being!'

Japanese that smelled on fresh lemon soap effortlessly liberated her hand a little, but kept her in his grasp diagonally over the desk edge. Breath from her mouth moisturized mahogany surface as she ravenously grasped for it.

'Listen now very carefully…, Bella, Beth or whoever you are, you are going to do something for us, you are going to provide some other things free of charge, which we require urgently. If you think to play some double game with us, Kintaro will rip-off you arm at first together with all other parts of your body, too…'

CHAPTER XV

Section 6.

CREATURE

December, 1998.

MONTENEGRO, THE DURMITOR NATIONAL PARK, MOUNTAIN OF DURMITOR, CANYON OF TARA RIVER, "ZMAJEVA PECINA" ("DRAGON'S CAVE") AREA, HIDDEN PART OF THE CAVE...

She examined the wound on her right upper thigh and confirmed that bullet hit the charging metal belt at her waist at first and then ricochets over to her leg. Skin surface ripped off together with part thigh muscle were artificially damaged moreover they looked much worse due to spilled blood, but no real harm had be done. Another thing that concerned her more than anything else was a fact that her "shield" stopped working immediately when she entered into the cave, which meant that some sort of "blocker" prevented it. In addition, her "beam" discontinued to emit signal of its existence, beside actuality that she was not out of its range, which confirmed an energy field activity in neighborhood. She applied healing patch to her wound, she collected Simon's Berretta with an additional magazine of bullets together with primeval strange curved blade and attached both of them on her back.

I have to be more careful with the other two of them. An American was good..., he nearly got me, and if I hadn't detected him on ultra violet range in a nick of time I would be there lying in the dust, instead of him...

Simon's splattered blood on her white clothes produced permanent stained marks, so since her protection gear is not working either and she was too noticeable in the dark, she stripped off her white clothes and as snake's discarded skin, she left it behind. Her dark brown colored, positively polarized heated suit gave her more freedom of movement, protection to cold temperature inside and combined safety of darkness with its functionality. Flickering lines on her charger indicated that she could use her "ion – weapon" two more times. She made few meters of slow progress in the course of narrow hallway, when female cry of horror echoed through cavern.

"AAAAAARRRRRRRGGGGGGGGHHHHHHH!!!"

She continued her steady, careful pace all the way through access strip with prepared Berretta in her right hand. She decided to keep her specialized advanced technical weapon as a back up in a case of an emergency. She reached nearly the end of it, when she stumbled on Jackie's bloody gray jacket on dusty floor. Three large ripped lines across the back and torn off left sleeve of the jacket stained with blood were everything left from her.

No dragged marks on the floor…, Like she'd been grabbed and lifted in the air…

Entrance of inner part of the cave was oval shaped and an empty shelled wide. It reminded her on Greek's burial chamber named "tholoi" dome outlined tomb, like a large toothless mouth. Illuminated by glare from the top, stalactites looked like giant monster's saliva crusted inside its enormous jaws. She slithered beside left pillar carefully sliding down the hall, keeping her back close to rough shell of the inner wall.

Low humming sound is coming from black smooth block of stone in the middle of it.

Surface protected by some kind of shielded glistening cover was glimmering under an artificial light from above. It reassembled generator or power charging box. There was polished object levitating in the middle air above the stone. It resembled mask, gold plated disk, smooth on surface and gold colored.

Everything staged in advance, very alluring, probably deadly too, perfect trap…

She did not see anywhere their leader Kirk nearby; all other parts of the cave covered in dimness were just perfect spots for lurking, sneaky bastard as he was. Something moved on top of her head, dark shadow soundlessly detached itself from above and dropped directly on her. She pushed with her legs twisting her upper body sideways parallel to the wall, as she gained additional four centimetres closer to its surface. That was all advantage position that she made and time that she got before human body enclosed with her partially extended right hand. Berretta fell from her right hand as heavy bloody torso landed on it, moderately bounced down on both her legs, knocking off her to the wall and she scrapped back of her skull down an irregular partition in the background. Metallic thud of her lost weapon resonance through the cave as warm salty liquid splashed on her face, breasts and legs.

What a hell was that…?

Shredded unrecognizable female body, gory straps of skin with gridded exposed white bones underneath and decapitated stump of neck, heedlessly rested beside her.

Breathless, shocked and wordless she caught glimpse of something large above her. Suddenly, she felt that coldness was emanating from The Being. Steamed breath came out from her open mouth. Terror of unexplained clenched her heart, unreasonable horror swelled in her brain and she felt some archaic fear inside her soul, as if all her primordial terrors multiplied themselves at once. She gazed up, against her will, and saw something dark grey, with folded wings in the background, distorted image at the edges, as The Being was completely unsubstantial, transparent in one second and fully flesh and bone, materialized in another second. Instead of head only two bright red almonds shaped pulsing, radiated eyes floated between its massive shoulders, eyes that were collecting her energy, soul and life in the same time, eyes which were deep inside her brain feeding on her knowledge and memories. Accessing one of her last thoughts, she bent her left hand, activated "ion – weapon", as bluish energy whip closed on the target, screeching sound filled the cave.

"Crrrreeeeeiiiihhhhaaaaggggg!!!!"

Her left hand without sensation collapsed, frozen breath exhaled against her numb lips and she fell through ice-covered river to the dark blue grave underneath.

CHAPTER XVI

Section 1.

TIC – TAC

February, 1999.

CANADA, ONTARIO, TORONTO, TORONTO POLICE STATION, DISTRICT SOUTH,

CHIEF'S OFFICE...

...

'Constable Bamford!'

The voice of the Chief Investigator Todd Stamford brought her back to reality for a second time

this morning.

'What happened back there?'

His face emerged from foggy background image of snow covered buildings near their police

station headquarter, which dissolved in smoke as she focused on his question.

'Sir, I sincerely don't know. Things get out of control.'

She was completely aware the their cover up operation had been gone for good, when their

suspect recognized the trap and run free and wild across casino parking lot in direction of his

previously parked van.

'How come he figured out there was a trap over there, so quickly that somebody did not notice

anything suspicious before in his behavior?'

'That was the question I was asking myself, for the last two hours, the question worth one million

for sure.'

'I really do not know. He just dropped there out of blue. One second nothing happened and he

was walking right into it, in the next one he stopped there as he hit some invisible wall in front of

him and acted weird and unpredictable...'

Todd's got facial expression of annoyed child, his cheeks colored circularly red like he hold his breath for too long.

'Hmmm..., that is not an answer, I was expecting from you Constable Bamford! Results! I want some results!'

Michelle hardly suppressed smile in the corner of her full lips, as she concentrated again on steamed window behind Todd's back, decorated with winter's frozen calligraphic art.

'Sir, may I said something..., Actually, may I make some suggestion which is going to sound weird to you at first, but I think it is worth to try...'

Stamford leaned back in his chair following her gaze across his left shoulder.

'Yes... Speak up!'

She nodded with her head and continued.

'Since we track down his movements around our province of Ontario for last month and a half, and he used the same vehicle all the time, I think we are able to pinpoint approximately location of residence, which would be somewhere between Oshawa and Kingston. Eyewitnesses reported the same truck descriptions associated with the driver who fits our photo robot sketch, so we can assume that he is not going to change his vehicle and his habits in the near future. Also, as he was spotted around gambling private clubs and casinos we can drop bait on him...'

Stamford rolled back his chair close to the edge of his desk anxiously and asked.

'What have you in mind?'

Michelle flashed on him thin smile.

'Casino Lottery ticket.'

Stamford raised his grayish eyebrows.

'What?'

Her stretched mouth went back to normal.

'Simple and effective. We are going to produce fake lottery ticket winner. Whoever owns the truck will come to us to pick up his prize - New GMC Pick - Up! Full tank fueled with all accessories!'

Todd pick up plastic package of freshly opened Tic - Tac and dropped two of them in his right palm.

'Not bad idea at all, if it is going to work...'

He put them in his mouth and played with them with a tongue for some time, as he was offering some to Michelle.

'It will work... No, thank you... Anything, which was given without tax and delivered for free in our society, becomes the main object of our interest, an open source for human greed.'

She caught approval to continue in a blink of his eyes.

'He's killer's first associate and our only link to him at the moment. Every crime scene location has been connected with this man, actually with his vehicle.'

Todd stopped chewing and pushed Tic - Tac's under his tongue for later. He reminded her on light version of Scotsman as he pronounced the sentence.

'Yes-h that's-h correct. He is-h like "Robin" - wonder-r boy, the "Bat – Man's" right hand helper-r...'

She couldn't hide her smile this time.

'We had luck with the snitch who was arrested prior to the previous drug related case; he gave us crucial piece of information's about him as our main suspect. Other surveillance tapes from sites helped us to track registered truck and his owner. After that, all pieces fell together without the problem...'

Michelle watched how Todd's face suddenly took surprised man expression and he partially opened his mouth like he is going to say something very important to her.

'Chief...?'

Nothing came out. No sound from him. He stayed frozen in the middle of it. Red circles, so characteristic for him, burst above his cheeks and painted all his face.

'Sir?!'

Purple color under his bulging eyes surfaced on his lips as well. He jumped from his chair desperately grabbing the edge of his working desk with both hands. Wheezing sound of punctured flat tire came from him.

'Hhhhhh...eeeeeee...iiiii...'

Michelle followed her chief's movements simultaneously kicking her chair aside. She closed the space between them in two long strides beside office desk.

'Todd!'

She kicked him hard across his back between his shoulders with her open hand. He swayed a little forward above the table. The sound coming from him stopped and switched to deep grunt.

'You are going to choke yourself!'

She screamed and grabbed him from the back, hugging him across his chest. She didn't have strength to lift him, but she pressed hard on his solar plexus together with both fists. She managed to shake his upper part of the body, as she gave three strong pulls to his stomach.

'LET - GO!'

She hung on his back giving him another pull – punch across his lungs this time. Another grunt surfaced on Todd's mouth and he straightened up, become rigid inside Michelle's bear hug. She struggle to stay on her feet, when all weight of his body leaned on her, and her grip loosened a bit in the same time as he released an additional support of his hands from office desk.

'LET...GO!?'

She was pushing one more time staying on the top of her toes in one second and then in the next one, he dragged her with his 97 kilograms of his body mass back to his desk.

'TODD?!'

CHAPTER XVI

Section 2.

FREE

March, 1999.

UNITED STATES OF AMERICA, CALIFORNIA, LOS ANGELES, SOUTH SIDE BOULEVARD...

Girl with a light brown hair crossed double lined Street Boulevard without looking left or right for an incoming traffic, or following the signs and automatic signalling sounds on displayed traffic lights. She did not care anymore for anything on this world, she was "high" on cocaine all last night and the drug hold her in its grasp even now on the late morning hours. Flippantly mood did not leave her yet, as she felt invincible and fearless, when she run through two – way, double line traffic jam in the middle of lunch hour brake and against all odds, nobody hit her with his car. Blown horns and yelled curses followed her on suicidal diagonal path across car's packed auto lines in both directions. She laughed at them, to all of them and to the world around! Milena just had a haircut and she dyed her natural blonde hair, so she was certain that her brother Stevan would like it now, if he ever saw her again in his miserable life. She made decision to left their home two weeks ago, but she made her move two nights ago, after her brother went outside to the city together with her father. As usual, both of them disappeared without any notice, without word, no message or explanations to their mother or her. Their reasons were known only to them, and she tried once to find out where were heading for, so she secretly followed them, but she managed to track them only to the subway station entrance. Her brother was waiting there and he delivered their father personal reminder, very short message to her. He viciously beat her with an electrical cord, three centimetres thick in diameter, approximately one meter long, doubled with an iron wire on the edge, covered by thick black rubber. She was eleven years old in that time and she still have nasty scars on her back and her upper thighs from that time, today seven years after.

It took one month of recovery, fifteen days in a private clinic and another fifteen at their new home, so only after that period of revitalization, she was able to properly sit in the chair and to continue her regularly school classes. She never ever asked them anything at all. Since then, her brother Stevan, who was eight years older, started to have a sex with her, at first she was able to satisfy his sexual urge only orally, but as the time passed, he insisted on anal sex too. She bled painfully at first, until she begged him to start using some lubricant, to which he didn't voluntary agree and initially declined. Later on, she learned to substitute his rough, sometimes an atrocious necessities with occasionally pleasurable, mild and gentle intercourses, but every time after he spend couple days of his free time with their father, on their mystery trips, he would become the same as earlier time, crueler even more, brutal and much worse than before... After the choking episode in December last year, when he already strangled her during the sex, once he performed PCR, during and following her reanimation process, increasable fear for her life reached the same level as severe fear of him in her soul. Two weeks previously, he crossed from aggressive and forceful over to vicious and sadistic sex act, as he tied her up to concrete polls inside rented garage, and he used an enormous oversized dildo on her anus and vagina for more than two hours without any lubricant. She submitted to his wishes for the last time as he urinated on her face forcing her to drink it together with his sperm. Two days ago, she collected his stashed drug money, around 20.000 dollars in cash together with 400 grams of cocaine, as compensation for everything that he owed her, and she hitchhiked two long haul trailers heading up on highways to the north, with her final unspecified destination somewhere in Canada. Finally, she had enough money to gain control of her life again and to start her new life on her own up there. Again, she had a purpose in life, another chance to start from the scratch. Warm sensation came from her womb spreading through her body when she thought about it. She laughed freely and honestly for the first time in years remembering widely used word of mouth that described one thing characteristic for Canadians.

"Welcome to Canada, eh?"

CHAPTER XVI

Section 3.

RECORD

November, 1989.

NORTH AMERICA, CANADA, ONTARIO, OTTAWA AREA, TOWN OF CARP, USA

DEPARTMENT OF DEFENCE PROJECT "AURORA BOREALIS"…

Extreme energy blast initiated through ionosphere and transported over Ottawa region, was

activating an electromagnetic shield roughly 60 meters in diameter. Silver color of it appeared as

pulsing liquid metallic shape floating in the mid – air above the ground near West Carleton, on a

top of Carp town and it was generating cold fusion radiation. Canadian military radar nearby

spotted it and alarm went on through their bases. Soundlessly, it stabilized itself 400 meters

beyond an open field spinning energized ion particles from an open air to the hard ground, and to

Maurice Oeschler, who were sitting outside his house on the porch, it looked like aircraft build

from a matrixes – dielectric magnesium alloy.

'Ssshi-T, Shhh-IT, SHIT - SHIT!'

Maurice jumped from his favorite rocking chair and almost ripped off his pants across his

overweight ass, as one of his back pockets flapped behind him as bluish small flag, when he

reached an entry and slammed his entrance flap screen door. Grounding point where free energy

flare had been connected to, scorched land surface burning everything that was touched by ions

burst, melting stones, dirt, grass and ground into compacted mass of swirling red and blue pool of

lava. The whole lot was moving in spiral magnetic field, together with centrifugal force created

around its epicenter. Lightning without thunder spread from it, as charged tentacles of power

were tearing atmosphere, formed cloud of liveliness in the area. Maurice emerged from its house

panting and puffing from his mouth, smeared saliva formed white circle around his lips, and he

swayed a little before he stabilized his Sony camcorder between his pudgy trembling fingers. He zoom his camera in direction of pulsing mass in front of him. He was preoccupied making an evidence of unprecedented event to realize that something strange is happening to him, too. Genetic changes through his body started in the same second as he witnessed environmental transformations, so mutation on his muscle and bone tissue become visible to him as he lost a grip on camcorder in front of his metamorphosed face. Belt that hold his Sony camera on his wrist snapped under his oversized, thick, unrecognizable swallowed hand and camcorder fell on soft cushion of his beloved chair. Tape was on; it was recording last 6 minutes of his life as a human being.

CHAPTER XVI

Section 4.

EUROPEAN

October, 1887.

UNITED STATES, NEW YORK, NEW YORK CITY, ASTOR HOUSE HOTEL, THIRD FLOOR...

She entered the building through an emergency fire door exit. To unlock simple door lock like that with improvised tool was minor task problem, the real problem for her is to convince the man that he needs help from her and that she has solution to his financial problems as well. The man was well known to his neighbors as very stubborn person, a little off the track for average American, person unusually tall, suspiciously clean behaviors, almost dangerously quiet and bizarrely well dressed, too European – classy outfit for a low class gentleman. The truth was that she desperately needed him.

He held the key, no – he was the key that can open secret door to her wildest dreams, light the path on her unsuccessful experiments make the final test... He is the only person on this world that was able to understand her. That understands her thirst for knowledge.

She would be able to unlock entrance door of his apartment without any effort, instead she knocked lightly on the door in front of her. After second knock, she heard incoming steps from inside, shuffling clothing noise and then everything stopped. The man on the other side of the door just stayed there for another 60 to 70 seconds without any movement. He couldn't see her through the full closed door, but she had a strange feeling of been watched and examined in the same time. She became uncomfortable, partially scared during the time off, by irritating silence and stretched seconds. At last, she heard lock clicking racket and secured door - chain clatter. The door went open with nobody inside the frame. Light was coming from the kitchen mostly and in partially visible living room only one bulb was on, one that was part of lamp positioned on the edge, in front of half open slide – window. She was standing at door's perimeter unsure what to do next, when she heard the voice from inside:

'Come inside girl, I am here behind the door in the first chair on the right. Please, close the door after you enter and do not switch on the light. Don't be afraid…'

How he knew that I am a woman, when he did not see me, before closed door?

She had male trousers; her long blonde hair hidden under oversized black cap, and upper body was wrapped inside wide pilot's leather jacket as well.

'I am very sorry, but my eyes are sensitive to the light, due to headaches developed for last three days and I do not feel well lately, but these are not the reasons for you to spend the rest of your evening standing there on the entrance of my humble suite. As I said, please come in, and welcome!'

His voice is warm and a little high for a man of his age sounds much younger than it is…

She stepped inside and firmly closed door behind her. On the right side of her, the man was sitting in the high leather chair and he was nothing more than a dark shadow with a grey picture less wall in his background. His silhouette radiated power through its tranquility and his eyes flickered inside the eye sockets of his large skull at this semi dark room. Again, unsettle sensation of been analyzed spread throughout her body and her soul as well.

'Could you please locked it and secured it additionally.'

With delicate motion of his long fingers, he took glass bottle of plain clean water and filled two empty glasses, which were positioned there earlier on the coffee table in front of him.

'And please, have a seat…'

She seated herself on another similar leather chair across him.

'Where are my manners…?! Welcome again and allowed me to introduce myself…, I am Nikola Tesla…'

He stood up in his full height and extended his right hand above the table towards her. She accepted it openly. His grip was firm, hard and very strong, that in one moment she thought that he is going to crush her hand, as her small hand disappeared inside his wide handshake. His palm was hard, cracked with scars, dry blisters and damaged stripes of skin that imprint themselves temporary on her totally opposite, soft, tender and wet palm skin.

'I am sorry, but my hard labor days of digging ditches left some temporary scars on my hands, but I can convince you that they were nothing and not so deep compared to my already healed emotional scars. I am proud by my honest physical, hard working job, as any other low paid labor worker in this country. Survival depends on our adaptation to certain situation in our life. And you are...?!'

'It is my pleasure and honor to meet you finally in person; I am Tanya – Tatiana Cherenkov.'

CHAPTER XVI

Section 5.

CALL

March 2010.

CANADA, ONTARIO, OTTAWA, HULL, BELL PHONE COMPANY, UNREGISTERED MOBILE PHONE NUMBER,…

…

'I did not expect any problems during our package delivery.'

The first voice said.

'And I did not have any either.'

The second one replied.

'How come that be, when I 've got a nasty phone call from D.C., last night about an additional police investigation on the case that was closed fifteen years ago. The case was reopened again by someone.'

An agitated tone of the first one.

'I am not aware of that, sir.'

Annoyance in an answer of the second one.

'Well, maybe you should be more informed prior to take another action against police investigators. And do your homework first.'

A hint of anger underneath.

'I collected necessary info on the main source of it from Toronto's office and...'

Nervously replied replica of fed up man.

'My sources confirmed dual parallel investigation on the same subject. One of them came too close to me. I want you to take care of that. Is that clear?'

He added it as underlined threat.

'Yes, sir! I will take care of our contra measures immediately!'

This worked perfectly on the other side.

'The woman will be your priority, as she is the one who has more connections and resources to do more harm than the man. Make it happen to look like an accident, nothing drastically, simple and clean, yes?'

Finally,... Now we are talking about the business.

'It is not going to be a problem at all.'

Of course, deal is done!

'The man is going to be blind and deaf without her. Do not proceed with any action against him, till I have more information on him and how much he knows.'

An additional assignment is on horizon, seems to be!

'Consider it done, sir!'

Good puppy! Sit! Sit down!

'Another thing, there is someone else on my trail as well..., but this one is far more dangerous than others.'

Touch of fear between syllabuses.

'I am listening...'

Naturally, you have to, there's no other choice!

'Our military operatives already failed to stop her and I cannot take other risky involvements through their channels this time. Too many questions would be asked from our agency anyway, after last action against her, that shouldn't be answered in near future. Cover up is already initiated.'

Whoa, we have lost some teeth, aren't we?!

'Am I going to hire someone else to do field investigation and footwork on her?'

Too much to handle. Look like...

'No, I already made some contacts overseas regarding that. I gave them your name and your phone number as primary contact.'

This is something new. Worth to investigate further...

'When I can expect their call?'

Sooner will be better...

'Within a month, in meantime stay low and do the job.'

So, I have time to dig up dirt around...

'Yes, sir.'

Confirmative.

'Bonus on top of your regular payment would be delivered prior to an assignment as always.'

Money as always is turning things around.

'Thank you, sir.'

You are welcome!

'Next time use secure line to contact me instead of public one. Only, in an emergency situation use this number. Otherwise, cryptic email will do the work, clear?'

We are now too cautious and suspicious? You should be...

'Yes, sir!'

But, it is too late my friend!

'From next on, do not "sir" me anymore, I was your commander long time ago and I am retired from the army more than two decades now, you can call me by my nick name.'

All habits as always die out hard.

'OK, Mac.'

Okey - dokey!

He removed earplug from his left ear which was attached to digital recording device in his black jacket left inner pocket. Microphone hidden under car's dashboard will remain there until he got his hands on the car again. Anyway, receiver range in his vehicle will lost the signal on next junction, after his target cross the bridge and reach Quebec side over the river. He got recorded proof that General is still an active player in the game.

My trip to Ottawa wasn't fruitless at the end; at least I've collected valuable information about all military personnel involved in their mission assignment at Bosnia during 90'-ies...

Now, he would be able to proceed to the second part of his plan. Blaquier dialed Toronto's private phone number which she left for him as contact number in a case of an emergency.

This is an emergency situation, indeed...

The phone ringed three times in a row and after a pause of two seconds, it switched automatically to the voice mail messaging box.

'Hello..., it's me again..., I am sorry to bother you on your days off, but I have bad news for you...'

CHAPTER XVI

Section 6.

THE BOX

June, 2010.

SERBIA, BELGRADE, DOWNTOWN AREA, CAFETERIA "BOOKSHOP AND TEAROOM"...

Miran took a long gulp of mixed - orange and grapefruit natural fresh juice, chewing slowly fresh fruit meat between his teeth and he enjoyed their taste and texture squashed underneath his tongue. He checked digital clock above the entrance area of new opened cafeteria "Bookshop & Tearoom" which was one of few coffee - patisserie spots, were smoking was not permitted, in this part of the city.

He is late as usually...

As everything else on Balkan, the law existed officially on the paper only, but it was never fully implemented, so non - smoking policy did not work in real life and it will pass years when the rule is going to be enforced in full. Late afternoon sun that was passing through glass window initiated strange shadows in the background of the coffee shop. They reminded Miran on the time when he was a small boy, left by his parents alone in his own room, just before the night time hours, when his mother closed the door after she wished him a good night. Under the moonlight beamed from above, the shadows of his toys would stretched across the floor towards his bed, in a long similar stripes which would be ending somewhere above the edge of his small bed, almost touching his legs under the cover. He had very strange erring filling inside his stomach, that they are going to grab his exposed foot and dragged him back to their dark holes, where they were waiting for him back there whispering in his ear all the scary, ugly things that will happen to him. The fear would grab him across his small chest, holding his heart in its cold grasp, squeezing the life from it, slowly and mercilessly.

It is amazing how lost fears from our childhood stayed with us and they uncontrollably resurfaced from the pit of our souls, when we do not expected them, just to remind us how vulnerable we are, forever attached to these moments from the past...

Miran activated phone screen and entered his four digit access code. "Inbox" message appeared in front of him.

"I stuck in the traffic jam across Branko's bridge over Sava river, please wait for me for another twenty minutes or so... I'll be there... Thanks."

He pressed end button on the phone and dropped it back inside his rucksack. He had a plan to visit flee market in a search for some old comics book that were missing at his private collection, anyway he has to stay longer in the coffee shop, but the scorching heat outside of 34 plus Celsius sounded like a very good reason to stay in cool air conditioned environment.

I hope that information is worthwhile of this lost time of mine. Unless, he was just pulling my tail for fun... Let's go and see what I have got...

Miran carefully peeled away paper from small package which he received early this morning through express post mail. The box inside has been neatly packed and protected by foam balls from accidental damage. He discovered small light weight metal, diamond shaped box between, which looked very old. Signs and letters carved on the top where unfamiliar to him and some of them were partially destroyed by the time and extensive usage.

They are similar to Greek language numerals and letters, or ancient Hebrew inscriptions and signs...

The lid was sliding easily from left to the right. Inside he found two polished black stones wrapped inside plain cotton blue cloth. The gems looked like onyx, semiprecious stones, almond shaped a little bigger then a regular human eye, carved from inside along their edges, with the same type of inscriptions signs and letters.

That was strange... I am not collector of the ancient's artifacts, or precious gem stones... Who and why send me this...

He checked an address of its sender, written at the left corner of the packaged paper, which raised even more questions inside his head, since he never had a contact with National Museum, plus he never knew anybody form there either. His name and address were correct, but somebody made a terrible mistake by sending him this package. For a brief seconds he was turning both stones in his left hand, considering what to do with them.

The best thing would be to return them to the sender...

A light touch of the hand on his right shoulder woke him up. He slipped the stones and wrapped them carefully by cloth inside the box, when waitress brought his tuna sandwich which he ordered ten minutes ago. She smiled to him wordlessly with light brownish Bambi's eyes as she was delivering his order, positioning knife and fork in front of the plate and a glass of fresh water beside it. Miran put packaging paper back to his rucksack together with metal box and thanked her for prompt delivery of his food. He chewed his third bite slowly, when his phone ringed for the second time. He swallowed quickly, checked displayed number and answered to unknown incoming call.

'Hello...?!'

CHAPTER XVII

Section 1.

RAGE

February, 2010.

CANADA, ONTARIO, TORONTO, QUEENS QUAY WEST. APARTMENT 9...

Cold January wind with occasional flurries played with the dry snow that was covering trees, land and flat rooftops of nearby buildings, triangular roofs of private houses, created seasonal idealistic picture of perfect winter's solitude. Through the windows of her warm bachelor apartment on upper level, an attic above the second floor, young woman was watching cheerful game of the wind with lonely bag of Lay's potato chips, named "Catch Me If You Can", feeling small nostalgic pang of memory in her heart.

It passed twenty years, as it was yesterday...

She clearly remembered the time when she played the same game with her younger brother at the back of their house, she would pretend that she cannot see him, as he would hide behind an old picket fence. His eyes were shinning wide opened from an excitement, between unopened rosebuds.

He would be a student now, one of the best for sure on his favorite University Of Modern Arts, with all his hidden talents which were buried together with small body four meters underground... Lost forever...

Streak of tears run across her left cheek marking, burning their path, warm and salty above lips all the way down to her chin.

Lost...

Silently she was watching through closed windows, dance of an empty potato sack around and frozen stoned table in a park down below, when her Toshiba laptop on the kitchen table gave her

"Bing-Bing" sound, announcing that she received an e-mail message. She crossed the space and touched lightly "tab" button on keyboard activating computer from its "sleep mode".

"Dear, E.

Well, it looks you're not the only one who'll be searching for our " G - target". When I got back here last night I found my roommate gone, along with most of her clothes and my stashed money, as well. She' d typed me a note saying she was going off on a very long trip with one of her new "friends" (I never been able to keep track of them), and that I should be on alert of some private detective, an ex – police officer who was sneaking and snooping around asking questions about me and you... She didn't even say that some locally hired thugs were interested about mine & yours recent whereabouts, and that she had some really "private conversation" with them, ending up with two cracked ribs and broken upper lip. I understand the reason why she's gone without any kind of warning - it seems obvious. She's always been extremely scared about everything, especially after the war. Incidentally, in a case it wasn't obvious to you; I had a hard time with them this weekend. They "convinced" me with their arguments last night on the parking lot, behind my office building, that this was just a little "bread-and-butter note" for you. I am writing this from an intensive care unit of Montreal's Memorial Hospital, only with three fingers of my left hand, which were not broken, only swollen at the moment. Thanks to good nurse Betty, who borrowed me her I-Phone..., Believe it or not, I did not reveal anything, because I had a trouble to keep my consciousness in that parking. I kept thinking about us back there, wicked and twisted persons in that camp all the time, when I lay down flat on the concrete ground..."

She had stopped reading it and she was just frowning in the screen for a moment. She fell silent, surprised by the vividness of her own memory, wondering what impression, feelings and nightmares it had made on the other woman. Somewhere deep inside her, where her thoughts were darkest, she felt the first sparks of unwelcome stirrings of a reawakened buried, hidden rage that she couldn't fought it down. Darkness filled the apartment - darkness and the weary droning inside her head, as if the two were coterminous, the droning the sound of mind power itself settled like a veil over the floors and furniture, stretching across opened doorways, moving books on shelves and pictures on the walls. It muffled all other sounds, the apartment become an isolated cavern of free energy, cut from the rest of the world and beyond the reach of time. Within the apartment every electric powered, an electronic device, starting with laptop in front of her sparked, as the force was passing across them, up to the high ceiling, slide down the walls, cracking, gleaming sweeping anything on its path. Darkness was unbroken all around her, her face was painted by rage, the shard of hard metal, streaks of tears emanated from her eyes painted it into white leather stretched mask, reassembling some inhuman female creature from horror stories.

Lost forever...

She smiled savagely to herself as first spark from an outlet beyond the window, jumped on the carpet and a little puff of foul smelling cone of light raised up. The flame sputtered once more on the spot, growing smoky, changing its color from black to red. It spreads outward and licks a newspaper stashed aside. She felt certain excitement at what was happening right now. Her soul was glowing with pride, the pain streaks curved on her cheeks get dry when she turned her head towards the exit door. The head twitched a little to the left, when she stand up and made her first step forward. Women's eyes gleamed quickly and dangerously under her eyebrows when she focused them on fried laptop lying on the table; the object flew through the air, crashing through tainted windows, following its free fall parabola to unoccupied wooden bench down at the park bellow. The name surfaced on her clenched teeth, as rage filled her cup of revenge.

"Mckenzie..."

CHAPTER XVII

Section 2.

COLLECTOR

April, 1999.

UNITED STATES OF AMERICA, CALIFORNIA, LOS ANGELES, CLUB,BEHIND HIDDEN DOOR,...

Loud music was coming from the large Bose's speakers above his head. The bas was drumming its own rhythm in his left ear, with high screeching voice of the lead female singer in his right one, together there were applying increased pressure on his brain tonight. Flashing light - show followed by music beat and people's voices from the background overwhelmed him. He tried to focus himself back to his task, that has been assigned to him for last two weeks, to get information of potential second black stone location and whereabouts of other relics - mysterious book inscriptions written on some ancient language which was long before Christ time forgotten. He has got some new information's last night, from one of his street's informants, a junkie addicted to "white powder" and "white supremacy" as well, that shoddy character nick - named "Stick" is going to be here tonight, and he will privately organize an auction on some stolen museums, private collection art goods, smuggled rare, an unconventional weapons and other high valuable small items brought illegally here. The bartender, young, green haired, colored homosexual with over feminized, wizardry movement pick up his fifty dollar bill, as an entrance fee, and he guided him to the back door entrance, masked by false oversized sliding mirror. Honestly, Markus did not care about any of them at all and he did not believed any of the crap which occupied Schuster's mind, about world white supremacy – forever lasting power, as long as he can earn enough money to stash aside and eventually fulfill his dream. He was recruited, trained and he became one of highest ranked members of their organization, but he was never completely wash brained like some of them, psycho killers politically colored, homosexually oriented, completely alienated from reality. Influenced by them, as a young man - teenager, he commenced and dedicated himself to an idea at first, provoked and stimulated in the same time by their methods, he absorbed everything from them, committing high crimes, ordered kills - yes, but without poisonous collective madness on their own cosmically pure reasons. Markus passed through mirrored door which opened from inside, in the same moment as he approached it.

Probably, they watched me from the beginning, since I made first contact with bartender and told him reference name.

Left of him enormous baldy, black man, ex pro wrestler by his body size, over developed muscles under his pink shirt and position of his legs, just stepped back without any word and let him in. Markus was really surprised by inner secret room. He expected something totally opposite. Instead of over packed, unorganized junkyard filled with everything and anything in the same time, like most of antic shops around the city, he entered wide and an empty middle space inside the room. All things were neatly stashed and packed beside the walls, leaned on them freely or arranged in visible fashion, covered by blankets and they just stayed there delivered in their original package, unopened in modified transport boxes. Small notes attached with content's pictures, which reminded him on postcards, were placed in front of each of them, naming and describing objects in brief details.

Very neat and clean for a smuggler and a thief. Hmmmm...

Across spacious clean area on the other end, opposite of him a man stands unmovable. Dim light made his figure stretched even more, if that was possible, due to the fact that his body was skinny, almost anorexic and his head has been equally thin, like needle head on the top of it. Markus couldn't see his face clearly hidden under wide hat which reassembled cylinder, shaped like a tube. It had similarity with an old comic character, named "Mandrake" from the same comic book series, which he adore as a kid.

Yes... He had an associate, huge black man dressed in leopards' skin, possessing an extraordinary strength, an African origin, similar as that one beside an entrance door... What was his name...?

Deep melancholic voice came to him across the room. It did not fit to thinly man's contours, spike like shaped head, together by his unconventional clothes just confirmed his personality obvious odd appearances. The man did not belong to this environment at all.

'Welcome to my humble shop! How we can assist you?'

Markus replied with to him by his bold, direct question.

'Do you have some of these items in your possession? "The Black Stone of Illyria" or "The Book of Cleitus"?'

Front teeth exposed under brimmed hat reminded him on hyena's smile before their feast on corpses.

'You are certain that the following items existed at all?'

It was Markus who smiled similarly this time in return.

'I have got info from a friend who has a friend.'

Needle head nodded to him without any further word. Markus felt that this is a critical moment for him. The man was considering and measuring odds for next minute in silence.

Patience..., Be calm and wait...

'Well..., since we have mutual friends of their friends, it's a custom between them to introduce ourselves prior to any future business.'

Good... I pass his screening...

'Markus is my name.'

'I don't care about your name, even if it's real one or a fake one either... Here, we are using our nick names only. Do you have one?'

Nobody asked Markus this in a long time. His inner alarm buzzed through his brain. He did not like it, not at all...

'Yes... I had. It was belonging to some other time and place. Long time passed, since I used it...'

'If you never liked it, I can fetch one for you..., if you required the new one...

Markus sighed before he responded. Weight of his past was on his shoulders again.

'No, it is ok! I do not need another one...'

'What was your nick - name, back then?'

There were hunting me as a wild beast again...

'"The Spider".'

Thin man seemed to be satisfied with his introductory game then he paused, self satisfying looked around the room before he responded.

'It is my pleasure..., "The Spider"..., My name is "Stick".'

Markus was getting annoyed by all this, but he needed the man, his possessions for time being, and he went with a flow of store owner.

'Now, we can continue our conversation in a much pleasurable way. Please join me and take a seat over there...'

"Stick" pointed at the left side of windowless room, wooden circular table made out of an exotic reddish wood with two similar low cushioned chairs beside it. Two of them were seated at the table across each other as chess players before the game.

'Now, let's talk about one of the items which I have and you desperately required, "The Book of Cleitus" and of course about the price which are you willing to pay for it...'

The man beyond him was blade thin, razor clean face with left eyelid slightly drooped, giving his eye a jocular look, as he was about to winked any second to Markus.

'How come you made a presumption that I need it desperately?'

His brown eyes quickly glimmered with gold in their depths.

'Everybody who came here is eventually desperate. I am the last hope and their savior on the path.'

'You have very high opinion about yourself.'

His face have got humorless, pinched and very tense expression. Then, in next second he pursed his lips, briefly turning them white.

'Objects for sale here are rare gifts from long forgotten Gods.'

He paused and swept with his right hand around.

'I am just a keeper... A mortal assigned to them.'

'Okay, cut your pompous advertising campaign! I can offer 10 clicks for it in green cash, now!'

There was a silence. "Stick" smirk his triumph inside his eyes, keeping the face unreadable.

I am straining myself not to kill you, you idiot!

At the conclusion of Markus last thought, man on the opposite side of old circular table drew a card from his left sleeve and consulted with it. Both of them fell back into respectful silence.

'The card just told me that you are a liar!'

In the same time when "Stick" placed a tarot card in front of him on wooden polished table, Markus heard squeaked sound of rubber shoes shuffling behind. He had time only to dodge on left side beside the table, when huge black man's fist like a cannon ball passed his temple. The voice followed him.

'GET HIM RHINO!'

Hunched next to fallen chair, Markus rolled over his left shoulder across the floor far away from his attacker. He sprung on both feet, still half - crouched, facing the large man sideways. Briefly an additional sound of "Stick's" muffled movement reached his ears. He looked in the opposite direction just in time to catch flash of metal in thin man's right hand.

A gun!

Markus left hand grab for the knife hidden inside the belt behind his back. Steel flashed in next second across the space between them.

'Gggggggghhhhh...'

Thin man was reaching for knife's handle that vibrated on his neck with his left hand, when legs gave up under him. He died with dilemma that occupied his last thoughts:

Should I ask for more...?

Black man reached him in next second. His large left fist caught Markus sideways between his armpit and shoulder, delivering an agony of pain to his rib cage, shoulder and right arm instantly. It also simultaneously kicked out the air from his lungs, so his scream sounded like raven's call for help. The other, right fist of his opponent was delivered fully to exposed right side of his face, on temporal bone area, partially covering right ear, right jaw's upper part and an edge of his brow bone. Blood erupted above his right eye, spraying like fountain, his sight was lost in a split of a second and in the same time, and he become temporary deaf as a post.

"Gorilla" is going to reap me apart...

The "Spider" blindly kicked with his right knee and left elbow, coordinating his attack on attacker's ribs and collar bone. It felt like he hit the concrete wall instead a person. Next instant, huge hands grabbed his neck, locking them around it. He felt full strength and weight of a man above him.

What an animal strength he has...!!!

Markus desperately use all his right hand strength hitting sideways trembling image in front of him. His knuckles crunched nose bone with his first blow, and he randomly delivered another three of them in the same area. The world was a blur, a roaring, earsplitting unclear aglow of blood. Wavering shape of huge mound looming blackly overhead produced hiss, some spit over his face with a grunt.

He is killing me...

Markus felt blood pounding in his head, the beating of his heart, floor beneath him sliding, life squeezing from his body, when he reached in vain the other knife hidden in his left boot. Movement was too slow, too vast as tremors from punctuated body above him screamed, once, twice, three times, and then released pressure around his neck.

Die... Die... Die...

He was no longer sure what he was seeing. He was sure that a great cyclopean beast was a man, ignoring neck pain, unseeing eyes, he lashed out his weapon where black man's head and face expected to be: darkened shape above at the end of extended arms. The body before him quivered at the blow, unyielding stab inside the soft part stuck home, through left eye socket into the brain. The giant body twisted and shriveled like a sliced - open worm, streaming warm fluid come out from wound, across knife's handle down his hand, it jerked twice and then fell limp upon Markus. The buzzing in "Spider's" head lightened in a pitch, become flashing light in the distance, when he pushed heavy limply corpse from him, revulsion filled his abdomen, but the corners of his mouth stretched in a smile.

This time ... She was closer to me then ever... Her kiss on my lips was magnificent!

"Die Spine" gurgled, coughed his own blood, moaned from pain and pleasure listening his own lunatic laugh.

CHAPTER XVII

Section 3.

VISIONS

January, 1999.

CROATIA, DALMATIAN COAST, CITY OF SPLIT, SAINT THEODOR – THE CHURCH OF OUR LADY, BELL TOWER...

Agent Willburn eyes burn inside out so badly, that he couldn't hold night goggles on them any second longer. He felt as someone stacked a very thin hot needle on the back of his skull pushing it all the way to the tip of his eye's pupil. He ripped off them from his face so violently that he almost broke them when he threw them on the cobbled stone floor. Suddenly, headache developed inside his head pushing and throbbing from his temples all the way to the back bottom of his neck, like someone is trying to extract that part of his brain through the vacuum tube. Pressure intensified immensely inside to the point that his vision blurred, distorted images of objects all around him stretched vertically, twisting around their axis and he lost his orientation and balance completely. He had sick feeling in his abdomen, like waves of hot liquid splashed inner walls of his stomach, filling intestines and his bladder with burning acid which it's going to burn everything inside out. He moaned, grinding his teeth until they were squealing from his hard bite. Whitening knuckles on his right hand were clenching on his gun as his life depended on that.

I..., I can't..., I... To...

He heard booming footsteps of an "Invisible Man" silent approach from above, his short exhaled breath hoofed across his face and loud cracking noise of his cloth brushing the smooth edge of rock wall.

Have... I..., ... Am... Move...

Willburn tried to move from an opening at the edge of the stairs, but everything around him seemed to float inside molted liquid lava, burning sensation on the surface of his skin told him that it will crisp any seconds over his flesh and bones.

...What...Is......On...Going...?

Lionel hungry grasped for air as a fish on dry land, when he stepped sideways and leaned his trembling body on the wall, intoxicated by strange visions which filled his mind.

The dark green eye filled him with its substance made of gold and silver.

Fangs of wolf snapped in front of his face and he felt fresh carnivore scent deep inside his nostrils. The wolf fed on someone's flesh recently, the human one undeniably, he was one hundred percent sure about it. Somehow he knew it, without any doubts. Saliva dropped on his face burning like an acid as wolf aimed for him again, but the bite of huge animal never reached his exposed pulsing neck's main aorta. Flash of silver with lightning speed arced from the background passing only few centimeters from his eyes. Pressure on him increased in the same time when beasts back legs scraped on his chain mail shirt and blood fountainhead from disjointed wolf's body, filling his tunic with its thick, sticky and smelly substance. He trembled from adrenalin surging through his body when shadow fell over him. He coughed spitting animal's blood between his teeth, confused and semi blinded when he raised his look up towards it. Huge fist held massive sword in front of him. Silver wolf's head was carved on its haft. Instead the face, polished golden mask watched him from above. The sound filled his skull bringing havoc to his senses.

"MMMMMMMMMMmmmmmmmmmMMMMMMMMMMM..."

Willburn blinked twice helplessly as images resolved themselves into tendrils of smoke before his eyes and he faced slim dark figure in front of him, outlined by grayish wall behind. Before darkness embraced him under its wing, words imprinted inside his brain surfaced with a thought:

"My Sign will be protected by Mask."

CHAPTER XVII

Section 4.

PORTAL

October, 1888.

UNITED STATES, NEW YORK, NEW YORK CITY, TESLA'S GRAND STREET LABORATORY...

Tesla was very pleased with Mr. George Westinghouse visit to his laboratory on Grand Street, promised financial help from his Westinghouse Company, an arrangements made between them for the manufacture of his motors on large-scale production. The man become impressed and interested for his inventions after he delivered his presentation of constructed models of poly – phase systems, alternative current dynamo and transformers specially of AC motor and introduction of an alternative energy solutions at American Institute of Electrical Engineers in May of 1888. Certainly, the man possessed money and power, but most importantly, he had vision and courage to foresee future developments of electricity and grab an opportunity to master them together with all other possibilities that were delivered in front of his feet, and the fact that Tesla have advanced knowledge, ideas and products were without the question.

Now, it is time to test this...

He initiated electricity current flow across his last version of modified design of high frequency test machine. Conical coil produced energy that flashed through the room. Stream of light, powered by transmitter connected to the end of his small machine charged through the air in the direction of antenna, which were positioned on the other end of his lab. Increasing energy blast connected both ends and kept them together for some time. Intensity of light increased, as frequency and sound disappeared completely, to the point that two ends fade away under delivered force shield. Nikola took one of the objects laying at the edge of his working bench, small oval; an almond shaped black stone a little bigger than average human eye. The stone has been highly polished, some type of gem – like stone, black like onyx, engraved with an ancient signs on its edges and Nikola was measuring it's weight on his palm, considering it's mass or its value in a split of a second, and then he throw it diagonally in the direction of energy shield visor. The stone flew across the room, entered the field, initiating sparks at first contact and then evaporated inside power screen completely, instead of passing through an energy belt and landing on the wooden floor on the opposite side.

Gone for good… Across an endless time and space… All the way to the other side…

CHAPTER XVII

Section 5.

VISITORS

April 2010.

CANADA, ALBERTA, EDMONTON, CITY OF ST. ALBERT, HOSPITAL, FIRST FLOOR, ROOM 109...

'Patient in coma was recently moved to the other room due to lack of space in this part of the building and due to fact that his condition did not improved for last three months. If you are planning to visit him at the moment, you should use entrance at the gate three, which is a back gate on the other end of a parking lot, opposite of power station compound. Just follow the signs on the left, after the exit!'

Nurse at the reception desk with raven black colored hair, oval face and small black piggy eyes waved with her left hand nourished by black manicured nails in front of her face, so Beth politely thanked and smiled back at her, as she took the exit door following given instructions. She did not expect any troubles to have with this assignment and everything went smoothly since she crossed the border back to Canada, when she took the trip to Edmonton, Alberta by her rented Avis car and her arrival at St. Albert Hospital had been unnoticed so far. Her fake ID and driving license worked out at the rental car agency, so she kept low profile as she drove her Toyota Prius in the range of speed limits on the highways, as well through the city. Canadians recently brought the law with "zero" tolerance for abusive, fast and drunk drivers, as well new monitoring systems with camera surveillance, helicopters and police patrols increasingly activated lately were factors which affected my habits to get "fast and furious", in and out of the job.

This time I had to change everything, since my last debacle episode in the States, Washington, DC. They have me in their grasp and I do not have any other alternative then sing to their song at the moment...

Additional to that, Beth did not get any word from Stella since she reached Ottawa two months ago, so she tried desperately to find her without any results so far, she activated again her long time ago severed connections with Serbian underground because they had extensive network over there? She missed her endlessly and enormously. Whoever harmed her in any way or killed her, he or they will pay dearly and painfully. She is going to hunt them down. Last update on her disappearance from Ramada Hotel where she was seen last time confirmed involvement of some radical terrorist group, affiliated with Neo – German National Radical Party subdivided fraction, which had their agendas, some ridiculous plans of regaining elemental power and wielded it over our fragile world.

Pretty standard wishes and dreams of concurred all existing world from masculine Alfa maniacs pumped by steroids, but lobotomized brains, in the black suits.

Beth entered "Hall of sleeping beauties" as she named part of hospital where comatose patients have been treated. She was pretending to wait for someone or something at information counter more than two minutes and then she sneaked around reception area when an opportunity opened. Some of the relatives - visitors, huge overweighed, woman in her late fifties fainted near buy, when doctor on duty, with enormous nose and these "geeks" stylish glasses, told her that someone of her keen finally died. Nurse from the reception counter called security guard to help, so together with another medical staff that was just passing by through the area, small skinny women in her late twenties, together they desperately tried to move big woman back to sitting position. Beth used commotion which increased as doctor broke his glasses in attempt to support his team and before she reached the stairwell to the upper floors, she was witnessing again their struggle to lift large woman.

I think guys that you will have to rent a forklift to assist you!

She stopped on the top of the stairs and peered around the corner, but she did not see anyone down the long corridor on the first floor. She checked the sign posted above on the wall, close to t he ceiling confirming that room 109 was somewhere in the middle of it, on the left hand side. She stepped to the corridor listening sounds that were coming behind closed doors on the left and right. First two on the right and one on the left were quiet as graveyards but from second one on the left came a whizzing sound of some medical equipment which reminded her on popcorn-machine. She quietly opened the door and craned her neck inside. She saw large bubble of smoky plastic cover over contour of small body inside its semicircular shape. Some rubber and plastic pipes were running out of it ending on squared electronic apparatus which was producing strange noise and sounds that she heard before in the halfway. She reached for white medical robe that hanged on the inner side of the entrance door. There was name tag plate attached to the left pocket.

Thank you J. T. Stewart. The coat is a little bigger and longer then my size, but it will do the job.
She adjusted coat's sleeves length to her size and used simple rubber band to make small pony tail of her red colored dyed hair as she step out back into hallway.

'Excuse me ma'am, do you know where is...'
The light blue eyes of the man in front of her squinted a little as he met her gaze close by, his fresh shaved face kept an expression of surprise and wonder in the same time. She recognized him immediately, Inspector Blaquier, the policeman who was after them for too long, last time she met him at Edmonton's Pyramids – Muttart Conservatory when she "tailed" the man in coma and him.

What the fuck is he doing here on Sunday morning?
'... nurse on duty, or doctor in charge of...'
The first instinctive impulse screamed inside her to attack him, as the fear of failure gagged her mouth and rage spread through her body. Blaquier read something of that in her eyes, or he felt instinctively some kind of threat emanated from her, and he reacted automatically before he get a clue what had just happen happening between them.

'..., Mrs. Stewart...'
His eyes briefly read the name-tag plate in the same time, when his right hand reached for a weapon attached to its holster under left armpit.

CHAPTER XVII

Section 6.

THE BEING

December, 1998.

MONTENEGRO, THE DURMITOR NATIONAL PARK, MOUNTAIN OF DURMITOR, CANYON OF TARA RIVER, "ZMAJEVA PECINA" ("DRAGON'S CAVE") AREA, HIDDEN PART OF THE CAVE...

Tanya struggled to put herself together and get on her feet, dizziness in her head spread through her leg muscles creating spasms effects through its tissue like electrical charges applied on their soft surface. She had feeling that she is going to throw up immediately, but she inhaled dusty air through her nostrils quickly and exhaled slowly holding her stomach muscles firmly, she lowered her abdomen full of applied air. It prevented her to vomit instantly. Sweet odor of blood hung around as she recollected previous events. Headless body of Jackie lay beside enormous black glossy humanoid arm cut above the shoulder. Blood on Tanya was mostly from woman stump corpse and thick human look like hand that ended with five sharp claws with five centimeters long nails. Blood on severed trunk arm coagulated much faster than human leaving smeared dark brown trail across the stone. Metallic taste in Tanya's mouth brought sickness throughout her arms when she unfocused eyes in front and moved head upright to an altar. What she had seen there, gave her shivers down to the end of spine. The Being, now made fully of flesh and bone, hold in its remaining left hand big blonde man by the neck. German man kicked the empty air underneath as he wordlessly struggle to escape from unbreakable grip of the creature.

Kirk...

The name surfaced from fogged memory. Tanya watched, unable to move from the shock, frozen under the spell, Kirk's useless fight in the midair. Something flashed in his left hand and disappeared in thick muscular Thing's forearm.

The knife...

Still bewitched by scene that played in slow motion in front of her, she felt that coldness, numbness of her hands together with the pressure in the head retreated from rushing blood that start circulating through her body. She heard her hearth frenzy rhythm, thumping in temples, kicking the blood back through veins. World spun around next second and she was completely blind in another second or two, but everything shifted back materializing from broken puzzled fragments.

The Being influenced my mind as well as my body...

Image was still flickering on the edges when two silenced gunshots came to her. Kirk left hand hold a gun in one brief second leveled to creature's head and in the same time his head went backwards as his neck snapped like a broken twig under grey colossus handhold. High piercing cry resonance inside the cave.

"Crrreeeeeeeeeee!!!!!!!"

The Being in pain discarded Kirk's body as a broken doll which flew five meters aside landing on hard stoned floor. It swayed a little which confirmed that Kirk's bullets made some damage after all.

"MMMMMMMMMmmmmmmmmmmm..."

Tanya initialized last charge of her "ion – weapon" as she pulled out strange sword with curved blade attached to her back. Her first two steps were unsteady, but she gripped the leather handle of old elementary weapon determinate to finish the fight, which was clearly stated in her steady gaze. The creature spun around detecting her slow advance and lands his almond shaped eyes on her. Tanya held her eyes low to the ground fully aware of emanated coldness that The Being sends through the space between them. She knew somehow that one contact with the gleaming eyes will be devastating for her; she will drop to endless pit of frizzing death forever.

Two more steps and he will be in the range of my weapon.

Deep hissing growl came from the creature. It's enormous wings similar to bats immersed from his wide back and in one powerful flap of them it disappeared from her view.

Damn it!

She tried to follow its ascending, but she got dizzy as her forehead hit the something hard, sparks of light flashed in front of her squeezed eyes.

Where did he go?

Her ionized weapon humming seized and the silence drop around. She heard only her breathing painfully loud in the cave. She did not have guts to move forward and she was too stubborn to give up. In an instant of her doubt, looming shadow appeared from above, creature soared from the dark ceiling catapulting itself directly to smooth squared stone protected by energy field. The Being vociferously released battle cry full of despair, rage and revenge as he collided in kamikaze stile with glimmering wall of radiant energy before her eyes.

"Crrrreeeeeiiiiaaaaaaaggggghhh!!!!!"

Instinctively, Tanya closed her eyes and she was shielding them additionally with curved blade in her right hand. Energy field almost instantly disintegrated the body in blasted flash, pillar of the force connected from the stone to an oval opening on the top radiated blazing light everywhere. Tanya felt cold wind of energy on her exposed skin, only the blade emanated heat wave in front of her face and even all sensations lasted not more than few seconds, she was burned.

"AAAAAHHHHH!"

She screamed in pain, as next brief second, huge pressure fist frontally hit her all body, kicking off the air, legs and ground under her feet. Tanya landed on her back in surprise when thunder deafening crack shook the ground under. She wasn't able to orientate herself in the space at first, till chopped stones hit her right shoulder and left leg. Large fragment of collapsing ceiling drop from above near her right leg. She rolled on her left side pulling her legs under and she was crouching using curved weapon at her right hand as support.

Cave's structure is collapsing; maybe I can get The Mask...

As an answer on her suggesting thought large portion of wall extended upward opposite of squared block of the stone in central part cracked and tumbled over blocking the path. Cloud of dust blocked her view and she backed up few steps semi blinded towards the main entrance.

I am going to end up here, buried together with the artifact, which I searched for...

Tanya heavily coughed and tried to cover her mouth by her left hand. Detection blinking light on her forearm in front of her face was steady green and charging line of incoming signal was full red.

Of course! Whatever blocked the "shield" now is gone...

Another wave of energy blasted in the background spreading the tremble of the ground under her feet causing vibration which knock off her again. Her right knee landed on hard rock surface, only two centimeters from ancient blade's sharp edge. She initiated "beam" retraction signal that activated her connection with her "receiver" at the room in Zabljak's Hotel.

CHAPTER XVIII

Section 1.

MEDICAL

March, 1999.

CANADA, ONTARIO, TORONTO, MEDCAN - PRIVATE MEDICAL CLINIC …

Michelle had expected that medical services, tests and an exam performed on her body are going to be over before her regular shift is going to kick in. She thought she heard a slow, agonizing moan which was coming from one of the rooms down the long private medical office corridor, and she was going weary of all smells and sounds around her. She left her seat by the entrance door; she walked to the second door on the left and looked inside. The man in white coat appeared in the same time in front of her, blocking the view of room's interior and he was the first man to smile at her all morning, as he softly asked her:

'Constable Bamford, come with me over here and please sit back, I have some important things to tell you...'

She blinked at him, feeling some strange discomfort spreading through her, prior to question which she asked him.

'Is it something serious,...I want to know...?'

She raised her head to look at him, she forced her face into a smile.

'Doctor...?'

He approached the chairs and stood starring down at her, thinking about something briefly, before he answered.

'Joachim. My name is Joachim. Please sit down...'

Doctor Joachim chose a chair on her right side, instead on the opposite one, which only filled up fear inside her, she could scarcely breathe. Suddenly, she felt so tired.

What is wrong with me? Why I have this strange feelings inside me...

'Constable Bamford, your first name is Michelle, isn't it? My I call you by your first name?'

Here we go...

'Yes, please..., Just tell me directly and honestly what it is wrong with me...'

Doctor Joachim's face glowered with pride.

'Michelle, I will be direct, there is nothing wrong with you and actually you are healthy woman, happily and proudly pregnant.'

Pregnant!?

'You are now in third - fourth month of pregnancy, your dizziness, weakness, short hot flashes and increased sweating are just regular symptomatic signs which were confirming successful adaptation of your body. You are going to have a healthy child. All performed blood tests were positively confirmed by our lab.'

I am going to become a parent, a mom!

'Congratulations!'

And Marc, my love, you will be a dad!

CHAPTER XVIII

Section 2.

PIT

May, 1999.

UNITED STATES OF AMERICA, CALIFORNIA, LOS ANGELES, KINGS CANYON

NATIONAL PARK...

The two men were working all afternoon in the shadow of the hill. The younger one, in his late

teens, was crouching over a human body neatly packed in a square shaped wooden box about half

a size of its regular size. Measurement of the box would fit maximum length of one meter long

and half of meter wide. From a strap on his belt hung carpenter's hammer parallel to his left leg, a

similar size of axe, shaped as hatchet was hanging upside down beside his right leg as well. Both

of them were smeared with fresh blood. Some drops were dried on the top of his leather working

boots. Two black horse flies were happily drinking and buzzing around his left foot. He swept

collected sweat from his forehead with genuine light blue silky female scarf strapped around his

right hand ankle, and he cursed under his breath, prior to his comment.

'The bitch was giving me hard time even now...'

The older man of the two grunted in an approval of his statement. He was tall, stoop - shouldered

man with thinning salt and pepper hair, maybe up to ten centimeters higher than the younger one

standing on the other side of the box. He was pacing around the base of modified greave pit

taking measurements and readings with a knotted rope, about one meter long. A Sony's

camcorder dangled around his neck.

'Now, my son, that time is over. She gave us more pleasurable times with her screams. It's the

only thing that counts.'

Squinting, he peered up along the length of the grave; he backed into the sunlight, holding his

camcorder in front of him, checking the dial on light meter as he focused its zoom on dismembered body.

'Think I'd better get a couple more pictures for our collection...'

The younger man stood watching him with a pride in his eyes, filled with joy inside his heart.

The blood rushed in his head and his cheeks blushed. Moments later he called out.

'Dad, may I have a second with her...?'

The other one, an older man lowered his camera, stepped back and turned around the mound.

'Oh, I don't mind at all!'

The old man cried, as he clicked quickly three more shots. He laughed to himself crookedly with his thin mouths, when his son hurriedly unzipped his pants.

'I am just finishing...'

The old man's eyes widened respectfully, he seemed impressed with the young man's penis size.

He nodded to himself, stepped forward, starred at nothing, listening his son moans behind him.

Seems like my boy is starting to enjoy this sport, quite a lot lately... Good for him...

Grunts and moans of younger man were coming now much faster as he persuaded his climax, standing, masturbating over gashed wounds of mutilated female body underneath.

'Unnngghhhhh.... You... FILTHY WHORE!!!...'

With two last squeeze of his right hand, he heard "heavenly choruses" booming voices of Saint's hoarse whispers through his ears, delivered through his final ecstasy. The old man came back to the pit with a small two litters red canister filled with gasoline. He dropped it beside the edge wordlessly.

'Father, isn't better to feed the vultures...? Like we did with the previous one...?'

The old man eyed the other one in silence; he shook his head glumly, the dark look growing on his face.

'What are you talking' about? 'Twas was the one from the neighboring a little town nearby. The one living' out of fifty kilometers radius from the closest suburb vicinity... Are you out of your mind...?'

The other one looked dubious for a second. He scratched his head and gave a genial node.

'The Lord wants us to live an continue our worship of His way, right enough, but He knows we're all just children, so in order to continue our game, we played it safe, and – well, He's always been good to us so far...'

The old man lapsed into silence.

And I am helping him, you young fool!

He wanted to add.

'And what might you be waitin' for?'

Younger one stood for a moment, watching his father, then he turned to face his grimly task. His sudden thought went back to his sister Milena. His father made a comment, like he read openly his last thoughts.

'We're gonna find her, soon..., And we're not gonna harm her any way, that wouldn't be right, not to our own blood..., Not to our "pearl"...'

CHAPTER XVIII

Section 3.

PROTECTOR

February, 1999.

UNITED STATES OF AMERICA, WASHINGTON, DC, UNITED STATES DEPARTMENT OF DEFENSE, GENERAL BRENDAN'S OFFICE...

...

Had he meant to keep an artifact as bait for a killer?

In retrospect General Brendan was forced to admit that perhaps there had been something slightly suspicious about agent's Willburn behavior towards missing artifacts and his lately actions against an unknown enemy, his detailed calculations and plans proved to be wrong at the end. And it seems that he paid highly for it, with his life.

His body never been recovered from Dubrovnik's or Split's location, or located nearby at the sea or the land, either.

Brendan'd merely hoped that Willburn would be still alive, after their trap turned into fiasco, but he already decided to keep a file open till the end of this winter. Never for a moment had he expected that the mystery – an invisible killer might show up in the city tower - together with a team of assassins.

Hired gunslingers from Eastern Europe and South America.

Further investigation confirmed their identities, connections to right-winged fascist, extremists group which operates in the States, too.

"Sweepers" did their job perfectly in the aftermath of church's fighting. Necessary strings had been pulled in the right moment through our embassy in Zagreb and military channels shushed Croatian government in the same time.

Computer terminal connected to an intranet, secured classified network, left of him produced a sound that broke his thoughts and caught his attention. Brendan touched tab button on his keyboard and pop up window of an incoming e - mail blinked on the screen.

General opened it with "enter" button and read:

...

"Sorry, I haven't written you in a while. It's easy to lose a track of time out here, and I am really pushing things up here and myself, too, to get through these tasks list which you send me last time. I have finished most of them, and everything went smoothly so far... There's also been some trouble with one of the subjects – that French boy, from Quebec, you remember him, the one that tried to escape and managed to kill three security guards and two of our scientists. He was been acting very wild lately and last week he run off into the woods. We thought he was gone forever, but it seems that last night he came back, sneaking into the compound, undetected by security systems, cameras, sensors and our sentries, and murdered two officers on spot, just for fun of the game... He was carrying his power like a sidearm and sounded very grim - almost shell - shocked, in fact: his power was deep, unstudied, filled with deep grief, uncontrollable rage and mind confusion. He informed me, in all seriousness that in a few months, another one like him is going to be raised and freed from its prison, from our testing area number two, the site back in Europe, and that he had telepathic connection between them for years. I can tell you Brendan that this subject started to give me creeps... I do not know which is more bizarre: what that French boy did last past months, or what he told me, but all this research will end up badly for all of us... Do come out again - soon. I mean it. I want you here to help me keep this Thing, or help me to kill It..."

...

I thought I'd go by that research facility again in a few days, just in a case that goddamned French – boy turned up to be right... And then, if the other guys have any afterthoughts...
Anyway, It sounded like I might be in a mood for some action, some killing of mutant's friends and his company. So here I am.

He was sending another e-mail message from another terminal on opposite side, right of him; it was nearly four o'clock AM; on a cold and cloudy Friday morning when he finished his typing. What struck him first was his clear presumption of truth, that he actually believed that things will get out of control, if he is not going to neutralized them, put them off the charts and plans once for all... He owed to himself this. How knew how methodical, stiff-necked and precise killing machine they could be, they become, one of those unconscientiously souls who proceeded with their grimly tasks, according to programmed, trained unstoppable schedule: first, second, third... When he took this job, he always knew that it would be his special obligation for his country, nation and people, to act as their semi- God, to become their Protector..

CHAPTER XVIII

Section 4.

BALLS

October, 1889.

EUROPE, FRANCE, EXPOSITION UNIVERSELLE, THE EIFFEL TOWER…

Wind was strong and unpredictable today, shifting between north-west and north-east in matter of minutes. Definitely not good for my experiments which I scheduled for this morning. Anything can happen, if I released it now...

Nikola checked once more gathering of dark clouds on west horizon and he returned two silver balls, fifteen centimeters in diameter, back to his leather bag, and he rested supporting above an iron fence on the top of The Eiffel Tower. His calculations were correct as always, but this time the weather shifted its course swiftly and he decided to postpone the test itself, up to late evening hours or eventually early morning hours next day.

The storm is coming; it is only matter of time... The location is perfect, so I am going to finish it after The Exposition...

Slowly and carefully he descend narrow stairs back to the last wide landing area. There, he stopped before solid construction frame leaning over the iron fence, upper part of his body extended dangerously over the edge as he peered down at the bottom of the tower. Something caught his attention, some movements down below caused that his mouth become thin and horizontal, it brought an additional line of concern over his wide forehead.

How that could be? They followed me back here as well?! They will never quit, aren't they?!

He considered one more option, but he was not sure when his assistant will arrive and probably he is not going to be here on time due to Exposition, so Tesla discarded that option without any further thought. Immediately, another one flashed before him clearly as always before, and he knew from the first spark, that it was the best option under these circumstances.

Americans, without any doubt... They followed me back here, as always... Scared to death not to fail to collect prototypes before someone else gets their hands on them, this time there will be another one to fight for...

He produced two silver balls from the leather bag and he placed them beside each other on the metal railing close to his left hand. The silver balls gleamed dully under the cloudy Paris sky when Tesla saw own distorted, stretched face reflection on their surface. His own two faces watched him silently, as they were expecting something from him. Subsequent investigation of particles inside employed medium of hydrogen, mercury, vapor and synthetic oil created very efficient flow of electrons inside the medium. Here, high above the ground, they are going to be employed by pure air only and powerful discharge of lightening, somewhere 300 to 900 meters above the rushing clouds...

The rotating magnetic field inside the ball itself will flashed current around the globe with such intensity that it is going to interrupt all radio communications...

Tesla knew that from this day on, he will become number one threat to United State's homeland security, highlighted name inside American's black book, associated together with other European's scientific and technological interest domains, as well primary target for their foreign intelligence agencies. He picked up silvery objects and pushed small button like bubble on its bottom surface. Without any sound produced back from the ball, he hold it at his large hands for another twenty seconds, as he was considering again his decision, and then Tesla raised them above his head for an additional ten to fifteen seconds rotating extended arms together simultaneously with strong, full force of his body, using its momentum to release them. Silver arc from his left hand passed above the tower high in the air following the small object at his parabola and when it reached the highest possible position, just when the Earth's gravity should take over, Tesla launched another one from his right hand using all his remaining strength. The second silver ball followed the first one on the same path above and started rotating around itself.

Nature stored up in the universe an infinite energy. The unseen resources of energy are all around us. We can use the power available for free in nature, which where are for a long period of time beyond our grip, to embrace all its potential and benefits and improve our quality of life.

Instead to fall directly to the ground below, two silver balls were floating in the air on its own, connected together; hold by an invisible shield force, and continuing rotation around their axis. Only grayness of the sky in the background made the experiment transparent to the naked eye, revealed magnetic field that hold them together, light bluish electromagnetic colored wall visible from the Tower above, where only Tesla stood and witnessed its existence. Everything lasted a little more than one minute altogether and it ended quickly within next few seconds.

Records of this are going too disappeared within seconds... It is time to take care of other things... Anxious people were waiting for me at the bottom of Eiffel Tower, men devoted to protect their country at any costs...

Narrow stream of energy pushed silver objects in the opposite directions, repealed by reversed electromagnetic polarity; they accelerated across the sky and disappeared from sight. Magnifying force left behind formed pillar of vacuumed concentrated beams of particles which flew upward through the free air, sending tremendous energy across the globe consisted of transverse and longitudinal magnetic waves. Reminiscent of Tesla's conducted demonstration evaporated completely till Nikola collected his leather bag. He smiled to himself, checking the wide opened space in front of him, as he was expecting some side effects, and then he descended metallic stairs to the lower level.

Tomorrow, they will crave for new sensations, but soon become indifferent to them. The wonders of yesterday are today common occurrences.

CHAPTER XVIII

Section 5.

REBIRTH

May, 2010.

UNITED STATES OF AMERICA, WASHINGTON, DC, WASHINGTON, "BIG BROTHER" OFFICE...

Stella had lost track of the time again, and with it her sense of direction. She knew only that she was their prisoner since beginning of this year, she was not completely certain about it, but she hazily remembered January, the winter time and some warm hotel room and that was extremely late when something happened... Her memory had been broken in pieces, like fragments of glass hanging on its edge, left inside the frame of broken window that represented her previous life. Despite her intentions of putting them together during previous months, some nights were filled only with blurred picture collections of faces without names, places shadowed by drug implemented in her veins, mostly clouded by wash - brained light blasts of hypnosis sessions. Stella fall under a drug addict rhyme, worshiping prophesy of needle, visions and wonders of hallucinogen substance became her obsession, she was now product of very successful experimental medical procedures, something they called "Rebirth". Suddenly throughout the midst of her own incoherent thoughts she heard footsteps in front of her doors, someone summoned her without words, he just implanted words inside her brain from somewhere...

Kintaro...

On some days he gave her enormous pleasures, and on some other only endless pain. This morning he arrived dressed in white kimono only. She thought he looked disconcertingly pale, thought it was hard to tell in the bad light above her head, so she waited for derisive little smile which was often the only way he signaled he was in good mood, but his mouth, and his eyes, remained serious. They were silent for a time, as if each were pondering the implications of this last day. Stella heard her breathing coincide with her heart rhythm, she was exquisitely aware of how little he cared about her, but she tingled from bursting emotions under her skin, if by some chance, he would reach out and touch her.

The time has come, I can feel it...

She felt when emotions stirred almost imperceptibly between them.

'Come on, do it to me...'

Her voice dismayed her, it sounded so breathless and frightened that she barely recognized it.

'Talk about anything you like. Tell me a lie. Or tell me the truth.'

He drew a little closer to her like he was sliding above the surface.

'I saved my secrets for this final confession, but I still cannot remember my life before, I had a terrible dream.'

She willed herself to relax and stay calm in front of him. She never witnessed rage outburst from him, but she was convinced that she wouldn't survive it.

'I already know all your secrets, there weren't any lies between us and I've told you the truth about everything. Your nightmares were part of your previous life experiences.'

Kintaro reached out with his right hand and touched her right shoulder. Her nervousness returned with a rush and she knew perfectly well what would happen now; the things he was going to do with her, and how she was expected to respond. It was like knowing all the answers without ever having been asked any of the questions.

'Come..., embrace him...'

Instantly when she saw his erection under, with a languorous movement she rolled toward him, keeping her eves on his, she darted out pink tongue to lick her lips. Beneath her pubic hair pulsing beat of desire start spreading between her thighs and her belly. Kintaro deeply sighed when she was butting her head and face against his genitals, controlling the pressure and her movements by his outstretched left hand.

'Your main task will be to kill...'

Stella gripped hardened penis through kimono's fabric with right hand, scratching cotton surface by her nails, and moaned, as Kintaro was giving her final instructions.

'MMMMMmmmmmmmm... Aaaahhhhh....'

CHAPTER XVIII

Section 6.

MONTENEGRO – MAN

May, 2010.

CANADA, ONTARIO, TORONTO, TORONTO POLICE SERVICE, MAIN BUILDING, 40
COLLEGE STREET...

More than two hours passed, and he was still on the same place as the day before. He did not
reach his target in last twenty four hours. There was no answer at her apartment, and the woman
he'd spoken to at Police HQ said that Michelle hadn't come to work today. He hung up, troubled,
almost indignant, at this unexpected absence of someone he'd regarded as reliable as Chief of
Main Police Investigation Unit, M. Bamford.

Where the hell was she, anyway? Who had she gone off with?

Well, "Montenegrian" would track her in a day or two, when she got back to her regular work
shifts and life schedule. He certainly wasn't going to wait around her apartment block any longer;
he had already wasted enough time today. The main street had been dull lately, with cars passing
but rarely, faces inside them occupied by their own mind and business, so nobody noticed him, he
was confident about that. He had drunk too many cans of beer, there behind waste container box,
and eaten too many potato chips bags. Now, as he got to his feet and moved slowly on the
sidewalk, the heat made him feel dizzy.

Damn it! I shouldn't drink so much...

He walked for more than one hundred meters down the street when he spotted an antiquated
Ford, black as a hearse, traveling from opposite direction. Buildings shadows lengthened
perceptibly with the passing day and stretched across the street, so he was able to see only two
black - garbed figures inside incoming vehicle. Instinctively, he hurried far away from the edge
of the pavement when the vehicle bore swiftly down upon him. He slithered two steps backwards

to gain more space for maneuver. Far from slowing as it neared him the Ford increased its speed and made a sudden swerve to the right. Crnogorac" ("Montenegrian") legs woke up just in time, when he jumped back to avoid being run down.

Assholes!

He was lying on the street, watching the car receding slowly down the street, until it rounded a band and disappeared, giving him a taste of their exhaust inside his mouth. He reached for a gun holstered to his right leg, hidden under pants, when Ford reappeared around the corner.

Mother fuckers are coming back!

Ascending car reflection was dazzling now, making rainbows in his eyes. Miso blinked and looked away. He crouched, partially leaning himself on the brick wall on his right, breathed deeply, holding the weapon now in both hands, targeting incoming vehicle driver. Eagerly he pressed the trigger, silencer whooped almost soundlessly as touch of a smile crossed his face, he repeated it two more times, before approaching car closed the distance between them. The man's eyes widened when he saw that the Ford had a bullet proof windshield glass and that his shots just chipped the surface, so he had pushed himself from the wall behind his back. He landed hardly on his left shoulder just few centimeters away from car's left bumpers that whooshed behind him. The car scrapped its right side on the building wall beside him, the screeching noise of metal filled Miso's ears and broken metallic shards, hard edged bricks particles flew around him, delivering cloud of dusts which hovered around him. He heard sound of brakes behind his back, as vehicle was creaking like the masts of a ship in a storm in an attempt to stop. Gradually, "Montenegrian" raised upper part of his body, squinting through cloudy vision of a car, aiming his weapon, looking, searching in vain for his attackers.

Where are you bastards...? I will kill you...!

Two stings bite him instantly, the first one behind his craned neck close to his right ear, and the second one between his cheek bone and his nose, just one centimeter below his right eye. His right hand went towards his face, then grows limp briefly, before his head dropped backwards and down on asphalt. "Montenegrian" eyes closed further, as he was about to fall asleep, the last lost thought stayed frozen on his brain's surface, but the man appeared not to notice that, or at least did not care anymore. All his fears and worries were gone. He was free... He was dead

CHAPTER IXX

Section 1.

COMANDER

April, 2010.

CANADA, ONTARIO, TORONTO, TORONTO POLICE SERVICE, MAIN BUILDING, 40 COLLEGE STREET, FIFTH FLOOR…

At two fifteen today, Chief of Investigation Unit, M. Bamford has been summoned to the fifth floor office by the assistant of Main HQ Police Commander, Mr. Andre Fournel, a graying, harried - looking man, whose desk, opposite Michelle's, was piled high with crime files, some of them marked by colorful note stickers.

Up to his neck in someone else's pile of shit, flashed on him from upper levels... Poor guy...

'You look like you could use some vacation or a change of job...'

He said to Michelle, dourly over the top of his glasses. Hint of sarcastic smile touched his lips. He checked her legs and curve of her hips with nonchalance of primate's interest for next female.

Arrogance of male was clearly readable on your face, then drop dead from work, you asshole!

'I am sending you upstairs. Commander's got fifteen minutes of his lunch break for you...'

Climbing the stairs, Michelle ignored hidden meaning of his words, she had discovered long time ago there was simply waste of time to complain and argue with Neanderthal male pieces like him. She have got a warning message from Blaquier last month, about her as potential assassin's target and she took it very seriously, since the man knew his job very well, so she started preciously measures towards her office and home security.

I've already installed additional sensors and cameras on both locations, changed my incoming - outgoing routes, schedules and regular behaviors, but everything up to now was regular and there was no surprises. This was more than good! Anyway, I have to think about personal security, to hire some bodyguard near buy...

Her footsteps echoed hollowly in the silence of the hall, only humming of electrical fans followed her, all floor was deserted and the air was oppressive and cold still. Michelle drifted toward large front door on the left side and knocked powerfully and shortly twice.

'Come in!'

The voice came from inside. She entered the room half-sized as previous ones downstairs, with single centrally placed working desk, and behind it, sat placidly the Commander. He was heavy, slow moving man, in his late fifties who perspired easily and who left his hair only with great reluctance. Left of him beside small bookshelf sat Canon photocopier machine that was chugging effortlessly, making some copies on its own.

'Chief Bamford, please...'

Commander smiled wistfully and blinked his mild eyes pointing to leather chair on the right.

'No, thank you Sir, I do not want to take too much time off your lunch break, I am more comfortable as it is...'

He was no taller then she when he stand up and came around the table straight to her, offering a handshake. Michelle had to admit to herself, that she did not expected this from her boss at all, that there was something rather strange about it, but anyway she couldn't refused it, so she accepted it. His hand was very dry, small in size with plump skin, but strong grip.

I hope this doesn't mean that I am fired...

Commander confirmed it with a nod, like he was reading her mind instantly, and posed a strange question instead.

'Chief, do you have any problems recently? Private issues?'

She was considering in a second, how much he already knew, but she responded quickly, honestly to some extent.

'I'm not sure I do. Not yet, as far as I am aware.'

He cocked his head and smiled.

'What I mean is, there's a bit of information about your recent purchase and installation of security equipment inside your home premises, this was, of course, totally domain of your privacy, but it is completely different issue when it comes to your office..., Do you follow me...?'

Ehhhh, now we are talking about...

'Well, I have some evidences about suspicious activities close to me and about possibilities that I am on someone's list, someone who hired a "Hit-Man" to take care off...'

He nodded again, not at all surprised.

He still hadn't said what he wanted...

'Most likely you are... Any name to connect to...? Someone showed particularly interest in you?'

Michelle felt that it would be better for her to keep the name of the main suspect for herself, somehow she believed in Blaquier's conspiracy theory, which sounded ridiculous at first, when she heard directly from Michael, but later on, proved itself to be deadly serious. When death took lives of almost every person involved in his investigation, Michelle become true believer.

'No, I don't have any names...'

He pursed his lips and shook his head in negative response.

'That was reason more to give you an additional protection..., considering this situation, by the way, that was the main reason for this short meeting...'

This cannot be just simple coincidence. There is much more then this... Hidden underneath...

CHAPTER IXX

Section 2.

INVESTIGATION

May, 1999.

UNITED STATES OF AMERICA, CALIFORNIA, LOS ANGELES, 140 NORTH LA
STREET, MAIN DISTRICT POLICE DEPARTMENT, CHIEF'S DETECTIVES OFFICE…

…

In November 1997, Europol supported Austrian and Hungarian police in identifying victims of
illegal organs trafficking and arresting the organizers of an illegal medical and human
trafficking network. Five young women, from Hungary and Romania, were beings heavily
drugged, used as potential donors in a house in southern Hungary and prior to removal of his
internal organs they were sexually and physically abused, raped and tortured repeatable on the
same location. Traces of their body fluids were found together with their DNA samples. Bodies
were then disassembled in peace and "distributed" on more than ten locations between Hungary
and Austria, mostly in small towns remote areas; where they were discovered later in garbage
bins, recycle dumping grounds and outskirts of rural roads. Without established contacts with
friends and family of the victims, we would never be able to identify them completely. DNA
samples collected from these locations kept updated in the same database at Europol Main HQ
central unit and compared later by other incoming results from the field units from different
countries and police districts. Three of them were tortured in similar way which detailed
descriptions were indicated in appendix of this e-mail. As a result of the operation, Hungarian
police arrested the main suspect, a 54-year-old Hungarian and his 36-year-old female Serbian
accomplice. During house searches, police seized guns, a considerable amount of cash, jewelry,
and other assets worth several thousand Euros.

In addition, IT and communication equipment was seized, along with a large amount of evidence relating to criminal activities over the last 10 years. Detailed files on these individuals were attached at the end of zipped folder, too.

...

Marc browsed through appendix and attachments saved inside the first zip folder and he made short notes as a reminder.

...

Radmila Jakovljevich - Rada, 36-year-old female Serbian accomplice of a Lajos Zsolt, 54-year-old Hungarian, will be my priority...

...

He skipped some sections that explained intelligence reports and facilitated techniques in exchange of collected intelligence, which also resulted in the discovery of new international criminal links between Europe and States.

...

Hmmmm..., this part would be interested, since it is identical to our recent discoveries...

...

Twenty eight cases were reported and documented so far by Intelligence Units which pinpointed the criminals modus operandi and helped to identify that 126 individuals that were part of a wider organized terrorist crime group named 'The Black Hand". The main source of their income were trafficking human beings (including internal trafficking inside 19 European Union countries and non-EU countries), as well overseas to USA and Canada, money laundering, production and distribution of synthetic drugs, cocaine, benefit fraud, child neglect, perverting the course of justice, theft and handling of stolen goods.

...

Marc already compared reports from CSI (Criminal Scientific Investigation) LA field units from last three murder scenes and he found a perfect match of DNA with the European CSI DNA samples.

DNA found on victim number 26, the crime scene...

...

Further investigation were finalized in October 1998, Intelligence indicated that this organization was using drivers, working for a legitimate transport company, to smuggle illicit body parts and organs into the US. The drivers stopped in major harbors en route to the US to load up. They were using the cover of their company vehicles and frequent trips to the US to facilitate the imports. The Europol analyzed key intelligence contributions which pinpointed the criminals' modus operandi and helped to identify the source of supply, people and vehicles involved. The operation concluded with two arrests and the seizure of nearly 277 000 Us dollars by the US authorities.

...

The transporting company was registered and operated by deceased person, classic sample of an identity theft...

...

Children from the Ex-European communities. The offenses include: trafficking human beings (including internal and external trafficking in the US). The operation's primary aim was to safeguard the potential child victims and involved 16 addresses being searched in USA and Canada. The children found were taken to a dedicated centre staffed by child protection experts from the police, the local authority and local health trust, where individual assessments were made on each child. The assessment process examined the welfare of the children and sought to identify if they had been subject to exploitation and/or neglect. Europol was an active member of the Joint Investigation Team (JIT) and provided assistance to the competent authorities by:

1. Giving expert advice on setting up the JIT and the planning of strategic and operational activities. Ensuring analytical support throughout the whole investigation.

One of the key outcomes from this analysis was the identification and prioritization of the main targets of the organized crime group, both in Romania and the UK.

2. Providing on-the-spot assistance through the deployment of its mobile office, in the UK and

Romania on four occasions. Each time, real-time checks were carried out on the database to support intelligence gathering operations and coercive British and Romanian police actions (searches and arrests).

3. Drafting and disseminating 67 analysis reports. Identifying key links to other EU countries, especially Belgium and Spain. The quality and quantity of analysis provided by Europol was crucial to the progress of the case. Europol is expected to provide further support in the near future...

...

The Europol sent its expert to the field to coordinate simultaneous operations in both the country of origin and destination. Moreover, dedicated operational analysis was provided by Europol which helped to detect international links through cross-checks on victims with data already held in the Europol databases, as well as establishing links with other reported cases at USA. Europol also analyzed data from individual cases and gathered during the day of action which resulted in more charges being brought against the suspects.

...

Running his finger down the columns of names and addresses, he squinted at the listing for San Fernando's Valley areas. The table arrests listings were not difficult to follow; there were footnotes to refer to the type of offenses, as well short descriptions of their nature, too; rows of tiny numbers that seemed to swim together with last names. But as near as he could make out, his search has been on right track. In fact, he saw now, if the tables were correct, in the past five years there'd been two occurrences of unusual brutal sexual assault and both of them were close to Burbank sub district...

...

In both cases charges were taken against the same person, an adolescent with problematic behavior, especially violent towards young females, registered physical and emotional assaults in and out of high school facilities, a teenage boy... The name and address were the same in both cases... It's worth to check it..

CHAPTER IXX

Section 3.

TEST TWO

June, 1943.

EUROPE, SOUTH - EASTERN EUROPE, OCCUPIED TERRITORIES OF BOSNIA,
SUTJESKA REGION, DOD (DEPARTMENT OF DEFENSE) TESTING SITE NUMBER
TWO...

(Today territory of Bosnia and Herzegovina, Sutjeska National Park)

...

Auroras were never seen in this latitude at anytime, consequently it was spotted only this time,
noticed by local residents on June, 06. 1943., above the mountains, in a form of a low arched
lights coming from somewhere in the north. Between the end of that night, in sunrise time,
luminous streak resembling cirrus clouds appeared and disappeared randomly, generally
extending from north - west to south - east, and extending past the zenith. Huge double arch was
formed above small town from the north. There were well - defined low curtains defined on the
sky, and the whole area was full of diffuse masses of luminous matter that was moving, filling the
space slowly, and pulsating like some living thing. Once in a while a very rapidly spread
transference of luminosity occurred, always from the horizon upwards in several quick pulses.
Nobody remembered or has seen this phenomenon before, the lightning without any sound,
thunders without rain and mute flash of energy. This activity was reaching small houses and
nearby farms, closing them with darkly green streamers from the north, which seemed like a robe
dropped above, unmoving from the west to the east and the sky stayed bright until down. Slight
moving of aurora above all area wasn't suspected for several hours, so people stayed in their
homes, scared by war atrocities before, but now additionally feared of its weird colors, trapped
under huge energy field for too long..." As always there are some exceptions, some people cannot

be stopped, or scared by anything, especially children... The woods were a patchwork of bright shadows and dark lights. Everything changed when green streamers covered the land. Wide - eyed, obviously dazed, the little girl, seven years old, stumbled down an uncertain path, following the green river bank, as it skirted the edge of the thick pine forest. In her arms she clutched something small, white, limp, that looked like a teddy bear, perhaps, or some other nursery toy. It wasn't a toy at all; the girl was clutching a dead dog, small puppy, her best and only friend. She stopped in front of an abandoned wooden hunter's or fisherman's cabin near the edge of the river. She had found a perfect spot, small shallow in the earthen floor to perform some kind of funeral ceremony for her friend. She put dead animal in the natural hole in the ground and went to the bushes nearby, picked up two small branches of dried wood, and she made a primitive wooden cross tied with her left shoelace. She reached for some additional branches and made improvised cover for her dead puppy dog. Tears were glistening inside her bluish eyes as she kneeled beside the small grave and solemnly stabbed small cross above upper edge. Touched by boiling emotions inside her, a child struggled with pronunciation of some words, but she was able to whisper few of them at the end.

'My dear doggy...'

The girl felt the customary lump formed inside her throat and she covered her eyes with her small white hands before the river of tears covered her face. Sobbing quietly trembling of small shoulders shook all her small body when she bent over all the way down to her knees overwhelmed with emotional pain.

'Sleep well... I miss you...'

She wasn't able to see the figure standing there, about ten meters diagonally from her, veiled in shimmering sunlight, as unmoving as the high trees, a man, tall, bearded, nearly naked, his clothing in ribbons, his hands black as dirt with darkly humus dried on his body, hair and face.

'I love you...so much...'

The flickering light rose slowly behind her back, the stream of gold corona swirled round her fragile body, head, and ankles joined together with greenish light fog that was forming at zenith.

She felt dizziness, weakness spreading through her body; the solemn stillness of strange warmth on the skin, like the sun seemed to die a little and shadows of the trees grew longer reaching for her where she was sitting. Gazing at girl from the distance, the figure raised its left hand stretched yearningly toward her, his all body become longer as slanting rays of sunlight hung like gold curtains before him, and it looked like his hand reached out other body, took her head imperatively in his grasp. For a moment, as his hand touched her body, she turned to cast a single, half regretful backward glance at the man still standing on the same place, and then the figure of a man became shrouded by spreading darkness in the same time as red energy arc connect and closed over them both.

CHAPTER IXX

Section 4.

THE BRUSH

November, 1890.

UNITED STATES, NEW YORK, NEW YORK CITY, TESLA'S GRAND STREET

LABORATORY...

...

The heating effects of high - frequency currents applied on the human body would help some

individuals with circulatory problems, but my proposal to local doctors was declined due to their

fears of electricity and enormous pressure from Thomas Edison's campaign against me.

Tesla realized that his "brush" of charged particles had its own distribution of intelligence

through different mediums, and that any motions of them could become easy measurable in the

space. Practical applications of the "brush" would be in telegraphy, to send dispatches across the

Atlantic by any speed since its sensitiveness was so great that the smallest, sightless change will

affect it.

Laboratory experiment performed on high frequency currents opened an electric field of

sufficient intensity and produced connection to light up electrodes vacuum tubes at the other end

of the room.

He picked up the small horseshoe - magnet couple of centimeters wide and waved with it at the

distance of two meters in front of tubes, witnessing interpretation of very strange phenomena. His

movements caused the movement of "brush" of beam in either direction, following the magnetic

field of electric charged particles, depending on the position in which the magnet was held.

If anyone approached the tubes from two – three meters away of the object, the beam - brush

would swing to the opposite side of the tube. If I walked around the tube even from a distance of

five meters away, the beam would make same movement likewise, keeping its center end always pointing directly at the moving object, actually me. The slightest movement of my finger, or even tensing of my any muscle, would bring a swinging response from the beam itself.

Nikola adopted this new technique of light inside his vacuum lamps without being connected to any direct source of electricity, as the permanent method of lightning his laboratories. The loop around the ceiling was always energized, and if anyone wanted to switch on the light in the room, he just had to take a glass tube and place it anywhere inside the room.

This time I am going to shoot charged particles in the cloud above, connecting terrestrial scale of surrounding atmosphere on greatest altitude, where the pressure of their was lower than down here... Something similar to natural phenomena effects of aurora borealis, but controlled and localized from this area...

Tesla opened the metal tube constructed from special light material that Tania provided for him last month, whose source and origin remind mystery for him, as she refused to tell him about her sudden disappearance from Paris Expo and her even strangest reappearance at Niagara Falls at Canada.

She was using my prototype machine too often... I am really concern for her health; the side effects were devastating on the human tissue... It drained its essential energy too fast and too much in a short period of time...

The tube - lamp was constructed so as to be used with different organic matter such as carbon, diamond, ruby or other hard material positioned in the center of the unit, wirelessly charged, energized by endless Earth's energy that was passing through glass tube inside.

Tesla aimed the tube, positioned it highly above his head on, on metal modified holder which was directed to the open sky. With one swift move, he press the switch on the end that generated tremendous charges from the Earth, the sound of ionizing field filled the room, and then pure electrified stream of energy, shaped in the form of a canon blasted from the tube.

"WWWWWUUUUMMMM..."

Yes! I have built it... And used it! Demonstration was finished! Only a little time will pass before I can give it to the world

CHAPTER IXX

Section 5.

REPORT

May, 2010.

CANADA, ALBERTA, EDMONTON, EDMONTON POLICE WEST SIDE, KINGSWAY

AVE, NW...

...

In the matter of minute's hospital corridor turned into the battleground... Red haired woman

almost physically bumped into me on my way back to reception area. She came out from the

second room on the right at the beginning of "special care" room areas, adjusting her white

coat's sleeves, so I assumed she was just finishing her regular doctor- patient visit, and I

approached her with a question. In the same moment when I opened my mouth everything went

wrong, since I detected some anomalies attached to her, first the size of her white outfit did not fit

her shoulders and length of her body, second I caught honest surprise, strange recognition flicker

in her pupils, a twitch of nervousness or panic under her right eye and sense of immediate danger

emanated from all her body in next instant. Instinctively, I have reached for my weapon, but she

thwarted it with lightning speed of counter attack. The name-tag reflected her name: "J.T.

Stewart" and I had time only to cover my exposed neck with my left hand in the same time as she

flashed silvery object in front of me, aiming high with her right hand. The sting of needle passed

through my skin, muscle and hit my bone, an impact broke it on half, so she managed to inject

some amount of liquid inside. I used my right elbow, to stunt her attack, hitting her face

sideways, pushing her temporary away from me. "Doctor" delivered me again surprisingly,

strong right leg low kick, which ended on my left hip bone. I've lost my balance temporarily, in

the same time when my left arm got numb completely from injected poison needle. Burning

sensation spread on my fingers, insensible arm condition clutched my elbow completely, as I landed on it painlessly, and I wouldn't feel anything even if I broke it on an impact. With non understandable vengeful cry unknown woman furiously closed the distance between us. I managed to pull out my weapon from its holster and that was all, before she crashed her full weight upon me. Blade clutched in her right hand penetrated my rib cage and effortlessly disappeared beneath. I screamed and made instinctive futile effort to escape from hers death grip, trying to push her and roll on the opposite side. Her vivid face close by, produced every detailed emotions, hatred look, raged flash of teeth and joy of savoring the final moments of human life, when she twisted the knife inside me. Scream came out unnaturally high from my breathless lungs, followed by body tremor which brought another pain agony cacophony through me. With final strain I pressed the weapon's trigger, maybe from shock that shook all my body, maybe fear of death tenfold my strength, and honestly I did not know and I did not care, either; I just want to escape from that iron death trap. All her body jerked back few centimeters, through spasmodic twitching of her flesh, once, twice, three times in a row, I knew that I hit something vital through her belly, but just precautionary I shot her one more time in very close range. She wrenched her neck towards me like she was going to give me her last kiss, then somewhere down below; I felt that she kicked her legs one more time, before all her breathing stopped. Nimbly my right arm released the weapon, which stayed trapped between our bodies, and simultaneously, I have lost full control of my left arm. The room spun around me, black vortex took over my body and my soul completely, and I welcomed its silence, it's dark blanket which fell above my whole body, that gave me a long lasting, expecting peace of mind, freedom from pain and misery...

...

CHAPTER IXX

Section 6.

DREAM

January, 1999.

CROATIA, DALMATIAN COAST, CITY OF SPLIT, SAINT THEODORE, THE CHURCH OF OUR LADY...

She watched his struggle to stay awake. His face turned in her direction, when she initiated her weapon. Fear surfaced across him emanating its power through his oversized bulging pupils. *He was dreaming with wide open eyes. Whatever nightmare took over his brain, it stopped now... He is fully aware who I am.*

The black man in front of her held his both hands on his temples, his right one pressed by gun's handle and the left one with his large fist, moaning, swaying a little on his wide positioned legs, before he crumbled like potato sack beside the stone wall. Tanya considered possibility to kill him immediately as preciousness to eventual problems, but he was the only one who has information about the artifact which she required. He planted the fake one, very good replica of original one, to fool her or eventually his employer as well, which she gathered from the other dead female agent, together with one of the dark gemstones. At least the stone has been original one and unique.

He lost his conciseness completely due to the shock, pain or something else... Anyhow, he is mine now.

Section 1.

April, 2010.

CANADA, ONTARIO, TORONTO'S SUBURB, OSHAWA, APT.14...

...

Walking through this part of hospital park area with two doctors beside her, she felt a tug of bad memories, almost akin to military compound where everything started. She remembered, even now, with perfect clarity, how a decade ago she stood there while soldiers smiled at her, command her to remove her skirt and all her clothes. She remembered that day in the white house, on the dirty floor, chilled air across her back, smell of urine, blood and sweat, the first man on her, inside her, the black form with fleshless mouth... And she was remembering exactly what she said to her mother later, next morning, as she hugged her favorite toy in her bruised hands... She remembered because her entire life changed after that, since that moment she was perfectly normal, regular person as anyone else, then later after the war, when she started with medical treatments, different drugs and medications, hypnosis sessions and an alternative medical treatments in Germany, Switzerland and Austria, the black Thing's eye opened and since then it glared through her, speaking, whispering, sharing the Words of Power with her. The Doctor on the left, said:

'You are going to be all right now.

The Beast whispered across her shoulder:

"I have been waiting for you for centuries."

She had stammered breathlessly a question.

'Why me?'

The doctor continued:

'We are trying to help you here, all of us.'

"I have been searching for someone like you, for too long."

'What do you want from me? What I have to do?'

The other one on the right, with black rimmed glasses responded coldly:

'To behave better and learn to control your emotions, specially your anger.'

"So Much - You are going to get your revenge, if you perform Ceremonies in my honor."

'How I am supposed to do that?'

Voice from the right added an advice.

'Take your medications regularly, control your breathing through yoga exercise which I showed you last time, the results will come...'

"I am going to teach you rituals, You will learn to find the sinners."

'What will happen, if I cannot..., control it?'

Voice from the left told her cold truth.

'Then..., you will stayed institutionalized and locked in similar facilities like this one, for the rest of your life.'

"You are going to burn."

She swallowed hard her own spit that tasted like acid.

...

The same taste filled her mouth now, it came back together with her memories. She inhaled slowly through nose, holding her breath deep down in lower stomach, preventing herself from vomiting instantly, and she exhaled even slower between her teeth relaxing her abdomen muscles, releasing pressurized air from inside. She felt a little better after showering this morning. She settled back naked on the couch, eyes half closed, listening to the adding of the morning news.

"Fireman in the Oakvile, section of Toronto suburbs, last night, battled a six - alarm blaze that took the lives of at least four persons, all but one of them was a child, four years old. And now..."

Behind her the buzzer sounded. She roused herself and went to the intercom.

'Good morning, FedEx Delivery, I have a package for Mrs. Forsyth Emmy.'

She buzzed him in and, stepping into the bedroom, wrapped herself in her yellow bathrobe. A minute later the doorbell rang, she turned down television and went to answer it.

...

His thoughts are clear, occupied by tight student's exams schedule and incoming girlfriend party on the following weekend days, on Sunday. He was not sure what to buy for her...

'Sign here, please...'

The delivery boy said, handling her flat brown cardboard box, then a slip of yellow paper and a pencil.

Hello sweetheart! What a cat! I...

He seemed bemused at finding an attractive girl in her robe waiting for him and it looked as he was struggling to think of something clever to say.

Cannot...

She blocked his thoughts, without any problems, cutting his intent to start a conversation and she felt his hungry eyes on her as she scribbled her official - false name, and instinctively pulled bathrobe tighter.

'Thanks, honey!'

He said, a flicker of a smile masked his confused thoughts. Frustrated by incoherent own thoughts, unable to speak and think intelligibly, he just managed to add.

Think..., think...

'Enjoy it!'

She saw, when she closed the door and she'd gotten the box open, that "Amelia" sent her another data on the *beast - man* who deserved to die. It was old – fashioned war criminal, the killer similar to her first one, with whom *Ceremonies* started in another century, on another continent, but she felt ambitious, thrilled to kill him like with same excitement like at the beginning.

"Picture, digital recordings, his personal files and correspondences were on memory stick.

Consider this a temporary replacement for Mr. G. At least this one can provide a path and open a back door to reach our primary target..."

In the box with memory stick, wrapped in blue tissue paper, she'd enclosed a second - hand book, a slim brown antique - looking volume whose spine had long since been rubbed clean of lettering. there was no any title on it. Idly, she flipped through it. There were several crude line drawings of mapped areas, various ungainly costumes - or strange dressed people, faces, sketches and pictures of strange animals, but most of the book was filled with diagrams, mathematical calculations, symbols, signs, a mass of old footprints and short notes on some archaically sign language. She thought she recognized a few pre-archaic maps of Balkan Peninsulas, South - East European territories that seemed right out of prehistoric period - but it was difficult to imagine that this area of Europe looked like it. She put small book aside and went back to the kitchen table where was her new Apple Pro Notebook which she purchased last month, since the last one burned to ashes due to her out controlled rage - fire two months ago.

Eventual evidences of my existence were incinerated together with that apartment... That was the only good thing after all... Besides, I released an energy collected in my body... Which saved my life at the end...

Inserted memory stick has been recognized instantly by computer's software program and it pop up a single folder file named 'Die Spinne'.

"The Spider" on German language..

CHAPTER XX

Section 2.

PICTURES

June, 1999.

UNITED STATES OF AMERICA, CALIFORNIA, LOS ANGELES, WESTSIDE, BEVERLY CREST, NORTH BEVERLY GLEN BLVD, MOUNTAIN COTTAGE...

Juergen moistened blue eyes were searching through "DEATH RAY" file report contents on some additional clues what went wrong on hidden artifact site at Canyon of Tara River, Montenegro. All Alpha Team members dispatched to the area were executed, plus the site was completely destroyed under unexplained explosion inside the mountain's caves.

Kirk was valuable and dedicated leader of the Cell, and is going to be hard to replace him, maybe Markus would be next one to replace him as an instructor, but that now depends on the circumstances of his recovery time, his body adaptation and his interest on the subject.

He was always a "Lone Wolf" in the action and his assignments so far, so final decision should be his, but I will pursue him by any necessary evil to accept it...

Schuster reached for small leather book, with yellow and cracking around the edges pages and stiff with age, from plastic zip bag attached inside file's binder. It looked at least half century old. His perpetually blue eyes were getting wider when he recognized the sign in almost upper left corner of slashed, scribbled surface of leather, an ancient mark of Lion.

It resembled Macedonian, No..., Maybe Roman... The symbol of Alexander the Great! The King of Macedonia...

He sifted through the pages and he'd felt the sudden pounding of his eighty years old heart. Rendering were crude, the pictures below were decorated with faded, old, luridly colored parts, they appeared to be some remnant of partial copies of some other much bigger picture, the images had stood out from the cracked, smudged and yellowed paper with terrifying clarity.

They seemed so alive... So detailed over there, somewhere were just smudges... Like there're going to spring to life any moment...

There were twenty one drawings in all, between two blank one, at twenty three book's pages, each on separate sheet and each, on his own way, filling his soul with inexpressible horror. There was white - gray bird like thing with blood on his long claws, standing before large piled human skull hill and dying a pool of darkened red water filled with humanoid body parts.

Sacrifices.. An altar of Death...

There was the hint of something crouched beneath it, a pale black and white book, fat and somehow repellent to him on the first look, levitating on the top of a low earthen mound of odd proportions, surrounded by strange monoliths, positioned circularly around and a red satanic - looking sun on one page and cold oppressive moon on the next page.

The same ritual... Just opposite sides of the same coin... Jin and Jung.. Black and White.. Good and Evil...

On the following page was image of round silvery shape of shield, positioned against a black background that Juergen at first took it for another heavenly body, a cosmic planet or another moon, until suddenly, he realized with a shudder, he saw it for what it was, a great round lidless eye, looking at him from the page, with squared letters written below, suggesting its name or something similar...

An Eye of legendary creature... Cyclops...

Schuster's face expression changed into a mask of disgust, when some of the pictures become so queer, he couldn't tell what they meant to be, or what they were representing, so he flipped through some of them feeling sickness and revulsion, till he stopped on next one, like a slim sticklike silvery object, long, with ornamented surface, which had features of...

A Spear...

It was impelled with two of the things that looked like oversized dogs, or very large wolfs, only the scene was so badly drawn, it was hard to be sure, and next one was showing the same spear like thing trusted through enormous, pulpy things that might be a coiled serpent or some kind of worm, that had huge smiling lipstick led with razor blades, sharp long teeth.

Favorite weapon of Gods...

Another figure was small, dark and shapeless creature with the half - formed body, that had a look of dead things, zombies, vampires and werewolf together, and earth covered by decaying leaves, like child's attempt to draw some creatures that, he had heard about but never seen...

An ancient representation of Evil... Dracula... The Vampire... The Dragon...

Juergen's mood changed with each other new image, his brain was stirred by impossible memories, images were activated in his subconscious, even the strangest of all the Pictures was the three concentric circles with the red slash down in the middle of it, seemed somehow familiar in ways almost painful to think about...

The Three... Father and Son and Holly Ghost... Three Circles of Life...

And there were others even worse a horrifying scene drawn entirely in white and another entirely in black, painfully decorative, showing struggle, fight, sometimes defeats and victories of humans, but mostly clashed forces of good and evil, until Juergen's blue gaze fall on the page that contained extremely unpleasant thing that may have been a man, except his bone structure and muscle composition, an abomination of human being, ugly creature holding a strange shaped weapon. A thing that glared and beckoned, it had what looked like an extra line of sharp teeth inside his wide, luminous inviting smile...

Evil... Smile of... Death...

He knew that it was beckoning to him. The room was tipping forward, he was slipping through, falling in an abyss, the world was spinning around him drawing him toward that terrible face, it's sharp teeth... Dizzy, he had somehow had the presence of mind to hide himself from the evil thing, lost from the penetrating eyes, he shoved the leather book beneath a stack of old files on the table, papers flew before him as he stumbling wild eyed across the room and he deliriously called for his bodyguards down which were securing cottage entrance downstairs.

'Kkkkkk..., Kurt...'

When they found him less than a minute later, Juergen Schuster was lying, crumpled, and unconscious on the stair's landing, later on, it was believed he'd had fall downwards due to hard work, exertion, his age and an unfortunate accident.

CHAPTER XX

Section 3.

POWER

March, 1999.

CROATIA, DALMATIAN COAST, CITY OF PULA, CATACOMBS UNDER PULA
ARENA...

Willburn lay in the dark. He saw a patch of grey, like daylight, but all around him it was
darkness. The daylight, if it was that, stood on some perch in the blankness, down beyond his legs
or up beyond his feet, or along. He was not sure that he was awake, or he had a dream again, he
ought to speak, but only three words came out into the air in front of him.

'Who am I?'

He said to himself, at little more than a whisper. The question, in what sort of place and position
he was lodged, now came at him again. He remembered flying through that cascade of silvery
moonlight, wolf's attack and nothing afterwards, but guessed that he had continued dreaming that
over and over, again before he arrived here, headfirst. Most likely he is in some kind of prison, at
the basement of some house, somewhere outside of city, since he did not hear any sounds of car
traffic, human noise, conversations or anything which indicated that he is near some civilized
environments.

Where am I?

Like one in a dream he stand up, made his way with slow, unthinking footsteps down the ancient
staircase and through lengthening shadows of the room, moving absently toward the weak stream
of light down below. He squinted with his eyes, adapted to the darkness around him, and
recognized shape of some kind of door in front of him, so he pushed it with his left hand
expecting bolt resistance of closed exit. Before he managed to touch it, the door swung without
any sound outwards, bringing light, stinging shards of pain into his pupils, flashing blindness to

his sight.

There were open...!

Stepping outside completely blinded, he gazed through his lashes unsmiling to an outer stone chamber which spread in front of him, bathed in yellowish - amber light. Framed as he was within the doorway, totally naked, he seemed the only truly alive dark thing in the old, large underground cavern. There were so many incoherent thoughts inside his head, too much to think about now, all previous events were clouded, too grave memories to contemplate and his mind refused, for the moment, to grapple with them and turned instead from logic to instinct. He surveyed space around with a practiced eye of a killer, for some signs of any unusual activity, looking for potential threats, stepping from the arched doorway, and the air around him was humming with kinetic energy emanated from his nude body. He felt strange force radiating from him, like all humanity was forgotten in a blink, just raw noise of power, patterns of killing instinct and waves of uncontrollable rage.

This..., This..., Power - Rage is great!

Jerkily he began heavy steps towards an entrance – an exit, the strain on his body was hard, his lips were tightening, red color was surging to his face, he felt it in his fists, the pumping of loathsome poor, the air before him ringed with ancient voices screaming for a kill inside the skull.

The Time has come. The Day is young. The Hunter is old...

CHAPTER XX

Section 4.

LONDON

February, 1891.

EUROPE, GREAT BRITAIN, LONDON, THE STREET WITHOUT NAME AND NUMBER...
Red brick house in front of him looked similar any of them in the row, up and down in the street.
Foggy patches floated above the ground reaching his knees, swirling around him as they have
been attached to his legs when he step of the sidewalk and crossed block paved street checking
his right side first as always, then in the second he realized his common mistake, he quickly
switched to the other side as well. He was able to adjust to the rule of the left side here in Great
Britain, partially to their food as well, but the weather was killing him with its rainy, never
ending days and constant moisture on the streets. Everything reminded him that he was
swallowed by some giant and he ended up somewhere inside giant's oversized intestines, walking
and breathing moisturized air, gliding throughout the long halls of sticky, cold and greasy stuff
around him. He removed annoying thoughts and unwanted incoming images from his head, as he
knocked on the reddish surface of heavy oak door. Since nobody responded to it after minute or
two, he used large circular iron brass that hanged in the middle and he banged it twice. Echo of
heavy thuds resonated back inside the house interior.

Matthew is going to be very surprised. I cannot wait to see his face, when I am going to present
him prototype of the "Shield". He will flip over the edge from excitement!

The door was opened by his wife Mrs. Walker. Her large brownish eyes went wide as she
recognized Tesla and her pure Oxford's accent were pinched by two octaves above her regular
velvety colored voice.

'Ah! My dear Mr. Tesla! What a pleasant surprise!'

She tiptoed to him to kiss him lightly at his right cheek, to close to his lips. She pressed her warm soft lips on his skin, as her breath brushed its cold surface from an excitement. It felt strange outwardly good, but deep inside his chest the feelings were wrong.

'Matt, look who is here! Our beloved friend arrived and he brought some sunshine to us! Please, come in Tesla!'

Behind Nikola's back sun settled above horizon and shined through gray clouds at his back to confirm her statement. He entered inside the house, welcomed by its heat and his owners. Tesla smiled to approaching man whose shadow stretched and disappeared on the opposite wall, when Mrs. Walker closed an entrance door behind.

'Hello Tesla my friend! Welcome to our humble home!'

Matthew Grenville crossed the hall in two long strides and gave bear hug to unprepared Nikola with his thick, short and meaty hands. Tesla lost his breath under Greenville's hard squeeze and he coughed between warm friendly patting across his exposed back.

'I cannot wait to hear all your stories! I followed your successful performance two years ago at Paris, in France on International Exposition Fair! That was something that shook the world, my friend!'

At first Tesla thought that Matt referred to an episode with Americans, but then he saw Matthew's face expression, his hand gesture with thumb up, he realized that Matt gave support to Nikola's technological demonstration at Exposition.

'My dear Matthew, that was all one big circus, back there, instead caged animals, artists and acrobats, the place was packed with greedy bankers, uneducated investors, fake inventors that were stealing someone else's ideas and self important scientists, they all together belonged to the same circus troupe, they were real clowns in the eyes of an audiences back there.'

Gina took Nikola's long black Kashmir coat, his cylinder and burgundy leather gloves as they advanced down the hallway. Tesla stopped in front of dining area and removed his black shoes before they entered the room. Gina strongly protested against his behavior.

'Tesla you do not have to do that!'

Nikola smiled to her, bowed humbly and promptly answered.

'My parents told me long time ago that was disrespectful for home owner to enter his house with your shoes on. Beside the fact that is not hygienic, they instructed me to do it in order to help the person who is taking care of the house itself, to show a respect for his or her work.'

'Thank you again our dear Mr. Tesla, you were always thoughtful regarding our women's responsibilities...'

'You are more than welcome! If our world resided on women more then on a man, it would be better world, it would be more humanity and peace around.'

Matthew raised his bushy eyebrows surprisingly as his forehead wrinkled and he made disapproving comment.

'Well, I think that woman has to know her place at our social life, especially in the family circles, she has to be dedicated to her man and their children, as well...'

Nikola smiled to his comment and knew that he shouldn't argue with conservative English attitude towards the women, but he could not resist his urge to answer.

'My dear Matthew, women are going to rule this world sooner or later, we are just peons used in never ending chess play. The game was played for a long time, and it will be played long time after we're gone! The future my friend, belong to dominant females!'

Grenville was watching Tesla directly in his eyes, as he was trying to read some sarcastic look or he was expecting a wink from Nikola, as a sign that he was joking. Since Tesla eyes kept deadly serious look, he realized the truth that this man had completely opposite opinions about almost everything which he, Matthew respect valued and stand for.

'Anyhow, I came here Sir. Matthew in great need for your help.

In the near future I would require your assistance in very delicate and private matter, matter which is going to be crucial for our future and future of our children as well...'

Grenville more felt Tesla's nervousness and tension then it was clearly visible on his face and body language.

'Tesla I will try to help you...'

'Please, Matthew, this will happen in the future, year of 1943, so documentation, files, schematics and pictures do not exists yet, but they are going to be delivered on your door by someone in that time instead of me...'

Matthew Grenville mouth opened and dropped down when he heard detailed future developments, incoming wars, visions, horrors' and he was listening Tesla's instructions about the non existing files named: "Death Rays" and "Shield".

Trying to forget the past is less painful, then trying to remember the future..

CHAPTER XX

Section 5.

KINTARO

June, 2010.

UNITED STATES OF AMERICA, WASHINGTON, DC, WASHINGTON, "BIG BROTHER"

OFFICE, THE BASEMENT – DOJO – TRAINING AREA…

…

CRACK!

The blade went deeply inside the man. Scattering pieces of flesh from the man's face and chips of his broken lower jaw bone flew from my mighty sweep of the Bokken. The body was standing at the place, still trembling from deactivated nerves which refused to give up. Brain was sending signals to the arms and legs which were shaking under the impact and his shock. The man fell apart in front of me dead as post.

"I am wrath of the God!"

Only one matter occupied my mind.

"I am part of him!"

Death.

CRACK!

Death to all.

"His vengeful right arm!"

CRACK!

I swung the weapon back above my head for another blow. I was not thinking about an attack or defense at all. I was just moving between them, reacting, sweeping their bodies with my Bokken everything that was moving around me.

CRACK!

I left my weapon buried in the middle of the next one and wiped out the face of the second one close to the left with a rough stone. Pensively I run my right hand thumb inside the neck of the third one, applying the pressure on his upper nerve meridian, blocking him completely. He did not feel anything in next instant when I smashed his 'Adam's Apple" with my left elbow… He was drowning in his blood perplexed by his sudden death. I yanked my weapon from the twitching dead body and hefted in my right hand, swung horizontally on the next one…

CRACK!

Lord knows that I offered them honorable death one hour ago, before the Shrine and they did not accept it. I delivered them mercifully death instead, as a fair payment for their grand - grandfather's sins, quick dead for any warrior…

CRACK!

…

Kintaro was deeply in his hatefully debt of blood which he inherited from his family and his attackers offered themselves freely to him. Same as his grand - grandfather had run his vengeance on Tanaka Clan a century ago, taking their heads off with his katana.

…

CRACK!

Somehow, the feeling of floating a few centimeters above the earth and taking their lives from the start, where I wanted, when I wanted, filled my soul with enormous pride that I mastered this art and skill… My Sensei had been right… I had strayed to identify myself as a Master…

CRACK!

A tiller of the Mother Earth…

CRACK!

Henceforth myself as a Maser…

CRACK!

A toiler in the vineyards of the Death…

CRACK!

And now… A stranger was due to enter my path, an outsider, someone ignorant on our beliefs, who did not have simplify sympathy, whose godlessness was obvious was in his every move, expression, word and act. He was determined to die… I will gladly provide it for him when I see him…
CRACK!

CHAPTER XX

Section 6.

THE BUS

March, 1999.

MONTENEGRO, BAY OF BOKA KOTORSKA, REGIONAL HIGHWAY ABOVE THE CITY OF KOTOR...

The open white bus was filling up with passengers quickly. She was about to slip into one of those seats in the middle, but the fat rude women pushed her aside, before she reached it and slammed her fat ass into it. She steered the other one in the rear.

It will be better here. At least I will be alone for some time.

Some undefined coldness tightened around her hearth and she swallowed it hard for no reason at all, when she thought about Miran again.

That was funny... I have already miss him, like I had not see him for months, and we departed just one day ago... I love him, it's just that simple truth... And I missed him...

'Okay...'

Natasha said to herself, plainly loud. The fat women in front looked at her with big question mark above her head. She felt chill sea breeze on her neck and sitting beside the partially opened window, she removed a light blue kerchief from her leather "Mona" purse and tied it around her throat; it was going to get older when the ride started. She was looking up again down the seat row, when the fat woman turned to her and frowned.

'What's the matter?'

She asked her ready for an argument and fight.

'Nothing...'

Natasha answered, fastened the handkerchief around her chin and huddled down on her seat. Her heart was pounding so hard she could almost hear it above the bus loud engine. She closed her eyes and tried to calmed down her breathing and relax. A burly driver came down the line at last a minute later and checked her ticket, ripped off one copy of last page and gave her back the other portion of it, without any words.

I have got a headache, but it's a minor one... The best thing will be to take a short nap in the meantime. No pills this time...

Natasha closed her eyes and relaxed a little; she was adjusting her body better between the bus seats and after two - three minutes, she was asleep listening groomed, deep sound of diesel engine behind her back. She slept for next forty minutes without dreams or any disturbances around her. Until powerful "Bang" woke her up.

...

The vibration through the bus instantly woke some other passengers and the sudden activation of breaks threw her aside and back against the seat, as they descended down the hill. Natasha gripped the seat in front of her with her right hand and opened fully her eyes. Everything around her seemed to slow down, and she gasped, for ahead of her the bus seemed to spilling into an abyss - and all of them, passengers were hurtling downward, faster and faster. They'd have fallen, faster than she ever thought she could go, and screams were filling her ears, her eyes were now completely open when she whispered a prayer to the God.

'Oh, dear God! Help us!'

Before the final run, they hit some large tree and the bus reached the top of the highest branches, and almost stopped there, for a moment they seemed poised, balanced between two worlds. And just as they were teetering on the edge, with the whole stoned abyss spread below them - the beach at the end with dark waters of Adriatic Sea down deep below. For a brief second she thought it might be this just a dream, or some trick that her mind played with ...

I want to live... I want... To see him only one more time... Please...

And then in the next instant they slide forward again, they were hurtling downward, ahead of her people in the bus were screaming in horrors, she was holding herself on the seat with all her might, and they were dropping again with additional speed she thought that straps and seat would break immediately under her pressure. Suddenly, like a vision, there was a huge white bird before her window, a seagull like, hanging angelically in the air, as it was reaching for her - trying to protect her. Something gleamed in the light, behind the bird, when roaring metallic noise get even with the screams of trapped humans, and it moved so fast, she wasn't able to see it, just a blur of movement... The rude, fat women in front of her, screamed again and broke her neck, when she slid and hit her head on the window, which cracked from its impact. Next moment she felt that her body flew up, the bus roof smashed against her, then she fell away behind, onto the floor. The blood poured from her nose, across her face, all over the front of her new white shirt. She ineffectually licked a dab of own blood, comforting herself with thoughts:

It is going to be Ok... The God will save me...

By the time she made her last thought, bus stumbled further down, reached the end and the sky had opened up with red, hot burning explosion which swallowed everything around.

EPILOGUE:

BATO

6 – TH CENTURY BC, TRIBE OF DAESITIATES, ARDUBA – AN ILLYRIAN SETTLEMENT...

(Modern day on territory of Bosnia and Herzegovina, Vranduk village near the town of Zenica ...)

...

The Death's breath was behind my back now...

Three days ago the last portion of massive invader's army had marched into Illyrian scout's camp. The first comers of "The Son of Gods", as they called themselves, had made boldly attack for the city walls and all Dardani's spears and arrows or Mithra's fire balls thrown at them, slowed them before the gates, but it did stop them. First two days city walls protected them and higher ground gave them an advantage to his tribe, they were brave as wolfs and strong like a bears, but it didn't make a difference at the end. Attackers mimed disembowelment, castration, beheading and rape of the citizens on the Dardani's city ramparts and they kept their expressions, promises and words to the last one.

The Great Goddess swallowed half of my people and the other half are still under protection of the God of Earth Powers...

The last of God's warriors screamed on and on, like slaughtered pig, while Daesitiates Chief, spilled their guts on the ground, their intestines smoked in the sun before the Temple Arch. An Illyrian warlord stomped on one of dying God's warrior spine and broke it like a dry twig and cut his lunatic screams. He rushed forward, about ten arm's length and cut the head of the shrieking wounded man without looking back at the city ruins. Amok inside his soul was singing for blood. Bato the Daesitiates cloaked himself inside the War Beast and did not care at all, he did not give so much as glance at those fell behind him on the walls and he swung his Illyrian fighting sword named "*Ulk*"("Wolf") once more, a master stroke across an exposed head and breasts. He pushed the corpse with his right foot, so that the touting neck spurted over his extended right arm.

My "Ulk" has been blessed by Varuna...

Bato tore off with his left hand shredded leather that used to protect his shoulder and left his clothes hanging in stripes. He ripped off spiked unblemished metal plate of some corpse near buy and fixed with leather straps on his right shoulder. Daesitiates Chief pulled apart cloth from the last killed God's warrior, wiping his blade clean as he retreated back to Temple's entrance. Cracked city stones under his sandals were still drying of intruder's blood under scorching sun, which stood at its zenith over the town's white roofs, when pack of hardly armed and armored silhouettes trembled in the shaking light in front of his eyes. He could not make out who or what they were.

They would step now for the last time on our native soil of Zalmoxis (God of Earth Powers), he will hear their sorrowful cry on the far side of Haemus Mons (The Balkans Mountains)...

The Chief of Daesitiates slid the golden circular shield off his back an hook it on his left arm and rose his "*Ulk*" *with a* right one high above his head, stretching sore muscles, sending to them an insult war cry, smiling grimly to the coming deaths of men before him.

BOOWVA - BOGH! ("BOSONA - WATER THAT RUNS!")

"Words of Power" echoed across the walls to attackers exposed minds, showing their hopeless fight, the force of it thinned their blood to water, froze them physically and emotionally, shattered their souls, power of words trapped them in a split of the time. "Shmarjet", pure silver metal helmet multiplied energy of his mind, killing a handful of warriors in the first row directly exposed to psychic force. Blood filled their eyes, mouths and ears, boiled through their skin and faces like burning venom, spreading through their bodies. They were collapsing in agony of sacrificed souls when he leaped to their second ragged line of five of them still standing.

The first of them at the left end took the edge of his sword clean through his neck and the head jumped off, eyes, hair and teeth were still in the air when he hit the neighboring one, further on the right, with his shield at once. The shield edge beat his face off leaving an unrecognizable mass of meat and bones and when the men fell in front of Bato, he stomped on the throat with his forward left sandal crushing attacker's windpipe in pieces. The Chief stepped to the right quickly, he shortened his sword aim and put razor, rounded point into the third man mouth and dropped his hand hardly down to thrust up it into the brain. Fourth one had a time to rise his huge scimitar above his head in a attack, before mighty swing of "Wolf", decapitated the top of his head, and he fallen in, jerked like a fish on the ground, gouts of bone, brain and blood from a severed head stayed on its hard blade. The fifth one valued his life the most and he retreated some steps back to gain distance between them. Bato was standing in the wreckage of the affray along with the legs and arms laying in a circle of human meat, spread in a stone dish below the arched shadow of the Temple. He waved his gold-shield in semi circle in front of him, so an astonished God's warrior drooping body went backwards impaled by one of his *"Abeis"*(Snakes). The man was chocking on the ground on Sica attached to his neck, his face frozen in the midst of its last smile.

"Sons of Zoroaster" were devoted worshipers of Angra Mainy ("The Evil Spirits") that raided on our King Bardyllis and almost wiped out his tribes of Daors. I am not going to allow them to do that with our tribes...

He lightly close the distance to got his weapon from the limply body of the man who was laying dead there, blood was still pumping from attacker's open flesh wound, and the air become sweet with it, the flies came feasting on it when Bato, like a man under a spell, half dead and half blind grasped his father's favorite weapon with his left hand. A shadow advanced above the ground, before dark hooded huge *Zoroaster's* Leader ran suddenly from nowhere into the space between him and pile of corpses, with a heavy black axe in his both hands. Bato - The Chief used one of his *Abeis* - Sica as a pivot to rotate around his left hand, pushed himself slightly to the right when enormous figure brought weapon on him, and he tugged out his *Ulk* - sword a little sticky from brain's blood and parried to an attack. Black clad Leader wrenched his axe against his sword and came straight at him with full force and mass of his enormous body, "Wolf" - sword rang from an impact and hissing sound came out, when huge axe slides down the blade to his right leg, just few centimeters over the knee. Muscles were ripped off, cut almost to the bone, as Bato ignored an exaggerating pain, he felt that his leg was still there attached to his body, and he took another wield with "Wolf", counter attack from right to the left, that created more space and time to escape another stroke of the black axe edge. Axe was in the air again, Zoroaster's Master warrior was standing astride of him aiming for Bato's head. "*Abeis*" flashed like a truthful serpent under the gold shield and reached behind humongous warrior's thigh, cut - bite him deep inside through flash and bone, bringing for first time strange words howled in rage.

"One with the Hand."

The axe made full force contact with exposed shield underneath, the impact shattered golden - iron surface in three pieces and Chief of Daesitiates dropped on his right knee in front of his opponent's brute strength. Bato's second "*Abeis*" sneaked out to the left attacking rib cage of a man, impaling body to the hilt. Grunt came out from man's lips under cloth covered face. God's Sons Leader smashed "Shmarjet" horizontally with thick iron axe's handle as a short club. Through waves of sparkling light Bato saw an opening between extremely large hands and he attacked viciously, revengefully and deadly.

"One with the Land."

Spear like upward with powerful thrust, "*Ulk*" vanished inside wide huge torso from the bottom to the top, was rupturing internal organs and a heart with its wide blade. Hollowed, broken rib cage acted as a kind of well from which blood had flowed to stain polished hard metal, they rusted themselves into one, as both of Chief warriors stayed together, embraced in a death spasm. Entrails went out of Leader's belly, dark blood run down the channel of "Wolf's" blade and made a little pool at the end of an ornamented silvery handle.

"AAAARRRGGAAAHHHHH...!!!!"

Howl made of frustrated vengeance, released anger and unbearable pain came up to Bato, through the smoked empty eyeholes, *Zoroaster's* black eyes flashed to him through the killing haze. Chief of Daesitiates hefted weightily with his weapon partially on the left side, unbalancing his dark opponent, and he grasped right colossus hand near the elbow, took statue stone like wrist by both hands and broke it.

"CRACK!"

Sound of fractured bones filled his ears, the black axe blade fell out from his sight on the ground below, when Bato use a body momentum and cracked The Leader directly in the forehead, using full remaining strength in both his fists. Black colossus went backwards, swaying on his feet, when Bato seized hold of "*Ulk's*" hilt, pulling it free downwardly from a falling body, as he crouched in front of, ready to attack one more time, if it was necessary...

He fought to quell the excitement, the urge to release a scream of victory that surged like heat inside his lungs, enveloped by incoming force in him, inside this raising union of his body and soul. The Words of Power emanated by his mind become beacon that carried victorious images and news to all tribe's survivors.

"BOOWVA - BOGH!"

AUTHORS' NOTE

THE DEATH MASK – "The Face of Illys" has been in part inspired by real historical events, which took place in last two centuries, which I have read and witnessed myself in my short life.

Tesla left his imprint on this civilization and our everyday lives enormously that he did not give me any other option then to become part of this book.

Illyrians were also part of our heritage and anything and everything which I have found about their history, way of living and civilization was written by destroyers of their civilization.

Conquers of different civilizations wrote our history so far.

I witnessed the end of the World myself through the War which ruined and scavenged the Balkan only twenty years ago.

Names, places and events happened for real, to real people.

Everything else is pure fiction.

The story will be continued…

In the next book.

The real true was always hidden somewhere between the lines.

That space was open to writers.

To be filled with their imaginations…

And their dreams…

Raymond R. Bosnic